FANTÔMAS

in America

Acknowledgements

First and foremost, thanks to Jean-Marc Lofficier for signing on to this project in the first place and for his extreme patience in seeing it to completion. For my amazing wife, Allison Trimarco, for reading it over and over and teaching me rules for comma placement. For my favorite mystery writer and dear friend Kathryn Miller-Haines for reading every word I've ever written and debating the proper use of the word "swoon." For my buddy Hope Gatto and the rest of my friends in the Passage Theatre Stage One Writers Unit–Ian August, Sonya Aronowitz and Lynne Elson. For Mr. Bradley's Musical Jam and Laura Spector's awesome Fantômas portrait. For Aaron Christensen (aka Dr. AC) for his encouragement, Robin Walz for his invaluable website and Tim Lucas for nursing and encouraging my Fantômas obsession, as well as letting me win the Fantômas press book on ebay.

I'm not done yet. Also, in no particular order, thanks to: Marcel Allain, Pierre Souvestre, *The Gray Seal* novels by Frank Packard, The Count of Monte-Cristo, The Penguin, The Fantastic Four, Eugène Sue's *Mysteries of Paris*, the films of Louis Feuillade, the Fantômas films of André Hunebelle, *Shadowman* by Georges Franju, Brian Stableford's translations of the Black Coats novels, the Arsène Lupin novels of Maurice Leblanc, Nick Carter, Old King Brady, Sexton Blake, D.W. Griffith's *Musketeers of Pig Alley*, The East Side Kids, Bela Lugosi in *Bowery After Midnight*, Lightning Hutch and Luc Sante's *The Low Life.*

Finally, for the dozen or so adventurous readers out there who have been dying to read a novel based on a lost serial inspired by a rarely translated French character from the early part of the 20th Century–this book is for you!

D.W.

in America

by

David White

based on characters and situations
created by

Marcel Allain & Pierre Souvestre

and

Edward Sedgwick & George Eshenfelder

for the serial "*Fantômas*" (1920)
produced by The Fox Film Corporation

A Black Coat Press Book

Thanks to David McDonnell for proofreading the typescript.

Visit our website at www.blackcoatpress.com

ISBN 978-1-934543-07-8. First Printing. November 2007. Published by Black Coat Press, an imprint of Hollywood Comics.com, LLC, P.O. Box 17270, Encino, CA 91416. Printed in the United States of America.

William Fox
presents
The
1921 American Serial
in 20 Episodes
Fantomas

William Fox
presents
Fantomas

Introduction

In 2007, it's nearly impossible to find a lifelong Parisian who remembers what daily life was like during the years 1900-1913. If you're lucky enough to meet one, and take the time to ask them about that period, their countenance will not be one of wistful nostalgia, but fear. They may attempt to tactfully change the subject but, when pressed, they will all answer the same way.

"I remember Fantômas."

France heard of Fantômas for the first time in 1911, when writers Marcel Allain and Pierre Souvestre began chronicling the true exploits of the master criminal, in monthly pulp magazines published by Fayard. To anyone familiar with America's fascination with its own criminals, detailed in magazines, novels, radio, television and the cinema, this exploitation of real-life suffering will come as no surprise. Society has always had a morbid obsession with its own fears and taken delight in the allure of danger and evil.

For years, the citizens of Paris had locked their doors and windows at night, fearful of the crimes they knew to be lurking on every boulevard, then woke up the next morning and purchased Souvestre and Allain's retelling of the Fantômas saga. The elite feared him. The rabble claimed to know him. The surrealists embraced him.

As the fear of Fantômas reached a fever pitch, two men became emblems of justice and instant celebrities–Inspector Juve of the Sûreté and Jerôme Fandor, reporter for the French newspaper *La Capitale*. During the 12 years of Fantômas' reign, the two men could be seen, and recognized, at virtually every crime scene in Paris, usually with Souvestre and Allain following close behind, pens and notebooks in hand.

Then, as suddenly as he had appeared, Fantômas vanished.

In 1912, *La Capitale* reported that its star journalist, along with Juve and Fantômas, had been lost at sea with the rest of the passengers and crew of the *RMS Titanic*. A little over a year later, Allain and Souvestre published their account of Fantômas' demise, and life in Paris, for a short while at least, returned to normal.

In 1920, Marcel Allain shocked the world by announcing that Juve, Fandor and Fantômas had returned. Or had they? Skeptics claim that Allain (without Souvestre, who died during the pre-war influenza epidemic) was merely cashing in on his former success. A more likely scenario is that Parisian society, having lived through the Great War, no longer felt threatened or challenged by a single criminal no matter how clever or violent he may have been. In any case, these later novels were written off as mere fiction, as were the reprints of the original Allain and Souvestre manuscripts. It seemed that everyone had ceased to believe in the existence of Fantômas. Or, perhaps, they had simply chosen not to believe.

In any case, if we are to take Allain at his word that Fantômas returned after the war, the question remains–where was he in the intervening years?

In 2001, my wife and I took a vacation to Paris where I decided to try and locate some of the original Allain & Souvestre manuscripts. They were surprisingly difficult to find, even among the famous green bookstalls along the Seine. I finally located two reprints, published in the 1950s, that had clearly been abridged. The accompanying illustrations depicted the "characters" in 1950s fashions, further cementing the idea that the stories were fiction.

Upon returning to the States, I began searching for the rare English translations of the original manuscripts. Of the 40 or so French publications, only a dozen had been translated and all but two of them had been out of print for over 70 years. In the process, I stumbled upon a number of interesting Fantômas artifacts. One evening, while searching e-bay, I bid on a press book for the silent American movie serial featuring Fantômas. It was produced by Fox Films, directed by Edward Sedgwick and starred character actor Edward Roseman as Fantômas. I had seen a listing for the film on the Internet Movie Database, but had assumed that it was simply an American remake of the French serial directed by Louis Feuillade. In any case, an accurate assessment of the serial was impossible, as it appeared to be one of many films from the era considered "lost." Further Internet research had supported this assumption. Nevertheless, one of the scans in the e-bay listing caught my eye. It contained plot information and character names that didn't appear in any of the original Souvestre & Allain accounts. I engaged in a bidding war with someone named "lostcinema20" and silently cursed him every time the price of the item elevated by another dollar. After much anxiety about how my wife would react if the asking price went up any further, I won the item, sent my $100 to the seller, received it a few days later and promptly set it aside without a thought. I still had not completed my collection of the English translations, so I turned my attention back to finding them.

It was around this time that I received the following e-mail:

Dear Sir–

Congratulations on your recent e-bay win! I regret that the auction ended in the middle of the day when I was unable to monitor my computer, but you win some, you lose some, as they say. You might be interested in knowing that I am a private collector of lost films and I have in my possession the first five chapters of Fox Films' Fantômas *serial. How they came into my possession is something I'm not at liberty to reveal, but given your fascination with the master criminal, I thought perhaps you might be curious about viewing the chapters. If so, feel free to contact me any night after midnight, at (xxx) xxx-xxxx.*

Sincerely,

Raymond Smythe (lostfilms20)

I couldn't believe my eyes! It was already past midnight, so I picked up the phone and called Smythe. He was still awake, in his mid-eighties but sharp as a tack. We stayed on the phone until the wee hours of the morning, with him sharing story after story of the years he had spent tracking down some of the most famous lost films of all time. He claimed to have a complete copy of Erich Von Stroheim's *Greed*, for instance, as well as *London After Midnight*. As believable as he sounded, however, I was still skeptical. Still, the opportunity to view the lost *Fantômas* chapters, as well as some of Smythe's other treasures, proved too much of a temptation to ignore. By the end of the conversation, he had invited me to his home in upstate New York. The only caveat, he said, was that I shouldn't arrive before nightfall and had to depart before the Sun rose the next morning.

An unusual, foreboding stipulation to be sure, but Smythe promised an explanation once I arrived. In late 2003, I left my home in New Jersey one Saturday evening, and set out for Raymond Smythe's house. I arrived at about 10 p.m. with my notebook and tape recorder. Smythe's home was enormous. I'm not sure why that surprised me. Only a wealthy man could have amassed the collection he claimed to have.

Smythe himself was a bit of an oddity–a tall man with long, flowing grey hair whose posture and confidence belied his advanced age. He wore a three-piece suit that matched his silver mane, as well as a curious pair of sunglasses with blue-tinted lenses. He wore these even inside and I never once saw him remove them.

After an hour or so of conversation, any misgivings I had about Smythe vanished. He was a well-spoken, kind man. His sunglasses and odd sleeping schedule were due, he said, to a severe form of solar urticaria. He was allergic to the Sun. Over the years, the condition had worsened until, fearful for his life, he simply reversed his sleep cycle. Just before dawn, he retired to his windowless bedroom, then rose at dusk and went about his business.

Eventually, I grew impatient with his stories and became desperate to view the lost Fantômas chapters. Perhaps I glanced at my watch one too many times, because he eventually chuckled, stood up and invited me upstairs to his film library. The room was secured by a large metal door–the type of which I normally associated with a bank vault. He spun the knob until he hit the right combination and led me inside.

The interior was stuffy and cold, but stacked to the rafters with film canisters. The desire to set up camp in that room and examine each and every piece of film was overwhelming, but time was passing and I had to forego my collecting instincts for the time being. Smythe led me to a corner shelf where, alongside the complete works of Louis Feuillade, there were five small canisters bearing the labels *Fantômas* (1920). "Marcel Allain hated this film, you know," he said. "He demanded that the main character's name be changed to '*Diabolos*.' Eventually, it was exhibited in Paris, but only in truncated form. Then all copies of it seemed to disappear entirely."

We left the vault and proceeded to the screening room where Smythe loaded the first chapter into the projector. The story, surprisingly, was standard serial stuff and nonsense. Fantômas tells a detective named Fred Dickson that he will quit his evil ways in exchange for a full pardon. Dickson refuses, and Fantômas kidnaps a famous chemist named Professor Harrington. Harrington, you see, has developed a method for manufacturing gold and Fantômas wishes to capitalize on the secret. Dickson is joined in his chase by the Professor's fetching daughter, Ruth Harrington, and her square-jawed fiancé, Jack Meredith.

Over the course of the five chapters, false identities were

assumed. Chases took place on foot, by car and by boat. Fantômas attempted to marry Ruth Harrington. The gold-making formula seemed to change hands over and over again like the worst example of Alfred Hitchcock's McGuffin.

Still, there was something mysterious about the film–a sense that the viewer was not being told the complete story. For instance, the proceedings were occasionally interrupted by a mysterious "Woman in Black" who seemed to have almost supernatural knowledge of Fantômas' crimes and felt a wrathful jealousy of Ruth Harrington, even making the occasional attempt on her life. It was a story in pieces, and the pieces on film only represented a portion of the entire tale.

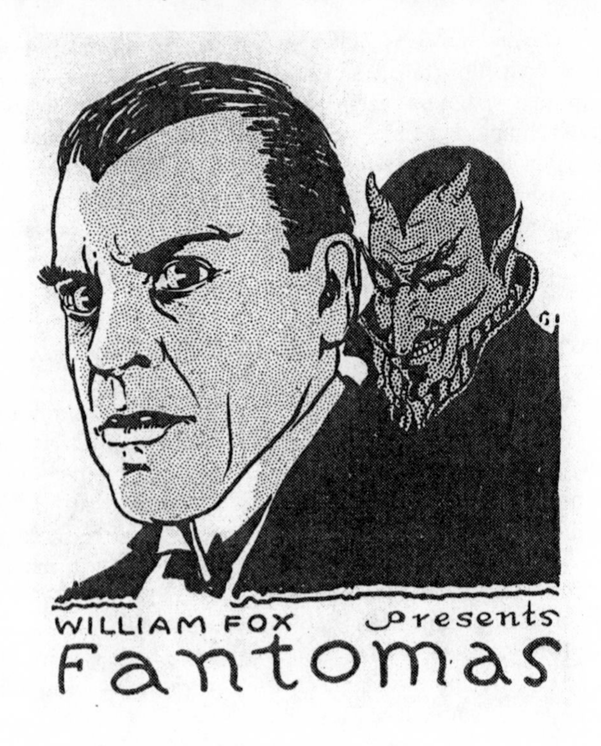

As we finally reached the cliffhanger for Chapter Five, which found Ruth and Jack trapped inside Fantômas' mansion on Long Island (!), the movie gave way to a screen of empty light and the last bit of film slapped against the spinning reel. Smythe rose and said he needed to get to bed as the Sun was due to rise in just a few hours. I thanked him, shook his hand, and expressed my desire that we might continue our acquaintance. He smiled and escorted me back to my car.

The story might have ended there if I hadn't received another mysterious e-mail the following day. It read:

My Dear Mr. White–

I am flattered by the attention that you have given of late to my exploits. I was beginning to grow concerned that my activities had been forgotten, or lost to the ravages of time, and it is gratifying to know that I can trust my immortality to collectors such as you.

Incidentally, I have already called on Mr. Smythe. While he was initially reluctant to part with the films of my American exploits, he eventually saw the light and I'm pleased to be able to add these crude bits of celluloid to my collection. In addition, since I had no place to be following our encounter, I helped myself to some of the other noteworthy films in his library as well. I've always wanted to see whether or not London After Midnight *was worthy of its reputation. I'm sure you understand.*

With Regards,

F.

I didn't conclude my initial reading of this communiqué with the sense of alarm one might expect. Surely it was a joke, I thought. Perhaps Smythe had more of a puckish sense of humor than I gave him credit for. After multiple readings, however, I began to grow concerned. I can't say for certain what made me decide to drive back out to Smythe's home, but I believe it was the phrase "saw the light."

That afternoon, I drove to upstate New York and waited for sundown to complete my journey to Smythe's home. Although my sense of dread was beginning to mount, a part of me felt I was over-reacting, and I didn't want to risk rousing Smythe from his sheltered room before it was safe to do so. Soon it was dark and I resumed my journey, finally parking my car in Smythe's driveway.

I noticed at once that his front door was wide open. It was madness to enter alone and unarmed. Furthermore, I was not so dispossessed of my wits that I failed to realize that fact. Still, the evil emanating from inside the house acted as kind of lure, and I found that I was unable to resist. Perhaps, I'm ashamed to say I thought to myself, I might even be able to rescue the films and keep them for myself.

I didn't get the opportunity to determine whether or not I would have been able to resist such temptation. I searched the house from top to bottom. Not only was there no sign of Smythe, but his film vault was entirely empty.

I still did not think Smythe had been the victim of foul play. There was every possibility, for instance, that he had simply packed up his wares and taken off for parts unknown. Even as I considered this, however, a nagging suspicion told me it was untrue.

Before leaving Smythe's house, I noticed that another door had been left open. It was a sliding glass door on the ground floor that led onto a back patio. From the foot of the stairway I could see a figure lying in a lawn chair, his silver hair shining in the moonlight.

As I approached the body, it was clear that Smythe was dead. He was lying in his lawn chair dressed in the same grey suit. His eyes were wide open and his mouth was twisted in pain. His pale skin had become a map of ruptured red blisters and scars, as if someone had roasted his body over an open flame.

I called the police and waited for them to arrive. Under interrogation, I told them everything I knew, omitting the small detail of the mysterious e-mail from "F" that led me back to Smythe's house in the first place. It seemed too incredible and, truth be told, I was afraid of looking like an idiot. Surely Smythe had simply had a heart attack in his lawn chair and, tragically, had spent the day in the sun before I discovered his body. The e-mail was the work of a prankster and the film canisters had been stolen by a thief who happened upon Smythe's house and took advantage of the open door.

This is what I told myself, but in my heart I didn't believe it. Not even after the coroner's report showed no signs of foul play and the investigation into the missing films reached a dead end. The truth of Smythe's death revealed itself to me on the most terrifying night of my adult life. It began with a dream.

I was lying in bed next to my wife, tossing and turning. Perhaps it was the summer heat that kept me from drifting into sleep, but for whatever reason my thoughts turned back to Raymond Smythe. Eventually, I fell asleep and found myself back on Smythe's back porch. It was daylight, and I was surprised to see Smythe seated in his lawn chair with his arms raised above his face in an effort to block out the sun. He began screaming in pain and I wondered why he didn't simply stand up and walk back inside. I turned my head to the left and saw a man seated opposite Smythe. The man was impeccably dressed in a top hat and tuxedo, complete with tails. He wore a thick black piece of cloth across the middle of his head, with holes cut out for the eyes. He carried a gun and was calmly pointing it at Raymond Smythe. He could have pulled the trigger at any moment and eased Smythe's suffering, but he chose to wait. It was clear that he found Smythe's pain amusing. Indeed, witnessing his slow, tortuous death seemed to be the stranger's *raison d'être*. Procuring the film canisters, several of which were resting at his side, was simply a bonus.

As I opened my mouth and tried to yell, the stranger turned toward me and smiled. It is impossible to describe the sensation I experienced at that moment, dreams being what they are, but I had the distinct impression that I had been "marked"–that the stranger had made note of me and I would never be free from his influence.

I awoke with a start, my face and chest bathed in sweat. My wife woke up next to me and asked me if I was okay. Suddenly, I became dimly aware of a rustling sound coming from my office. I leapt from my bed and made my way down the dark hallway to my office door and threw it open. I turned on the light to the room to find that the window was open, its curtains billowing in the hot wind.

Sitting on my desk was the manuscript you are about to read. On top of it was the following note:

William Fox
presents

Fantomas

Mr. White–

A trade, if you will, or a small thank you for leading me to the missing chapters concerning my adventures in America. In exchange for those priceless treasures, I leave you this–the complete story of my first year in your fine country. The serial was, of course, based on incomplete accounts of my exploits. As is often the case, however, the truth is slightly more... blasphemous. I hope this manuscript brings you no small amount of pleasure, and trust that you will continue searching for the remaining 15 chapters of the 1920 Fantômas serial. As you locate them, I will provide you with more narrative. Until then, this chronicle, which covers the period of time also covered by the first five chapters, will have to suffice.

With Regards,

F.

I leave it up to the reader to decide how much of the following work is fact or fiction.

David White
2007

Fantomas (1920)
1. *On the Stroke of Nine*. 2. *A Million Dollars Reward*. 3. *The Triple Peril*. 4. *Blades of Terror*. 5. *Heights of Horror*. 6. *Altar of Sacrifice*. 7. *Flames of Sacrifice*. 8. *At Death's Door*. 9. *The Haunted Hotel*. 10. *The Fatal Card*. 11. *The Phantom Sword*. 12. *The Danger Signal*. 13. *On the Count of Three*. 14. *The Blazing Train*. 15. *The Sacred Necklace*. 16. *The Phantom Shadow*. 17. *The Price of Fang-Wu*. 18. *Double Crossed*. 19. *The Hawk's Prey*. 20. *The Hell Ship*.
Producer: William Fox; *Director* : Edward Sedgwick.
Scenario: Edward Sedgwick & George Eshenselder, from the well-known detective novels by Marcel Allain & Pierre Souvestre.
Director of Photography: Horace Plympton.
Cast: Edward Roseman (Fantômas), Edna Murphy (Ruth Harrington), Lionel Adams (Professor James D. Harrington), Eva Balfour (The Woman in Black), Johnnie Walker (Jack Meredith), John Willard (Detective Frederick Dickson), Irving Brooks (The Duke), Ben Walker (The Butler), Henry Armetta (The Wop), Rita Rogan.

DRAMATIS PERSONAE

Emile Cortez–Master detective of Barcelona, Spain
Frederick Dickson–Detective with the New York City Police Department
The Woman in Black–A woman in mourning, with her own reasons for seeking Fantômas
James Dale–The mysterious "Saint of 14th Street"
The Torch–A member of the Fantômas gang
Brian Shea–Another, rather unfortunate, member of the Fantômas gang
Sally Shea–Brian's unfortunate wife
Geoffrey the Slasher–Owner of *The Hog's Head*, a tavern on the Lower East Side of Manhattan
The Council of Ten–Mysterious organization dedicated to ridding Manhattan of vice and corruption
The Musketeers of Pig Alley–Snapper, Muggs and Glimpy, three street urchins from the Bowery
Father Rose–Priest of the Our Lady of Perpetual Sorrow parish in the "Five Points" area of the Lower East Side
Sergeant Corona–Dickson's corpulent superior officer
Professor James Harrington–Eccentric explorer and brilliant chemist
Ruth Harrington–His beautiful, tempestuous daughter
Jack Meredith–Ruth's wealthy, Oxford-educated fiancé
Poturu–Harrington's Amazonian houseboy
Officer Jenkins–A young policeman with a penchant for pulp
Boris "The Prince" Zaitsev–A young Russian immigrant and member of the Fantômas gang
Dr. Hans Voitzel–A brilliant German scientist and member of the Fantômas gang.
Fantômas–?

LA CAPITALE
(April 1912)
SEARCH FOR *TITANIC* SURVIVORS ENDS

Authorities have ended their search for survivors of the luxury cruise liner *RMS Titanic* after more than two weeks of searching. It is thought that over 1400 people lost their lives in the tragic accident that sank the ship, its passengers, crew and cargo on April 14th. The cause of the tragedy is well known, but rumors persist that Fantômas, the man responsible for some of the most heinous crimes in Paris since the turn of the century, was among the passengers and may, in fact, have contributed to the tragedy.

Regular readers of *La Capitale* will recall that Fantômas was believed to be responsible for the murders attributed to the young painter Jacques Dollon, the disappearance of the American detective Tom Bob and the murders of the Marquise of Langrune and Lord Beltham, among many others. Survivors of the *Titanic* report having seen the heroic Inspector Juve of the Paris Sûreté fighting an unidentified man alongside *La Capitale*'s own star reporter, Jerôme Fandor. Regrettably, the bodies of Juve and Fandor have yet to be discovered, and they are believed to have gone down with the ship. It is this writer's sincere hope, that the heroism of these two men was not in vain, and if they are currently lying lifeless beneath the waves, that the wretched corpse of Fantômas is lying there beside them. Perhaps, due to the diligence of these fine men, the crimes of Fantômas will cease with the sinking of the *Titanic*.

WILLIAM FOX PRESENTS
FANTOMAS
1921 American Serial in 20 Episodes
FROM THE WORLD FAMOUS STORIES OF MARCEL ALLAIN & PIERRE SOUVESTRE
Scenario & Direction by EDWARD SEDGWICK
EPISODE ONE
"ON THE STROKE OF NINE"

ACT I

In which Fantômas arrives in New York, matches wits with Detective Frederick Dickson, and makes use of the unfortunate Mr. Brian Shea.

Chapter One: The Arrival of Fantômas

Allow me, if I may, to deliver a warning to the Reader. The story that is about to unfold may shock, disturb and terrify you. It concerns a personage so sinister, so evil as to strain credulity. It is difficult to imagine in these enlightened times that such a fiend could have existed. Nevertheless, he did exist and his atrocities are a matter of fact, not superstition. Although the story began in 1900 at the Château de Beaulieu in France, and encompasses a parade of horrors that includes the brutal slayings of the Marquise de Langrune and the painter Jacques Dollon, it does not end there. Nor does it end with the tragic sinking of the *RMS Titanic* in April 1912. Instead, the trail of Fantômas leads us to America–specifically, New York City in the year 1917.

Before we settle in to that time and place, however, let's take a look at a steamship somewhere in the Atlantic, about a month after the *Titanic* tragedy. We'll start down below, in steerage, where hundreds of peasants, pressed against one another for warmth, struggle to find comfort during their long journey to the new world. Above them, in much roomier, more luxurious quarters, are the first and second-class passengers, many of them lucky enough to be provided for by relatives already in the United States.

Now we travel up to the deck of the ship, under the moonlight, where we observe two men engaged in conversation. The man on the left is Emile Cortez. You can tell by his bearing that he is a Spaniard, and more than happy to display his nationality in mixed company. Despite the lateness of the hour and the conspicuous absence of other passengers, he has made every effort to keep up appearances. His perfectly styled hair and moustache are slick enough to catch the moonlight, and the cigar between his lips takes on all the significance of the Spanish flag mounted on foreign soil as a symbol of national pride.

The other man is, for all intents and purposes, almost completely nondescript–a study in averages, of medium height, medium build and hair of indeterminate color. His deep-set black eyes are his only real distinguishing feature. We can assume that it was his almost complete lack of outward personality that led Emile Cortez to engage him in discussion. The soul of a Spaniard never shines as brightly as when it is placed against a bland foreigner.

Emile Cortez exhaled a mouthful of smoke, waving his cigar hand to waft the scent of tobacco around the deck. "Direct from Cuba," he said. "The best tobacco in the western hemisphere." He offered the man a second cigar. The man held up his hand and shook his head. "Are you certain?" Cortez asked.

The man nodded his head and relaxed under Cortez's watchful gaze. "Do you speak English?" Cortez asked.

"Yes, of course."

"Ah," Cortez nodded. "Then we will speak in English, for it is a beautiful tongue. Is this your first trip to America?"

"No."

"An interesting country, America." Cortez exhaled a puff of smoke and settled back into his deck chair. The two men gazed out at the Moon as it shone gold over the lightly tossing ocean. "One or two more generations, and I suspect that America will become the receptacle for the whole of Europe's working class. Not that I'm cynical, you understand, about the 'land of the free,' but one look at a ship of this size, its steerage stuffed with penniless merchants and arthritic craftsmen, it's difficult to believe that life will get any easier once they've completed their journey. But mark my words, my friend. When the story of America is finally told, it won't be told by kings or presidents or captains of industry. It will be told by the poor, the infirm, the downtrodden…"

"The criminals?" the man asked.

Cortez considered this for a moment. "Yes," he said, "if you like. Why not? The story will be told by the criminals."

The man smiled.

"What is it you do for a living, my friend?" Cortez asked.

"I'm–a businessman," the man answered, blowing away the foul cigar smoke and briefly turning his head away.

Cortez didn't seem to notice. "Well, you're headed to the right country, then!" He laughed heartily, which led to a chest-shaking cough. He brought his arm to his mouth, and expelled a mouthful of brown fluid on the back of his sleeve. "Cuban or no," he chuckled, "these things will be the death of me."

The man chuckled.

"But what can I do?" Cortez gesticulated. "Life is short. Our bodies, depressingly mortal." He hooked his index finger around his cheek and pulled it to one side, revealing a row of golden teeth. "The results of age, tobacco and a childhood of poverty. And years from now, when I've rotted in my grave, a handful of gold will be all that's left of me."

The man laughed. "A handful of gold, a pocketful of dust." Cortez laughed as well, and stifled another cough. "And what brought you to France before this journey?" the man asked.

"What brings any man to France?" Cortez said, waving his cigar through the air. "The steps of Montmartre, the steeple of the Sacré-Coeur…" he leaned in, "…Pigalle, the Moulin-Rouge," he whispered, with a wink. "And, of course… Fantômas."

The man raised an eyebrow and gazed, for the first time, into Cortez's eyes. "Fantômas, you say?"

"Indeed," said Cortez, his eyes alight. "Fantômas!"

"The Lord of Terror," the man said. "*L'homme sans visage.*"

"Exactly!" Cortez exclaimed, jabbing his cigar perilously close to the man's face. "The Terror of Paris. Responsible for some, if not all, of the most heinous crimes of Europe."

"Relentlessly pursued by the intrepid Inspector Juve and the wholesome journalist Jérôme Fandor," the man added with a hint of sarcasm. "Tell me, Señor Cortez. I remember hearing that Fantômas, in an attempt to feign his own death, once killed an entire shipload of passengers by releasing a horde of rats on board, each of them infected with the plague."

"That is not even the most sinister of his crimes, my friend." Cortez's eyes grew wide with excitement. "Maybe you remember the case of the young painter, arrested for murder, who died in his jail cell. After his death, the Princess Sonia Danidoff was robbed of her priceless necklace and the young artist's fingerprints were discovered in her room!"

"Impossible!" the man exclaimed.

"Fantômas, hideous fiend that he is, had stripped the flesh from the dead man's hands and fashioned from them a pair of gloves with which he continued to commit his crimes, leaving the dead man's fingerprints in his wake. The poor young man. Like so many others, to be used as a pawn in Fantômas' horrible crimes. What was that man's name? Pity, my memory isn't what it used to be."

"Pardon my cynicism," the man scoffed, "but I don't believe a word of it."

"No?" Cortez asked in amazement.

"It seems to me," the man expounded, "that whenever the authorities, or for that matter the general populace, are confronted with crimes too horrid to imagine, or too inexplicable, they accuse this mysterious Fantômas."

"Not true," Cortez insisted. "Fantômas is a master of disguise who can take on many different identities. He leaves no evidence behind at the scene of the crime, therefore his presence cannot be determined by modern police procedural. Instead, one must follow one's instincts. Often, it is impossible to see or hear Fantômas. Instead, you sense his presence. The scene of the crime bears the unmistakable whiff of evil and violence. That is how you know Fantômas."

The man laughed. "You are not describing a man, Señor Cortez, but rather the Devil himself."

Cortez leaned forward with excitement. "A man! Yes, a man! But a man who employs the Devil's tricks! A master of deception whose weapon is pure terror. He strikes randomly, wreaks havoc with no obvious motivation. Creates fear for no other reason than to grip the imagination. Once you have been confronted with Fantômas, it is not uncommon to dream of Fantômas. To see Fantômas everywhere, to imagine his hand in every sinister crime. That is the power of the illusion the fiend creates. But make no mistake–Fantômas is a man. And like all men, he can be discovered, caught, arrested, guillotined."

Cortez sat back in his chair and gazed wistfully at the full Moon. "My father was a police officer in Barcelona. He often spoke of the famous Paris Sûreté with a great deal of fondness, having apprenticed there for many years, and following their exploits in the papers. It was his great wish, God rest his tired soul, that I take up the family trade. After his death, I corresponded with Messieurs Juve and Havard of the Sûreté, and made arrangements to be their guest in Paris. I was eager to join in the chase for the wretched Fantômas." With this, Cortez uttered a deep sigh, and his words betrayed a sense of melancholy and regret. "Alas, the forces of evil do not wait for the forces of good before plying their wicked trade. By the time I arrived in Paris, the *Titanic* was already at sea, and my pursuit of the scourge of Paris ended before it had begun. I waited with Havard for news of the tragedy, and as the *La Capitale* came in every day, shared in his grief for a man I had never met, but whose ruthless pursuit of justice I happily shared."

"It must have come as a great disappointment, having traveled all that distance."

"At first," Cortez confessed. "But then I received word that Fantômas had survived."

"Really!" the man exclaimed, with no small amount of alarm.

"And furthermore," Cortez continued, "that he was headed for America!"

"You don't say!" the man whispered. "I wonder who betrayed his confidence."

"I will tell you who." Cortez glanced around the deck of ship, scanning it for prying eyes. "A cowardly tramp named Bouzille. A foolish ragman, one of thousands that peddle their worthless wares on the streets of Paris. A man of endlessly shifting allegiances, he allied himself with both Fantômas and Inspector Juve. He confessed all to Monsieur Havard after disguising himself as kitchen help to gain entrance to this ship while it was still docked in France. Before it departed for the continent, Bouzille secured documents allowing Fantômas secure passage."

"This ship?" The man's eyes grew wide with fear.

"*Si*," Cortez replied. "I have reason to believe that Fantômas is on board this very vessel!"

"*No*! It can't be! After sinking the *Titanic*…what will we do if he unleashes his fury on the ship's crew or, worse yet, its passengers?"

Cortez rose from his chair and placed his hands on the man's shoulders. "Try not to panic," he said. "Tomorrow, we dock at New York Harbor and will have made safe passage to the city. If Fantômas is on board this ship, I will arrest him." Cortez sat back down and stubbed out his cigar on the rail of the ship.

"You are a brave man, Emile Cortez," the man exclaimed, with genuine admiration.

"Thank you, friend," Cortez answered. "I am as my father would have me."

"God rest his tired soul."

The ship began to pitch, the winds to blow. "We have a rough night ahead of us, my friend." Cortez said. "I feel a storm rolling in. Perhaps it's time for us to retire below."

"Retire?" the man said with a start. "How can I have a moment's peace knowing that Fantômas is on board!"

"Ssssssh!" Cortez placed a finger to his lips, as much to calm the man as to silence him. "Be calm in the knowledge that Emile Cortez is here, and will protect the lives of you and every passenger on board this ship. My father was a daring but cautious man, full of strength and self-sacrifice–qualities, I dare say, that have been passed on to his son."

"I will rest easier," the man said. "Knowing that you are on the job."

"Come," Cortez said, standing and offering his arm to the man. "We should go below. A pretty fix I'll be in to be tossed overboard by the wind before having the opportunity to make my arrest!"

"Much thanks for the conversation, Señor Cortez," the man said, shaking the other's hand.

"The pleasure was all mine, Señor… Señor…" Cortez laughed. "My apologies, my friend. I fear I have spoken only of myself all evening, and have neglected to ask you your name."

"Dollon," the man answered. "Jacques Dollon."

"Dollon," Cortez repeated, eyeing the man carefully. "Your name is familiar. Have we met before this evening?" The ship pitched once again before the man called Dollon had a chance to answer. "Come," Cortez said. "It's getting dangerous here in the open air."

His need for companionship temporarily sated, Cortez entered his stateroom and turned on a small oil lamp. He then opened a large steamer trunk resting at the foot of his bed and drew out a sheaf of paper–each page containing details on Fantômas' crimes and exploits. After tossing the pile on the bed, he drew out an envelope of photographs–each one depicting one of Fantômas' many disguises and portraits of his confederates–an obese woman named Big Ernestine and a sinister-looking fellow with the sobriquet "Guillotine."

Cortez withdrew a pair of spectacles from his shirtfront, then stripped off his jacket and tie before dropping to the bed, kicking off his shoes and resting with his head against the wall. Once again, he began poring over the evidence procured through the good will of Monsieur Havard of the Paris Sûreté. Here were all the gory details of Fantômas' devilish past-times–on one page, the hideous story of the Marquise de Langrune, her throat cut so deeply that her head was virtually separated from her neck. On another, Cortez reviewed the case of Lord Beltham–his body discovered locked in a steamer trunk that narrowly avoided being shipped to Australia. Each detail was more bloody and gruesome than the last. Within the pile of photographs was a picture of Etienne Rambert, the disguise Fantômas took in order to assassinate the Marquise. Beneath that was a portrait of the once-famous actor Valgrand, imprisoned and guillotined in place of the master criminal. And there, at the bottom of the pile, was a picture of Jacques Dollon, the unfortunate young man who…

Jacques Dollon. A horrible thought suddenly dawned on Cortez. *For the love of God, the name of the artist was Jacques Dollon.*

The door to Cortez's stateroom flew open, hitting the wall with a bang. Before the Spaniard could register what was happening, an arm clad in black cloth smashed the lamp, plunging the room into darkness. Cortez tried to rise from the bed, but a hand pressed hard against his mouth, pushing him backwards and pressing his head against the wall. Cortez grimaced in pain and his right arm reached up to grab the intruder's wrist, his left arm groping hopelessly for his spectacles which had fallen to the floor during the struggle. By this time, the other hand of the intruder had found Cortez's throat and was squeezing, cutting off the stale air to his lungs. Cortez continued to struggle, but the two powerful arms held him fast, and as his eyes adjusted to the darkness, he found himself staring into the familiar dark eyes of his deck chair companion–eyes surrounded by a hood of black cloth.

"What a shame," the intruder whispered, barely audible over the roaring winds that had begun violently tossing the ship. "Written out of the drama before the close of the first act. What would your father say?" A tear fell from Cortez's eye onto the strong black-clad hand. "Perhaps he'd say 'Such a shame that Barcelona lost its one true champion.' " Still holding on to his captive, the intruder kicked the door closed.

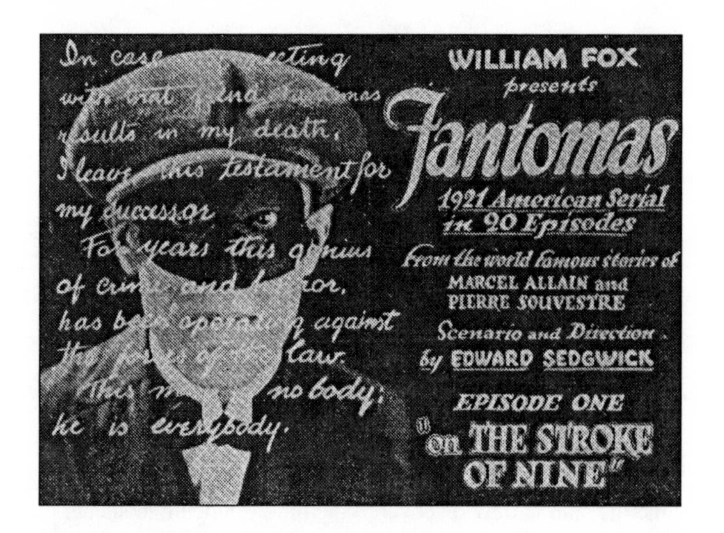

A few minutes later, a man clad head to toe in black exited the room, dragging behind him a steamer trunk of considerable weight. After making sure that he was safe from prying eyes, the man carried the trunk into the stairwell, up the stairs, then exited on deck. The waves were tossing, and several times the man in black had to take one hand off the trunk and steady himself against the railing. Eventually, the ship settled, and the man picked up the trunk, balanced it on the railing, then tipped it overboard and watched as it crashed into the tossing waves.

The next morning, the man who had called himself Jacques Dollon stood on the upper deck, staring down at the bow of the ship while hundreds of passengers disembarked into the New York Harbor. He observed the passengers from first and second-class easing their way through the officers of the Port Authority without having to show any paperwork, while the hundreds of disheveled and dirty passengers from steerage were being forced into a queue while stern-faced authorities demanded identification and letters before sending them off to Ellis Island.

Of course, he thought to himself, *only the wealthy–those who can afford luxurious passage–have the advantage of not having to identify themselves*. It was a curious thought, and the man calling himself Jacques Dollon made his way down to the bow of the ship and prepared to exit. After easing his way into the mass of people waiting to leave the harbor, he looked out onto the New York City skyline. *How*, he wondered to himself, *can so much dirt and filth erupt from a city that is so... new?*

Eventually, the man found himself at the front of the line, where he offered the officer in charge his identification. "Good morning, Mr. Cortez," the officer said after examining the man's paperwork. "Welcome to New York City."

And with that, the man–who now went by the name of Emile Cortez–found himself in the new world. And by the time the ship's crew discovered the bloodstained bed sheets in Emile Cortez's room, a man with a head full of plans and a pocket full of gold teeth had disappeared among the huddled masses of Manhattan.

Fantômas had arrived in America.

Chapter Two: A Trap for Fantômas

Unlike the rather abominable "sensationist" fiction that was so popular during the early 20th Century, the story of Fantômas and his rise to power in New York begins modestly. Like all immigrants struggling to find their way through the rapid turns of the burgeoning industrial age, Fantômas began small, with a handful of gold teeth. Within a few short years, however, he rose to prominence as the "Terror of Manhattan" before finally abandoning the island in order to return home to Paris. By the time he left, he had established a crime network the likes of which New York had never seen. It began in the dirt and grime of the Five Corners on the Lower East Side, along the famous Bowery, and spread outward through all five boroughs, striking fear into the hearts of the poor and rich alike. He did this not only by securing the cooperation of hundreds of desperate, and often deadly, European transplants, but by obtaining a secret so powerful that it threatened New York–indeed, the whole nation–with financial ruin.

But please pardon your humble narrator for getting ahead of himself. All answers will be delivered in good time. What's important to realize is that this is not just a story of Fantômas, nor of the poor unfortunates who found themselves hopelessly trapped in his web, but also of the brave men and women who sacrificed much, and risked all, to stand up to the Master of Evil. In a very short time, their lives were forever changed.

Were this tale a mere work of fiction, the reader would be forgiven for expecting a hero with enough charisma and strength to match the malevolence of his adversary. Little doubt, then, that you will find yourself disappointed by Detective Frederick Dickson, an awkward socialite and a chronic mumbler. Dickson's father founded one of the most successful textile mills in the east, and upon his death, left the mill and his entire fortune to his son. Young Dickson, however, was more obsessed with the brutal treatment of the mill workers than he was with maintaining a successful business, much to the delight of both his employees and his competitors. After several years of ensuring safe conditions and living wages for the mill laborers, young Dickson succeeded in driving his father's business straight to the brink of bankruptcy.

His fortune in jeopardy, and his reputation even more so, Dickson finally sold the mill for a pittance, from which he managed to eke out a small living. Unfortunately for his former employees, the story of Dickson's ill-fated inheritance doesn't end there. In the spring of 1912, the new owner of the textile mill, a callous young industrialist who had reinstituted all the abusive business practices that Dickson had fought so hard against, refused to replace some faulty equipment. Not long after, the machine caught fire and the industrialist, who had locked all the workers inside to prevent walk-offs, watched as his business investment burned to the ground with all of his employees still inside.

Not the most encouraging background for a protagonist destined to clash with one of the most malevolent fiends the world would ever know, but consider this–in the wake of the mill tragedy, Dickson found that a thirst for social justice began to well up inside him. His peers rolled their eyes and clucked their tongues. His father's associates wondered what the elder Dickson would have thought of his son, who lacked both charisma and business acumen. Dickson, meanwhile, against the wishes of his relatives, became a Detective. Driven by a need to ferret out corruption in the most destitute areas of the city, Dickson became acquainted with the immigrant communities of Manhattan.

Dickson first heard the name Fantômas in the summer of 1917. It was uttered in whispers by the poor and downtrodden of the Lower East Side. If the name were spoken aloud, women would cross themselves and quake with fear. Children's eyes would well up with tears and grown men would gather their families and secure them behind locked doors. Even before a single crime was attached to Fantômas' name, he had managed to manufacture an aura of terror around his persona. In those days, petty crime ran rampant and violence erupted randomly in the streets, but the notion of fear and destruction being created and spread by a single man was unheard of.

The first crime attributed to Fantômas, however, did not occur on Dickson's watch. An original Matisse owned by a prominent art collector living on the Upper East Side vanished one evening after its owner fell unconscious after downing a drugged cup of tea. There was no sign of forced entry and the art collector's elderly mother, who was asleep in the same room as the painting, was discovered dead at the foot of her bed. Presumably, she awoke to find the thief removing the Matisse from the wall and attempted to stop him, whereupon he slashed her throat from ear to ear. In place of the painting, the villain had left his calling card on which was printed, "*With Regards, Fantômas.*"

A week later, the entire vault of the Manhattan Savings & Loan was cleaned out between the hours of two and four in the morning. A policeman strolling 54th Street observed a group of men, clad head to toe in black, running out of the building carrying bags of money. He gave pursuit, whereby they disappeared into an establishment known as Casino Joe's and subsequently vanished. The owner of Casino Joe's was released after a brief interrogation and an investigation failed to turn up any worthwhile clues. Once again, Fantômas' calling card was discovered in the now-empty vault.

By this time, rumors of Fantômas' existence had spread from the ragged gin joints along the Bowery to the decorated dens of the St. James Club. Still, Sergeant Corona of the New York Police Department refused to discuss the incidents with the press, and did his best to convince others that Fantômas was just a myth.

Like all great discoveries, the incident that led Frederick Dickson to proof of Fantômas' existence was an accident. It was sweltering hot, and an Italian named Garibaldi had attempted to carry off an icebox from a shop on the Lower

West Side. He had kicked the door in about midnight–so far so good–but found himself unable to lift the heavy appliance onto the street. After about an hour of pushing and sliding, Mrs. Pantino, two doors down, saw the glass on the street and called the authorities. Mr. Trentini, she said, was in the hospital with the flu and his wife had asked Mrs. Pantino to keep an eye on the shop for a few days. Luckily, she was out of bed waiting for that worthless nephew of hers to come home when she heard the ruckus.

Garibaldi was crouched on the floor, trying to shove the icebox with his shoulder when Dickson walked in, accompanied by two police officers. Garibaldi laughed when he saw them, said something in Italian, then said "Fantômas," stressing the second syllable by mistake so that it came out "Fan-TOE-mas." Garibaldi, as it turns out, was a numbers runner for a Baxter Street flophouse. After being delivered to a jail cell, Garibaldi continued to invoke the name of Fantômas, insisting that "The Master" would deliver him from his cell in due course, which seemed to cause considerable distress among his cellmates. The anxiety was exacerbated once Garibaldi began waving around a curious charm, worn on a chain around his neck. During the interrogation, Detective Dickson saw that it was a gold tooth.

Garibaldi's boastfulness didn't last much longer. After two weeks of enjoying his advanced jail-cell status, he was found dead–strangled with a shoelace. The other prisoners claimed innocence (of course), and said that they woke to see a mysterious man dressed in black assaulting Garibaldi. The police rolled their eyes and laughed, citing the reliability of the jail cells and trustworthiness of the guards, but Dickson felt the prisoners were telling the truth. For one thing, Garibaldi's gold tooth necklace had vanished.

Over the following months, the name "Fantômas" was being uttered by every petty thief on the Lower East Side. His presence was reported in Bleeker Street saloons and the houses of ill-repute on Cat Hollow. Dickson's colleagues still considered the name a myth–a superstition carried over from the home countries of the foreign population. Not only were petty thefts being blamed on the mysterious Fantômas, but murders as well. Before long, mothers were putting their children to bed at night with a stern warning–"Be good, or Fantômas will get you..."

And so it went, week after week, month after month. The more Dickson's superiors tsk-tsked the notion that crime on the Lower East Side was controlled by a single mastermind, the more stubborn in his convictions Dickson became.

Then one night, he set a trap for Fantômas.

Detective Frederick Dickson

During the day, the ship docks along the Hudson were packed with barges unloading their cargo into warehouses. From dawn until dusk, men and boys from the ages of five to

75 sweated under the blistering Sun, lifting barrel after barrel, crate after crate. Their flesh burnt, their muscles torn, the men and boys worked for pennies a day, and when night fell, they went home to the rooms they shared with two other families, or spent their hard-earned cash on spiked liquor at Stephenson's Black and Tan. By 2 a.m., it was unusual to see any life whatsoever dwelling in the riverside warehouses.

Except on this particular morning, when a man named Krakowski, sporting a thick white beard and eyeglasses, pushed open the door and sent a dozen pigeons scattering into the rafters. He made his way to the center of the cavernous space carrying a locked briefcase, until he found a small table accompanied by two chairs, one of them pulled out from the table as if anticipating his arrival.

Krakowski sat down, placed the suitcase on the table, checked his watch, then folded his hands on top of it. At exactly 2 a.m., the specified time, a door opened from the opposite side of the warehouse. Framed in the doorway was a tall man with slicked-back, black hair, dressed in a black suit. The smoke from his cigarette rose in circles toward the ceiling. In the distance, as if it were portending some inexplicable, random act of evil, a clock chime began to sound.

The man in black thrust one hand into his pocket and made his way casually but purposefully toward the table. The smile on his face reminded Krakowski more of a dilettante dinner-guest than a criminal mastermind, and Krakowski had to take a deep breath to calm his nerves. "Morris," he said. "Morris Krakowski."

The man in black extended his hand. "And I," he said, with a smile as bright as fire and eyes as black as pitch, "am Fantômas."

Krakowski took the man's hand and felt his own sweat well up in his palm. His breath caught in his throat and, involuntarily, he began to cough. "Are you all right?" the man in black asked. "Would you like some water?"

"Begging your pardon," Krakowski said. "I am honored.

I had expected someone, I just hadn't expected…expected…"

"The man himself? The myth? The legend?"

"I have known for some time that you were no myth, but it is still surprising to…"

"I know," the man in black laughed. "You didn't expect such a brazen introduction. You thought, perhaps, I'd send an underling to do the dirty work."

An awful thought crossed Krawkowski's mind. "What will you do, now that I've seen your face?"

The man in black laughed, long and loud, causing Krakowski to shift uncomfortably in his chair. "This is not my face," he said. "Make no mistake. You will never, ever see my face." Krakowski breathed a sigh of relief and the two men made eye contact with one another. Krakowski found himself stunned, immobilized by the dark eyes of the man in black. His reverie was broken when the man in black cleared his throat.

"Yes?" Krakowski asked.

"Not to rush things along," the man in black said, "but daylight will be here in a few short hours and it would be best if I found my way clear of this room by then. You have something to show me?"

"Yes," Krakowski said, and snapped open the briefcase, drawing from it a stack of file folders and envelopes. "Payroll records," he said, "contracts, evidence of funds diverted, tax evasion, cash exchanges…"

"In other words," the man in black interrupted, "enough information to have the local police precincts falling at my feet."

Krakowski began to speak more animatedly. "Virtually everyone of any importance is represented. Bribery, corruption… You now have enough information to secure the cooperation of every major law-enforcement official in the city."

"And, I imagine, you are requesting a payment of some sort for this treasure trove of information."

"A small payment," Krakowski answered. "Minute,

really. A pittance. A fair price."

"You understand," the man in black said, sitting back in his chair and kicking his heels onto the edge of the table, "that I expect to examine the documents before we discuss a fair price."

"Of course," Krakowski said, sliding the folders across the table. "Take all the time you need."

The man in black looked around for a suitable place to extinguish his cigarette and, finding nothing acceptable, dropped it to the ground and ground it out beneath his heel. Krakowski's heart leapt when the man reached into his jacket pocket, but all he retrieved was a handkerchief, which he methodically brushed the ash from his brightly polished shoe. "Let us see," he said, replacing his handkerchief and picking up the sheaf of papers from the folders to examine them. "Hmmm. Fascinating stuff, really. Very interesting. All in all, Detective Dickson, I'd say this is a commendable job of forgery."

"Pardon?" Krakowski asked.

"Right down to the official departmental stationary. Did you have their cooperation or did you have to put in long nights, after the offices had been abandoned for the evening?"

"I don't understand."

"Really, Detective, when I first heard that you were asking questions about me, it was my intention to kill you right away, but before I did, I wanted to see what you were capable of. Let me say that I am very, very impressed. You've obviously spent hours doctoring these files, making sure that the false information isn't painfully blatant. And, here again, there's your disguise. As someone who has spent more than his share of time in front of the mirror, trying to perfect the art of applying a false nose, I applaud your achievement. Why, I can barely tell where the plastic ends and your real flesh begins."

"You are mistaken," the man said, a tone of panic in his voice. "My name is Morris Krakowski."

"Your name," the man in black sighed, "is Detective

Frederick Dickson. Failed businessman, champion of the oppressed with a guilty conscience for letting all those people in your father's textile mill die. And that is why you have become so obsessed with finding out who, or what, I really am. Well, I admit that I have developed an almost equal interest in you. Since I arrived in this foul-smelling country, a few years ago, I have found myself virtually unchallenged. True, I am quickly becoming a legend on the Lower East Side of this overpopulated, overrated city, but what is that to a man who once had all of Paris trembling at his feet? Have you ever been to Paris, Detective Dickson?"

Detective Dickson, for it was he beneath the heavy makeup and false face of Morris Krakowski, weighed his options for a brief moment, before finally deciding to admit his part in the charade. "No," he said. "I haven't."

"What a shame," the man in black said. "It's really quite exquisite. Not a day goes by that I don't dream of walking along the Seine, or into the Paris Opera House, my opera glasses in one hand and a bomb in the other."

"What are you going to do with me?"

"I am undecided," the man in black answered. "You present something of a problem. You remind me very much of an adversary I had back in Paris."

"Inspector Juve," Dickson said.

"Yes! You've done your research, Detective Dickson. While I find the prospect of matching wits with an intelligent opponent an intriguing one, my plans are too delicate to gamble them away in such a manner. To be constantly thwarted in a city as grand as Paris is one thing, but to risk being taken in by a common American in a city that reeks of sweat and fish… the humiliation would be too great."

With a sudden movement, the man in black reached into his jacket and drew out a gun. Like a bolt of lightning, Dickson stood up, kicked his chair into the air, caught it with his hand and threw it at the man in black. Dazed by the sudden movement, the man in black dropped his gun just as Dickson shouted, "Now!"

From everywhere they came, their guns drawn. Two dozen police officers spilled out of the dark corners of the warehouse, their guns trained on the man in black. One of them stepped on the fallen gun, and slid it away from him. Dickson pulled off his wig, false nose and beard. His heart racing, his legs shaking, he stared into the man in black's eyes. "Surrender, Fantômas!" he said.

"I am not Fantômas," the man in black said. His voice had changed. The man who, a few moments ago, had appeared for all the world to be a vicious murderer, was cowering in his shoes. "Please," he said. "Have pity. I am not Fantômas."

"No tricks," Dickson said, cocking his gun and aiming it between the man's eyes.

"No tricks," the man in black repeated. "I swear to you, on my mother's grave. I am not Fantômas! He sent me here."

"Who did?" Dickson's gun didn't waiver.

"Fantômas! He told me what to say! He said if I didn't, they'd kill her." The man in black swooned and fell forward, catching himself on his knees.

"Kill who?" Dickson said. "Who are you?"

"My wife," the man cried. "He'll kill her. God help me, good sir. Have mercy. Please have mercy."

"You are Fantômas!" Dickson yelled.

"I am not!" the man said, choking back a sob. "I swear by all that is holy I am not! Please, for the love of God, don't let him…"

Before the man could finish his plea, a shot rang out, echoing through the rafters. The man pitched forward, clutching his chest. Dickson quickly turned around, and the policemen began aiming their guns at the ceiling. "He's up there!" one of them said. Dickson looked up toward the broken skylight and spotted a man clad entirely in black from head to toe, aiming a gun.

"After him!" Dickson yelled, and the man disappeared onto the roof. Dickson addressed the officer standing next to him. "Gordon! Stay with this man," he said, thrusting the sobbing criminal toward him. "The rest of you, follow me! To the roof!"

Dickson and the other officers darted out the door, guns drawn. They emptied onto the pavement surrounding the warehouse, then scattered in separate directions, looking for cover. Dickson and two other officers took refuge behind a trash barrel in the loading dock, all of them aiming their guns upwards toward the roof. The night was black as pitch, and the men were waiting desperately for their eyes to adjust, straining to see any trace of movement. A shot was fired on Dickson's left side, and he turned with a start in time to see something large and black float to the ground. More officers opened fire and the black object twisted to and fro. "Hold your fire, men!" Dickson shouted. "It's just his coat!"

Dickson quickly looked above where the coat dropped, and spotted the figure of a man, darting across the roof. He took aim and fired. A loud shriek tore through the night air, and the man spun around before dropping out of sight. "Got him!" Dickson muttered to himself. "Gregory! Burch! Follow me!" The two men broke ranks and followed Dickson to the side of the building, where a ladder ascended the length of the wall. "I'll go first," Dickson said. "You two, behind me." The three men followed the ladder upwards, and as Dickson cautiously craned his head over the edge of the building, he spotted the man, flat on his back, holding his side and groaning. The man's gun was lying away from him. "Gregory, help me keep him covered. Burch, you get his gun." Dickson and Gregory, their guns trained on their captive, approached the fallen man from two sides. He rolled back and forth and moaned. Blood spilled onto the roof from the fresh wound in his ribs. He was wearing a black hood that completely covered his face, except for two tiny eyeholes. "Cover me," Dickson said, and bent down to pull off the man's mask.

The man was balding, and sported a large black eye and what looked like a knife scar across his face. His front teeth were missing, and Dickson noticed that beneath his clothes, the man looked obscenely thin and malnourished. "Please," the man groaned. "Do not hurt me." Dickson took notice of the man's European accent. "I don't know. I don't know him. He say he give me money. He say he hurt my family."

"Who said?" Dickson shouted. "Who are you?"

"I, Sergei," the man stammered.

"Who hired you?"

"I not know. He say, follow man in black suit. Watch from roof. If man fall to knees, fire gun. He say he give me money. Hurt my family if I say no."

Burch approached Dickson, holding the man's gun. "Blanks," he said. "Nothing but blanks."

"He knew," Dickson muttered. "It was a set-up. That means the man in the suit was…" A horrible thought crossed Dickson's mind. "Oh, my God. Gordon!"

Dickson took the ladder two rungs at a time and shot down the side of the building. Gun drawn, he leapt into the first entrance he could find and ran to the center of the warehouse where the table stood. Just on the opposite side laid the dead body of Officer Gordon. His throat had been garroted. His eyes and tongue bulged out of his head. Next to the body was a rubber mask, tanned with slicked black hair. Before Dickson could speak, a sinister laugh began echoing through the rafters. Dickson aimed his gun upward. "Where are you?" he shouted. "Show yourself!"

The voice seemed to come from everywhere at once. "Where the Devil am I?" it said. "More importantly, who the Devil am I?"

"You killed him," Dickson said, a quiet venom in his voice. "Murdered him in cold blood."

"Pish, tosh," the voice continued. "What's another officer of the law more or less? What's one useless official enforcing the ineffectual, antiquated laws?"

"Fantômas? Are you Fantômas?"

"You see what I am capable of, Mr. Dickson, and I, in turn, see what you are capable of. I will contact you soon. I have a proposition to offer you. One that I'm sure will be of great interest."

"Face me, coward!" Dickson shouted. "Hello?" No

answer. "Hello?" Dickson stood poised for several seconds, but the voice, and the man who owned it, had vanished.

After a lengthy conference with Sergeant Corona, followed by a pained phone call to Officer Gordon's wife, Dickson stumbled into the Broadway building where he kept an apartment. His eyes heavy, and his heart more so, Dickson made his way up the three flights to his door. Placing the key in the lock, he almost failed to notice the door giving way without the telltale click of the lock snapping out of place.

Someone was inside.

Dickson drew his gun and slowly allowed it to lead him into the room. Passing it back and forth in front of him, Dickson smelled the unmistakable scent of… "Perfume," he said to himself. "It's a woman." Reaching over to the lamp, Dickson flipped the switch, but the room remained in darkness. "Hello?" he said aloud. "Is someone there?" With his gun in his right hand, he pulled open a desk drawer with his left and retrieved a candle and match. He set the candle on the desk, struck the match with his free hand, and lit it. With his gun still aimed in front of him, he picked up the candle and thrust it forward, following it further into the room. Suddenly, the light from the flame illuminated a woman, unarmed, her face covered with a black veil, the rest of her covered by a long, black dress that revealed her lithe figure.

"Who are you?" Dickson said. "What do you want?"

"Do as he says," the woman choked, a hint of panic in her voice. "You have no idea what he is capable of." Dickson could detect a faint British accent.

"Fantômas?" Dickson asked. "Are you talking about Fantômas? Who is he?"

"Please," the woman said. "He is a monster, a master of deceit. Do as he says. Obey him, or he will rain horror down on this city, the likes of which you cannot, dare not, imagine."

"How do you know him?"

"I can say no more," the woman said. "Remember me." With that, the woman lurched forward and blew out the candle. Dickson reached for her, but she pushed him away and darted out the door, slamming it behind her. Dickson groped wildly for the knob, opened the door and stepped into the hallway.

The perfumed woman in black had disappeared.

Detective Dickson meets the mysterious Woman in Black.

Chapter Three: The Saint of 14th Street

To the wealthy and privileged of New York City, Manhattan's Lower East Side is a den of corruption and sin–a sweaty, over-populated morass of filth and despair. The immigrants spill out of their cracked and broken houses onto the tenement stoops and into the streets, dodging splintered fruit carts and toothless salesmen desperate for pennies. The alleys are dank, cramped with children draped in rags, making their way through the narrow maze of buildings like rats in a trap. During the day, the tumult of sound includes shouts in several different languages–Polish, Spanish, Italian, with only a hint of broken English rising above the den to remind us that this foreign land, this cracked mirror of the American dream, lives in the backyard of New York's elite. Safe behind the walls and windows of their Upper East Side homes and Midtown haunts, Manhattan citizens dread the thought of finding themselves lost in the rust and mold-filled catacombs, its streets reeking of rotten cabbage and unwashed flesh. While the immigrant population had tapered off in recent years, the more respectable German and Irish families having left the tenements south of 14th Street for slightly more prosperous housing elsewhere, the general impression among New York's citizens is that the Lower East Side is still a breeding ground of sin and crime, and is responsible for the corruption that has slowly been leaking into their fair city.

You will no doubt be dismayed, Dear Reader, that it is into the heart of this foul section of the city that we are now headed, for it is here that the next chapter of our story takes place. Your escort is a man named James Dale, and his feelings about this much maligned neighborhood are wholly different from the popular opinions that pervade public conversation. He first appeared on these streets two months ago, and although he keeps no lodgings here, the local residents are growing familiar with him. A few weeks ago, he aborted a knife-fight between 12-year-old Danny Simmons and a drunk with a murderous temper. Rather than turning the boy over to the police, he returned him to his mother with whom he spent hours in conversation before finally making his exit at the break of day, leaving behind a crisp, new one-dollar bill. In no time, word got out that James Dale was a kind man who understood the problems of the poor, and was happy to leave behind a few coins in exchange for certain nuggets of information.

The unfortunate denizens of the Lower East Side

There he is, in the middle of the street, with his bowler hat and thick black moustache, winding his way past the butchers and news vendors. Notice his eyes as they dart back and forth, searching the store fronts for a particular sign. Although he has walked these streets before, he is unfamiliar with tonight's destination, which was given to him an hour ago by a young man with frightened eyes who said, in broken English, "You want to find Fantômas, go to the pig head." Moments later, he stops in front of a small tavern, shoved between two tenements at the edge of an alleyway. The sign above the door, its paint chipped and color faded, reads "*The*

Hog's Head" and bears a picture of a severed pig head with an apple in its mouth.

James Dale is entering. Follow him, but keep your eyes open and your head down. It is night now, and this place is a den of thieves.

No matter how familiar James Dale had become with the neighborhood, he always stayed alert when he walked the Bowery. Often, he found himself distracted while treading a familiar alleyway, only to find that he had taken a wrong turn and was suddenly in unfamiliar surroundings. He felt the same way here at the *Hog's Head* on Bleeker, although tonight his detour was intentional. Scanning the stifling, smoke-filled room, with its splintered walls and creaky dance floor, he was relieved to notice that very few people noticed him as he entered. It was dusk, and the drunkenness was starting to take hold.

Smoothing down his jacket and pressing his moustache to his face, he approached the counter and sat down.

"What'll you have?" said a large, ruddy-faced man with a pockmarked nose.

"Something strong," James Dale answered.

The man laughed. "Everything I got here is strong. Wouldn't serve it if it wasn't."

"You must have a specialty, then," Dale smiled. "Something to ease the mind after a long, hard day."

The man snorted, then turned around and pulled a large jug of clear liquid from a nearby cabinet. "We have our own still. Best stuff in the city." He poured a drink for Dale, then one for himself, and raised his glass in a toast.

"To your health," Dale said, then took a sip and set the drink down. "The name's Dale. James Dale."

"Geoffrey," the man said, narrowing his eyes, as if trying to place the stranger's face.

"I've heard of you," he said. "The Saint of 14th Street."

"Is that what they call me?" James Dale smiled.

"You don't get to choose your own name on the East Side. The people here choose it for you."

"Like Geoffrey?"

"Naw. Geoffrey's my real name." The man leaned in toward Dale and show him a quick wink. "Folks here call me Slasher."

"Why Slasher?"

With a wry smile and a proud nod, Geoffrey reached under the counter and undid the latch of a small ice chest. Cool mist rose into the air as he reached in with both hands, lifted out a frozen pig's head, and landed it on the counter with a hard thump. The eyelids were open, but the eyes had been removed. The flesh was a pale grey and the snout still bore traces of thick black whiskers.

"One slash across the throat and he's dead," Geoffrey said, making a slashing motion across his throat with his index finger. "When I was a boy, I could do a dozen in under a minute."

Dale covered his mouth with a closed fist, ostensibly to stop a small cough, but more to mask his nose from the foul stench emanating from the severed head. "Hence the name," he said, with a casualness that seemed more than a little forced.

"I would've preferred Butcher, but whattaya gonna do?" Geoffrey said, placing the head back into the chest and kicking the lid shut. "Slasher's a guy who'll stab you in the back. The Butcher's your friend."

"Given your clientele, perhaps Slasher provides a certain amount of insurance."

"Nah. That's what those guys are for." Geoffrey leaned in to Dale with a certain amount of confidentiality and pointed to two men standing at the back of the room. Dressed in grey trenchcoats, buttoned to the collar, with grey hats pulled discreetly across their brows, they eyed the room with an intensity that belied their otherwise casual posture, leaning against a support column, their hands resting in their coat pockets.

"The Councilmen," Dale said, more as an assertion than a question.

"A lot of folks got plenty bad to say about them, but they never done me wrong yet. They keep everyone in line. Got a thing about the 'lack of morality' in the city. Ha! They like to make sure no one gets out of hand. They say they don't care much for public drunkenness, but I've seen a couple of 'em sneak a swallow or two from the tap."

"They charge protection money?"

Geoffrey nodded. "It's a steep price to pay, but what's a fella to do? Bristol Bob on Second Avenue tried to start a side business in his back room. Nothing too bad, just some real friendly ladies, eager to please, if you know what I mean. Councilmen got wind of it, and Bob found himself on the wrong end of a blackjack. I've built this place up from the dirt. It's nothin' too pretty, but it's all I got and I'm damn proud. The customers don't care much for 'em, but as long as they're here, no one gets too out of line."

Dale's eyes settled on a dirty, wiry gentlemen at a nearby table, holding a lit match in one hand, while passing his other slowly through the flame. "Who's the gentleman with the match?"

"Torch, they call 'im. Has a thing for fire. Eyes light up like a crazy person when he sees it. He's the only one in here makes me nervous, anymore. Shake your hand one minute and stab you the next."

The next moment, Torch was joined by a pale, blonde, nervous fellow, whose eyes darted about the room, stopping more than once on the Councilmen. "The fella with 'im is Brian Shea," Geoffrey added. "Another mysterious fella."

"How so?"

"Disappeared for awhile a few months ago. Around the time his friend Garibaldi died in lock-up. Looks over 'is shoulder a lot. No idea why. I serve drinks. I don't ask questions. But word out on the street is that they work for that guy… Fantômas!"

From his vantage point at the counter, James Dale is too far away to hear the conversation that arises between the Torch and Brian Shea. You and I, Dear Reader, have no such boundaries. The table next to them is empty. Let us take our drinks there and sit, but be warned, these men are associates of one of the most dangerous criminals in history, and it would not behoove us to reveal our curiosity too openly.

"I got your message," Shea said. "What do you want?"

Torch snuffed out the match with the tip of his tongue and tossed it to the floor. "Relax, Shea. I'm your friend, ain't I? Guy can't walk into a nice friendly place and chat up a friend?"

"We're still friends then?"

"Course we are," Torch said, slapping Shea on the shoulder. "Have I ever steered you wrong?"

Brian Shea pulled out a cigarette and placed it between his lips. With unusual eagerness, Torch produced a matchbook and offered his companion a light.

"He makes people do unusual things, Torch," Shea said. "Things they wouldn't normally do."

"You didn't play by the rules."

"Jesus, Torch. I know I messed up. I was worried about Sally. I was worried about the baby."

"But Garibaldi? What were you thinking, Shea? Father Rose had good reason to keep him out of the fold. The guy was a loud mouth. Now every beat cop in the Bowery is wandering into saloons asking about Fantômas. They raided the *Black and Tan* and found Sammy Milligan going over bet sheets. Beat him so bad he ain't gonna be able to walk right no more. Good thing he's more afraid of Fantômas than he is of the pigs, otherwise we'd all be in for it right now."

"Garibaldi needed the money," Shea said. "He got down on his knees and begged me. Said he was broke. Said he wanted to send his sister to Albany to stay with their cousins."

"Keep it down, Shea," Torch said, glancing over his shoulder. "Garibaldi hasn't got a sister. The guy was a liar and he deserved everything he got. If there's one thing I can't stand in a crook, it's dishonesty."

"Jeez, Torch," Shea shook his head. "What can I do?"

"Relax, Shea. There may be a way to rectify the

situation. Get yourself back in."

"How?" Shea asked.

"Go to Father Rose. Make your confession."

Brian Shea downed his drink, wiped his face with his sleeve, steeled himself, then rose to leave. James Dale spotted this movement out of the corner of his eye. As Shea headed for the door, Dale dropped some coins on the counter, pulled down his hat and headed through the door as well.

Let us follow them, shall we?

Brian Shea walked quickly down the alley, and it was late enough that the only sound was the clip-clop of his shoes as he faded into the night. James Dale followed behind him at a discreet distance, dimly aware that he was being followed by the two men in grey coats. The Councilmen had exited the bar and were on opposite sides of the alley, skulking from doorway to doorway, trying to keep Dale in their sights.

In seconds, James Dale lifted open the steel grate leading to a storage basement and dropped himself through, the metal door slamming shut above him. The Councilmen quickly converged and attempted to lift the door in order to continue their pursuit, but to no avail. After a brief discussion, they returned to the *Hog's Head*.

While the Councilmen cannot follow James Dale, we can meet up with him a few minutes later. After maneuvering his way through the darkness of the basement and finding his way into the attached tenement, he dashed up four flights to the roof and leapt to an adjacent building. He then descended down a fire escape and made his way to a small garden on the corner of Bayard and Park. It was protected by a metal fence, and the entrance was padlocked shut. Dale looked around, then climbed the fence and dropped quickly to the other side. Under the cover of a grove of trees, a group of boys, visible only by the light of their cigarettes, were playing dice. They were raggedly dressed in wrinkled clothing, their belts too long for their malnourished waists and their ball caps cocked to one side. Each one of them had by their side a box containing rags, used nails, old brushes and other discarded items that they had rescued from the garbage heaps. The three boys considered themselves the toughest kids on the Bowery and referred to themselves as The Musketeers of Pig Alley.

The tallest kid blew on the dice nestled in his hands, then sent them spinning out across the pavement. "Snake eyes!" he said. "That counts for somethin', don't it Muggs?"

A smaller boy, with a torn fedora resting lengthways across his thick black hair, snatched the dice from the ground. "What are you, some kinda moron?" he said. "Snake eyes ain't nothin' but two, Glimpy."

"Don't let Muggs lie to you, Glimpy," said a third boy. "Makes up his own rules as he goes along."

"Put a sock in it, Snapper!" Muggs said, shaking the dice. "All I gotta get is higher than a two and you owe me your box o'rags, Glimpy."

"Jeez, Muggs!" Glimpy said, reaching under his cap and scratching his head. "The shoe shine guy gives me a penny a rag!"

Muggs pretended not to hear and tossed the dice to the ground. "Fork it over, Glimpy!" he shouted, once the dice had come to rest. "Read 'em an weep! Box cars!"

"Hold on there, Muggs," said Snapper. "That's a two and a three. That ain't boxcars."

"Mind your own, Snapper," said Muggs.

"I think Snapper is right, Muggs!" shouted Glimpy, "and I ain't givin' you my box!"

"Why you dirty, no good…" Muggs snatched the cap from Glimpy's head and threw it to the ground. "Come on, ya double-crosser! Put up your dukes!"

"Aw, jeez," Glimpy whined. "Not again! You know how cross my ma gets when I been fightin'."

"Serves ya right, ya big lump!" Muggs shouted, slapping Glimpy on the side of his ear.

"Hey, quiet, you guys!" Snapper whispered. All three boys stopped and listened. "I thought I heard somethin'."

"Evening, boys," James Dale said, approaching them from beneath a nearby tree.

"Relax, men," Muggs said. "It's just Mr. Dale."

"Evenin', Mr. Dale," Snapper said.

Muggs pulled off his hat and slapped Glimpy on the head. "Ain't you got nothin' to say, Dumbo? Show Mr. Dale some respect, will ya?"

"Sorry, Muggs," Glimpy said, rubbing his sore face. "Evenin' Mr. Dale. To whom do we owe this honor?"

"I need your assistance, boys," Dale said.

"Anything, Mr. Dale," Muggs said, grabbing Dale's hand and shaking it vigorously. "You know that. I always said you can count on us. Ain't I always said that, men?"

"I heard 'im say it, Mr. Dale," said Muggs.

"I did too!" Glimpy said with an enthusiastic nod. "I heard 'im say it every day!"

"Put a lid on it, clowns!" Snapper snapped. "Mr. Dale's got somethin' to say."

"Thank you, Snapper," Dale said with a chuckle. "I want to know if any of you boys have heard of a man named Brian Shea."

"Sure, I have," says Snapper. "Mr. Shea and his wife and son live down on 18th, right across from my dad's clothing store."

"What does he do for a living, Snapper?"

"Jeez, Mr. Dale, I can't say for sure. My ma's friends with his missus, but says Mr. Shea's up to no good. He's always tellin' me to keep my nose clean, to keep out of trouble."

"What about the man they call the Torch?" Dale asked.

"Aw, jeez, Mr. Dale," Muggs said. "That guy scares me. Don't go messin' with him or you're liable to get hurt!"

"We don't want ya gettin' hurt, Mr. Dale!"

"Thank you, Glimpy," Dale said, mussing Glimpy's hair with his hands.

"Bunch a' burnt out trees over at the park," Muggs said. "I smelled the smoke one night, and snuck out to see what was up. The whole grove was goin' up in flames and the Torch was just standin' there, starin'. Like he was droolin' over a

42nd Street showgirl, or somethin'."

James Dale crouched down and motioned for the others to follow suit. "Listen to me, boys," he said. "I need you three to keep an eye on this Brian Shea. But don't let yourself be seen. Is that clear?"

"Clear as day, Mr. Dale!" Glimpy said.

"I don't want any of you following him inside anywhere. If he goes into a building, I want you to wait outside until he leaves. And above all stay clear of this Torch fellow."

"You don't gotta convince us of that!" Snapper said, shaking his head.

"How will we find you?" Muggs asked.

"You won't," said Dale. "I'll find you."

We will now take our leave of Mr. James Dale and his rugged band of street urchins and turn our attention to a church on the corners of Baxter and Park. In the late 1700s, this was the site of Coulter's Brewery–a business that made good for about 15 years, then closed up and became a dumping ground for the poor and infirm of the Bowery. At one time, more than a thousand people called its cramped cellars and dank stairwells home. It was razed the following century to make room for an Episcopal mission, which eventually died out due to an embezzlement scandal, giving way to Our Lady of Perpetual Sorrow.

The façade is only 20 years old, its spires ornate but modest–in tune with the community surrounding it and the calloused hands that built it. This simple church stands with pride on this otherwise foul and odorous corner, promising salvation and hope to the ragged souls that cross its threshold. The church is empty, save for the man currently kneeling in the front pew–the man we know to be Brian Shea. It is minutes after his departure from the *Hog's Head* and he has entered not only to rid himself of his notorious pursuers, but to make confession. After crossing himself, he rises and steps into the confessional.

"Forgive me, father," Shea said, "for I have sinned."

"Hello, Mr. Shea," a voice in the accompanying booth answered.

"Father Rose," Shea said.

"Yes, Mr. Shea. It is I."

"Father, please forgive me. I..."

"Tut, my boy," Father Rose interrupted. "Not another word. The damage is done, I'm afraid, and we are here to make amends."

"Please," said Shea. "Allow me to explain."

"Explanations are an unnecessary extravagance. I have neither the time nor the patience for them, Mr. Shea. You had a job to do. And instead of performing your relatively minor duties with the precision that I hired you for, you gave your duties to that fool Garibaldi."

"My child was sick," Shea cried. "I had to go home. He had a fever..."

"My organization," Father Rose continued in a calm voice, "depends upon every one of us pursuing our individual objectives with the utmost dedication. We are a collective, a machine, and when one of us fails to perform..."

"I know, Father Rose, I know..."

"Then why, Shea? Why give the task to that insipid fool?"

"Because he begged me. He needed money. And I didn't mean to give him the gold charm. He stole it from me."

"That charm," Father Rose said, his voice beginning to quake with anger, "is a symbol. When I arrived in this country, I had nothing but a pocketful of gold teeth. I have been very selective about who I bestow those symbols upon."

"Yes, I know," said Shea, beginning to panic. "I made a mistake. What can I do to make it up to you?"

"It is clear to me, Mr. Shea, that your wife and son are of the utmost importance to you, yes?"

"Yes."

"And I sense that you would prefer it if you could extricate yourself from my organization so that you could devote more time to your duties as a husband and a father."

"If only I could," Shea said, his voice betraying a small sense of hopefulness.

"Your wish is my command," Father Rose said, his lips curling into a smile. "I have one more task for you, Mr. Shea, and in return for this favor you are going to do me, I promise to provide your beautiful wife and your adorable child with everything they need. A weekly supply of food, fresh clothing and monthly doctor visits. All of it provided by me, anonymously, with no questions asked. And all you have to do is give me something of yours."

"What?" Shea asked. "Anything."

Father Rose smiled. "Your liberty, my boy. Your liberty."

Moments later, Father Rose was alone in the church. Brian Shea had left to ponder his fate, and Father Rose, safe from prying eyes, stepped behind the altar and released a small lever in its side. As the metal rod thumped against the side of the podium, a small door revealing a stairwell fell open at the front of a raised platform. Lifting his clerical robe above his knees, Father Rose stepped through the doorway and started down the stairwell, the heavy door slamming shut behind him.

Down a circular staircase he walked, lower and lower, as if descending from a house of God into the depths of Hell. Upon reaching the bottom, he pulled a large lever embedded in the wall, and the sub-basement flooded with electric light.

We are here now in the subterranean stronghold of Father Rose. The room is enormous, the cavernous ceiling reaching nearly up to the floor of the church. What was once storage for hundreds of beer kegs, then shelter for hundreds of destitute New Yorkers, is now a plush den, dripping with European class and sophistication. The walls are lined with bookshelves, each of them crammed with hundreds of well-read volumes–Vidocq, Gaboriau, Sue, Féval, Balzac, Zola, Leblanc, Leroux. A veritable library of French literature including translations of Tolstoy, Shakespeare and, resting on a music stand, an original folio of John Webster. On the other side of the room are racks of wine, hundreds of bottles and a selection of the finest crystal. In the center of the room rests an armchair and a dining table. In the far corner is a cage containing a man. He is hunched on the floor, clad in filthy clerical robes, his hair mussed and his beard untrimmed. He winces from the light as Father Rose enters the room.

"You will be happy to know," Father Rose said to the caged man, "that if everything goes according to plan, you will be free to leave."

The man raised his scarred head and stared at Father Rose. "You're setting me free?" he gasped, his throat thick and dry.

"Setting you free, or killing you," Father Rose said. "Either way, your torment is nearly at an end."

The man buried his face in his hands. "Why have you done this me?" he cried. "Imprisoned me. Stolen my identity. To what purpose?"

"I have made many observations since coming to this country," Father Rose said, stripping off his clerical robes to reveal a black, three-piece suit underneath. "It is a land of great hope but, if I may say, very little substance. In such circumstances, when the poor immigrants have nary two pennies to rub together, hope, and by extension religion, become the new currency. Wouldn't you agree, Father Rose?"

"You are the Devil. The Devil…"

"No, Father Rose, thanks to you and your trustworthy persona that I have successfully adopted, I am, in fact, an angel. A purveyor of hope in the darkness of poverty. I will be sad to see it all go, but we must move on, I suppose. Man is nothing if he does not grow and change according to circumstance. Come, Father Rose…" And here, the man we now know to be Fantômas unlocked Father Rose's cage and helped him to his feet.

"Be careful," Fantômas said. "Your muscles have atrophied somewhat and I wouldn't wish you to fall. Phew!" Fantômas exclaimed, waving his hand in front of his nose while escorting the authentic Father Rose to the dining room table in the center of the room. "What do you say to a nice dinner, then a warm bath, eh?" Fantômas lowered Father Rose into a dining room chair. "On the menu for tonight is one of my favorites–lean steak sautéd lightly in butter, red wine and crushed black pepper. Exquisite! A perfect final meal, if final meal it turns out to be. Have a glass of wine, Father Rose," Fantômas said, uncorking a bottle of wine and pouring it into a glass. "An 1864 Chardonnay. Sweet, but not terribly so." Fantômas swirled the liquid in the glass and wafted in its scent. "Mmmmmmm…" he swooned. "Perfect. I can see why you insist on ascribing such delightful properties to the blood of your fictional savior. Were I a god-fearing man, such smooth, delicious seduction would inevitably lead me to a life of fervent religious zealotry."

"God help me," Father Rose cried. "Please… God help me."

Fantômas placed the wine glass in front of Father Rose and gently stroked his matted hair. "God is not here, Father Rose," he said. "Never has been. I'm afraid that you will have to make do with me."

Chapter Four: Frozen in Fear

The headquarters of the New York City Police Department buzzes with activity 24 hours a day. Step inside the front door and your ears will be assaulted with sounds of ringing telephones and clacking typewriters. A group of policemen are standing in the corner by the coffee pot admiring the sexual allure of a beautiful, but unfortunately deceased, woman–her clean face and hair captured for posterity on a dull black and white photograph. Near the door, an Italian officer questions a German witness, both of them fighting their way through the difficulties of the English language in order to share information. If we stay here much longer, we may be lucky enough to witness the subduing of a violent suspect or the firing of a pistol. Alas, our schedule will not allow for loitering. Walk briskly past the rows of teary-eyed victims and scowling thieves. Ignore the sign over the stairwell admonishing us to turn around if we aren't authorized personnel. Walk down the staircase, two flights to the basement, then cross the long, empty corridor with its walls lined with pipes. Step lively through the boiler room and through the door on the other side.

This is the office of Detective Frederick Dickson.

Dickson didn't mind the solitude. The noise of the upstairs chaos was consistently drowned out by the racking and clanging of the boiler. The occasional burst of sweat brought about by the sucking in of warm stale air kept him focused and the cracked windowless walls were a blessing–sunlight, after all, being an unnecessary distraction.

Dickson awoke at 6 a.m., which, in his office, looked the same as midnight. His suit rumpled from the previous evening's sojourn, he had fallen asleep at his desk once again, and raised his head only to discover a piece of notebook paper stuck to his chin by way of the spirit-gum residue left over from his false moustache. Tearing the paper from his face, he examined the notes he had taken a few hours before:

The Hog's Head
Geoffrey the Slasher
The Councilmen
The Musketeers of Pig Alley

Since Sergeant Corona had ordered Dickson to stop wasting time on the Lower East Side, Dickson had found it necessary to adopt the disguise of James Dale. As the weeks went by, he found the confidence he gained through this false identity to be strangely liberating, and he often did his best work after Dale had vanished with the light of dawn, leaving Dickson alone in his vault-like office, the night bleeding insignificantly into the day. Time stopped, or rather seemed to stop, here in this bunker, hidden from the rolling eyes and furrowed brows of the police force.

Shortly after waking, Dickson heard a knock on the door. "Come in," he answered, sliding his fake moustache into his desk drawer. The door opened and in walked a small bespectacled man carrying a large mail bag.

"Hello, Lumpkin," Dickson said, rubbing his eyes.

"You sleep here, Detective?" Lumpkin asked.

"A long night."

"I'll just bet," Lumpkin chuckled. "A public servant's work is never done, right?"

Dickson smiled. "Something like that."

"Hope you don't mind me coming down here like this, Detective. You've got a post from London here and the boys told me to just bring it down direct. When they gonna give you a mail box upstairs, Detective?"

"Your guess is as good as mine."

"Kinda cramped down here, ain't it? I wouldn't be able to stand not having any windows."

Dickson changed the subject. "How're the kids, Lumpkin?"

Lumpkin smiled from ear to ear. "Ah," he said. "Willie Jr. just started wiggling his ears the other day. He's smart, that one."

Dickson smiled. Lumpkin was one of the few friendly

people he dealt with on a daily basis. "Maybe he'll grow up to be a mail carrier like his pop," he said.

Lumpkin laughed. "Why, I was just thinking 'bout that the other day! Great minds think alike, right, Detective?"

"Right you are, Willie. Right you are."

Lumpkin stared at Dickson, nodding his head and smiling. Both men sighed.

"You had a letter for me?" Dickson asked.

"Oh! Right! Sorry, Detective. Here it is." Lumpkin pulled the letter from his bag and examined it. "From a Harry Dickson of London, England. He a relative of yours?"

"Yes," Dickson said with a scowl, snatching the envelope from Lumpkin's hand.

"Something wrong, Detective?"

"No. Thank you, Lumpkin. Tell the family I said hello."

"Right as rain, Detective!" With a wiggle of the ears and a brief salute, Lumpkin turned on his heel and walked out the door, leaving Dickson alone with his curious correspondent.

Dickson stared at the envelope for awhile, admiring the impeccable handwriting and the perfectly centered stamp. Cousin Harry had spent summer vacations at his uncle's home in New York, as a young boy, but had since set up shop in the cooler, and damper, climate of London. Since then, he had become the Dickson family pride and joy by becoming an amateur detective, serving in Flanders during the Great War and embarking on a series of adventures in Berlin as an agent for British Intelligence. Dickson had corresponded with his cousin only rarely. Jealousy had come between the two cousins ever since childhood, when young Harry would entertain at the dinner table by making quarters disappear or placing a napkin over a spoon and levitating it above the dinner plates. The applause that followed always led to a casual dismissal by Harry that it was all an illusion–one that anyone with a modicum of intelligence could perfect. Dickson found his cousin's faux modesty to be the utmost arrogance, although he would often sneak down to the dining room after the lights had gone out, examining Harry's place setting and searching for wires, magnets or secret compartments beneath the table.

In any case, Harry had somewhat lost touch with his stateside relatives and Dickson promised himself that he'd never subject himself to his cousin's arrogance again. It's a promise he would have kept too, if it weren't for that damned Fantômas.

Dickson willed himself to tear open the envelope, then unfolded the letter and began reading:

Dear Cousin Freddy,

How delightful to hear from you! It's been simply ages. Why, the last time I saw you, you were scuttling about the kitchen in your daddy's slippers. Running away from the family cat, I believe you were. What was that hideous beast's name again? Well, no matter. Good memories fade as often as bad ones. I was so sorry to hear about uncle's death, and certainly intended on sending a telegram, but a consulting detective's work is never done, you know. If I'm not mistaken, at the moment of uncle's funeral, I was warding off hordes of idol-worshipping Chinamen. I'm sorry that taking over his business didn't quite work out for you, but we aren't all cut out for the industrial life, are we?

Imagine my surprise, then, when I heard you were a detective for the New York City Police Force! Bravo for you, cousin! And no simple wallet-lifters for our boy Freddy, no! Rather, Fantômas! How frightfully ambitious of you! The Lord of Terror has surely met his match in little Freddy Dickson!

A few words of advice, if I may–I met Fantômas several years ago during the Affair of the Man in Grey. *His goals have less to do with the attainment of wealth than they do with spreading fear. Fantômas' power lies in his sadism, his predilection for perpetrating violence for the sake of violence. Yes, he may make off with a treasure here, a bejeweled necklace there, but the spoils of the crime are less important to him than the chaos he creates in the process. This is not a man driven by simple greed, but by a lust for destruction, and if he happens to obtain a fortune in bonds, well, so much the better.*

So, how to deal with such a creature? I know that there is a movement in certain law enforcement circles to put one's faith in things as small as a fingerprint–to examine dust particles and threads from jackets and tobacco stains on forefingers, etc. Such forms of detection have their place, but I fear they will do you no good in tracking down Fantômas. My advice is to try to forget everything you may have learned about detection. It will only get in your way, Cousin. One never has proof of Fantômas' existence. Rather, one simply feels his presence and intuits his activities. The French call it a pressentiment, *and if you spend your time examining doorknobs with magnifying glasses, you are more likely to receive a knife in the back than you are to discover the truth. Be warned, Cousin. To track Fantômas means leaving the rational world of logic and coherent motive behind. The closer you get to him, the more you will become subject to events that seem illogical, even absurd. To stay on his trail, you must forever keep in mind the intrepid Alice, and allow yourself to tumble down the rabbit hole.*

As for the mysterious Woman in Black that you mentioned, I'm mystified. Years ago, Fantômas assassinated Lord Beltham. It is generally thought that he did so with the intention of marrying the Lord's wife, Lady Maud Beltham. During Fantômas' reign of terror, Lady Beltham consistently made herself a player in Fantômas' games, sometimes siding with the madman, and other times assisting Inspector Juve in tracking him down. It seems the poor woman was in love with the monster, but couldn't stand to be a party to his horrid crimes. The Woman in Black could certainly be Lady Beltham, if the poor woman hadn't committed suicide in September 1910. Still, where Fantomas is concerned, the discovery of a corpse doesn't necessarily mean that the deceased won't miraculously reappear at some point in the future. As unlikely as it seems, stranger things have happened when it comes to the fiend.

Finally, never forget that Fantômas is human. A sinister human, yes, but not a wraith or a phantom. Every human has a weakness. Find his. Again, it won't be found through poring over old photographs or making plaster casts of footprints. Listen to your gut, cousin. In the end, it may be all that saves you.

And on that cheerful note, I'm afraid I must bid you a fond adieu. Duty calls in the form of the Indian ambassador who has asked me to look into an assassination attempt on the Maharaja. I find India tiresome, but the food is not without interest.

I remain cordially yours,
Harry Dickson

While Dickson was glad for Harry's advice, he was still left with an overpowering urge to toss it in the waste basket. Before he had the chance to debate the letter's fate, however, there was a knock on the door. Dickson barely had time to say "Come in," before the door swung open to reveal the enormous, puffing, sweaty frame of Sergeant Corona.

"For the love of God, Dickson," Corona gasped, his forehead moist and cheeks inflamed, "can't we get you an office on the main floor? A man's lucky to make it down those stairs and past the boiler without having a heart attack."

Especially if that man weighs in excess of 300 pounds, Dickson thought to himself. Sergeant Corona was, it must be said, shockingly large. Even people that dealt with him every day were surprised by his girth when he walked into the room. "Did he actually get bigger?" they'd ask one another. Corona tried to mask his size beneath facial hair and oversized clothing, but the effect was that he looked even larger. Topping the scale at over 300 pounds, Corona was nonetheless the voice of authority within the Detectives' Unit. No one really knew how old he was. Given his appearance, he could have been anywhere between 30 and 60, although given his health, most people agreed he couldn't possibly be older than 45. Coming to work every day, framed in a double-breasted tan suit with shoulder pads and a gold watch fob, Corona successfully staved off any pity by scaring the hell out of everyone he met. It was common knowledge that within the ranks of the New York City Police Department, one word from Corona could either make or destroy an officer's career.

"Good God, Dickson," Corona gasped, sinking into a chair and dabbing his forehead with a used handkerchief. "How can you stand this rat hole?"

Dickson tensed as the pitiful folding chair groaned under Corona's weight. "I like it here," he said. "It helps me concentrate."

"Well!" Corona choked, "I rarely find the opportunity to drop in for a visit and I can hardly say I'm sorry about that. No reflection on you, Detective, merely an observation."

"To what do I owe this… honor?"

"I spoke with Gordon's widow today."

Dickson sank into his chair and felt his grief over the fallen officer begin to surface.

"A fine woman," Corona continued. "Very bad business, of course, especially with those two children and another one on the way. Still, she has family, I'm told, and I'm sure will muddle through."

"Sir," Dickson interrupted. "I can't tell you… I take full responsibility for… If I had known…"

"Oh, for Pete's sake, Detective, stop stammering. You did as much as any officer could. That's not what I want to talk to you about. I want to talk to you about Fantômas."

Dickson looked up, stunned, and quickly slid Harry's letter into his desk drawer. "What about Fantômas?" he asked.

"You're a curious man, Dickson. I must admit that I took you on more in deference to your father than any other reason, and I'm sorry to say that I always expected your timidity and lack of gumption would prevent you from being an exemplary detective. You may have proven me wrong."

"Thank you, sir," Dickson muttered. "I guess."

"When I interviewed Burch and Gregory and all the other officers at the dock that night, a picture of you emerged that I found very intriguing. Really, Dickson–donning disguises, kicking chairs and opening fire on suspects. You're not at all the man I thought you were. Some of the officers said that they couldn't ever remember hearing you actually speak out loud before."

"Pardon me, sir. But what does this have to do with Fantômas?"

"I want him caught, Dickson, and I think you're the man to do it."

"I beg your pardon, sir?"

"Yes, yes, Detective. I will admit a certain amount of reluctance, in the past, when it came to this paranoid fantasy of yours. But one of my men is dead, Dickson. Whether this Fantômas is a single human being, as you say, or a dozen human beings, I want him–or them–arrested. Taken off the streets." Corona paused while Dickson stared at him quizzically. "Something wrong, Dickson?"

Dickson snapped out of his reverie. "No, sir," he said.

"Good! It's settled, then." Corona began to rise out of his chair, huffing for all he was worth, until he was standing fully upright. "The entire force will be at your disposal."

"I beg your pardon, sir?" Dickson repeated.

"Is there something wrong with your ears, Detective? I have just offered you the full support of the New York City Police Force to track down your boogeyman. Most detectives would be flattered by this show of good faith."

"My apologies, sir," Dickson stammered. "It's just that…" Dickson glanced at his desk drawer and remembered Harry's advice. "I think in this particular case, I'd rather go it alone."

"Now it's my turn to say 'I beg your pardon?' "

"Fantômas is no ordinary criminal, sir. I fear that traditional police methodology will be of no use. The best way to track him down may be to… well… use my instincts."

Dickson waited nervously for Corona's reply.

"Your instincts, eh?" Corona huffed. "You're going to sniff him out like a bloodhound, are you?"

Dickson stood his ground. "Yes, sir," he said.

"Very well then. It is, of course, against my own instincts to allow it, but you seem to know more about this man than anyone else. I will trust you for two weeks. No longer. If, after that time, this Fantômas is not in prison, I will take you off the case and bring the full force of the NYPD to bear on him. Until that time, I expect you to share every scrap, every morsel of information with me. Is that understood?"

"Yes, sir. Perhaps…" Dickson paused.

"What is it, Dickson? Spit it out."

"That man," Dickson continued. "The one on the roof in the black mask. Fantômas' pawn. I wonder if I might…"

"Let me stop you before you go any further," Corona interrupted. "The man's name was Sergei Growtowski, and I'm afraid he's no longer with us."

"Dead?" Dickson asked.

"Not dead," Corona replied. "At least as far as I know. We had him in custody and he… well… he disappeared."

"I don't understand."

"Damndest thing. He was in the back of the paddy wagon when we left the docks, but by the time we arrived at the station… nothing."

"Incredible."

"All the more reason why I want this Fantômas arrested. Are we clear, Detective?"

"Crystal," Dickson answered.

"Good. It's settled. In that case, I will now embark on my day-long journey back to my office. Dear God, Detective, if you succeed in this–and I sincerely hope you do–I'm insisting on a new office for you. Preferably one on the ground floor."

"Yes, sir," Dickson said, and remained standing until Corona had waddled his way out of the room.

Something about the entire exchange had struck Dickson as curious. Corona had never given him much attention before, and had certainly never shown great faith in his opinions, much less his talents. Why now? What was it about the

Fantômas case that had sparked Corona's interest?

Dickson began pacing, running his fingers through his tousled hair. What did Corona want? Who was the Woman in Black? Was he searching for the original Fantômas or an imitator? Or a dozen imitators?

Dickson and a gang of villains

Dickson looked up as the doorknob to his office turned. Unusual. Who could it be and why didn't they knock? Half expecting to see Corona's girth fill the doorframe, he was surprised to see Willie Lumpkin smiling at him.

"Hello, Dickson," Lumpkin said, moving toward the detective with uncharacteristic swiftness. "I have a message for you that you may be interested in."

Dickson's instincts screamed that something was wrong. Lumpkin never addressed him as "Dickson," nor was he ever seen without his mail sack. Furthermore, what possible reason could he have for being here? On the other hand, he looked like Lumpkin. Sounded like Lumpkin.

A moment's hesitation was all it took. By the time he

had decided to trust his gut reaction, the syringe clutched in Lumpkin's right hand was already sinking deeply into Dickson's forearm.

"Just relax, Detective Dickson," Lumpkin said. "In a moment, you will have no choice anyway. Your muscles will feel weak, then you will be unable to move altogether. You can still speak, of course, but don't try to move your arms or legs. You'll only be frustrated by the attempt, and it will prolong our meeting beyond that which is comfortable for either one of us."

"Fantômas."

"Clever man. Try not to panic. I have not immobilized you permanently, only for an hour or so. Long enough for us to come to an agreement." Fantômas pulled a chair forward and sat opposite Dickson, who was slumped forward, his arms hanging useless by his sides. "Lift your head, Detective. I want to be able to see your eyes. It's unpleasant engaging in a summit with another man's forehead."

Dickson could sense all feeling leaving his extremities as he lifted his eyes to address the man who looked exactly like Willie Lumpkin. "Lumpkin," he muttered, his words beginning to slur. "You killed him?"

Fantômas laughed. "I'm flattered that you know me so well, Mr. Dickson. But no, as a gesture of good faith, I have allowed him live. Believe me when I say that no one is more surprised by that choice than I am, but the business we have to discuss is far more important that the life of a lowly mail carrier."

"What do you want?"

"Why, Detective Dickson, I thought you'd never ask. It is, after all, the reason I'm here. I…" Fantômas began, standing up from his chair and drawing from his shirt pocket a small American flag. "I want to be an American." He began waving the tiny flag to and fro in front of Dickson's eyes.

"You're insane," Dickson snarled.

"Of course, I am!" Fantômas chortled. "Who but an insane man would charter a filthy room at the bottom of a ship, travel for months to this country with barely a penny in his pocket, only to set up shop in a filthy, disease-ridden hellhole for the express purpose of waiting for the angel of freedom to bestow her graces on me? To shower me with wealth beyond imagining? There are thousands of people like that here, Detective. Are they all insane?"

"They are poor. They are honest."

"And that will be their undoing. Lured to this rotten island with the hope of finding two or three extra potatoes a year, they file in and out of the factories, shovel coal, stitch rags, risk life and limb so that a handful of industrialists prosper. And they do it every day, 24 hours a day, with smiles on their faces."

Dickson was beginning to grow impatient. "Stop wasting my time, Fantômas. You want to be an American? Is that really why we're having this conversation?"

"It is precisely why we're having this conversation, Mr. Dickson. But I can't do it without your help. I have a deal to make with you."

"I don't make deals with the Devil."

"Even if, by making a deal, you could ensure that the Devil ceased to exist?" Fantômas raised one eyebrow and waited for Dickson's reaction.

"Go on," Dickson answered, his curiosity piqued.

"The agreement I wish to offer you is this, Mr. Dickson. You will end your pursuit of me and I will cease my criminal activities."

Dickson stared at Fantômas, waiting for him to speak again. "You expect me to believe you?"

"I may be a violent, hateful man, Detective, but my word is as good as gold. You leave me alone to pursue my dreams, to follow my bliss and I, in turn, will end all of my criminal activities."

Dickson was stunned. Something told him that Fantômas was telling the truth, but the other part of him, the instinct that he had ignored, leading him into these dire circumstances, told him there was something dreadfully wrong. "You will end your life of crime," said Dickson, "and what? Live the rest of your life as an honest, ethical, moral philanthropist?"

Fantômas began to laugh. Not the sinister, ironic laughter that Dickson had seen before, but a series of uncontrollable guffaws, leading him to brush tears from his eyes and clutch his sides in hysteria. After a few moments, he collected himself. "Very good, Dickson," Fantômas said with a smile, "And here I assumed you were a humorless champion of the oppressed. It's a funny thing about America, Detective. Freedom is valued, but honesty is not. The ethics of hard work are trumpeted by everyone, but hardly adhered to by those in control of the city's wealth. And as for morality…" And here, Fantômas leaned in to Dickson and met his eyes, "In what fairy tale world do you live in, Detective, in which being a law-abiding citizen is somehow synonymous with morality?"

Dickson said nothing. Fantômas leaned back in his chair and drew a cigarette from his top pocket. "Crime, as an occupation, is far too easy in this city. All it takes is a little influence and charisma and one can easily persuade a handful of desperate individuals to do their dirty work for a few pennies a day. The allure of fear, of terror, of chaos, have always been more profoundly rewarding to me than that of crime. I see endless possibilities for me in this country. Why, with my ambition and drive, surely I could become a captain of industry. Is there anyone more powerful in this city than its entrepreneurs? They are gods! They can save or end a life with a signature, destroy a family's livelihood on little more than an impulse. That is power, Detective Dickson. You know it as well as I. I've done at least as much research on you as you have done on me, and I know that it was precisely because you had such empathy for the working class that you failed miserably as a businessman. You were forced, by your lack of foresight, to abandon the people you cared most about. And what happened? 148 innocent souls perished in a fire that could have been prevented. The man responsible for their deaths, the man you turned your company over to, didn't serve a day in prison. Do you know why, Detective Dickson?

Because he committed no crime. A crime against humanity, perhaps, and certainly he possessed rather questionable morals and ethics, but was he strictly speaking, a criminal? It's a conundrum, and one that I find endlessly fascinating.

"But I also find myself at an impasse. Do I really want to give up the life of crime that I've nursed so carefully for so many years? Even now, I have planted seeds all over the city that could bloom at any moment into some of the most remarkable acts of lawlessness that I have ever committed. Do I wish to abandon these opportunities after so much… hard work?

"So you will make this decision for me, Detective Dickson. Quit your infernal pursuit of me and I will never again commit another crime."

"And yet," Dickson interrupted, "you will continue to exploit the poor immigrants of this city. You will remain a force of evil."

"Well, you can't have everything."

Dickson suddenly remembered the warning he had received from the Woman in Black. "She warned me," he said. "The Woman in Black told me to do as you say."

Suddenly, at the mention of the mysterious woman, Fantômas stopped and stared with curiosity at Dickson. His eyes darted back and forth and he cleared his throat. It was a brief moment, scarcely a fraction of a second, but Dickson saw it happen. A moment later, Fantômas had pulled himself together. "Women that dress in black are, indeed, the most alluring, Mr. Dickson. But I'm afraid I don't know who you could possibly be talking about. Perhaps you have been the victim of a cruel prank. In any case, let's not speak of mysterious women. We haven't much time left and I would rather return to the subject at hand. Will you, or will you not, accept my offer?"

"And how do you propose I do this? I can't just stop searching for you. You have crimes to answer for, Fantômas. You are a thief and a murderer. Your resolution hardly matters in light of the atrocities you have already committed."

Fantômas chuckled. "Arrest me, Mr. Dickson. Put me in prison. Throw away the key."

"I don't understand."

Fantômas crushed out his cigarette and removed from his pocket a small photograph and tossed it on the desk where Dickson could examine it. "His name is Brian Shea," Fantômas explained, "and he made the mistake of disobeying me. After a recent conversation, he and I agreed that the best thing for him and his family would be for him to admit that he is Fantômas."

"You would pass your crimes off on an innocent man?"

"Ha! He is hardly innocent, Mr. Dickson. He is a thief with a history of wrongdoing. He was bound to end up in prison sooner or later. At least, this way he will achieve some small amount of fame in his lifetime. You will arrest him, with my cooperation, and he will become Fantômas. I will provide you with the evidence to charge him with every crime that has ever been attributed to me, and many that haven't. He will go to jail, you will be a hero and I will… I don't know… become a newspaper publisher or something. Wouldn't that be grand? Then I could retire and write a self-serving autobiography about how I was born with ink in my veins.

"But back to the unfortunate Mr. Shea. In any case, his family will be well provided for, you will have the notoriety you seek, and I will become a very wealthy man. Everybody wins."

Dickson's eyes narrowed sharply and his lips stretched tight in anger. "I can't listen to this nonsense any longer," he said. "If you think I will allow you to harm the hard working people of this city while you sit in your high tower, completely above reproach, then it's possible that you are even more insane than I give you credit for. The answer is an emphatic *no*, Fantômas. A thousand times *no*!"

Fantômas suddenly burst from his chair and clutched Dickson by the collar, lifting his still frozen body and driving it to the floor. "I could kill you, Detective. I could kill you right at this moment and spend the rest of my life wreaking havoc on this city and there would be no Frederick Dickson to stop me. What makes you think I won't?"

Dickson strained to raise his head and stared Fantômas in the eyes. "Because," he said, "with the exception of a handful of disreputable petty crooks, I am the only one who knows for certain that you exist."

"And?"

"And," Dickson smiled, "I rather think you like that."

Fantômas continued to stare at Dickson, his eyes bloodshot and full of venom. He held Dickson by the collar, straddling his inert body as it lay on the floor, his anger rising as he snarled hot air into Dickson's face. "I want you to see it happen," Fantômas said. "I want you to witness the terror that you helped create. I want you to go to your grave knowing that you could have stopped it, but refused. I want you to know that you are responsible for all the misery, all the suffering that is about to descend upon this city."

Fantômas lifted Dickson and placed him back in his chair. He dusted himself off, regained his composure and walked to the door. "Tomorrow night, at the stroke of nine, I will kidnap Professor James Harrington. Prepare all you like. Take all the precautions you will. You will fail to stop me, Mr. Dickson. When the clock strikes nine, Professor Harrington will be in my possession. I will show no mercy to this city, Detective. Nor will I, the next time we meet, show any mercy toward you."

Fantômas reached into his pocket and removed his watch. "Fifty minutes to go, Mr. Dickson, and you will regain your mobility. I suggest you take the time to enjoy the relaxation. These minutes will be last moments of peace you will ever experience."

Fantômas turned on his heel and left the office. As the door swung closed, Dickson could hear Fantômas greeting someone with the voice of Willie Lumpkin. "Afternoon!" he said. "Top of the morning!" the other voice replied.

Dickson sat in his chair, waiting for sensation to return to his hands and feet, and remembered Fantômas' curious reaction to the mention of the Woman in Black. He had clearly been caught off guard. For the first time, Dickson had observed in Fantômas a moment of confusion–of weakness.

Fantômas was not impenetrable. He was afraid of something.

And her name was Lady Beltham.

WILLIAM FOX PRESENTS
FANTOMAS
1921 American Serial in 20 Episodes
FROM THE WORLD FAMOUS STORIES OF MARCEL ALLAIN AND PIERRE SOUVESTRE
EDWARD SEDGWICK
EPISODE ONE
"ON THE STROKE OF NINE"

Chapter Five: On the Stroke of Nine

"Dash it all, I'm sorry, but it strikes me as a lot of rot, by God!"

The man with the false British dialect is actually New York born and bred. He is standing by the hearth, holding a cigarette in one hand while smoothing down his moustache wax with the other.

"I mean no one appreciates a good adventure as much as I do, by God, but it all seems rather silly, don't you think?"

Six years ago, Jack Meredith was a student at Oxford where he found his British classmates frightfully exciting and rather more refined than his former playmates from upstate New York. At the age of 23, he returned to New York to take over his father's munitions plant, and became one of the wealthiest arms dealer in the country. He is one of Manhattan's favorite sons.

"A Parisian master criminal on Long Island! It sounds like a jolly good hand-wringer, that, and if I were reading it in a dime novel, I'd be up all night chattering away at my fingernails. But surely, such people don't actually exist!"

We are in the home of Professor James Harrington–inventor, chemist and explorer. He owns one of the most ornate and luxurious homes on the north shore of Long Island. Built on the side of a small cliff, the living-room windows looking out onto the ocean, the Harrington mansion has long been the envy of residents and travelers alike. The floors are polished redwood, and the walls are hung with dozens of trophies from Harrington's many expeditions–the head of a buffalo, several spears from an unknown race of Amazonian tribesmen, a golden Buddha and shelf upon shelf of maps, globes, statues and icons. There is hardly enough room for the large leather chairs and oversized grandfather clock against the back wall.

"Not people," Dickson explained, "but a single person.

Fantômas."

"And you think he wishes to kidnap me?" Professor Harrington asked, puffing on his pipe and stroking his bushy white beard.

"He made the threat," Dickson answered, "and to Fantômas, a threat is as good as a promise."

"But don't you worry!" Corona chimed in, shifting his girth in the leather chair and making an extraordinary noise in the process. "This house is surrounded by the finest policemen in the country!"

"The world's finest," Harrington chuckled.

"Right!" Corona shouted, then punctuated his enthusiasm with an elongated coughing fit that left his face a distressing shade of red. "Great Gravy!" he sputtered. "That steak from Delmonicos is not sitting well with me at all."

The grandfather clock began to chime.

"Odd," Corona said. "It's 8:30 p.m."

"Yes," said Harrington, "The damned clock is a half an hour ahead. Can't figure out what's wrong with it."

"Professor Harrington," Dickson said, turning the conversation back to more important matters. "Can you think of any reason why Fantômas would target you for kidnapping?"

"For robbery, yes. But for kidnapping?" Harrington shook his head and thought for a moment, tapping out his pipe on the side of the chair. "As you can see, every corner of this house is crammed full of priceless treasures, but what would someone like this Fantômas do with them?"

"Sell them to a collector, I gather," Jack offered.

"Doubtful," said Dickson. "Fantômas is no gentleman burglar or mischievous thief. He is bent on power and destruction. I have no doubt that whatever he's planning has ramifications that go far beyond anything we've thought of yet."

"Well I, for one, am sick and tired of all the lazy foreigners trying to ruin this great city!"

Meredith's outburst was such a non-sequitur that it was

met, for a moment, with confused silence.

"Think about it," Meredith proffered. "Just what is it that allows some dastardly Frenchie to commandeer this great American metropolis? Why, it would certainly be all right with me if some of the shiftless immigrants were rounded up and shipped back to where they came from. Don't get me wrong. I know we're all from someplace else–Plymouth Rock and all that–but really it's getting out of hand."

"Don't tell me you're going on about that again, Jack," the female voice came from the other room. "Really, gentlemen, you mustn't let him start speaking or he'll never stop."

Ruth Harrington entered the room in a way that only Ruth Harrington could–with an effortless confidence that many people referred to as masculine and a coy lilt that pegged her instantly as feminine. The combination was so apparent and disarming that Dickson felt himself begin to blush the moment she turned to extend her hand.

"Good evening. You must be Detective Dickson."

"Yes, ma'am," Dickson mumbled. "Nice to meet you."

Although Ruth had no memory of it, this was not the first meeting between her and Frederick Dickson. Years earlier, she and her father had given a presentation at Columbia. Dickson attended, partly out of interest in hearing of the Professor's exploits, and partly out of loneliness following the factory debacle that had driven him to hermit himself in his home. For more than an hour, Dickson listened to Professor Harrington regale the audience with stories of his adventures in the Amazon jungle. Dickson was, if not rapt with attention, at least distracted. He hadn't counted on seeing Ruth Harrington, sitting behind her father on the dais and assisting him with his displays of maps and trinkets from Brazil. While she didn't capture Dickson's eye immediately, he found himself gradually unable to concentrate on what the scientist was saying, and more enchanted by her grace. She was wearing a dark green dress made of fabric that seemed to anticipate her every move and shift accordingly. By the time Harrington had finished speaking, Dickson was almost breathless with longing.

Following the presentation, Dickson ambled around the adjoining hall, pretending to examine Harrington's collection of artifacts that had been placed on display. Knowing that Harrington would have to leave by a nearby door in order to greet his colleagues, Dickson loitered as closely as possible, waiting to catch a glimpse of Ruth and her enchanted green dress. As time rolled on, Dickson decided to forego his silly fantasy and simply make his way back to his home. Suddenly, the door opened and Dickson, for the second time that night, found himself stunned by Ruth Harrington.

For reasons he could not guess, Ruth had taken the time to change out of her dress and into a pair of pants and a white collared shirt. She seemed suddenly so brash that Dickson was afraid of even approaching her. The contrast between her public self and this, her private self, only thrilled Dickson more.

Ruth Harrington was two people.

His head spinning, Dickson approached Ruth and her father, both of whom were now swarmed with well-wishers and representatives of the press, and tried to make his way through the crowd. By the time he was within striking distance, the pair had made their way to the exit. Dickson offered his hand to Professor Harrington, mumbling congratulations of some sort, but a quick whiff of Ruth's perfume drained him of any courage he had, and he brushed past her with a "hello" that came out a little too loud and awkward.

Professor Harrington and Ruth left the building and Dickson never saw her again.

Until tonight.

"Well I'm dreadfully sorry if I offend, but it's the truth," Jack continued. "If we could simply get control of this immigration problem, we wouldn't be holed up here tonight like rats in a trap!"

"You are suggesting some sort of screening process for

master criminals trying to sneak into the country?" The sarcasm in Dickson's voice surprised everyone, not the least of whom was Dickson himself.

Jack lifted one eyebrow and delivered a polished smirk. "You misunderstand me, Detective. I'm merely suggesting that some sort of barriers must be put into place to prevent the more lazy and shiftless immigrants from planting themselves in our fair city and gumming up the works. That's all."

"Ignore my fiancé, Detective," Ruth said, giving Jack a playful slap on the shoulder. "The only foreigners he comes into contact with are the ones that spend all day putting together his toy guns."

Dickson was trying to listen, but he felt his face flush after hearing the word "fiancé."

"Well, I'm sorry!" Jack protested, "I know that there are probably good, upstanding, hard-working people out there, trying to make better lives for themselves, but I haven't been able to hire any. Do you know that we've spent the past year charting their work progress, their rate of speed and productivity, and the data shows that virtually nothing gets done after three o'clock in the afternoon? Why, I may as well end the work day four hours early. It's as if someone has pumped sleeping gas into the building."

"Perhaps they're hungry."

Once again, the quiet venom lurking behind Dickson's comment brought silence to the room. "Well," Jack said, with an awkward tinge to his voice. "They ought to buy some food, then, oughtn't they?"

Jack's comment led to more silence, until the sound of the grandfather clock ticking became the loudest noise in the room.

"Detective Dickson," Corona grunted, breaking a sweat as he pried himself from his chair. "Perhaps I could see you in the other room for a moment."

Corona planted his cane on the floor and ambled toward Dickson. The detective, his head spinning with fury and embarrassment, followed the sergeant into a neighboring room. "Would you mind telling me," Corona began, once they were out of earshot, "just what, exactly, you think you're doing?"

"My apologies, sir," Dickson stammered. "I didn't mean…"

"Didn't mean what?" Corona snapped. "Didn't mean to insult one of the most influential young men in the city? For God's sake, Detective. I'm counting on you to resolve this Fantômas matter and I'm more than willing to play things your way. But if your way includes blatantly chastising the families that have built this city into the great metropolis that it is…"

Dickson interrupted. "I have no intention of criticizing his business acumen, Sergeant. But anyone who claims to know about the lives of the immigrant population without ever setting foot among them…"

"And have you set foot among them, Detective Dickson? Have you worked beside them? Breathed the same air that they breathe? Broken bread with them? Because the last I heard, you were still living quite well off of your father's money."

The accusation was delivered with fierce intensity and succeeded in silencing Dickson. He stared at the ground, his face flushed with humiliation.

"Let's get something straight, Detective. Your father was a good friend of mine, and I have no intention of dishonoring his memory by firing his son. Tom Meredith is also a good friend of mine. He is also a good friend of the Mayor's, as well as every person of influence in this city. We will capture Fantômas, but we will do it without angering the good men who run this city. Is that clear, Detective Dickson?"

Dickson cleared his throat and continued staring at the ground. "Yes, sir," he said.

"I didn't hear you, Detective."

"I'm sorry, sir."

"Good. Now get back in there and make nice with Jack Meredith."

"Yes, sir."

"And for God's sake, stop ogling Ruth Harrington. It's making everyone nervous."

Dickson blushed even further, and broke out into a cold sweat. "Yes, sir," he repeated.

The lovely Rurth Harrington and her esteemed fiancé, Mr. Jack Meredith

Corona turned his back on Dickson and lurched back into the living room. Dickson followed close behind. "A fine house you've got here, Professor Harrington!" Corona exclaimed, in an effort to break the tension.

"Thank you, Sergeant," Harrington replied. "Over the years, my home has become my own private museum. When I'm not traveling, I like nothing more than studying and cataloguing my various treasures."

"Excuse me," Dickson said, drawing a threatening glare from Corona.

"What is it, Detective?" Ruth asked.

Dickson found his confidence and addressed Jack Meredith. "I just wanted to apologize to you, sir. Please understand that I bear you no ill will, I simply grow concerned when the plight of the poor and downtrodden is addressed."

"Think nothing of it, Detective," Jack said with a brief laugh. "It's a conversation that's more likely to go round in circles than it is to come to any serious conclusion. Take a hundred people from a hundred different countries and plop them down in the same neighborhood, there are bound to be problems."

"If I may," Harrington began, relighting his pipe and adjusting his smoking jacket. "As someone who has spent much of his life traveling to the far corners of the world and rubbing elbows with the natives, perhaps I can speak to this whole issue of foreign cultures in America."

"Of course, Professor Harrington," Corona chimed enthusiastically. "We'd love to hear your educated opinions. There are those of us, far too many of us, that offer opinions without the benefit of personal experience." He shot a sideways glace at Dickson.

"First of all," Harrington began, with the air of a man who had seen it all and, furthermore, knew he had seen it all, "Americans aren't the only civilized people on the planet. That much is obvious, I know, but too many people have never given themselves the gift of traveling to a foreign land and prefer to think that America is the pinnacle of intelligence and ambition. Not true. The Germans–also very ambitious. The Spanish are a very proud people, and the English make the best tea I've ever had. Drop down below the equator, though, and you'll find all sorts of races and tribes that, while fascinating and beautiful in their own way, still maintain a bit of old world savagery. For instance, did you know that some of the tribes still partake in the custom of eating human flesh?"

"My God!" blurted Corona, mopping his brow with a handkerchief. "Gruesome!"

"And yet," Harrington continued, "the more time one spends with them, observing their daily routines and customs, the more one begins to accept these kinds of practices as normal."

Jack laughed. "Cannibalism? Normal? Perhaps that's the solution to the foreigner problem right there, Professor. Allow the immigrants to simply feed on themselves. Only the strong survive, yes?"

Dickson bit his tongue.

"Yes, normal," Harrington declared. "And that is the danger of immersing one's self in the beauty of another culture. One runs the risk of losing sight of one's own civility. Perhaps this Fantômas, whoever he may be, is someone who engages in behavior that, while it may seem brutal to us, is simply his nature."

"Pardon me for interrupting, Professor," Dickson began, noticing Corona's threatening glance out of the corner of his eye. "But you can hardly compare the two. Fantômas acts out of sheer maliciousness, not from some inherent primitivism. He is nothing if not sophisticated. By contrast, the Indian tribes you speak of do not engage in their native customs out of evil."

Jack laughed again and clapped Dickson on the shoulder. "Cannibalism?" he chortled, "Not evil? There is evil everywhere, Detective. I'm sure the good Professor can attest to the fact that despite the so-called 'beauty' he experienced in the wilds of the Amazon, he saw and experienced things that could only be described as evil."

Professor Harrington grew quiet, and it was clear to Dickson that he was remembering some horrid experience or distant suffering. "Yes," he said. "However!" he charged, shaking off his reverie, "the Amazonian Indians are not unintelligent! Quite the contrary! They can be taught, and reasoned with and–yes, I'll say it–civilized. You all had the privilege of meeting my houseboy, Poturu, didn't you?"

"A charming boy!" Corona said. "Took my coat and everything. Hardly even noticed he was there."

"You'll be surprised to learn," Harrington added, "that Poturu comes from Fortoleza, on the coast of Brazil. Poturu!" Harrington shouted, which was followed almost immediately, by Poturu's entrance. He wore an impeccable uniform and stood, with complete confidence, in the doorway with his hands comfortably by his sides.

"Poturu and I hit it off immediately, the day we met," said Harrington. "Isn't that right, Poturu?"

"Yes, sir," Poturu said, with a deep, rich voice that betrayed only a hint of his South American accent.

Harrington laughed. He clearly had a great deal of affection for the native boy. "Why, when Poturu told me that he wanted to learn how to read English, I thought–by God, here's a golden opportunity to make a difference in a young man's life. Isn't that right, Poturu?"

"Yes, sir."

"We're still working on the reading, but in the meantime, he has become the perfect houseboy. Right, Poturu?"

"Yes, sir."

"Pardon me for interrupting, Dad," Ruth said, causing Dickson's heart to leap into his throat, "but it is 8:50 p.m. Isn't that the time that the 'Terror of Paris' is supposed to whisk you away to parts unknown?"

"Not a chance in the world!" Corona shouted. "My men have the place surrounded. Every door is barred, every officer is well armed."

"Nevertheless," Dickson added, "it could be fatal for us to lower our guard at this point. Fantômas can be lethal if underestimated."

"My God, Dickson," said Corona. "You don't have to scare them, do you?"

Dickson ignored Corona and made his way around the perimeter of the room. While the others watched, he shut and locked every door leading to other parts of the house. He then turned his attention toward the windows. After checking to make sure there was a police officer below each window, he tested the bolts on each window frame, and drew the curtains.

"Goodness," Jack declared. "An awfully thorough detective you have here, Sergeant. Window bolts and everything."

"Everyone should remain calm!" Corona said, taking charge of the room. "You are all in the protective hands of the New York City Police Department."

Dickson finished his rounds and stood in the center of the room, his eyes trained on Professor Harrington.

Harrington grew uncomfortable under Dickson's gaze. "Now what do we do?" he asked.

"We wait," Dickson answered.

Inside the Harrington mansion

And wait, they did. Each of them glancing from side to side at one another, but none of them stirring a muscle for fear that the noise might startle the others. Corona drew out his pocket watch and stared at the second hand as it drove the clock closer to 9 p.m.

A hush fell over the group. At first, all they could hear was one another breathing, until the sound of the grandfather clock ticking seemed to grow louder and louder. It was Corona that broke the silence. "It is now 9:01 p.m.," he said.

"Impossible," said Dickson. "Your watch must be fast."

Another minute of silence.

"My watch is not fast, Detective," said Corona. "Furthermore, it is now 9:02 p.m."

"We're not moving," said Dickson. "No one is to move until I say so."

Five minutes of silence.

"This is silly," Jack said. "And I have a cramp in my foot."

"It's 9:07 p.m.," Corona said. "I think we have to admit the fact that we have outsmarted Fantômas."

"It's not possible," Dickson said.

"Not possible?" Corona snorted. "You would rather we fail? You think Fantômas can't be outsmarted?"

"Of course, he can," Dickson said. "If he were unbeatable, why would we..." Dickson looked around the room and met everyone's eyes for the first time since the countdown to nine had begun. "For him not to even make the attempt..."

Suddenly, Dickson dashed to the window, threw open the curtains, unlocked the frames and raised the glass. "Jenkins!" he shouted. "You OK out there?"

"Just fine!" Jenkins answered.

"Have you seen anything? Heard anything?"

"Not a thing, Detective!"

"Damn!" Dickson swore, turning from the window and marching back into the center of the room.

"I'm very confused by your behavior, Detective," Harrington said, tapping his pipe. "I'm still here. I'm safe. I'm well. Surely that's a good thing."

"A very good thing," Dickson answered. "Something just doesn't feel right."

"Well, of course not," Jack offered, sitting down and

rubbing his cramped calf. "Here we were expecting the worst and nothing happened. I dare say we were overreacting."

"I'll tell you what I think!" Corona puffed out his chest with pride. "Our good friend Fantômas realized he was no match for the New York City Police Department!"

"Hear, hear!" Harrington cheered. "Poturu! Some drinks please!"

"Yes, sir." Poturu said.

"Martinis? Everyone? Everyone?"

Everyone but Dickson nodded.

"Martinis for everyone, Poturu," Harrington said. "And don't spare the olives!"

"Yes, sir," Poturu said, and left the room.

"A cigar, Sergeant?" Harrington said, and produced an ornate gold and red cigar box from the fireplace mantle.

"Don't mind if I do, Professor," Corona answered. "Don't mind if I do."

"India's finest tobacco leaves," Harrington said, passing one of the cigars under his nose.

Corona planted the cigar between his lips and stood proud in front of the fireplace. "Let this be a lesson to all the criminals in New York," he said. "No one, not even the infamous Fantômas, gets past the NYPD! Ten minutes past nine, Dickson. As much as it pains you to do so, perhaps you ought to admit that we've won."

Suddenly, Ruth stepped further into the room and stood next to Dickson. "I agree with Detective Dickson," she said. "Something doesn't feel right." Dickson turned to look at Ruth. Ruth stared back in turn. A feeling of unnamable dread passed between them.

"What do you mean, darling?" Jack said, placing his hands on Ruth's shoulders. "Maybe you're just tired."

"I don't know," Ruth said, slightly twisting away from Jack's grasp. "It's just a feeling, that's all," she added, meeting Dickson's gaze once again. "I can't explain it."

It was Dickson that finally broke the gaze. "Professor Harrington," he said, walking toward the scientist and unconsciously waving the cigar smoke from his face. "You have said that you can't imagine why Fantômas would want to kidnap you..."

"That's correct," Harrington answered. "I haven't the slightest idea."

"What does that have to do with anything?" Corona asked. "From what you've told me of Fantômas, it strikes me that punctuality is one of his very few virtues."

Dickson ignored him. "You've recently returned from one of your expeditions, haven't you?"

"Well, I don't see that it matters, but yes, I returned about a week ago. Ruth and I spent two months in the rain forest. Poturu stayed here and took care of the house."

"Did he see anything strange while you were away?"

"You can ask him yourself when he returns, but I'm sure he would have mentioned it."

"While you were away, Professor, did you discover something significant? Did you bring back anything of importance?"

Dickson knew by the look in the scientist's eyes that he had struck a nerve. Harrington's glance shot toward his daughter. "No," he said. "Just the usual. A wood carving or two. Some native coins."

"Professor," Dickson pressed forward until he was nose to nose with Harrington. "If there's something you're not telling me, if there's some piece of information you're withholding, I entreat you to tell me what it is, regardless of whether or not it seems important."

"Give the man some air, Dickson!" Corona shouted. "If it was important, he'd tell you!"

Dickson realized he had overstepped his bounds, but was determined to ascertain the truth. He was left with two mysteries–the reasons for Fantômas' threats, and the reason for his failure to follow through on them.

Poturu entered with a tray of drinks.

"Have a cocktail, Detective," Jack said, lifting two off of the tray and handing one to Dickson. "We may as well relax for the rest of the evening."

Relax they did. At least, everyone but Dickson. While the conversation continued, punctuated by amusing anecdotes and ebullient laughter, Dickson remained silent and troubled. He turned the facts over in his mind, but it wasn't the facts that were distracting him. It was his gut. Cousin Harry had instructed him to forget about logic and rationality and trust his instincts. He had almost begun to feel on the edge of madness when he happened to glance over at Ruth. He realized then that she hadn't spoken in several minutes. She turned and met his gaze. She had the same feeling, and wore the same haunted look. *Something that Fantômas said that night in my office...* he thought. But what was it?

And then the clock began to chime.

Everyone looked up with a start.

"Damn clock." Harrington said. "I really must get it fixed. Ever since Ruth and I returned, it strikes on the half hour. Damnedest thing I've ever seen. Can't figure out what's wrong with it."

...Clock strikes on the half-hour...

...Clock strikes...

The clock struck.

... At the stroke of nine...

Fantômas had said, "At the stroke of nine, I will kidnap Professor James Harrington."

Not at nine, *at the stroke of nine*!

The clock was striking now. One... two... three...

"Everyone!" Dickson shouted. "Into the room! Now!"

Jack leapt from his chair. "What the Devil...?"

"Nobody move!" Dickson shouted again, then ran to the window and shouted at Jenkins. "This is it, Jenkins! Look alive!"

"I'm here, sir!" Jenkins answered. Dickson bolted the window shut and drew the curtains.

"The doors!" Dickson shut and locked all the doors leading to the living room after pulling the confused Poturu through the doorway.

Seven... eight... nine!

Dickson turned to Ruth. Her hands were pressed to her face in sheer panic. She understood.

And then the lights went out.

"Bloody Hell!" Jack shouted. "I'm terrified of the dark!"

There was the sound of a rusty hinge.

Everyone screamed. Dickson begged for them to calm down. Harrington's voice rose above the din. "Help! For God's sake, help!"

"Dad! Dad!"

Dickson leapt blindly into the darkness toward Harrington's chair. He caught a handful of the scientist's robe and pulled his way into the fray. He felt two muscular arms pushing him away, so he lashed out with his fists, trying desperately to subdue Harrington's attacker. A single fist caught him on the side of the jaw and he felt himself letting go of the robe and falling to the floor.

When the lights came back on, Dickson was still on the floor, facing away from the chair toward Corona, Jack and Ruth–all of whom were staring in horror at something over his shoulder. He turned with a start. Professor Harrington was gone, and in his place was a single business card, carefully placed in the center of the chair. Dickson pulled himself to his feet, picked up the card and read it:

With regards, Fantômas.

It is here that Act I of our dreadful story reaches its close–with the strange disappearance of Professor Harrington and the threat of Fantômas more dangerous than ever. Take a break to calm your nerves, if you must, for the horror will only grow worse in Act II–in which Fantômas' true motives are revealed and Detective Dickson is set upon by hundreds of blood-thirsty rats.

ACT II

In which Fantômas' true motives are revealed and Detective Dickson is set upon by hundreds of blood-thirsty rats.

Chapter Six: Messengers of Evil

We are back on the Lower East Side, 24 hours after our previous visit. We are inside a tiny, cramped tenement building occupied by Brian and Sally Shea. Sally is changing the baby while Brian sits on the windowsill, blowing the smoke from a handmade cigarette out the window.

Although Brian Shea had never read a work of literature from beginning to end, he was still intimately familiar with the concept of irony. The tiny room that he had viewed as a prison had, now that the threat of a real prison loomed, become the only place he could experience freedom. He found himself unable to turn and look at Sally, though he knew she was staring at him. He could hear the baby's gurgling and the sound of the cloth diaper being changed.

Shea had never really thought about prison before. His childhood in Ireland had been spent in a house little bigger than a horse stable. Room enough, perhaps, had it not been for his three brothers and two sisters. Still, Shea looked forward to the day when his siblings would leave for America, while he, the oldest son, would stay behind and take over the land. A reasonable enough plan, and one that would have worked out, had he not fallen in with the Irish Republican Army when he was 16. By the time the family's emigration plans were in place, Shea, whose real first name was Liam, was on the run from the authorities. Were it not for the sacrifice of his brother Brian, who allowed Liam to take his identity in order to gain passage to America, Shea might have entered prison long ago.

Years later, he was still living life under his younger brother's name and in trouble once again. His relief at having successfully fled the IRA had lasted less than two months before he found himself in league with a group of petty thieves. One of those men, the one everyone called the Torch, had taken Shea in, let him sleep on his bed and eat his food. They became fast friends. They cracked safes together, starved together, and when Shea married Sally in front of the Justice of the Peace, the Torch was the only witness.

The unfortunate Mr. Brian Shea

When a mysterious criminal, calling himself Fantômas, began recruiting able-bodied men in the Fall of 1912, Torch was one of the first to jump at the opportunity. Shea, never one to turn down an adventure with a friend, went along for the ride. For over an hour, Brian Shea and the Torch sat through the passionate sermonizing of the captivating Father Rose until the service was over, the doors locked and the Torch introduced Shea to the smiling priest.

"Hello, Father," Shea said.

"Actually," Father Rose replied, "My name is Fantômas. And I have need of your talents."

Now he was trapped once again in a prison he had created, dreaming of Ireland's rolling hills and the too crowded stable. He tried to picture jail–its rusted bars and dank scent. He wondered if he'd be able to visit with Sally, or if he would be shuffled off to Rikers Island, too dangerous for contact with anyone from the outside. Would he ever see his son again? Would his son ever recognize his Da, or would he know him only as Fantômas?

"Brian," Sally said, breaking the silence. "Maybe you could come here and hold him for a bit. He's squirming something terrible."

Brian didn't answer, but tossed his cigarette out the window and stepped over to his wife and child. "Good Lord," he snapped. "Just went an hour ago. We go through a dozen pair of britches a week."

Sally stared at her husband. "He's only a baby, Brian," she said.

Brian turned toward Sally and could see the confused look in her eyes. "I'm sorry," he said.

"What's wrong?" Sally asked.

And Brian told her everything.

He began with Fantômas. He recalled the day the baby was sick and he decided to give the job to Garibaldi. He told her about Garibaldi's murder in prison. Finally, he told her about his meeting with Torch and the subsequent orders from Father Rose. Sally sat in silence, rocking the baby, until he was finished.

"I thought we were honest people," she said.

"I'm sorry," Brian offered once again, knowing it couldn't make up for what he had done, but also knowing he had little else to offer. "I'm doing this for you," he added. "He swore that he'd take care of you."

"And you believe him?" Sally snapped. "A creature like him? What happens when he changes his mind, Brian? What happens when he decides we're just too much of a nuisance to care for anymore?"

"What choice do I have?" Brian shouted, pacing furiously around room. "I've seen what he does to people that try to betray him. He'll kill us both, Sally. He'll kill the baby. Maybe if I do what he says…"

Sally finished his thought. "Maybe our child will grow up without a father. And I'll spend the rest of my life listening to people talk about how you're a horrid criminal. What happens when Denny grows up? When he's old enough to fend for himself? Will Fantômas come for him too? After taking care of us for so long, do you really think he won't expect a payback of some kind?"

Brian stared at his feet, taking it all in. He knew Sally was right. His chest beginning to heave with sobs, he sat on the edge of the bed and held his face in his hands. Sally stood and walked over to the stove and took down a sugar jar from a small, rickety shelf. Balancing the baby on one arm, she opened the jar and withdrew a roll of bills. Brian looked up and she tossed the roll into his lap.

"It ain't much," she said. "Been saving it from the extra laundry I do. Would it be enough for three train tickets?"

Brian unrolled the bills and began counting. "It might be," he said. "But train tickets to where?"

"Does it matter? We may only make it as far as Boston, but would we be any worse off than we are now?"

"How can I ask you and Denny to sleep in the streets?"

"How can you ask us to give up a husband and a father? How can you ask us to enslave ourselves to that… that… beast?"

Denny began to cry and Sally paced the floor and bounced him gently in her arms. Brian stared at the roll of bills in his hands, then again at his wife and child. The conversation was over, for now, but the problem remained and Brian could imagine no resolution.

Hours later, his wife sleeping by his side, clutching their son to her breast, Brian stared at the ceiling, listening to the ticking of the clock and the clanging of the pipes. He glanced at his watch–it was 2 a.m. Taking care not to jostle Sally and the baby, he slid out from under the covers and stood beside the bed. Once Sally's labored breathing had convinced him that she was asleep, he got dressed, pulled on his jacket and left the apartment, taking care not to let the door squeak too loudly on his way out.

It was madness. Furthermore, Brian Shea knew it was madness. Standing across the street from the dimly-lit Our Lady of Perpetual Sorrow church, Shea stood in the shadows, mustering the courage to go forward. It had taken him 20 minutes to run from his tenement to this alleyway. If he could get in and out of the church in ten minutes, he could make it back to bed before daylight and Sally would never even know he had gone. By the time they made it as far from the Lower East Side as Sally's laundry money could take them, Brian would surprise Sally with the spoils from tonight's adventure. They'd rent an apartment in Boston. Brian would get honest work. Sally would raise their son. The three of them would grow old together, far from the shadow of Fantômas.

Shea looked up and down the street to make sure no one was watching, then darted toward the back of the church, finally crouching between two bushes on the edge of a small garden–two rows of vegetables planted by the children in the parish. Shea made his way, knees crouched, head down, to the wooden gate separating the garden from the back door of the rectory. Peering over the fence into the rectory window, Shea tried to focus as intently as possible through the darkness, trying to see if Father Rose was asleep in his bed. If Father Rose was gone, he had nothing to fear.

After several seconds of staring, Shea was unable to determine whether or not the rectory was occupied, and considered his next movement. If Father Rose was inside the rectory, there was no chance of success. If, however, Father Rose was inside his underground sanctum, the existence of which Shea had only heard as a rumor, he had a chance.

Just then, Shea saw a light come on inside the church, the

stained glass shining out over the parish garden. He retreated back to the bushes. It had to be Father Rose inside the church. For the moment, anyway, the rectory was empty. Shea forced himself forward, giving himself no more than three minutes to complete his task. He rushed forward, gathering momentum, and pulled himself over the fence. Dropping to the ground, he crawled quickly to the back of the rectory, positioning himself beneath the window. From his jacket, he pulled out a small hammer, then removed his jacket and wrapped the hammer inside of it. He counted to three, then stood up, swinging the hammer at the window. The glass shattered and clattered to the floor. Shea stood up, glanced around, and knocked the remaining edges of the glass into the room. He lifted himself through the window and moved quickly over to the other side of the room, where the safe containing all of the money collected by the church was recessed into the wall.

He glanced around again and stood still for a few seconds, listening for any sound that might betray another presence in the rectory. Hearing nothing, and convinced of his solitude, he donned a thin pair of gloves and began turning the dials on the safe. He tried to relax, knowing full well that it took patience to feel the tumblers falling into place, but the sweat on his brow was dripping into his eyes, stinging them and breaking his concentration. The first tumbler fell. He listened carefully. Still no noise. He brushed his shirt sleeve across his eyes and dialed frantically in the opposite direction. One more minute. The second tumbler fell. His toes were clenched. The back of his neck began to ache. Thirty more seconds. The third tumbler fell and the door to the safe swung open.

Picking up his jacket, he quickly tied the arms together, turning the back of the jacket into a pouch. He quickly scooped the contents of the safe into the jacket, secured the pouch in his arms and walked quickly but quietly back to the broken window. He tossed the bundle out the window to the ground, then hauled himself through. Once outside, he rushed toward the fence, bundle in tow, and climbed over, darting once again to his hiding place between the garden bushes. There he waited for a moment, trying to catch his breath. He closed his eyes for a moment, breathing deeply, steeling himself for the run back to his apartment.

A light came on. Then another. Not in the rectory, but in front of him, in the church. A third light sent the stained glass image of a crucifix directly into Shea's eyes. He squinted and turned away, then heard movement. From the front of the church, a group of men were darting down the front stairs. "The alarm in the rectory!" one of them said. Shea had heard no alarm but it made sense that the opening of the safe would have triggered some safeguard in another part of the church. It was sneaky, but then that was Father Rose's style.

Shea bolted across the street, clutching his stuffed jacket to his chest. A cry of "There! Over there!" broke the night silence and Shea heard a dozen footsteps running toward him. *No time to turn around*, he thought, his legs driving him as fast as they could toward the safety of an alleyway and complete darkness.

The footsteps continued as Shea dashed between the two buildings, grabbing garbage cans and tossing them behind them in a futile attempt to distract his pursuers. At the end of the alley was a wooden fence. Shea leapt as high as he could, clutching the splintered wood, his body slamming into the fence, sending out a noise that echoed between the brick walls. He climbed, hand over hand, to the top and dropped over onto the other side.

He kept running as fast as he could, his chest heaving, the muscles in his legs aching, until he suddenly realized that he could no longer hear the sounds of Father Rose's men running behind him. He stopped, resting against a wall, his hands on his knees, feeling his lungs ache with the exertion.

Where did they go? Why did they stop?

Because they recognized him. And they knew where he lived.

Sally was asleep. The baby was asleep. They'd never know what was happening until it was too late.

Shea felt the welling of grief in his chest and forced it down, threw himself away from the wall and began running again toward home. During the final block, his legs began to cramp and he felt as if his lungs would burst. He could see his tenement in the distance. There was no movement, no sounds of struggle, but outside of the building, Shea could make out the outline of a long, black automobile. As he moved closer, he could hear the engine idling, and standing next to the car was the figure of a man, his face barely illuminated by the flame of a match being held between his thumb and forefinger.

The Torch.

"Hello Brian," Torch said.

Brian staggered over toward the car, gasping and trying to catch his breath. "Where's Sally? Where's Denny?"

"They're in the car."

"Let them go, Torch. In the name of all that's holy…"

"I can't do that Brian."

"For God's sake! It was a mistake, Torch. Here," he said, handing over the jacket stuffed full of bills from Father Rose's safe. "Take it back. I don't need it. Just don't hurt them."

"You idiot!" Torch snapped, glancing around him and passing the jacket back to Shea. "Do you really think you'd get away if any of these men thought you had stolen from Fantômas?"

"Then, what…?"

"I saved your life!" Torch put his hand around the back of Shea's neck and pulled him closer. "I've been ordered to kill you and take your wife and child while Fantômas decides how to proceed."

"Torch, listen," Shea said, tears coming to his eyes. "This is insane."

"Fantômas is insane, Shea. Dangerous and insane. I wanted to warn you in time for you and your family to leave New York, but when I recognized you running away from the church, I knew I had no choice. Either allow Fantômas' men to catch and kill you or divert them from the chase by leading them here."

"Here? But why?"

"I put my life on the line for you, Shea. I might already be on the outs for allowing an intruder to break into Father Rose's house. If he were to find out that you and your family escaped, I'd be done for. I'm sorry, but Sally and the baby are my insurance policy. He has me, Shea."

"What do I do?"

"Nothing. I just saved your life. You can return the favor by disappearing and never coming back."

Just then, a group of men pouring gasoline from large canisters ran out of Shea's tenement building. "It's all ready, Torch," one of them said.

"Fine," Torch said. "Get in the car. I'll be along in a little while." Torch rapped on the front window. The driver rolled it down and Shea could see Sally's face, terrified and in pain, glaring at him accusingly from the passenger seat. Torch whispered instructions to the driver, and moments later, the car had traveled down the street and out of sight, leaving Shea and Torch alone in front of the building.

"I really am sorry, Shea," Torch said.

"Don't hurt them," Shea pleaded.

"Why in God's name would you steal from Father Rose? I was willing to put my life on the line to help you escape, but now..." Torch walked toward the building, drawing a matchbook out of his jacket.

"What are you going to do?" Shea asked.

"Fantômas is angry, Shea. He tried to make a deal with the police and they just laughed at him. Now, he's giving everyone a warning."

"What kind of warning?"

Without answering, Torch lit a match and dropped it into the puddle of gasoline at his feet. In seconds, the flames had spread through the front door of the building and began leaping up the staircase. Shea looked up and saw people darting from room to room, screaming to rouse one another awake. Black smoke began pouring out of the first floor windows as residents leapt onto fire escapes, dropping their belongings onto the street outside. Shea fell to his knees in shock, watching people dart from the building in tears, screaming babies in their arms. He glanced over at Torch who was staring as if hypnotized into the bright lights of the flames. His eyes were unmoved by the light, his skin unhurt by the heat, and Brian could see that the look on his face was one of elation.

Chapter Seven: Tunnel of Doom

"Oh, God. Oh my God." Ruth stifled a sob with her hands and stared at Fantômas' calling card.

"Is this a joke?" Jack asked. "Because if it is, I don't find it very funny. No, sir, not funny at all."

"It's no joke, I'm afraid," Dickson sighed with defeat, sinking in the chair that Harrington had occupied mere seconds earlier. "We've failed. I've failed."

Corona collected himself, smoothed his hair back with his palms and addressed Ruth. "Don't be afraid, Miss Harrington. The New York City Police Department is on the case!"

"And a bloody splendid job you've done so far!" Jack shouted. "Perhaps you can explain how Fantômas was able to spirit the good Professor away when every door and window was locked shut!"

Dickson suddenly sprang back to life. "We haven't got a second to lose," he said. "Every moment that we waste means Professor Harrington is being taken further and further away from us."

"How?" Ruth cried. "How could he have been kidnapped? We were right here! No one could have gotten in!"

"No one got in," Dickson answered. "But one of us left."

"Have you lost your mind, Detective?" Corona snapped. "We're all standing exactly where we were when the lights went out."

"Not all of us," Dickson said. "Poturu is missing."

Jack drove his fist into his other palm with a loud smack. "I knew it!" he said. "I never trusted that shifty little Indian boy. Why he's probably making a meal of Professor Harrington right now!"

Ruth slapped Jack on the shoulder.

"Ow!"

"Don't be ridiculous," Ruth said. "Poturu has been loyal to my father for years. He would never do something like this!"

"If," Dickson offered, "the man in the room was actually Poturu."

"What are you suggesting?" Corona asked.

"Quickly!" Dickson rushed to Ruth's side. "Where is Poturu's room? Where does he sleep?"

"The third floor. But I don't understand…"

"Follow me, everyone," Dickson called, rushing through a door and toward the staircase. "Time is wasting!"

Dickson rushed up the stairs with Ruth and Jack following close behind.

"For God's sake, Dickson!" Corona shouted, huffing his way slowly up the stairs, pulling himself along the handrail. "Slow down, will you? Not all of us are as spry as we once were!"

"Second door on the left," Ruth called ahead as they darted down the dark hallway.

Dickson approached the door and tried the knob. "Locked," he said. "Everybody stand back." Jack grabbed Ruth by the shoulders and moved her out of harm's way. Dickson stepped away from the door, then charged forward with all his might, driving his shoulder into the door and knocking it off its hinges.

The moment the door opened, all three were assaulted by a pungent, horrible smell that wafted aggressively from the room and into the hallway. "Good God!" Jack shouted, pressing his hands to his nose. "Did someone die in here?"

"My guess?" Dickson answered. "Yes. Someone died in here."

"Christ!" Corona's shouts traveled down the hallway as he continued to make his way up the staircase. "What's that horrible stench?"

Without waiting for Corona to catch up, Dickson, Ruth and Jack pressed their hands over their noses and entered the room. There, in the middle of the floor, was a giant steamer trunk. “A crowbar, a hammer…something!” Dickson shouted.

Ruth darted from the room and passed Corona who stumbled in, breathing heavily, and collapsed into a nearby chair. “This is really too much,” he said. “Dickson, would you mind telling me what’s going on?”

“I’d rather not, sir,” Dickson answered. “I have an idea but I pray that I’m wrong.”

“Does your idea include hundreds of pounds of year-old cheese?” Jack said, pinching his nose and wiping tears from his eyes. “Because that’s the sensation I’m experiencing at the moment.”

“Here!” Ruth said, re-entering and handing Dickson a crowbar.

“Stand back, everyone.” Dickson said. He shoved the end of the crowbar underneath the lid of the trunk and pressed down with all his weight, until the padlocks shattered and the lid flew open. The origin of the horrible smell was no longer in question. There, stuffed into the trunk, was a human corpse–its arms and legs broken and bent into impossible positions. The eyes were wide open and the tongue was protruding from the open mouth as if the man had died in the throes of extreme fear.

“Poturu,” Ruth said. “It’s Poturu.”

“But that’s impossible,” Jack shouted. “We just saw him a moment ago!”

“Miss Harrington,” Dickson said. “You are absolutely sure?”

“Absolutely,” Ruth answered.

“Miss Harrington!” Corona choked, pressing his handkerchief to his nose. “Do you mean to tell me that during the ten seconds the lights were out, someone managed to not only kidnap the Professor but snagged Poturu, carried him upstairs, murdered him, stuffed him in a trunk, locked it, then made his escape?”

“Preposterous!” Jack said.

“I agree,” said Dickson. “That’s not what happened at all.”

"But that's Poturu's body!" shouted Ruth. "I'd swear it on my life!"

"Yes," said Dickson. "The corpse is that of the unfortunate Poturu. The man we saw downstairs, however, was not Poturu."

"Not Poturu?" Jack asked. "Then who the bloody hell was he?"

The question was met with silence as the realization dawned on everyone at once.

"Fantômas…" Corona said.

"Or one of his confederates," Dickson added.

"But when?" Ruth asked. "How?"

"Judging by the condition of the corpse," Dickson said, trying in vain to bend Poturu's hands back and forth, "and the fact that rigor mortis clearly set in ages ago, I'd say the murder took place three to four weeks ago when you and your father were in the rainforest."

"But…" Ruth stared again at Poturu's corpse. "He looked just like Poturu. Sounded just like him."

"Don't underestimate Fantômas' genius," Dickson said.

"If no one minds," Jack pinched his nose, giving his voice an unpleasant, nasal quality. "Perhaps we could leave this room and adjourn to where the air is a mite cleaner."

"I second that," Corona said. "And if I can avoid the stairs at all costs…"

But Ruth ignored them, marching her way down the hall to the master bedroom while Dickson and the others followed close behind. "Miss Harrington," Dickson said. "If there's anything your father didn't tell us about why…"

"There's plenty my father didn't tell you," Ruth said. "And I pray to God no one found out."

"Found out what?" Jack asked. "Really, darling, you're behaving very mysteriously."

Ruth said nothing, but threw open the door of her father's room and walked to his bed. Lifting the top off of one of the bed poles, she revealed a small knob, encircled in numbers and embedded in the wood. After dialing frantically, a section of the east wall began to rotate until a large safe, previously hidden behind the wall, was now on view for everyone to see.

"Good Lord!" Corona said. "Your father a bit paranoid about security?"

"He had every reason to be," Ruth answered. "He didn't trust anyone but me with the location of this safe. Not even Poturu."

"The question is," Dickson added, "did the false Poturu somehow discover it?"

"That's what we're about to find out," Ruth said, grabbing the giant dial on the face of the safe and working the combination. In seconds, the safe was open and everyone in the room saw what was inside–a small, leather-bound journal. Ruth grabbed the journal as if her life depended on it and began quickly turning the pages. "Thank God," she said. "It's all here."

"What's all there?" Jack was growing impatient. "For the love of God, Ruth!"

"I agree with Mr. Meredith," Dickson said. "If this is anything that can help us track down your father's abductors…"

"I don't know if it is or isn't," Ruth said. "He didn't want anyone to know, but now…"

"You can trust us," Corona said, taking Ruth's hand.

Ruth looked each man square in the eyes as if to weigh their trust and fidelity. Then she moved toward the bed, sat down, and motioned for the others to do the same.

"It started with our last trip into the Amazon," she began. "Father had, against all odds, located a small group of Indians from the Panara tribe living deep in the forest. The tribe is an ancient one–descended from the much larger Southern Kayapo tribe, until the constant attacks by the Portuguese drove them further and further into the wild. They were extremely distrustful of outsiders but over a period of several weeks, my father and I were able to ingratiate ourselves to them. One night, my father asked the head of the tribe about a story he had heard–that somewhere in the Amazon was a lost city of gold."

"Nonsense!" Corona said.

"Balderdash!" Jack shouted.

"Go on, Miss Harrington," said Dickson.

"If the head of the tribe was to be believed, the lost city of gold was not a myth, but a fact. Furthermore, several Indians from the Ava-Canoeira tribe had been there and seen it. They brought back with them several gold coins, which they had used to trade with the Panara. My father saw the coins. Held them in his hands. That night, we packed our things and set out to find the Ava-Canoeiro.

"It took days of searching. The Ava-Canoeiro tribe is made of up of runaway slaves from the Carijo Indians. They became nomads, wandering through the forest from place to place. Eventually, we were able to find a small settlement, but my father's questioning had gotten the attention of the brutal Carijo. Once again, my father was able to make friends with the Ava-Canoeiro and finally showed them the gold coin that he had taken from the Panara. The Ava-Canoeiro agreed to lead us to the lost city the following morning.

"That night…" The words caught in Ruth's throat. Jack took her hand and she continued. "That night, I woke up to hear my father screaming. I ran out of my tent in time to see the Carijo Indians slaughtering the small band of Ava-Canoeirio. My father was trying to fight them off with his rifle but they were too fast. I grabbed my walking stick and leapt into the fray but, by that time, the Carijo had set upon my father. He shouted at me to run and, although I shouldn't have, I did.

"After days of walking, with nothing to eat or drink, I stumbled into the Panara village and passed out. I have no idea how many days I was unconscious, but the Panara fed me and nursed me back to health. Once I was back on my feet, I tried to organize some of the men to help me search for my father, but they were too afraid of the Carijo. I spent a week there, wondering if I'd ever see him again. I was about to give up hope and set out for home, when he stumbled into the village. He looked as if he hadn't eaten in days and had a tremendous fever. I spent all night at his bedside, cooling him down with a wet cloth, and at one point in his feverish delirium, he looked up at me and said, 'I saw it.' "

"Saw what?" Jack asked. "For God's sake, darling, don't keep us in suspense!"

"He said he saw the lost city of gold. The Carijo had taken him there, held him prisoner while they plundered jewels and gold from the vaults of the ancient city. My father was able to escape while they were transporting him back to the Carijo village to be killed."

"He spent the next several days scribbling in his journal–this journal–writing down everything he had seen, as well as directions and landmarks indicating how he could find the lost city again. When we finally returned to the States, he began studying the gold coin he took from the Panara and discovered that while it was genuine gold, it was synthetically produced."

"I don't understand," Jack said.

"They were alchemists," Dickson explained. "The people of the lost city had discovered how to manufacture gold."

"Exactly!" Ruth said. "My father swore me to secrecy but I suppose that doesn't matter now."

"Did you and your father ever discuss this in front of Poturu?" Dickson asked.

"Yes, but he had such limited knowledge of English."

"Perhaps Poturu didn't understand English," Corona sniffed. "Fantômas' henchman, on the other hand…"

"So he didn't get what he came for," Jack said.

"Unless," Dickson added, "he intends on trying to make a trade–your father for the journal."

"That won't do him any good either," Ruth explained. "My father writes everything in his own personal cipher." She flipped open the book and showed them the pages, which were riddled with odd symbols and numbers. "He's the only one who knows how to decipher it. The secret is locked in his head. He's never even shared it with me. The only way

Fantômas will be able to discover the secrets of the lost city is by capturing both my father and the journal."

Once again, the clock began to chime.

"That's it," Dickson said. "That's it. That's the sound I heard. Follow me, everyone!"

Dickson raced out of the room and took the stairs two at a time until he arrived back in the living room. The others followed close behind as the clock continued to chime. Dickson spun around and addressed the group. "Professor Harrington was taken by the false Poturu and smuggled out of the house under our very noses."

"But how?" Corona said, his voice tinged with frustration. "Every door was locked!"

"Not every door," Dickson explained. "When the lights were out, I distinctly heard the sound of a rusty hinge."

"Yes," said Ruth. "I heard it too."

Dickson marched over to the back of the room and faced the grandfather clock. He grabbed the handle of the clock door and swung it open. "Dickson!" Corona shouted. "What are you…"

"One moment, please!" Dickson snapped, cutting off Corona who sat down with a great "harrumph!"

"Ah-ha!" Dickson cried in triumph, after examining the inside of the clock. "The false Poturu was not idle during the many weeks you were away!" Dickson pulled a lever and suddenly the back of the clock slid away, revealing a dark cavern. The others rushed to Dickson's side and gazed into the abyss.

"Someone! A candle!" Dickson said.

Ruth retrieved a candle from a nearby cupboard, lit it and held it inside the clock so that they could examine the dark passageway.

"The construction is obviously new," Dickson said. "Built while you were away, no doubt." He stopped the pendulum from swinging so that they could get a clear view. "He halted the pendulum every time he stepped through, then started it again. After coming and going a number of times, the chime went out of sync."

"Which is why," Jack surmised, "the clock would only chime on the half-hour!"

"Exactly!" Dickson said.

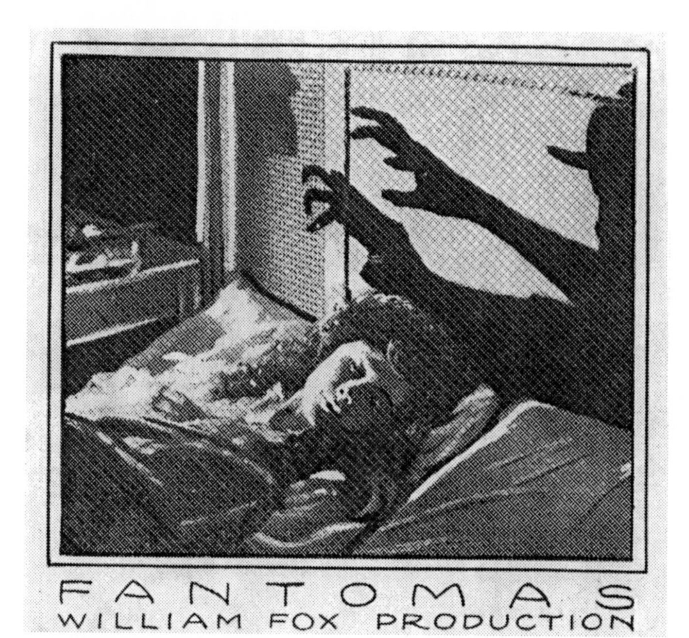

"But why?" Ruth asked. "Fantômas could not have known that we'd return to Long Island with the secret of the lost city, for God's sake."

"No," Dickson said, "but he did know your father was a renowned explorer with a collection of eccentric and priceless artifacts. My guess is that there are dozens, perhaps hundreds, of secret passageways connecting Fantômas to the homes of the wealthy throughout New York City. I wouldn't be surprised to find that he has infiltrated many of those homes with his own agents, replacing the family servants with his sinister followers, much as he did with the unfortunate Poturu. No doubt those criminals are Fantômas' eyes and ears, reporting to him anything of interest. Once the false Poturu told Fantômas about your father's discovery, Fantômas set his plan into motion."

Ruth suddenly brushed past Dickson and squeezed herself into the passageway. "Ruth!" Jack shouted. "Where are you going?"

"After my father!" Ruth answered.

"I would advise against that, Miss Harrington," Dickson said, grabbing Ruth by the shoulder.

"I've survived quicksand. Surely I can survive a wooden staircase." Ruth glanced at Dickson's clutching hand, then set her eyes against his. "Now," she added in a steely voice, "if you don't mind…"

"Fantômas is dangerous," Dickson said.

"So are piranhas," Ruth said, "so get out of my way."

"Miss Harrington!" Corona shouted. "It could be treacherous!"

Ruth disengaged herself from Dickson's grip and began descending the stairway. "Dash it all, Detective, do something!" Jack shrieked. "I'd go after her myself but the blasted dust will make me sneeze horribly."

"Hold on, Miss Harrington!" Dickson said, chasing after Ruth. "I'm coming with you."

Dickson caught up to Ruth and the two began following the stairway downward. "I don't need your help," Ruth said, without turning to look at him.

"I have no doubt that you're fully capable of taking care of yourself, Miss Harrington, but when it comes to Fantômas, there is safety in numbers."

Suddenly, and without warning, the doorway leading to the living room slid shut. Were it not for the glow of the candle Dickson and Ruth would have been left in darkness.

"Blast!" Dickson heard Jack shout from behind the door.

"The lever!" Dickson yelled. "On the right hand side!"

"I'm trying!" Jack yelled back, "but the bloody thing

won't move!"

"I'd try to reach it myself," Corona shouted through the door, "but... uh... I'm afraid I don't quite fit!"

"Don't bother!" Dickson yelled. "The thing might be booby-trapped. Miss Harrington and I will follow where it leads. You two go outside and draft Jenkins and the others into searching for a hidden exit of some kind. This passageway must lead somewhere."

"Right-O!" Jack shouted. "This way, Sergeant..."

Dickson and Ruth heard their footsteps run farther and farther away, then turned back around and continued their descent. They walked in silence, side by side, listening to the creaking of the stairs as they headed lower and lower. "Surely," said Ruth, "we're beneath the house by now."

"We must be far underground at this point," Dickson answered.

"How far down can it possibly go?"

"I have no..." Dickson stopped and grabbed Ruth by the hand. "Wait. Did you hear that?"

"Hear what?"

"Every step creaked except this one."

Ruth gasped. "We're in danger."

Suddenly, the steps folded underneath them, turning the staircase into a smooth chute which sent them plummeting, head over heels, against its surface. Their bodies gained speed as the momentum caused by the sudden drop drove them forward and downward. The candle flew out of Ruth's hands, struck the wall and quickly extinguished, leaving the two of them to continue their rapid descent in blackness.

After what seemed like an eternity of battering their heads and backs against the walls and trying in vain to get their feet underneath them, the chute ended and Dickson and Ruth found themselves free-falling into space, still unable to see the ground that was undoubtedly rushing up to meet them. With a sudden splash, they found themselves chest deep in a pool of dirty water.

"Miss Harrington," Dickson said, once he had regained

his balance. "Are you OK?"

For several seconds, there was no response and Dickson began to panic. "As well as I can be," Ruth finally answered. "What happened? Where are we?"

"That stair we stopped on must have been a triggering device of some sort, designed to discourage intruders. Is it as dark as it seems in here or have I gone permanently blind?"

"It's dark," Ruth answered. "We appear to be in a well of some sort."

"There must be an exit. Feel your way along the walls."

They did so, wading through the water and pressing their hands against the hard stone that had become their prison. Eventually, they found their way to one another when Dickson inadvertently pressed his hand on top of hers. "Sorry," he said.

"That's all right, Detective," Ruth said, letting her hand rest beneath his for a short moment before pulling it away. "Find anything?"

"Nothing," Dickson answered. "But it's curious that my eyes are adjusting to the dark."

"Why is that curious?"

"Because it means that some amount of light must be entering from somewhere."

"Above us!" Ruth said, noticing a small beam of moonlight coming from a spot in the ceiling.

"There's our exit," Dickson said. "Climb on my shoulders and take a look."

Ruth waded over to Dickson, placed her hands on his shoulders and pushed herself up onto him as he braced himself against the wall. He tried to ignore the scent of her perfume as it wafted downward. Ruth crawled upward against the wall, placing her feet on Dickson's shoulders and standing on her tiptoes. "It's a door, all right," she said. "It leads outside. But it's chained and padlocked.

"Is there any give?"

Ruth banged on the door, rattling the chain as hard as she could. "No more than five inches," she said. "Certainly not enough room for either of us to squeeze through."

"Do you have a hairpin?"

"Yes. Why?"

"You can pick the lock."

Ruth laughed. "Who do I look like? Raffles?"

"Give it a try," Dickson answered. "I'll instruct you from down here."

"It'll never work," Ruth said. "Help me down." Dickson grabbed Ruth under the arms and set her back down in the water. She held out the hairpin to Dickson.

"What's this?" Dickson asked.

"You're going to pick the lock. Get on my shoulders."

"Are you insane?" Dickson asked. "I'll crush you!"

"Listen, Detective Dickson," Ruth said, wagging her finger in front of his face. "I carried a 300-pound Mayan statue on my back through two miles of leech-infested water. Surely I can handle a lone 180-pound detective."

Dickson knew when he was beaten. "As you wish," he said.

While Ruth pressed her hands against the stone wall for support, Dickson took off his shoes, sent them floating through the tank, and mounted himself on Ruth's shoulders. Once he had his balance, he groped for the lock, inserted the hairpin and began working the mechanism. "Are you OK down there?" he said.

"I'm fine, thanks," Ruth answered. "Just hurry."

Dickson moved the hairpin back and forth, but his hands were slippery and he dropped it into the water. "Damn!" he said.

"Come down," Ruth said. "I have another hairpin."

Dickson dropped back down into the water beside Ruth.

"Sorry," he said.

"I only have one left. Don't lose it." Ruth removed the second hairpin and shook her hair free, allowing it to hang loose over her shoulders. Their eyes had adjusted to the dark enough for them to see one another in the dim light. Their eyes met.

"What are you looking at, Detective Dickson?"

"Nothing, Miss Harrington," Dickson turned his head away, thankful that it was too dark for her to see him blush.

"Let's give it another try," Ruth said.

"Wait," said Dickson. "What's that sound?"

Ruth stood perfectly still and listened. In the distance, she could hear a distinct squealing, like a small child crying. Then, the sound grew louder and louder, like the sound of several children squealing.

"Where's it coming from?" Ruth asked.

"The same place we came from," Dickson surmised. "The chute."

"It's getting louder."

Dickson and Ruth leaned their heads toward the noise and listened as it grew in volume and pitch. What once sounded like a handful of crying babies had become a cacophonous sound of high-pitched squealing. As the sound grew nearer, they could hear the additional noise of hundreds of small bodies slapping the wooden floor of the chute.

"What was that?" Dickson said, feeling a shock of soft fur brush past his cheek.

"I felt it too," Ruth said, as a small, soft object landed on her head and bounced into the water with a light splash.

The sound grew louder. So loud that Dickson and Ruth had to yell in order to be heard among the din. "Great God!" said Dickson. "What are they?"

Suddenly, Ruth felt a tiny set of claws pierce her blouse and take root in the flesh of her stomach. She let out a shriek and instinctively grabbed for the small creature trying to dig its way through her clothing. A set of teeth bit her fingers and held tight while she flailed her arm through the air, trying to shake the object from her hand.

The squealing noise was deafening now, as Ruth and Dickson saw dozens, then hundreds of the dirty, furry animals spill out of the chute and surround them in the water.

"Rats!" Ruth screamed, seeing Dickson struggle with one of the rodents that had dug its teeth into his ear. "They're rats!"

Chapter Eight: Meetings at Midnight

When Ruth Harrington was 16, she accompanied her father on one of his expeditions for the first time. The journey took them to the wilds of Africa, and although Professor Harrington had misgivings about exposing his daughter to the dangers of the jungle, he had the utmost trust in the native guides to keep an eye on Ruth at all times.

Traipsing for hours at a time through the trees and grass while giant insects tried to find their way through the mosquito netting, Ruth Harrington observed their guide with admiration and envy. She imagined herself holding the machete blade, leading a troupe of explorers through the brush, hacking away at the branches that stood in their way.

One morning while the expedition was packing up for another trek, Ruth set out on her own. Her plan was to be gone for an hour or so, then return to her father demanding that she be allowed to lead the group. She absconded with the guide's machete while his back was turned, then set off into the jungle, confident that she could handle whatever hardships came her way.

Within 20 minutes, she was lost.

She panicked for only a moment, and then used every skill that her father had taught her to guide herself back toward the camp.

Then, the snakes came.

Two King Cobras approached her from the front, springing up from the sides of the path and blocking her way. They were each about three feet long, with their heads fanned out and rocking gently back and forth, staring at her and daring her to move. Their tongues darted back and forth and Ruth could see their fangs dripping with venom.

She stared at them, eye to eye, for what seemed like an eternity. They challenged her to move forward, back toward the campsite, but Ruth knew that one small move would be a signal for them to strike. The cobras were quick and deadly.

One swift move and they would infect her with their venom and she would die, there on the jungle path, and her father would never be able to find her.

Ruth stared. And continued to stare. And soon, the challengers became the challenged. She felt their anger rising as the hissing became more intense and the gentle swaying of their heads became more aggressive. They were ready to strike. Ruth felt the handle of the blade clenched tight in her fist and, in a moment that went by so fast that she hardly had time to take notice of it, Ruth whisked the blade through the air, beheaded both snakes and watched their severed bodies drop lifeless to the ground.

Ruth Harrington

We relate this story to you, Dear Reader, not to horrify you, but merely advise you not to underestimate Ruth

Harrington.

"Get on my shoulders!" Ruth shouted at Dickson while both of them were busy swatting away the blood-thirsty rodents.

"Are you insane?" Dickson shouted. "You can't fight off hundreds of rats by yourself!"

"Neither can you!" she protested. "And if we don't find a way out soon, we're going to wind up as two piles of fleshless bones! Ow! That's my shoulder, you furry little bastard!"

"Ouch!" said Dickson. "I think I'm bleeding. All right. But you should know that I'm very opposed to this!"

"Write a letter to the editor!" Ruth snapped, placing her hands on the stone wall while Dickson climbed on her shoulders and reached toward the padlock, hairpin in hand.

"I'm having trouble getting hold of the lock!" Dickson said. "Could you not squirm around so much?"

"Ow!" Ruth shrieked as yet another rat sank its teeth into her flesh. "Sorry to inconvenience you but I'm trying to strangle hundreds of rats with my *bare goddamn hands*!"

"Almost got it," Dickson said. "Damn!"

"What?"

"You don't want to know."

"Don't tell me you dropped the hairpin."

"I dropped the hairpin."

"Dammit!"

"It must be floating around down there! Can you feel it?"

Ruth began fighting off the rats with one hand, while running the other through the water in an attempt to locate the missing hairpin. "Don't make waves!" Dickson said, "or it will drift away!"

"They aren't my waves," Ruth shouted. "They're the rats' waves! Now shut up while I find this thing!"

Despite the horrifying nature of his surroundings, Dickson found himself oddly intoxicated by Ruth Harrington's spirit. Gone was the frightful young girl worried about her father, and in that girl's place was a strong, vicious survivor. Dickson's attraction was tinged with no small amount of envy.

"I found it!" Ruth said, extending her hand upward toward Dickson. "Now get us out of here, quickly!"

Dickson reached down, almost losing his balance, and took the hairpin from her hand. Without a word, he clutched it tight and began working once again on the lock. Ruth continued thrashing about in an attempt to drive the rats away. "Uh... Detective?" Ruth said, in a voice that Dickson found disarmingly calm.

"What is it?" he asked, still working the hairpin into the lock.

"I'm going to lower myself completely underwater. Will you still be able to reach the lock?"

"Are you kidding?" Dickson could hardly believe his ears. "For God's sake, you'll drown!"

"Trust me!" she said, and submerged herself completely underwater, while Dickson stood on his tiptoes, unsteadily balanced on Ruth's shoulders. Stretching his arms as far as he could, he continued to work the hairpin back and forth.

Ruth was underwater, her eyes pinched shut against the dirt and grime. With both arms, she began pulling the rats beneath the water, squeezing their throats and snapping each neck as they fought to find their way to the surface. With most of the rats floating above her, her body was protected from their claws as her hands darted to the surface, dragging the rodents under two at a time. After the first few, she found her rhythm–grab, squeeze, snap, reach. Within minutes, there were dozens of dead rats floating on the surface of the water.

"I got it!" Dickson cried, pushing the door upward and letting it fall on top of the well.

"Miss Harrington! Miss Harrington!" Dickson leapt off of Ruth's shoulders and landed beside her in the water.

Ruth raised her head above the surface and began gasping for air. "Blacking...out..." she said, then fainted in Dickson's arms.

"Miss Harrington!" Dickson said, slapping her lightly on the cheek while the remaining rats began closing in on them. "Wake up!"

Ruth began to stir and her eyes slowly opened. She started to speak, but Dickson placed his forefinger against her lips. “Quiet now,” he said. “You’re going to have to climb on top of me to reach the door.”

“What about you?” she whispered.

“Let’s get you out first, then we’ll worry about me.”

“Ruth! Darling!” Jack’s voice came from above and echoed through the well. “Dash it all! Are you down there?”

“Down here!” Dickson shouted. “Help!”

“Wait!” Dickson heard Corona’s voice, obviously trailing significantly behind Jack. “I’m on my way!”

Jack’s head suddenly appeared in the doorway at the roof of the well. “Oh, God!” he said. “Ruth! Is she OK? Detective Dickson, please tell me she’s OK!”

“She’s fine,” Dickson said, “but we’ve got to get her out of here!”

“Sergeant!” Jack shouted to Corona. “Get a rope!”

Here we’ll leave our band of heroes with assurance to you, Dear Reader, that Dickson and Ruth will be lifted safely from the well, thanks to Jack and Corona. While the rat bites they suffered are indeed painful, they will shortly be discharged from the hospital with instructions to get some rest and drink plenty of fluids. The wounds are horrible to look at, of course, but to the best of the Doctor’s knowledge, neither Dickson nor Ruth have been infected with rabies, the plague or any other ailment that one tends to fear while one is being gnawed on by hundreds of ravenous rats.

And so, with their health and safety temporarily assured, we’ll move our story ahead to the following evening. We are in midtown, in the catacombs beneath the skyscrapers that make up the awesome skyline of this great, modern city. The meeting we are about to observe is secret–known only to a cadre of righteous men known as the Councilmen. We would reveal more to you, Dear Reader, but in this case a little knowledge can be a very dangerous thing.

At around midnight, a lone figure in a dark grey coat and

hat made his way across the dance floor of Diamond Dave's saloon, then stepped through a dark doorway behind the bar. He descended a flight of stairs until he reached a long hallway lit by a few dim bulbs that hung from strings attached to the ceiling. He continued walking, and when he reached the large iron door, he pounded on it five times with his closed fist. Moments later, a metal plate slid away from a window located in the center of the door and another man's mouth became visible.

"Yes?" the mouth asked.

"It's me," the man said. "Number Four."

The window on the door slid closed and a loud clang on the other side indicated that the lock had been thrown. The door opened and the man entered. The room was lit by candles that circled its perimeter. In the center was a long table where ten similarly dressed men sat, about to begin their unholy conference. Against the wall, a small wiry man was tied to a chair with a black hood over his face. At the head of the table was a large mechanical box–a voice amplification device with wires that attached it to a hole in the wall. The box was hissing static and a disembodied voice crackled from the mesh surface. "Are we all here?" the voice asked.

"We are," one of the Councilmen answered.

And it is here, Dear Reader, that we find ourselves in attendance at the secret weekly meeting of the ten men and their hidden leader who make up the society known as The Council of Ten.

"Let us begin," the voice from the box squawked.

The Councilmen known as Number Eight and Number Two left their seats and approached the bound man in the corner. They pulled the hood from his face, revealing the frightened countenance of Sergei Growtowski–Fantômas' henchman who had been arrested, and subsequently vanished following the recent warehouse raid.

"What is your name?" the voice asked.

The man quaked with fear. "I... Grotowski..." he answered.

"And what a fine grasp of the English language you have, Mr. Grotowski."

Grotowski said nothing, but continued to tremble.

"I'm uncertain as to how much of what I'm saying you can understand, Mr. Grotowski, but you have been detained by an organization called The Council of Ten. We feel, as do many other prominent citizens of New York, that there are criminals who aren't punished severely enough by modern-day law-enforcement techniques."

Grotowski looked confused. "I…not…understand…"

The voice chuckled. "Of course you don't. You felt you could simply bring your family to our little island and live as if you were still in Europe, consorting with criminals and dealing in every sort of violent subterfuge you can manage. Who is Fantômas, Mr. Grotowski?"

Grotowski may have been confused by the questions hissing from the disembodied voice, but at the sound of Fantômas' name he began to struggle against his bonds. "No!" he shouted. "Fantômas…he kill me…kill my family…"

The Councilmen heard a deep sigh come from the electronic voice. "He is useless," the voice said. "Kill him and find me someone who speaks English."

Number Eight pulled a blade from the inside of his coat and drew it across Grotowski's neck. Grotowski's head slumped forward as his blood spilled across his bare chest. His hands and feet twitched for a moment accompanied by a sickening gurgling from his throat. In moments, Grotowski was dead.

"Take him away," the voice said. "And toss his body into the Hudson. We'll have to look elsewhere for an informant–someone with more to lose than a worthless wife and sickly child."

Number Two and Number Eight dragged Grotowski's body to a nearby trunk and tossed it inside.

The voice moved on to its next item. "Number Four, you have a report?"

"Yes," Number Four said, withdrawing a sheaf of rolled

papers from his inside coat pocket. "A good collection from the Slasher at the *Hog's Head*. He's a good man. Pays up on time every week. We took in the weekly rate from the *Three Deuces* and *Chick Tricker*. Number Eight hit a couple of nearby shock houses. Gave him a little trouble at first..."

"Just at first," Number Eight chuckled. The rest of the men laughed as well.

The electric box was silent save for the ever-present hiss. Finally the voice emerged once again. "Idiots!" it said.

Number Four looked at the other men with trepidation. "I don't understand, boss."

"Perhaps," the voice hissed, "you have forgotten that it's our holy mission to clean up this city! To rid it of corruption and deceit! You've gotten greedy. All of you! Reveling in your money–behaving worse than the petty thieves you have sworn to regulate. The money you collect is for the good of this organization and not for your own pockets! We live in a city where even the police engage in vice. Someone has to maintain control of this city, gentlemen. And you are the men who have sworn to maintain it!"

"Sorry, boss," Number Four said sheepishly. "We just thought..."

"You didn't think!" the voice interrupted. "The only way to fight sin is to immerse yourselves in the dens that promote sin. But you must be careful. You will be tempted to stray from the path of righteousness whenever you expose yourselves to such wickedness."

The ten men shifted uncomfortably in their seats. "The thing is, boss," Number Four began with no small amount of nervousness. "It isn't that easy. Used to be there was just the occasional gang. Now we have Fantômas to deal with."

The static continued but the voice remained silent for what felt like an unbearable length of time. Finally a fierce whisper slithered from the box with an elongated, malevolent hiss. "Fantômas," it said. "And why are we afraid of this pathetic Fantômas?"

It was as if Death himself had crept through the room,

aiming his scythe at each of their throats. "The guy scares us, boss," Number One said with fear in his voice. "I know it's our job to keep the city clean and everything, but Jesus...people talk about him like he's a ghost or something."

"He's the Devil," Number Three added. "And the people who work for him are the walking dead."

"It's true!" said Number Eight. "I've heard the people at the *Hog's Head* say that when a crook gets gunned down, he comes back from the dead to work for Fantômas."

"Idiots!" the voice shouted, which was followed by a shrill burst of electric noise that had all ten men clasping their hands over their ears simultaneously. "While the ten of you have been busy collecting your penny-ante change from the local gamblers and whores, would you like to know what this Fantômas and his gang have been doing?"

"I don't get it, boss," Number Four said. "Fantômas..."

"Has been making fools of us," the voice replied. "Week after week, he succeeds in looting scores of money and treasures from the wealthy citizens of this city, then vanishes without a trace. His organization is growing and his crimes are becoming more daring. The key to controlling this city is wealth, gentlemen, and Fantômas is well on his way to becoming the wealthiest man in New York City!"

"So what do we do, boss?" Number Six asked. "No one knows what the guy looks like or where he holes up? Every time someone puts his gang on the run, they take cover in some gin joint or flop house and completely vanish. Besides, the police will track him down sooner or later."

"You think so, eh?" The voice scoffed, "You think the police department has the best interests of the city at heart? Feh! All they care about is taking bribes and stuffing their pockets. We have an opportunity, gentlemen. What if I told you all that I had recently acquired knowledge that one of the greatest treasures of all mankind was right here in Manhattan and the only person standing in the way of our acquiring it was Fantômas? What if I told you that if Fantômas were to obtain this treasure, it would put the greatest source of wealth in this country into the hands of the poor."

The Councilmen shuddered.

"How much wealth?" Number One asked.

"Enough wealth and power to unseat the leaders of this city. You see the riff-raff that wander the filthy streets every day. They are profane human beings given to violence and drunkenness. They refuse to speak the English language. They spend their nights dancing with filthy prostitutes. They are the people who work with this Fantômas and they are the people that Fantômas will share his wealth with.

"Now I ask you, my friends, if this wealth suddenly becomes available, who deserves to have it? Certainly not the wretched Fantômas. Not the corrupt politicians, not the so-called law-makers."

"Then who?" Number Three asked.

"Us, gentlemen," the voice answered. "The Council of Ten. Wealth is power, my friends. And once we have that treasure, we can make over this city in our image. We can finally create the city of morality and holiness that we've always dreamed of. Our one obstacle is Fantômas."

"But how do we find him?" Number Seven asked. "No one knows who's working for him."

"One of you will be contacted shortly to enact Phase One," the voice said with terrifying intensity. "As for the rest of you, once you receive word from me that Phase One has begun, you will go block by block, door to door. Someone on the Lower East Side knows where Fantômas is, and they will tell us what we want to know, or they will face the consequences. You will divide the area into segments, with each one of you taking a separate area. You will knock on doors. You will ask questions. And when they refuse to tell you what they know, you will force the information out of them. Assume that Fantômas is everywhere. Assume that everyone is an enemy–the sick, the weak, women, children. No one is safe. No one is innocent. We will take the Lower East Side back from Fantômas. We will destroy him. And then the treasure of the ages will be ours."

At the same time, just outside Our Lady of Perpetual Sorrow, a young man crouches in the shadows. He has lost his family and his home. As he stares at the sinister church, he begins to wonder if he's lost his hope. For the past two days, Brian Shea has lived from doorway to doorway, corner to corner, alley to alley. By not allowing himself to slow down or rest until night falls, he has carefully avoided his former associates–men who, like Fantômas, believe him to be dead.

For the second night in a row, evening has fallen on the Lower East Side and Brian Shea has been able to stop moving, hoping to find a few hours of dreamless sleep under the open sky, praying all the while that he won't fall prey to the prowlers and criminals that stalk the night. On this night, however, sleep will not come to him as he stares across the street at the church and home of Father Rose–the place where he lost his soul, his liberty and finally, his happiness.

He knew his wife and child were somewhere inside, unless they had been murdered–a thought that he shoved to the back of his mind as quickly as possible, unable to bear the thought of something so tragic and horrific. *No*, he thought to himself, *they are there. I'm sure of it. In one of the many maze-like underground catacombs, Sally and Denny are being held captive, waiting for their husband and father to rescue them.*

He tried to will himself to stand, but fear and hunger kept him from doing so. If he were to attempt to break into Father Rose's underground chamber, there was every chance that he would be discovered and killed before he had the chance to rescue his family. On the other hand, even if he survived and Fantômas discovered that he was still alive, he would be putting his family at risk. Fantômas was very likely to murder them out of sheer spite at having been deceived.

Not to mention the fact that he was so very tired.

No, he thought to himself. *I can't just sit here. I have to do something. If I don't die at the hands of Fantômas, I'm likely to die of starvation here in the streets. And as for Sally and Denny, better to risk their lives now than condemn them to lives of imprisonment, torture and hopelessness. If we die, at least we will die together.*

His brain clouded from lack of sleep, his legs weak from hunger, Brian Shea was still able to lift himself to his feet and make his way across the street toward the church. The memories of Father Rose's sadism struck terror into his heart but his love for Sally and Denny drove him forward. Soon he was standing in the garden beside the rectory. The window he had broken had already been replaced and the lights were blazing inside.

"Don't go. It isn't time." The voice belonged to a woman. Brian spun around but saw nothing. After a few moments of peering into the adjacent graveyard, he spied a woman clad completely in black. Her face was hidden behind a veil, and even her hands were covered with long, black gloves.

"Who are you?" Shea asked.

"Come quickly," the Woman in Black said. "Out of the light."

Shea tentatively stumbled toward the graveyard to where the woman was standing. She clutched him by the hand and quickly led him behind a grove of trees. They stood among the tombstones and the woman ran her hand along his cheek.

"Who are you?" Shea repeated.

"I am no one," the woman said. "I lost my identity some time ago."

"I don't understand. What do you want with me?"

"I'm here to help you. Please. For the sake of your wife and child, Brian Shea, listen to me. It would be suicide to go into that church right now."

Shea brushed the woman's hand away from his face. "How do you know me?" he asked. "How do you know my family? Where are they?"

The Woman in Black raised her finger to her lips to silence him. "Fantômas has them," she said. "But they are alive and safe for the moment."

Shea slid down a tombstone and collapsed onto the ground. "I don't understand," he said.

The Woman in Black

The Woman in Black knelt down beside him and took his hand. "I was like you," she said. "I trusted Fantômas. Much to my shame, I fell in love with Fantômas. And even when I witnessed his horrible crimes and was an accomplice to his terrible violence, I continued to love him. I stood by while Fantômas slaughtered my husband and my love for him never faltered. I lost everything–my integrity, my pride, my self. That is why I wear this veil. I am in mourning for my very soul.

"I followed Fantômas from Paris and I have been watching him. It is my hope that I can prevent others from making the same mistake I have made. I am one step away from the grave, and then I will suffer eternal damnation for my sins. There is no hope for me–no redemption. But there is hope for you, Brian Shea. Have patience. I will come for you when the time is right."

Shea was dumbfounded as he watched the woman turn and walk away from him. "Wait," he said. "How will you know where to find me?"

The woman turned around. "I will be watching." The two stared at one another for a few moments and Shea got the distinct impression that the woman was beginning to weep behind her black veil. She turned her head away. "Remember me," she said, then darted around the grove of trees and vanished.

Fantômas and the Woman in Black

Chapter Nine: The Queer Tale of Boris Zaitsev

"Sir. Wake up, sir."

Professor Harrington heard the voice as if it were coming from the top of a deep well and he was trapped at the bottom, unable to stir, unable to open his eyes.

"Good. Wake up, sir. It is important."

Harrington couldn't open his eyes, so he tried to raise his hand. Feeling a single finger begin to stir, he attempted to rock his head back and forth. It was a Herculean effort but Harrington drew encouragement from the disembodied voice.

"Professor Harrington. The secret is in jeopardy. Wake up, Professor."

Harrington's eyes began to open, the lids heavy, his head continuing to throb.

"It's me, Professor. Potoru."

At the sound of his old friend's name, Harrington forced his eyes open and found himself gazing through stalks of bamboo. He tried to pull himself upright, but his head hit the wooden top of his prison, increasing the throbbing tenfold. His legs crumpled beneath his weight, and he observed that there was no room for him to extend them. One thigh screamed with cramps and the other was void of any feeling whatsoever, either asleep or paralyzed. Or perhaps–Harrington tried to put the thought out of his head–the leg had been removed completely.

His arm shot to his thigh and he felt his way down the calf to the foot. The leg was intact and Harrington managed to raise himself just enough to release it, allowing the blood to flow back into the extremity and sending a thousand pinpricks to his toes.

Where was he? Through the makeshift bars he was able to see the familiar foliage of the Amazon. But where in the Amazon? His cage wasn't lying on the ground–his view of the trees attested to that–so what was the jostling that continued to shift him from side to side?

He was being carried. Carried by the Carijo. He was their prisoner.

"Professor!"

The voice came again, and this time Harrington could see the kind face of his friend walking alongside the moving cage.

"Potoru!" Harrington said. "How..."

"Not now, Professor. Time is of the essence."

A voice in the back of his head told Harrington that something was wrong, but his relief at seeing his friend triumphed over his misgivings.

"How are you here, Poturu? I left you back home. Left you to take care of my home in Long Island."

"That isn't important, Professor," Poturu said. "What is important is that you listen to me."

Potoru continued to walk next to Harrington's cage, almost as if his feet weren't touching the ground.

"Help me, Poturu," Harrington said.

"I will help you, Professor. But you must listen. The Carijo are carrying you to the lost city."

"The lost city!" Harrington's voice rose with excitement. "I'm going to see the lost city?"

"Yes, Professor. Your precious lost city exists and you will finally lay eyes on it after all these years."

"How do you know this, Poturu?"

"Later. Once you arrive at the lost city, you will escape the Carijo and make your way back to camp."

"Ruth!" Harrington shouted, suddenly remembering his daughter. "How is Ruth?"

"No harm will come to her, Professor." Poturu's voice soothed despite its urgency.

"I will make my way back to camp," Harrington said. "My head... so tired..."

"Stay with me, Professor. Just another minute and then I must leave."

"Yes, Poturu, yes."

"Before leaving the lost city, you will find a gold coin and hide it on your person. You will run from the Carijo never letting go of the gold coin."

Harrington began to swoon. "Extraordinary... the gold coin... extraordinary..."

"After returning home, you will examine the coin and determine that it is not organic."

"Extraordinary..." Harrington's eyes closed and he began to drift back to sleep. "Synthetic gold. Extraordinary."

"You will write down the composition of the gold in your notebook."

"My red notebook. With my maps."

"Yes, Professor. With your maps. And you will hide the notebook."

"In my bedroom... in the safe..."

"Yes, Professor. What is the combination to the safe?"

"Your English has improved considerably, Poturu," Harrington mumbled.

Poturu clutched Harrington's head with both hands. "What is the combination to the safe?"

Harrington's eyes opened and he stared at his friend. He uttered the combination and as the last digits left his lips, he saw that the bamboo cage and the jungle had disappeared, replaced by a dark room built in stone and illuminated by a single dim light bulb. He lost consciousness and his last thought was that the man before him was not Poturu.

Fantômas, clad in the robes of Father Rose, paced back and forth beside the locked door waiting for "the man who would be Poturu" to emerge. After a few minutes, he heard the inner latch begin to move and waited for the door to open. "Well?" he asked, as the man disguised as Poturu exited Harrington's cell.

The man, who went by the name "The Prince," uttered three numbers–the combination to Professor Harrington's safe.

"Ha ha!" Fantômas shouted in triumph. "Good man! Good man, Prince! You have proven yourself an invaluable ally! First, by impersonating Harrington's servant so convincingly that not even he, nor his daughter, suspected a thing. Second, by drawing the combination out of Harrington's lips when I, I confess, could not. Ha! A little bit of narcotic and a familiar face. All we needed to draw the truth from Professor James Harrington."

"Thank you, sir," the Prince said. "It was a pleasure to serve you."

"Come with me, Prince," said Fantômas. "Let's call a meeting of my apaches, shall we? I have a surprise for you that I'm sure you'll enjoy."

"Yes, sir," said the Prince. "Thank you, sir."

While Fantômas was contacting his apaches and summoning them to his subterranean sanctum beneath the cathedral, another unholy meeting was taking place in Midtown. A tall man, clad in a grey coat and hat, made his way down several flights of stairs into an abandoned subway tunnel. Ignoring the "no entrance" sign, the man, who was called Number Seven, entered the dark tunnel, drew a match from his pocket and lit a series of candles along the tunnel wall, each one held in place by a stone fist garbed in a thick grey glove.

Number Seven tossed the match to the ground and crushed it beneath his heel. Shivering against the underground chill, he drew his pocket watch out of his coat to mark the time. 8:59 p.m. And the meeting was scheduled for 9 p.m.

"Number Seven." The deep, resonant voice came from somewhere deep within the tunnel.

"Yes, Master," said Number Seven. "I came as soon as you called." He put his watch away and began walking toward the sound of the voice.

"Stay where you are," the voice said. "Remember, should you ever lay eyes on me, your position within the Council will be compromised."

"Sorry," Number Seven stammered. "I didn't mean any harm."

"Enough," the voice said. "There is no time to waste. I wish to make use of your specialized skills."

Number Seven frowned. "But, Master," he said, "I left all that safe-cracking work behind me. You said we had to live lives of purity if we wanted to…"

"Sometimes," the voice interrupted, "we must use the tools of sin in order to combat sin. You are going to commit a robbery tonight. You are going to break the law. But in doing so, you will be serving the greater good. Do you understand?"

"Yes, Master," Number Seven smiled, cracking his knuckles one by one. "Lay it on me."

"You are familiar with some of the larger homes on Long Island."

"Am I! It was sneaking into one that got me five years in the stir. I don't know, boss. Those places are pretty secure."

"Don't be afraid," the voice said. "The house I'm referring to has a secret entrance. I have a map of the grounds that will lead you to it."

"A secret entrance? Geez, boss. What's in this place?"

"The first step toward achieving our ultimate goal."

"You can count on me."

The voice suddenly began moving further and further away as Number Seven realized it was retreating back into the tunnel.

"Return home," the voice finished. "There you will find your instructions, as well as the map of the grounds and a layout of the house itself. Return here within 24 hours."

Number Seven was suddenly alarmed. "Hey, boss," he said, his voice quivering. "If you don't mind my asking, how do you know where I live?"

There was no answer. The voice, and the man who owned it, were gone.

Back in Russia, Boris Zaitsev never considered himself part of the nobility. He knew that his home was large, his clothing bright and his aunts and uncles haughty and ostentatious. He knew that he occupied a different world from the scores of shoeless, red-faced people he occasionally spied wandering the countryside and the streets of town, peddling their wares from large carts made of splintered wood–their planks strung with smelly sausage wrapped in nets of fat.

Despite this, he never considered himself privileged in any way. Less because he was uneducated or lacking in worldly knowledge, than because he was a boy of 15. And boys of 15 never think they're privileged.

When the fearful grumblings began behind closed doors, Boris wasn't allowed to listen. He tried by placing a glass against the wall to eavesdrop on his father and the authorities that often visited–their gold buttons brightly polished and their demeanor fraught with trepidation. The word "revolution" was uttered more and more often as time passed. Finally, the doors of the private rooms opened and his parents began to speak openly of the danger threatening them. People were killing one another in Petrograd. Boris didn't understand who was doing the killing or why, but he soon realized that his life, the security of which he had always taken for granted, was about to come to a violent end.

He heard stories of violence, of killing, of Cossacks and peasants joining one another to attack landowners. In a matter of days, it seemed, Boris' young life turned upside-down.

Years later, a dangerous fever robbed him of any telling memories about his journey to America. Vague images of his parents waving goodbye to him as the boat sailed away remained locked in his mind, as did the memory of an illness that claimed most of the ship's crew, including his uncle Nicholas who had intended to deliver him to his American cousins. And so it was that on a chilly winter night in 1917, the 17-year-old Boris Zaitsev wandered, cold and hungry, onto the streets of Manhattan's Lower East Side.

Sleeping in alleys, sneaking into tenement basements for warmth, Boris met a handful of others in similar circumstances. Some Russian, some Irish, some German, all bitter. Boris' assertion that he was of Russian nobility led to laughter and much cajoling from his homeless companions. So much so that one of them endowed him with the name "Prince"–a nickname that stuck, particularly among people who were unable to pronounce "Zaitsev."

Toward the end of winter, the sickness took hold. After days of coughing and shivering in an abandoned basement, Boris realized that the feeling in his hands and feet had left him, and his face was flushed with fever. His last, fever-induced hallucination was that of his mother and father, their images fading in the distance.

Boris' next memory occurred weeks later when he awoke in the church–its stained-glass windows filling the room with light. Above him stood a tall man with a kindly face. At first, Boris thought he was an angel. Later, he discovered that the man's name was Father Rose.

Father Rose nursed Boris back to health and allowed him to live in the church. The fever, which had plagued him for weeks, left him confused and prone to disorienting headaches. Nevertheless, Father Rose took him under his wing and granted him kindness–gave him a home and, for the first time in months, a family.

Soon afterward, another change took place. Not to Boris but to Father Rose. Boris was unable to put his finger on it but the man who wore Father Rose's robes didn't seem like Father Rose. He looked like Father Rose, even spoke like Father Rose, but his kindness had hardened. With his pounding headaches and lack of focus, Boris had trouble putting his finger on the difference. Eventually, it didn't seem to matter. Father Rose seemed amused by Boris, even allowing him to aid in the construction of his underground dwelling–a chamber only accessible from a hidden door on the altar and a secret staircase hidden under a tombstone in the adjacent cemetery.

In time, Boris grew to idolize Father Rose. He often dreamt of becoming a priest–of donning the robes and ministering to people like himself. Indeed, when Father Rose was away one afternoon, Boris snuck into the rectory. Feeling mischievous and slightly daring, he discovered one of Father Rose's robes and put it on. Walking back to the deserted church, he stepped onto the altar, looked out into the empty pews and began to speak. In moments, his confusion and headaches disappeared as he immersed himself in the role–as he not only imitated, but became Father Rose. He had no idea how long he stood there, quoting scripture that he never knew he had committed to memory and adopting Father Rose's tone, gestures and mannerisms, but his reverie came to an end when a single figure seated in a back pew made himself known by applauding Boris' performance.

"Bravo! Bravissimo!"

"Father Rose." Boris hung his head in shame. "I'm sorry. I... I..." the headaches were beginning to return.

"No, no, my boy!" Father Rose said, walking briskly toward the front of the church. "Such talent! I had no idea there was a prodigy in my midst!"

Boris was confused. "What?" he asked, squinting his eyes against the pressure in his forehead.

"You have a rare talent for mimicry," Father Rose said. "I have work for you, my boy."

"What kind of work?" Boris asked.

Father Rose smiled. "God's work, my boy." He put his arm around the Prince. "God's work."

In time, Boris ceased to wonder about the nature of God's work, and instead reveled in his newfound talents and basked in the glow of Father Rose's affection.

"Friends and neighbors, gather 'round!" Fantômas, still clad in the robes of Father Rose, stood on the altar while dozens of men with calloused hands and brutal faces filed through the doors. After kneeling and giving the sign of the cross, each man removed his hat and took his place in one of the front pews. "Quickly, quickly," Fantômas said, clapping his hands, "time is of the essence and there is much work to be done."

The men eyed one another curiously. Some of them, old acquaintances or friends, greeted one another with brief handshakes. Others politely nodded their heads at one another or gazed curiously at faces that were unknown but familiar. While it was rare to know every one of the thousands that dwelled in the neighboring tenements of the Lower East Side, every face still delivered a shock of recognition to every other. They all had Fantômas in common.

These men made up the Fantômas gang–each one of them a specialist in his army of criminals. There was the Torch, who is already well-known to us. Lunch Pail Eddie was a childlike fellow who, nevertheless, could fire a bullet into a forehead at a hundred paces. Sammy the Siren was one of the best card sharps on the East Coast, until he turned his talent for prestidigitation to pick-pocketing. Since the disappearance of Brian Shea, the safe-cracking was being handled by a gentleman known only as "the Scar"–so named because of a knife wound that began in the corner of his upper-lip and ran northward toward his eye. In all, there were roughly a hundred rogues and villains occupying the pews of Our Lady of Perpetual Sorrow–each one of them culled from the throngs of parishioners that attended weekly mass, hand picked by Fantômas because of the individual talents they could bring to his organization.

"First of all," Fantômas continued, "I gaze on all of you as a father gazes on his children or a shepherd on his flock. I have been disappointed recently by the actions of someone I thought was one of our greatest assets. I'm speaking, of course, of Mr. Brian Shea who took it upon himself to usher a petty, foolish man into our ranks and almost jeopardized everything we are striving to achieve. I know you will all miss Mr. Shea, as will I, but I hope that you have learned a lesson from his betrayal.

"We are very close, my friends. The day will come when we will obtain a great measure of power that will allow us to reign over this city. I was recently blessed with… a revelation, if you will. An opportunity to obtain enough wealth to pull this neighborhood out of the gutter and make it the center of commerce for all of New York City."

The men glanced at one another with confusion.

Fantômas continued. "Do you feel it is your destiny to starve? Of course not. Do you feel it is your destiny to beg? No. And why should you? You are the workers of this city. Why shouldn't the kings of this unfair and unjust state be begging money from you? Our Lord said 'the meek shall inherit.' It is time, my friends, to claim your inheritance.

"To that end, I ask each one of you to aid me in my quest for this wealth. In 48 hours, we will strike Manhattan with a crime wave the likes of which has never been seen. I want the name of Fantômas to be on the lips of every citizen of New York and on the front pages of every newspaper. We are springing forth from the shadows, my friends, into the light. Mr. Torch is walking among you now with envelopes. Each one of you will receive one that bears your name. Enclosed are instructions, including the names of people you'll be working with, your intended targets and your escape routes. Destroy anything that gets in your way. Break anyone who tries to stop you. If you are arrested, have no fear. I will come to claim you when we have accomplished our task. Does everyone understand?"

The men began nodding. Some of them were nervous behind their cruel smiles, while others were itching to wreak destruction.

"Now," Fantômas said, "I wish to draw your attention to one of your own. You know him as the Prince, but for the last several weeks, he has been on an undercover operation for me. It is due to his selfless efforts that we now find ourselves on the precipice of greatness. Boris, please step forward."

Nervously, the Prince rose from his pew, stepped onto the altar and kneeled before Fantômas. Fantômas placed his hand on Prince's head, closed his eyes and lifted one of his arms toward the Heavens. "Lord, bless this young man who has put himself in danger to do your will. He is a sinner, Lord. But it was only his dedication to your ultimate work that led him to destroy one of your creatures and take his identity. We know that in times of war, this ultimate sin is often necessary to achieve the greater good. We know that you will smile on him, dear Lord, and grace him with your love, forgiveness and acceptance."

A tear broke out of the Prince's eye and rolled down his cheek.

"Stand up, my friend," Fantômas said, guiding the Prince up with his hands. "And take this gift that God has bestowed upon you." From inside his robe, Fantômas pulled forth a thin chain with a small gold tooth on the end–the same tooth worn by Brian Shea, then passed off to Garibaldi. The same tooth that mysteriously vanished after Garibaldi's twisted corpse was discovered in prison.

"Go forth," Fantômas said after the ritual was concluded, "Go and do my work."

The men quickly filed out of the church, waiting to speak until they had exited onto the street. "Torch!" Fantômas called, as the Torch was about to leave. "A few minutes, please."

The Torch looked around nervously and discovered that with the exception of the Prince, who was still staring in rapture at the gold tooth hanging around his neck, he was alone in the church with Fantômas. He thrust his hands into his pockets in an effort to appear casual, then walked up the aisle. "What is it?" he asked.

Fantômas put his arm around the Torch's shoulders. "I wanted to thank you for the fine job you did in the Brian Shea affair. I know it must have been difficult."

The Torch stammered. "It was no problem, boss. Really." There was a long pause as Fantômas stared into the Torch's eyes. "Is that all, boss?"

"No," answered Fantômas. "I have another job for you. Tonight. On Long Island."

The Prince raised his eyes in time to see Father Rose speaking with the Torch. He couldn't hear their conversation but could tell that it was an important one, not to be interrupted. Eventually, Father Rose clapped the Torch on the shoulder and walked toward the Prince with a big smile on his face.

"Get up," Fantômas said. "I have another surprise for you."

The Prince stood and followed Father Rose through the secret entrance beside the altar and down the circular flight of stairs to the study. Once there, Father Rose pulled another lever and a piece of the bookcase spun open, leading to a darkened path that went deeper underground. He grabbed a torch from a stand on the nearest wall and lit it. He then motioned for the Prince as he went through the door and walked down the dusky path until he came to a small cell. He stopped and turned toward the Prince. "I'm proud of you, my boy," he said with a smile.

"Thank you." The Prince was smiling as well.

"Tell me, son," Father Rose said. "What is the one thing you've always wanted? Forget about wealth and power and all that other nonsense. What is the one thing that would make your life complete?"

The Prince remembered the image of his waving parents, getting smaller and smaller as the boat pulled away from the shore. "A family," he said. "My own family."

Fantômas waved the torch across the door of the cell and saw Sally Shea, her legs chained together, holding her child to her breast. There was fear and hatred in her eyes. "What do you want with us?" she snarled. "Where is my husband? What are you going to do to us?"

Fantômas pretended not to notice her protestations, and instead turned to the Prince. "Take them," he said. "They're all yours."

Chapter Ten:
The Distressing Savagery of Ruth Harrington

For most of us, sleep is a reward–the final payment for a day's work well done. Laid out securely on our beds, covered in the safety of our warm blankets and surrounded by our most prized possessions, we vacate the tired bones and heavy heads of the workaday world and submit to life-preserving slumber.

For Ruth Harrington, however, sleep was a necessity. While she was certainly in the lap of luxury beneath her canopied bed, resting in the midst of her childhood toys and trinkets, she was not at rest. For a woman who, as a young girl, was forced to find sleep in the most inhospitable of places, Ruth often found the comfort and softness of blankets, springs and pillows to be disorienting. Indeed, she found she did not completely trust the whole idea of comfort. Comfort, after all, lowered one's defenses and made one vulnerable.

And so it was 24 hours after her father's abduction, she lie awake in her father's room, staring at the ceiling and watching the candlelight bounce shadows along the wall. Asleep or awake, however, her senses were fully alert–alert enough to hear the slight squeak of a hinge two floors below.

Her eyes, which had just begun to close, snapped open. She didn't bolt upright in alarm but continued to listen. The bottom of the grandfather clock was slowly sliding across the floor. Someone was breaking into the house.

It was the event she had been waiting for. Indeed, it was the reason she had chosen to sleep in her father's room in the first place.

The hidden clock door was open. The squeaking of the hinges had ceased and the sound had been replaced by the barely perceptible sound of footsteps. Ruth slid silently across the bed and picked up the telephone receiver. She whispered a number to the operator, then waited for an answer. It came in the sound of a slurred, sleepy voice.

The distressing savagery of Ruth Harrington

"Dear God. What is it? It's the middle of the night."

"Jack," Ruth whispered. "Someone is in the house!"

"What? Speak up, good man, I can't hear a word you're saying."

"Jack!" Ruth hissed. "It's me!"

"Ruth?" Jack shouted. "What is it, old girl, what's wrong?"

"Come quickly!"

"What is it? Dear God, are you okay?"

"I'm fine, Jack. Just come quickly. As quickly as you can!"

"Yes! Yes! I'll be right there! Do I have time for a quick wash up?"

"Jack!"

"Right, right! Sorry! Someone in the house, did you say? Don't move, darling. Stay right where you are! Arm yourself, if you can!"

"I'm fine, Jack! Just get over here!"

"Right, old girl, right! Be right there!"

Ruth hung up the phone, then froze in her tracks. The footsteps were ascending the staircase. She turned out the light.

The Torch had made his way across the living room and found the staircase leading to Professor Harrington's bedroom. After reaching the top of the stairs, he tread lightly down the hallway, dragging his fingers across the wall to guide him through the darkness. Harrington's bedroom door stood closed at the end of the hall. The Torch groped for the knob and turned it as slowly as possible before pushing the door open just wide enough to let himself in. He stepped inside, stood with his back against the wall and lit a match. He passed the flame in front of his eyes in an arc, scanning the room for signs of life. The bed was unmade but the room looked empty.

Satisfied that he was alone, the Torch shook out the match, dropped it to the floor and crushed it beneath his heel. He felt along the wall for the light switch and flipped it on, flooding the room with light. He walked to the far side of the room and pulled the curtains aside. No one. He kneeled down and peered beneath the bed. Nothing. He walked to the closet and opened it, moving the clothing from side to side to examine the inside. Empty. From his jacket pocket, he drew out a list of instructions. Crossing the room to the bed, he lifted the bedpost and quickly dialed the combination contained within. The wall in front of him quickly spun around revealing Professor Harrington's safe. The red journal was sitting inside, ready for the taking. He removed it from the safe, dropped it into his pocket, then quickly made his way toward the bedroom door.

The natives in the Bengali jungle had a curious way of capturing and slaughtering swine. When a group of them were nearby, the hunter would scurry up a nearby tree with his knife between his teeth, and wait for a pig to leave the group and walk beneath him. Once the pig had reached the appropriate spot, the hunter would drop from the branch, straddle the pig, cut its throat, then ride the animal while it bucked and tossed in its death throes, eventually losing blood, growing weak and turning over as the light faded from its eyes.

Needless to say, Ruth Harrington had observed this procedure dozens of times.

The Torch felt two bare feet land on his shoulders and force him to the ground. His knees hit the floor with a crack and he threw out his hands to catch himself as he pitched forward. A hand grabbed his hair and yanked his head backwards. From the corner of his eye he could see the flash of the knife as it came to rest underneath his chin, the blade dangerously close to his neck.

"Who sent you?" Ruth said.

The Torch was still in shock–winded from the pressure of her weight on his back. "Where did you come from?" he gasped.

Ruth pressed her lips against his ear. "The Bengali jungle," she said.

"The journal is in my pocket," Torch choked. "Don't kill me."

"That really depends on how cooperative you are. Did Fantômas send you?"

"Can't...breathe..."

"Yes, and there's only so long one can go without breathing."

"Take the journal... take it..."

Putting the Torch's head tightly under her arm while still holding the knife to his throat, Ruth reached into the Torch's pocket until she found her father's journal. She tossed it behind her onto the bed, then turned her attention back to the Torch. His face was turning beet red and Ruth knew she only had a few moments before he passed out from lack of oxygen. "Was it Fantômas? Answer me!"

"Of course, it was Fantômas." The voice didn't belong to the Torch, but to the stranger in the grey coat and hat who had just entered the room with his gun drawn. "Who else would send a petty thief to do the work of a professional?"

"Who are you?" Ruth asked.

"Not important," the man answered. "What is important is that you release that man very slowly, then retrieve the journal for me."

"Don't do it!" said the Torch. "I know him! I seen him at the *Hog's Head*! He's one of the Councilmen!"

The Councilman–the one known to the others as Number Seven–pointed the gun toward the ceiling and pulled the trigger. The loud boom shook the furniture and sent a deafening echo around the room. Bits of wood and plaster rained down on Ruth and the Torch. "Listen, I'm the one with the gun here. Maybe you should both take a step back and give me what I came here for."

Slowly, without taking her eyes from Number Seven's gun, Ruth Harrington let go of the Torch's head and dropped him to the ground, dismounting him as she did so. "Very good," Number Seven said. "Now, about that knife..."

Ruth continued to glare into Number Seven's eyes as she tossed the knife aside, as far away from him as possible. "Nicely done," he said. "Now, the journal."

Ruth backed slowly toward the bed and reached behind her until her hand gripped the book. The Torch was still on his knees, rubbing his throat and choking. Ruth held the journal in front of her. "Throw it here," Number Seven said. Ruth tossed the journal to Number Seven, who caught it with his free hand.

"Much obliged," Number Seven said.

With surprising swiftness, the Torch leapt up, grabbed an unlit oil lamp from a nearby table and tossed it into Number Seven's face. Number Seven screamed as the glass shattered, sending blood streaming down his neck. He fired his gun, just missing Ruth and striking the leg of the bed. After rubbing his eyes, which were still stinging and burning from the oil, he saw the Torch standing before him, a lit match in his hand. "Put down the gun," the Torch said, "or I'll toss this tiny little match into the tiny little puddle at your feet. In no time at all, your valuable grey coat will be on fire with you inside of it."

"Easy," Number Seven said. "I'm dropping the gun."

"Drop it quicker," the Torch snarled.

Number Seven tossed his gun on the floor. The Torch blew out the match and flung it aside.

"Hand over the journal," the Torch said.

Number Seven drew the journal from his pocket and held it aloft. "Come and get it," he said.

Ruth had slowly, silently, inched her way back to the dagger lying on the floor. She bent down and clutched the handle.

"I was hoping not to turn this into a fight," the Torch said. "But if I have to, I have to."

From the side of the room, the dagger spun end over end until the blade sank into the Torch's calf. He screamed in pain, then grabbed his leg and sank to the ground. "Much obliged, ma'am," Number Seven said, tipping his hat and turning to leave. Ruth leapt forward, sailing over the Torch's slumped body and grabbed Number Seven around the ankles, tackling him to the ground. His chin struck the ground with a thud and the journal went spinning across the floor and into the hallway. Number Seven flipped over until he was face to face with his attacker. His hands shot out and began squeezing her throat. "You're beautiful, babe," he snarled, "but you just made a huge mistake." Ruth flailed with her arms in an attempt to strike Number Seven, but he kept hold of her throat, extending his arms so that she was just out of reach.

Unknown to either Ruth or Number Seven, the Torch had made his way to his feet and was limping toward the hallway. With one hand on his thigh to stop the blood, he used his other arm to brace himself against the wall as he made his way out of the room. Ruth's face was beginning to turn red as Number Seven's hands continued to squeeze. "Whaddaya got to say now, Panther Lady?" he sneered.

Ruth choked out her answer in short gasps. "The...journal..." she said, "Stop...him..."

Number Seven threw his head backwards toward the hall, which allowed Ruth to free herself from his grip.

Grabbing his arm and forcing it away from her throat, she spun him over, driving his bent arm up between his shoulder blades. "Are you crazy?" he cried out. "He's getting away!"

Ruth looked up in time to see the Torch, journal in hand, limping down the stairwell. She slammed Number Seven's head into the floor, then leapt off of him and ran toward the staircase. Leaping with her arms outstretched, Ruth tackled the Torch, who was precariously balanced on the top step, and the two went tumbling forward, turning end over end down the stairs until they slammed into the floor with Ruth perched on top. "Ow! Christ!" the Torch said. "Enough, already!"

Ruth was breathing heavily, her hands pinning the Torch's arms over his head. "The journal," she said.

"Take it! Just take it! But stop hitting me for chrissakes!"

Ruth grabbed the journal, which was lying beside the Torch's head, and stood up. "Stay on the ground," she said, "or you'll get more of the same."

The sound of a gun rang out, the bullet creasing Ruth Harrington's shoulder. She dropped the journal and sank to her knees, clutching the wound. She looked up to see Number Seven standing at the top of the stairs, gun in hand. "Stay put," he said, "or you'll be the one that gets more of the same."

Exhausted, weak and in pain, Ruth stayed on the ground while Number Seven walked toward her with his gun raised. "You're a tough one," he said. "And pretty too. Shame I'm in a hurry or you and I could throw a log on the fire and get to know one another." He picked up the journal and headed for the door.

"Where is he?" Ruth called after him. "Where is my father?"

Number Seven turned around. "Lady," he said. "I'm here for this crazy book of yours. I don't even know who your father is." With a tip of his hat, Number Seven turned on his heel and left.

Ruth tore a piece of fabric from the hem of her nightgown and wrapped it around her shoulder. "Good," she said to no one in particular. "The bullet didn't go in." She turned around to see that the bullet had lodged in the face of the grandfather clock. Splinters of burnt wood lay on the ground at its base.

Suddenly, the Torch began to stir. "Did he get it?" he mumbled. "Did he get the journal?"

"Yes," Ruth said. "He got it. Now maybe you'll tell me a little about Fantômas."

"I don't have to tell you a damn thing," the Torch said, rubbing a lump on the top of his head.

Ruth sat down in her father's armchair and picked up a cigarette from the end table. "I suppose, then, that not even a million dollar reward would sway you?"

The Torch looked up with a start. "Lady, are you crazy? No one has a million dollars."

Ruth lit her cigarette. "I do," she said. "A million in cash. My trust fund. All I want is my father back."

The Torch thought for a moment, then stood up slowly. "Got another cigarette?" he asked.

Ruth motioned toward another chair and the Torch sat down. She placed a second cigarette between her lips, lit it, then passed it across the coffee table to her guest. "Now," she said, "let's chat."

Outside, Jack and Detective Dickson were driving onto the grounds of the Harrington estate. "Much obliged, old bean," Jack said. "Couldn't get my bloody automobile to start. It's a damn good thing you own a car."

"It belongs to the department," Dickson said. "How long has it been since you spoke with Ruth?"

"I haven't the foggiest. I was half-asleep. Ten minutes, maybe? Fifteen on the outside."

"Be on your guard," Dickson said. "If what she said is true and there was an intruder in the house, there's no telling what kind of a situation we're going to find ourselves in."

"Poor Ruth," Jack said, shaking his head and placing his fist in front of his mouth. "Not that she isn't a capable woman, Detective, but I hesitate to think what one of Fantômas' blackguards might have done to her!"

"Try to stay strong," Dickson replied. "We'll have to charge in, guns drawn. Ruth may be incapacitated... or worse."

"Or worse?" Jack sobbed in fear. "Detective, you don't think..."

"I don't think anything, Meredith," Dickson interrupted. "I'm just suggesting that we be ready for anything."

"Oh!" shouted Jack. "That wretched Fantômas! I swear if he's hurt one hair on my darling girl's head, I'll give him such a horrible bruising!"

"Here we are," Dickson said, pulling the car alongside the house. "Save the bruising for inside."

Jack started to leap from the car but Dickson's arm held him fast. "Slowly," he said, "and above all, quietly."

"Right," Jack nodded. "Slowly and quietly."

Jack slid with utmost precaution from the car seat while Dickson exited from the driver's side. Dickson drew and cocked his gun, then pulled a second gun from the pocket of his coat and tossed it to Jack. "You've fired a gun before, haven't you?" Dickson asked.

"Many clay pigeons," Jack answered with confidence.

"Good enough, I suppose," Dickson said, with a barely perceptible roll of his eyes. "Follow me."

Dickson crouched beneath the living room windows and made his way to the front door, which led into the study. Jack followed close behind and Dickson could hear him talking to himself. "Teach that Fantômas fellow a thing or two..."

Dickson pulled a lock pick from his inside jacket pocket, inserted it into the keyhole and began working the knob. In a matter of seconds, the lock gave way with an audible click. Dickson opened the door as noiselessly as possible as he and Jack crossed the threshold. They could hear the soft sounds of conversation coming from the parlor.

"They're in there," Jack said. "I can hear them."

Dickson nodded. "On the count of three," he said. "One...two...*three*!" Dickson kicked in the door and the two leapt into the room with their guns drawn, each of them aiming at the Torch who was sitting comfortably in an armchair with a bandage around his head and a biscuit in his hand.

"Put your hands in the air!" Jack shouted.

"How wonderful of you gentlemen to come," Ruth said. "The Torch and I were just having a chat about Fantômas. Would either of you like some tea?"

Jack looked befuddled. Sweat poured from his brow and he kept his gun trained on the side of the Torch's head.

"Lower your gun, Meredith," Dickson said. "I understand. Are you OK, Miss Harrington?"

Ruth smiled. "Never been better," she said. "A bruise here and there, but I'll survive."

"Darling!" Jack said, rushing to her side. "Did he hurt you?"

"Yes," she answered. "But we've gotten past it. Biscuit?"

"No, thank you," Jack answered. "I'm afraid I suddenly have a very upset stomach."

"This man works for Fantômas?" Dickson asked.

"I do," said the Torch. "And this fine lady has offered me a very generous reward for his whereabouts."

"A million dollars," Ruth added.

"What?" Jack shouted. "Are you insane? A million dollars?"

"Relax, dear," Ruth said. "It's my money and I can do whatever I want with it."

Jack sidled next to Ruth and spoke in a low voice. "But… what about the business? There's no war going on, so it's in a bit of a slump. Our first years of marriage will be very lean years indeed if we don't have some sort of cushion."

"Are you suggesting we let my father rot inside one of Fantômas' death chambers?"

Jack caught himself. "No," he said. "No, of course not."

"You know," the Torch interrupted. "I've been asking myself what it might take for me to give up Fantômas to the authorities. A million bucks just might do it."

The Torch apprehended

"I'll call Corona," Dickson said. "If he's willing to cooperate with the police, I want to take him down to the department so Corona can be present."

"Fair enough," the Torch said. "But after I deliver Fantômas to you, I take the cash and I walk. Understood?"

"Are you insane?" Jack shouted.

Ruth stopped him by stroking his arm. "Completely understood, Mr…uh…Torch."

"I have an automobile outside," Dickson said. "It looks like he may need some medical attention."

"That's not all, Detective," Ruth said. "Someone else was here too."

"Who?" Jack asked.

"I don't know," Ruth answered. "I didn't get a good look at him. He was wearing a long grey coat and a grey hat with a wide brim that covered the top part of his face."

"A Councilman!" Dickson cursed, striking his fist into his open palm. "But what could the Council of Ten possibly want with you? How could they know about any of this?"

"Perhaps Fantômas is a Councilman himself!" Jack

offered.

"I don't think so," Dickson answered. "The Council prides themselves on their perverse sense of justice. Fantômas has no need for such pretensions."

"But the question remains," Jack said. "Just what was the Councilman doing here?"

"That's not all," Ruth added. "Before he escaped, he stole my father's journal."

"Good God!" Dickson yelled. "The journal with the formula?"

"With the formula," Ruth answered. "With the formula, the maps…everything. Everything needed to synthesize gold and locate the lost city of the Amazon. It's all in that journal."

"And now it's in the hands of the Council of Ten," Dickson said.

"Ahem," Jack cleared his throat. "Excuse me."

"What is it?" Ruth asked.

Jack's head was slightly bowed and he was chuckling to himself.

"What's so funny?" Dickson asked.

"I'm sorry," Jack said, pressing his hand to his smiling lips. "It's just all very amusing, that's all."

"What is?" Ruth asked.

"He doesn't have your father's journal."

"I saw him take it, Jack," Ruth said with some annoyance. "The three of us fought over it, he picked it up off the floor and left."

"Nevertheless," Jack said with a smirk. "The Council does not have your father's journal."

"I don't understand," Ruth said.

"He doesn't have your father's journal," Jack said, reaching into his jacket pocket, "because I have your father's journal." He drew the journal from his jacket and handed it to Ruth.

Ruth was dumbfounded. "How did you…"

"After our little adventure last evening," Jack continued. "I thought it might be wise if the journal were spirited away to an unknown location. After all, anyone who came looking for it would come here. While you three were busying yourselves with dead Indians and secret doorways, I switched the journal with a blank duplicate I spied on your father's dresser. Cunning of me, wasn't it? Dashed cunning, you might say."

"I might say it was rather foolish," Dickson said. "Suppose one of these men had chosen to examine the journal while he was here, then decided to torture Miss Harrington until she told them where the real journal was. Your deception was clever, but it might have put Miss Harrington's life at great risk."

"Oh, pooh," Jack said with a dismissive wave of the hand. The Torch was growing more and more confused by their banter. Jack put a hand to the side of his face and whispered to him. "He's just jealous," Jack said.

The Torch smiled.

"FANTOMAS ESCAPES WITH THE MILLION DOLLAR REWARD"
WILLIAM FOX PRESENTS
FANTOMAS
1921 American Serial in 20 Episodes
FROM THE WORLD FAMOUS STORIES OF MARCEL ALLAIN AND PIERRE SOUVESTRE
SCENARIO AND DIRECTION BY EDWARD SEDGWICK
EPISODE TWO
"THE MILLION DOLLAR REWARD"

Chapter Eleven: The Million-Dollar Reward

We are back in Midtown Manhattan, roughly an hour or so after the preceding events. It is just past midnight, and although the police station is often filled to bursting with all manner of rogues and criminals, none of the policemen on the overnight shift could have anticipated the flurry of violent criminal activity that has erupted this night.

At approximately 10:13 p.m., a group of men began throwing bricks through the window of Bloomingdale's and stripping the mannequins of the latest fashions. Their hands full of hats and dresses, the men ran four blocks before they were intercepted by Officer Edward White. Officer White was able to lay hands on two of the men, but without sufficient backup, he had no choice but to allow the other four to escape.

Of more serious consequence was the group of a half-dozen men who attempted to rob the First National Bank of Manhattan. Armed with drills and blowtorches, the men broke into the bank, disabled the alarm, then went to work on the vault door. Officer Billy Hannigan of the ninth precinct was off duty and on his way home when he caught the flash of the blowtorch out of the corner of his eye. After calling the department for backup, Officer Hannigan kept his eye on the place until more policemen arrived. All six criminals were arrested and taken into headquarters.

These were the successful collars, but for every man who failed to escape the long arm of the law, another five successfully made their way to safety bearing the spoils of their trade. An original Gutenberg Bible disappeared from the New York Public Library, along with several worthless copies of the complete works of Horatio Alger. Several valuable pieces of Byzantine and Islamic art also vanished from the Metropolitan Museum of Art, and over $50,000 was looted from private homes occupied by the Manhattan elite. The members of Fantômas' gang left behind them thousands of dollars worth of damage and, when all was said and done, the estimated loss to the innocent victims was over half-a-million dollars.

Detective Dickson knew something was wrong as soon as he, Jack Meredith and Ruth Harrington climbed the stairs to headquarters with their prisoner in tow. The main hall was crammed with all manner of low life, most of them standing upright and handcuffed to water pipes. Off-duty officers had been roused from their slumber and were rushing into the squad room, still rubbing the sleep from their eyes. The phones were ringing off the hook and Dickson could see Corona at the back of the room, frantically giving orders to two rookie policemen.

"Good God," Jack said. "What the devil is going on?"

The Torch chuckled. The others turned to look at him.

"You know what's happening?" Dickson asked.

"What's the matter, folks?" the Torch said. "Ain't you guys ever seen a crime wave before?"

"*Dickson*! *Get back here*!" From the back of the room, Corona had spied Dickson and his entourage.

"Follow me," Dickson said, and the others fell in step behind him. Corona charged across the floor to meet them half way.

"Where the hell have you been?" Corona shouted. "I've been trying to reach you for hours!"

"I was at Professor Harrington's house, sir. There was an incident…"

"Never mind that!" Corona shouted. "Can't you see all Hell has broken loose?"

"But, sir," Ruth Harrington interrupted, "we have captured one of Fantômas' men."

Corona stopped dead in his tracks and noticed the Torch for the first time. "God in Heaven," he said. "How?" he began to stammer. "Where? Why?"

"It's a long story," Dickson said. "Is there some place we can talk? Some place quiet?"

"Yes," Corona said, shaking off his stupor. "My office.

Follow me."

The group followed Corona into his office, Dickson and Jack on either side of the Torch, leading him through the din. Once inside, Corona shut the door and locked it behind them. He went behind his desk and dropped into his chair. "Now," he said, "suppose you tell me exactly what's going on here, Detective. I told you I wanted to be informed of any action you took on the Fantômas matter. I hope you haven't been conducting this investigation behind my back!"

"No, sir," Dickson responded. "Maybe I should let Miss Harrington explain."

Ruth stepped forward. "I have offered this gentleman–Mr. Torch–a reward of one million dollars for delivering to us both my father and Fantômas."

Corona spit out his coffee. "Great Gravy!" he sputtered. "A million dollars?"

"That's what I said too, Sergeant!" Jack interrupted. "I think it's too large a sum of money to risk on a distrustful, roguish blackguard of the most deceitful and violent kind!"

The Torch rolled his eyes in amazement. "I'm sitting right here!"

Corona ran his hand over his face in exasperation, then got up from his desk and opened the door to his office. "Officer Jenkins!" he said. "Front and center!"

The young rookie appeared in the doorway. "Yes sir," he answered.

"Jenkins, please keep an eye on this man, will you? Put him out there with the others, but don't let him speak to anyone. Understood?"

"Yes, sir."

Jenkins led the Torch out of the room by the arm. Corona closed the door behind them.

"I agree with Jack," Dickson said once the Torch was out of earshot. "I'm not sure we can trust him."

"Well, then," Jack said with a sigh of relief. "We're all in agreement."

"Does anyone want to know what I think?" Ruth asked,

with no small amount of annoyance.

"Yes," Jack said. "Sorry, darling."

"I think that at this very moment, my father could be suffering the worst kind of torture imaginable. If I have to send myself to the poor house to see his safe return, I'll do it."

"I agree with Miss Harrington," Corona said. "Every minute wasted is another minute that Fantômas has the upper hand. If we act now, we can take charge of the situation on our own terms, before he has a chance to react. Fantômas may not even realize that the Torch has been arrested, but once he does, he will act."

"Unless, of course," Dickson countered, "we're playing right into his hands. How do we know the Torch didn't allow himself to be captured on purpose?"

Ruth addressed all three men with steely resolve. "It's just a chance we'll have to take."

Outside Corona's office, the Torch was seated between two members of Father Rose's congregation. Officer Jenkins was seated at his desk, ignoring the racket and thumbing through a copy of *Nick Carter* magazine. Torch eyed the crowd. Every man in handcuffs was an associate of Fantômas. They had taken his entreaty to rob the city blind very seriously, and trusted him to bail them out, somehow. On the Torch's left was Lunch Pail Eddie–so named because of his habit of carrying a loaded pistol to work in his lunch pail. Eddie was one of Fantômas' lieutenants, and when he recognized the Torch and started to speak to him, the Torch silenced him with a quick shush.

The Torch continued to scan the crowd, desperately trying to figure out a way to get a message to Fantômas.

"Hey, Jenkins! Get your feet off the desk and put down the kiddie book! We gotta send some of these guys home. We got nothin' on 'em." One of the detectives slapped Jenkins' feet with a file folder and threw it down on his desk. "Sign some of these and let's get a little more room in here, okay? Gettin' hard to breathe!"

The Torch stood up.

"Not you," the detective said, "You're not going anywhere 'til we get the OK from Corona." He looked at Lunch Pail Eddie. "Eddie, today's your lucky day. Keep your nose clean, all right?"

"Hey!" the Torch shouted as the detective was turning away. "You gotta phone directory in here somewhere? I gotta call my lawyer."

Jenkins pulled a phone book from his drawer and tossed it onto the desk. "You got two feet," he said. "Use 'em."

The Torch walked over to the desk and began thumbing through the book with his cuffed hands. "Much obliged, Officer," he said. While Jenkins was busy taking the cuffs off of Lunch Pail Eddie, the Torch snagged a pencil from the desk and scrawled a note on one of the phone book pages. He tore out the page, masking the sound with a quick cough, and stuffed it in his shirt. "Thanks, Officer," he said to Jenkins.

"Sit down," said Jenkins, turning back toward his desk.

As quickly as he could, the Torch grabbed Eddie by the hand and stuffed the phone book page into it. Eddie put the page in his pocket, winked at the Torch, then turned and left.

Corona threw open the door. "Jenkins!" he shouted. "Get him back in here!"

"Here's the deal," Dickson began once the Torch was back in the room. "We want Fantômas and Professor Harrington in the next 24 hours. You'll get the money once we're sure they're safe and sound, not before. After that, you're on your own. Live it up in some other city, if you want, but the first time you get back into trouble, I'll be there. And I'll make sure that whatever's left of that money won't even pay your bail."

The Torch stared at the others as if he was weighing his options. "Mind if I smoke?" he asked. Corona tossed him a cigarette. Dickson took out a matchbook and offered it to him. The Torch took a few puffs before continuing. "Tomorrow night, Fantômas is meeting with some of his lieutenants to transport the Professor to another location. This one is a lot more remote."

"Where is the meeting taking place?" Dickson asked.

"Not a chance," the Torch laughed. "It's on Long Island but that's as much as you'll get out of me. I'll lead you there after you've handed me the money."

Corona interjected. "Miss Harrington will withdraw the cash tomorrow morning and leave it here under lock and key. You," he pointed at the Torch, "will spend the night in a cell. Tomorrow night at 11:30 p.m., we'll meet at the Harrington mansion. I'll arrange for a chauffeur and an unmarked car to drive us to the location."

Ruth held out her hand to the Torch. "Deal?" she asked.

The Torch gripped her hand firmly. "Deal," he said.

At 11:30 p.m. the following evening, a long, dark automobile pulled up alongside the Harrington mansion. Ruth Harrington met the party at the door. The chauffeur remained in the car while Dickson and Jack escorted the handcuffed Torch into the house. Corona followed, with a briefcase containing one million dollars handcuffed to his wrist.

"Not much time," the Torch said once they were all

inside. "The meeting's gonna start soon."

Ruth took her coat from a nearby rack. "Let's go, then," she said.

Jack grabbed her loosely around the wrist. "Uh…Ruthie…"

"Yes?" Ruth asked. The others had dropped their heads toward the floor, averting their eyes.

"I think," Jack began, "That is…we think…perhaps it might not be so…seeing as how you're…"

"What Jack is trying to say," Corona continued, "is that Fantômas is a very dangerous man and it might not be prudent for you to…er…that is…"

"I can't believe what I'm hearing," Ruth said. "You don't want me to go, do you? You want me to stay behind while my father's life is at stake!" She turned to Dickson and implored him. "Detective, surely you can see that there's no sense in this course of action."

Dickson looked Ruth in the eyes. "I'm afraid I agree with them, Miss Harrington. We've discussed this thoroughly and decided that it might be best for all concerned if you weren't put at further risk."

"It's for your own good, darling," Jack added. "What would I do if someone hurt my little peach pit?"

"Oh, Christ!" Ruth threw her hands in the air and walked away.

"Miss Harrington," Corona continued, "you've been under a great deal of strain. We don't wish you to be hurt."

"I pulled a pygmy out of a python's throat, for Christ's sake!"

"But New York," Corona answered with a wag of his finger, "is a jungle of a different kind."

"And you!" Ruth said, suddenly turning on Dickson. "If you're attacked by any rats out there, you're on your own."

"Miss Harrington," Dickson addressed her in a low voice. "I apologize. It was my idea. I just couldn't bear the thought of you coming to any harm."

Ruth turned toward Dickson and, for the first time, saw

softness in his eyes completely divorced from his awkward mumbling or his man-of-action posture. Something different. She turned away, placing her hand to her face to hide the sudden flush of redness.

Outside, Corona's chauffeur glanced at his pocket watch and began to mentally tally up his hours of overtime. "Take all the time you need," he said to no one in particular, "Daddy needs a new ice box."

The chauffeur barely had time to turn around and investigate the sound of the back door opening when he felt the rope slip quietly around his neck. He clutched desperately at the thick cord, but the strong hands in back of him held tight, continuing to squeeze until the chauffeur weakened, then collapsed lifeless on the front seat of the car.

The tall figure leapt quickly from the car and gently pressed the back door shut to avoid a noisy slam. He quietly dragged the chauffeur into a nearby grove of trees and removed his clothing. Thirty seconds later, the tall stranger emerged from the brush dressed as the chauffeur, and took his place in the front seat of the car.

Just in time.

The front door to the Harrington mansion swung open.

Corona opened the passenger door and hauled himself in. Dickson and Jack shoved the still secured Torch into the backseat and sat themselves on either side of him.

"What did you say to her, Detective?" Jack asked. "I thought for sure she wouldn't take no for an answer."

Dickson stammered. "I...uh…just told her what you said. That we were, that is, concerned for her safety."

"Well good show, old chap. It's enough to make me wish you'll be around after we get married. How else am I going to get the old girl settled down?"

"While I hate to interrupt any discussion of domesticity, I suggest we hand the reins over to Mr. Torch back there," Corona said.

The Torch leaned forward to glance at the chauffeur's

profile. "Yes," he said. "Drive straight to the main road, then make a left."

Back inside the Harrington mansion, Ruth was pacing back and forth, unable to reconcile the insult of being asked to stay behind with the mysterious longing she felt when Detective Dickson had looked into her eyes. Surely the socially awkward, chronic mumbler hadn't affected her somehow.

Or had he?

She dismissed the notion with a wave of her arm and a quick march upstairs, forcing herself to remember the condescension dealt her by Corona, Jack and, yes, even Detective Frederick Dickson. On reaching the top of the stairs, a small object, half hidden in the space underneath the bathroom door, caught her eye. She bent down to retrieve and discovered that it was a matchbook–its cover folded back and three matches exposed. She read the lettering on the cover–"*The Hog's Head*."

The matchbook must have fallen from the Torch's jacket when she tackled him at the head of the stairs. What was it he had said during the fight over her father's journal? "I know him! I seen him at the *Hog's Head*! He's a Councilman!"

The Hog's Head

The Council of Ten

Fantômas wasn't the only person after her father's secret.

Clutching tightly to the matchbook, Ruth charged into her bedroom, sat at her vanity and removed a makeup kit. After applying copious amounts of powdered rouge to give herself a ruddy complexion, she brushed her hair flat and back to mask her curly locks. From her closet, she fetched a black coat and trimmed several large tufts of fur from its sleeves. With a dash of spirit gum, she attached the fur to her upper lip.

Her face altered, Ruth walked down the hall to her father's bedroom, where she threw open the closet and began trying on hats. She settled on a brown bowler, then began searching for a shirt and jacket, suspenders, pants and finally shoes. She gazed at herself–her new masculine self–in her father's mirror, turning side to side to examine the disguise.

"I'd make love to me," she said aloud.

Back outside, a strong lean figure dressed head to toe in black climbed a tree next to the Harrington mansion. He perched himself on a branch and watched the lights go on and off in various rooms on the second floor. Once all the lights were out and he began to see movement on the ground floor, he leapt from the branch onto the rooftop, the cushioned soles of his feet making a barely audible thud.

After securing himself on the roof, Fantômas–for it was he–crawled on all fours to make his way over the arc of the roof and found himself perched behind the chimney overlooking the driveway. From above, he could see the lifeless body of the chauffeur, stripped of his clothing and lying amongst the trees.

Good, he thought to himself, *everything is going according to plan.*

Maneuvering himself around the side of the chimney, Fantômas positioned himself directly above Ruth Harrington's room. He removed a strap from his waist and swung it around the chimney, clasping one end to the middle of the strap on the other side. The free end he attached to a harness he had strapped onto his back. He checked his belt to make sure the glasscutter was intact, then began, ever so slowly, lowering himself toward the bedroom window.

From the other side of the house, he heard the front door slam. Quickly, he pulled himself back onto the roof and detached the strap from his harness. With quiet precision, he tip-toed to the sloped end of the roof just in time to see a man exit through the front door and make his way to the car park.

A man?

With only the light of the Moon, Fantômas could barely make out the brown hat and suit worn by the curiously thin and slight stranger. He waited for the young man to drive off the estate, then lowered himself to the front door.

Removing a lock pick from his belt, he forced the door open and tread softly inside. Remembering the succession of lights flashing on and off upstairs, he walked quickly up the staircase, made his way to Professor Harrington's bedroom and switched on the lights. Several suit jackets, hats and pairs of pants lay scattered about the bed and floor.

"Hmmmm..."

He walked back down the hall and gazed into Ruth's bedroom. On her vanity were several open boxes of makeup and a tiny, curious object that looked like it didn't belong. Fantômas picked up the object and stared at it with his steely black eyes. It was a matchbook bearing the name *The Hog's Head*.

From the driveway of the Harrington mansion, it took approximately 20 minutes to find the meeting place along Long Island Sound. The chauffeur parked at the edge of the road and stayed in the automobile while the other four made their way down a short embankment toward the water.

"This way," the Torch said. "At the end of this cove, just beyond that outcropping of rocks, is the entrance to a cave."

"One of Fantômas' hideouts?" Corona said with no small amount of excitement.

"Yes," the Torch answered. "Something like that."

The four men flattened themselves against the wall of rock and slowly inched their way toward the opening in the cove. In moments, they were standing in line and prepared to storm the entrance. "On my count," Corona whispered. "One...Two...*three*!" The three men leapt forward with their guns drawn and aimed them into the cave entrance. After a moment, they realized that not only was the cave empty but it was only four feet deep.

"What the Devil?" Dickson said.

The Torch grabbed Jack's left arm and bent it behind him, then wrenched the gun out of his right hand and threw Jack to the ground. "Hand over the journal," he said to Jack, then turned to Corona. "And you, hand over the money."

Dickson aimed his gun at the Torch's head. "Don't be a fool, man."

From behind them, the lights of a car flashed on and the phony chauffeur was driving toward them down the beach at breakneck speed. Jack and Corona ran to one side and hid behind an outgrowth of rock, while Dickson stood in the car's path and pointed his gun directly into the windshield.

"Dickson!" Jack shouted, "For God's sake!"

Dickson fired. The bullet exploded into the windshield and struck the false chauffeur between the eyes. His head snapped back as he clutched the wheel and slumped over, turning the car so it was heading straight for Jack and Corona. The car's right wheels veered up onto the wall of rock, sending Jack and Corona scurrying into the shallow cave. When it finally came to rest, the car was blocking the entrance, preventing either man from exiting.

Dickson had leapt the other way and was on the other side of the car. Suddenly, he felt the barrel of a gun poke into his ribs. "Drop it," the Torch said.

Dickson dropped the gun, raised his hands and turned until the Torch's gun was aimed directly at his heart. "Where's Fantômas?" he asked.

"Right now?" the Torch laughed, "I haven't got the slightest idea. Now move. Stand against the car."

"Don't do it, Torch. Don't add murder to your rap sheet."

The Torch pressed the gun deeper into Dickson's chest. "Maybe I will and maybe I won't," he snarled. "But a good way to help me make my decision would be to do exactly as I'm telling you."

Dickson turned around and marched toward the car which was virtually perpendicular to the ground. He raised his hands and placed them on the hood.

"Now," the Torch shouted, "Toss me the keys to the handcuffs, Sergeant!"

A vague sound of muffled curses and frantic fumbling came from the cave. After a few moments, a single key sailed over the front of the car and landed at the Torch's feet. He picked up the key, undid the handcuffs, then grabbed Dickson and forced him to the ground so that he was laying just underneath the driver's side window. He snapped one handcuff onto Dickson's wrist and the other to the steering wheel, then turned and tossed the key into the water. "Now," he shouted again, "toss out the journal and the briefcase!"

"Are you insane?" Corona yelled back, "I will not!"

Jack swallowed hard. "And…uh…I haven't got the journal."

"You're lying," the Torch said.

"For the love of God, I'm not!" Jack squeaked. "Do you think I'd carry around something that valuable? Particularly when I'm going to meet a master criminal?"

The Torch clenched his fists in frustration. "The briefcase, then. Throw it over."

"I told you," Corona shouted. "Not on your life!"

"Toss it over or I'll put a bullet in the back of Dickson's skull!"

After a few moments, Corona stood up and pushed the briefcase over the upturned hood of the car. It slid down the front of the car and landed on the ground by Dickson's head.

"Well done, Sergeant," the Torch said. He tucked his gun in his belt, picked up the briefcase and made his way over the embankment until he was back on the road. Hovering above the three trapped men, he shouted down. "I'll give your regards to Fantômas!"

The three men lay in humiliated silence for several long minutes, each of them trying in vain to figure out what, exactly, they should have done differently. Finally, after a long while, one of them spoke.

"Well," said Jack with a petulant whine. "Now what?"

We regret, Dear Reader, that we must leave our heroes in such a state of profound embarrassment, but this chapter is drawing to a close and the evening has not yet ended. For now we must rejoin another cast member of our sordid tale back on the Lower East Side.

The small, mustached man with the brown bowler and jacket stepped into the *Hog's Head* and made his way through the smoky haze to the counter. Geoffrey was there, manning his post and mixing illegal drinks for his customers. Two Councilmen, Number Four and Number Six, were standing in the back, eyeing the patrons.

"What'll it be, young man?" Geoffrey said.

Ruth lowered her chin and tried her best to deepen her voice. "Well…er…how about a scotch?"

"On the rocks?"

"Straight up."

Geoffrey chuckled. "I like a man that drinks his liquor straight."

"Uh…thank you very much. Love my liquor straight. Mmmmm, boy, I love it. Just like all real men."

"So," said Geoffey, handing Ruth her drink. "You new to the neighborhood?"

Ruth took a swig and wiped the back of her mouth with her sleeve. "Yeah," she said, "new to the neighborhood."

"You look really familiar," Geoffrey frowned, trying to place the disguised face. "You been in here before, yeah?"

"No," Ruth said. "No, sir. Never been in here before."

"What brings you here tonight, friend?"

"Well…" Ruth hesitated, unsure of how much information she should ask for right away. After a moment's consideration, she took the plunge. "Seeing as how you're the owner of this establishment, I imagine you're pretty wise to everything that goes on in this neighborhood."

Geoffrey laughed. "Mister, I'm the king of the whole damn neighborhood!" He leaned in toward Ruth to take her into his confidence. "They call me Geoffrey the Slasher. You know why?"

Ruth shook her head.

Geoffrey showed her the pig head.

Ruth was unfazed. Slaughtered pigs, after all, were something she had seen plenty of. Geoffrey swept the pig head off the counter and dropped it back into the cooler, slightly resentful that he hadn't gotten more of a reaction from his customer.

"Impressive," Ruth said in a futile attempt to boost his ego.

"When I was a boy–a dozen a minute," Geoffrey said.

"Fascinating." Ruth tried to change the subject. "Listen," she said, "Since you know everything that goes on around here, I was wondering if you could tell me about the Council of Ten and Fantômas."

Geoffrey slapped his hand to his forehead. "Now I know why you look familiar! You remind me of that other fella was in here askin' about him."

"Other fella?" said Ruth. "I don't understand."

"Sure! Looked a lot like you. Not exactly. Bigger guy than you. Bigger shoulders. But had the same hat, the moustache… sure, that's why you look familiar."

"And this man, he asked you about Fantômas?"

"Yeah. The Saint of 14th Street, they call him. Name of Dale. James Dale."

At the sound of James Dale's name, Number Four got Number Six's attention. "You hear that?" he said. "The Slasher just called that guy James Dale."

Number Six looked at the disguised Ruth. "Dale. That the guy that was askin' about Fantômas?"

"Asking a few too many questions," Number Four answered. "Sure looks a little like him. Brown derby, that moustache, the suit…"

Without another word, Number Four and Number Six walked toward the bar and each put a hand on Ruth's shoulder. Ruth jumped a bit, then turned to eye her interrogators. "Yes, gentlemen, can I help you?"

"You James Dale?" Number Four asked.

"Me? No. No, never heard of him. I'm uh…uh…" Damn. Why hadn't she thought of a name? "Willard. John Willard."

"Really?" Number Six said. "Are you sure you're not lying? That sounded to me like a lie."

"Fellas!" Geoffrey interrupted. "This ain't James Dale. I seen James Dale. This fella looks a little like him, but..."

"Why are you protecting this guy, Slasher?" Number Four said. "Maybe you told Dale stuff about Fantômas–stuff we need to know about."

"No...no..." Geoffrey said, his voice betraying signs of panic. "Fellas, please. I wouldn't do that. I wouldn't cross you like that."

"Yeah?" Number Six said. "Maybe Mr. Dale here will tell us why he's going around askin' about Fantômas."

"Gentlemen," Ruth said, trying her best to assuage all three men. "Obviously, there's been some sort of mistake."

"I'll say there has." Number Six brought his arm back and struck Ruth across the face. She fell to the ground and Number Four watched as her false moustache skidded across the floor.

"What the hell?"

Ruth looked up at both men, her eyes ablaze with anger. "Holy Hell!" Geoffrey shouted. "It's a lady!" Ruth reached up for her face and felt that the moustache was no longer attached. Number Four came from behind and pulled off her hat, sending her hair tumbling down her shoulders.

"I'll be damned," Number Six said.

At this point, all conversation in the *Hog's Head* had stopped. Every patron had left their seats and surrounded Ruth, staring drunkenly and, in some cases lasciviously, at the woman who dressed like a man.

"She's a cute one!"

"What ya got under that jacket, dearie?"

"I wish my ol' lady would dress like a man!"

"Gentleman!" Ruth shouted, louder than she had intended. The room fell to a hush at the feminine tenor of her voice. "It was a mistake, my coming here. I apologize. I'll be leaving now."

"Not until you tell us your name," Number Four insisted.

"Edna," Ruth said. "Edna...Murphy?"

"Yeah?" Number Six looked doubtful. "And where do

you live, Miss Edna Murphy?"

Ruth froze. Where did the Irish families live? Why hadn't she done her homework before embarking on such a foolish errand? "Down the block?" she said meekly.

"You're lying," Number Four said.

It would be rude, and rather pointless, to describe in detail what happened next. The two Councilmen made a foolish attempt to subdue the woman who had once wrestled an alligator along the Nile River in order to protect a group of children trying to cross. The Councilmen fought as hard as they could, but were no match for the fury of Ruth Harrington. Unfortunately, when violence breaks out at the *Hog's Head*, it soon becomes a fast moving virus, infecting every last one of the customers, no matter how drunk they may be.

A brawl at The Hog's Head

And so, the result was that Ruth Harrington soon found herself overwhelmed and outnumbered. She stayed at the center of the fray, fists flailing, but soon even the Councilmen were able to catch their second wind just as Ruth Harrington was almost down for the count.

"Filthy whore," Number Four said.

Ruth lay on the floor, surrounded by two dozen drunken men. Her blouse was torn. She wiped a drop of blood from her mouth with the back of her hand.

Number Six grabbed a dishrag from the top of the bar and wrapped it around his fist. "Needs to be taught a lesson," he said, bringing his arm over her head.

The following happened so quickly that none of the two dozen men there that night could remember with any alacrity what exactly had taken place. Suddenly, Number Six screamed as a man with a moustache wearing a brown bowler grabbed his arm and cracked it across his knee. The sickening sound of the snap momentarily jolted everyone from their drunkenness and they all stepped back to get a clearer look. The stranger was standing above Ruth Harrington with both hands bending Number Six's arm behind his back, twisting it at an impossible angle. Number Six's face was flushed red with pain. "God almighty!" he screamed. "You broke my arm!"

"You've still got one good one," the stranger said in an oddly relaxed voice. "Why don't you quit while you're ahead?"

"I give!" Number Six shouted.

"Take her," Number Four said. "Everyone step away from the girl."

The crowd slowly backed away from Ruth, leaving a wide berth around her and the mysterious stranger. "As you were!" the stranger hissed, arms to his side and fists clenched. "Back to your drinks, everyone."

The crowd dispersed in silence. The stranger offered his hand to Ruth. "Let's quit this rotten place, shall we?"

Ruth's suspicion was trumped by relief at having been delivered from the crowd's intoxicated wrath. She rose to her feet, but found herself dizzy and half-collapsed in the stranger's arms. "There, there, dear girl," the stranger said. "Let's get you outside. The night air does wonders for a wounded soul."

The stranger led Ruth by the arm through the doors of the Hog's Head and into the fetid streets. "Thank you," Ruth managed to say as she felt her strength returning. "I'm grateful for your kindness. If you hadn't come when you did…"

"Pish-tosh," the man said. "Merely doing my gentlemanly duty. I adore traveling about, saving young women who dress like their fathers."

Ruth smiled. "Yes, well…" She stared at him a moment, a touch uncomfortable under his gaze. "I'd better be going."

"I'm sorry," the man said, leading her by the hand. "But you're far too weak to walk. I have a car nearby. Perhaps you'll let me drive you home."

Ruth's instincts warned against such an act, but ultimately she relented and followed the stranger to his car.

Moments later, the two companions were traveling out of the east side toward midtown. "So," the stranger said, "perhaps, if I'm not prying, you might try telling me exactly what you were doing dressed as a man and antagonizing a couple dozen drunken brutes."

"It was a bad idea," Ruth confessed. "I was looking for information." She fell silent, not wishing to reveal anymore.

"No need to explain," the man said. "I've been on many searches for information myself."

"How so?"

"Well, if you must know, I'm a detective."

Ruth stared at him, wondering if she had seen him before. "A detective. With the police department?"

The man laughed. "Heavens, no. At least, not with the New York Police Department. Some years back, I did some work with the Paris Sûreté."

"Ah!" Ruth said. "I thought I detected a European accent of some sort."

"Spain!" the man admitted. "I was born and raised in Barcelona."

"Oh? What brought you to the States?"

The man's face suddenly grew serious. "I have, for many years, been on the trail of the criminal Fantômas!"

Ruth stared at him, stunned. “Fantômas!” she said with no small amount of excitement.

The man turned to look at Ruth. “Where are my manners?” he chuckled. “May I trouble you for your name?”

“Ruth Harrington. And yours?”

The man extended his hand to her. “Cortez,” he said. “The name is Emile Cortez.”

"DEATH BY TELEPHONE"
WILLIAM FOX PRESENTS
FANTOMAS
1921 American Serial in 20 Episodes
FROM THE WORLD FAMOUS STORIES OF MARCEL ALLAIN & PIERRE SOUVESTRE
SCENARIO AND DIRECTION BY EDWARD SEDGWICK
EPISODE TWO
"THE MILLION DOLLAR REWARD"

Chapter Twelve: Fantômas in Love

Allow us to take a short reprieve from our story and ask the reader to try and remember the rush of first love. Perhaps it was years or decades ago. Perhaps you are currently suffering from the pangs of an intense infatuation or, God help you, the terrifying reality of genuine love. In either case, Dear Reader, your humble narrator hereby offers you his sincere condolences. There is no pain like love. Even as it lifts us, it threatens to destroy us. All rational thought is overturned. The time we are away from the object of our affection ticks by as slowly as the imperceptible turning of the Earth, while the time we are together ends all too soon. Day breaks, our loved ones leave and we are left with heartache and damnation.

The last time Fantômas was in love, it was with an unheard of intensity. Unheard of not just for Fantômas, but for most of the civilized population. So jealous was he of the husband of the desirable Lady Beltham, that he had strangled the man to death, stuffed his corpse in a trunk and attempted to mail it to Australia.

That, Dear Reader, is love.

And so it was that Fantômas, in his disguise as internationally renowned detective Emile Cortez, found his chest beginning to burn with passion as he drove through the city with Ruth Harrington at his side.

"So," Ruth said, trying to break the awkward silence. "How long have you been in New York?"

"A few years," Cortez answered. "I followed Fantômas here from Paris. My father was a police officer in Barcelona. He often spoke of the famous Paris Sûreté with a great deal of fondness, having apprenticed there for many years and followed their exploits in the papers. It was his great wish, God rest his tired soul, that I take up the family trade."

"And how do you like America?" Ruth asked.

"An interesting country, America," Cortez answered.

"One or two more generations and I suspect that America will become the receptacle for the whole of Europe's working class. Not that I'm cynical, you understand, about the 'land of the free,' but one look at some of these neighborhoods, their tenements stuffed with penniless merchants and arthritic craftsmen, and it's difficult to believe that life will ever get any easier for them."

"My oh my, Mr. Cortez. That's awfully pessimistic, don't you think?"

"Oh, don't misunderstand me. I'm very optimistic about the possibilities inherent in coming to a country with so much…freedom. Often, I think of Barcelona with its history and its beauty and I confess that I feel a longing for my home. But here, in America, I wake up every morning knowing that anything is possible. That if I so desire, the world is mine for the taking."

Ruth stared at Cortez as he continued to drive through the streets. The early morning had laid a quiet across the city. The sky was still black as pitch, but even the night owls had retired to their beds, leaving the streets barren of life. All was still and silent and Ruth leaned back in her seat and looked out the car window. The noise and bustle of the city had ceased. It was a feeling of calm she had never experienced before.

Cortez broke the silence. "Miss Harrington…"

"Please," Ruth interrupted. "Call me Ruth."

Cortez smiled and pressed one hand to his heart. "No, Miss Harrington, I would never do you the dishonor of assuming such familiarity."

Ruth laughed. "You are not assuming it, Mr. Cortez, I am giving it to you freely."

"Nevertheless," Cortez added, "I am a gentleman. Still, Miss Harrington, I'm wondering if you will allow me to show you something."

"Perhaps," Ruth answered, somewhat warily. "What is it?"

"Only the most beautiful sight in New York City."

Parked outside a warehouse along the shore, Cortez and Ruth looked at the lady draped in grey–the symbol of freedom visible in the early morning light, rising like a phoenix from the waters. Her left hand held the mighty torch aloft and her garment hung from her massive shoulders. The crown that rested on her head was an emblem of her humility and pride.

"I've never seen it," Ruth said. "I mean…of course I've seen it. Hundreds of times. But I've never really looked at it. She's quite extraordinary, isn't she?"

"When I first arrived in this country, huddled among the poor masses, forced to spend weeks and weeks in cramped steerage, this was the first sight I beheld when I stepped onto the deck of the ship. And it was then that I knew that I would have everything I ever wanted. That while I regretted the life I left behind, a new life was possible. I knew at that moment that I would do whatever it took, for as long as it took, to achieve my dreams."

Ruth stared at Cortez, moved by the look of wistful nostalgia in his eyes. "Fantômas," she said.

Cortez turned to her suddenly. "I beg your pardon?" he said, with some alarm.

"You were searching for Fantômas."

Cortez laughed. "Ah, yes. The dreadful criminal Fantômas. The savage human beast that I have dedicated myself to apprehending."

"Mr. Cortez," Ruth began, a bit regretfully.

"Of course," Cortez interrupted. "It's time for you to go home."

By the time Cortez's car pulled up to the Harrington mansion, the Sun was just beginning to rise. The grey night had begun to retreat, allowing the colors of the day to return.

"Well," Ruth said, turning in her car seat to address Cortez. Her hand was on the door handle but she was making no attempt to leave.

"Well," Cortez said.

"Perhaps you would allow me to make us some morning

tea. You did, after all, save my life."

"My dear, dear, Miss Harrington." Cortez nodded with a graciousness Ruth had only seen in royalty. "As I said before, I am a gentleman. And a gentleman does not invite himself into a lady's house after a long night."

"Well, Mr. Cortez, technically it's no longer night. The Sun is rising. A bit of tea is the least I can do."

"Well then," said Cortez, acquiescing. "A bit of tea it is then."

Ruth stepped into her home with Cortez following closely behind.

"Quite a large house for just one woman," Cortez observed.

"Oh no," Ruth said. "I share it with my father." And it was here that the night's reverie came to an end. She had been so intoxicated by her brush with violence, followed by the poetry of the city and Cortez's charming and assured manner, that the weight and worry of the previous days had taken a brief respite. Now, however, with the coming of the dawn, Ruth's anxiety returned.

The next thing she thought about was Jack.

"Are you all right?" Cortez asked. "You look strange. Did I say something to upset you?"

"I'm sorry," Ruth said. "I'm engaged to be married."

"Congratulations!" Cortez said. "Wipe those guilty thoughts from your mind, Miss Harrington. We are merely acquaintances and our union is one of complete innocence."

"Yes," Ruth smiled with some relief. "Of course it is."

"Tell me about him," Cortez said, sitting down on the sofa.

Ruth sat next to him. "Hmm. What's to tell? I've known him since I was a child. He lives three houses down from here. Always has. We played together as kids. As I got older and went off on journeys with my father, I was always relieved to come home and see his face. We grew apart over a number of years, but it was always assumed by everyone around us that we would be married. And a couple of years ago, when he returned from Oxford, we reunited. A few months ago, he asked me to marry him and that was that."

"I'm always delighted to hear when a woman as beautiful and charming as you finds someone who appreciates her assets. And who is the lucky man, pray tell?"

"His name is Jack Meredith."

Cortez threw his hands to his face in surprise. "No!" he gasped. "The Jack Meredith? The munitions heir?"

"The same," Ruth said, slightly confused. "Have you heard of him?"

"Heard of him? I went to Oxford with him!"

"You did?"

"Old Jackie boy! I can hardly believe my ears! Well, well, well, Jack Meredith has certainly done well for himself, hasn't he? What a strange world we live in! What a very strange world!"

Ruth was aghast. "So you know him well?" she asked incredulously. "He's never mentioned you."

"Well of course not," Cortez said, lowering his voice. "Secret Societies, blood brother, vow of silence, that sort of thing."

"Blood brothers?"

"And now here he is in America with a fortune at his fingertips and a beautiful woman at his side. Will wonders never cease? Well my dear, I'm pleased and a little proud to say that I knew Jack Meredith when the only women he knew were the kinds that never told anyone their real names, if you catch my drift."

"Pardon?" Ruth stood up from the sofa.

"Ladies with little on their minds besides a clean bed, a warm body and a crust of bread."

"Excuse me!" Ruth was growing suspicious.

"But you've tamed him!" Cortez said, leaping up from the sofa with a burst of enthusiasm. "The great playboy Jack Meredith has settled down. How unexpected and delightful!"

Ruth felt her anxiety begin to rise. Something about Cortez didn't seem right all of a sudden. "Wait a minute," she said with an accusing tone. “When did you go to Oxford? You spent your life in Barcelona until you left for Paris. You said so yourself.”

“Semantics, my dear,” Cortez stepped toward Ruth. “Oxford is the Barcelona of England. Surely you’ve heard that before.”

Ruth stepped backwards, away from Cortez. She was suddenly very unsure of herself. “You don’t know Jack Meredith.”

“Oh, but I do, Miss Harrington. We know one another very well. As I say, we were like brothers.”

Ruth stared at Cortez through steely eyes. “Prove it,” she said.

Cortez walked to the wall and picked up the telephone receiver. “Call him and ask.”

Ruth stepped slowly to the phone and Cortez moved to one side. She took the receiver from him, dialed the operator and gave her Jack’s number. The phone rang once…twice…three times…

“Hello?” Jack’s voice was tired and haggard.

“Jack?”

“Ruthie, old girl. Is that you?”

“Jack, I have to ask you something.”

“Hold on, old girl, I can barely hear you.”

“Jack?”

“Ruth? Can you hear me? What’s that ticking? Is that coming from your end?”

“Jack! Hang up the…!”

From the end of the line came an enormous explosion. The sound was so deafening that Ruth recoiled from the phone, dropping the receiver in the process. Even Cortez was somewhat stunned by the sheer force of the blast. Ruth ran back to the phone and picked up the receiver.

“Jack! Can you hear me, Jack? Operator! Hello, operator! What happened?”

From the window at the end of the living room, Ruth could see smoke rising in the distance. She ran to the window to get a better view. "That's Jack's house! What's happened?" Flames were growing and rising, sending thick black clouds of smoke billowing into the air. Ruth turned around to face Cortez. All at once, the charm and savoir-faire of the respectable Spaniard had fallen away and he scowled at her through his false moustache and heavy black eyes.

"Fantômas!" Ruth said.

Ruth and Cortez

Cortez reached into his jacket pocket and pulled out a syringe. "In the flesh," he snarled.

Outside, a woman clad entirely in black stared through the window at Ruth and Fantômas. She was hidden by the trees, but still close enough to see the hideous look of perversion on Fantômas' face. A pang of jealousy welled up in her breast and her face flushed red under her long black veil.

Once again, Dear Reader, we have reached the end of an act. Your humble narrator now recommends that in order to calm your nerves, you set this book aside and read something a little less shocking. Perhaps a story about Tom Brown, or something by the delightful and clever Miss Austen. Then, when you feel your constitution has been restored, join us back here for Act III–in which Muggs, Glimpy and Snapper give refuge to some unfortunates and the Woman in Black seeks revenge on the Lady in White.

WILLIAM FOX PRESENTS
FANTOMAS
1921 American Serial in 20 Episodes
BLADES OF TERRO

ACT III

In which Muggs, Glimpy and Snapper give refuge to some unfortunates and the Woman in Black seeks revenge on the Lady in White

Chapter Thirteen: A Narrow Escape!

While we are certain that the reader, in his or her current state of shock, is experiencing a pressing need to learn the fates of Jack Meredith and Ruth Harrington, there are probably a number of issues that require explanation. For instance–how, exactly, did Jack Meredith extricate himself from the space between the shallow cave and the overturned car and make his way back to his Long Island home in time to receive Ruth Harrington's frantic phone call?

For the answer to this quandary, we ask the reader to go with us back in time, a few hours prior to the events of the last chapter. As I'm sure you recall, Jack and Corona were trapped behind the automobile that was destroyed when Detective Dickson fired a gun through its window, mortally wounding one of Fantômas' agents and causing the car to careen onto a large platform of rocks, upending it and preventing Jack and Corona from leaving the cave. The Torch, before leaving the scene with a briefcase containing one million dollars, handcuffed Detective Dickson to the steering wheel of the car, leaving him face down in the sand along Long Island Sound.

We rejoin our heroes at the moment we last left them at the end of chapter ten.

"Well," said Jack, "What now?"

"Now," Dickson answered with a deep sigh. "We wait."

A frantic, rustling sound came from behind the car and Dickson was certain it was Corona, trying in vain to wriggle himself free. "Wait for what?" Corona yelled, his booming voice full of rage. "I'd like to know, Detective. I really would! Our only link to Fantômas is getting away!"

"And," added Jack, "he's getting away with one million dollars of my fiancé's money!"

"Yes!" agreed Corona. "There's also that! Any brilliant ideas for getting us out of this scrape, Dickson?"

"I told you," Dickson answered. "We wait. We wait for Jenkins."

"Jenkins!" Corona erupted with a chortle. "How is Jenkins going to find us out here?"

"In case something like this happened, I told him where we were. I said if we didn't show up by 2 a.m. to grab a patrol car and come looking for us."

"Jolly good show!" Jack exclaimed.

"But Jenkins?" Corona interrupted. "The man can't be counted on! If 2 a.m. comes and goes and he's in the middle of a King Brady Dime Novel, he's likely to forget all about us!"

"He's also the only one at police headquarters who can leave without anyone really noticing," Dickson countered.

"Good thinking, Detective," Corona agreed. "This isn't necessarily something I'd want the rest of the force to know about."

"So when," Jack began, with a shrill, impatient tone to his voice, "can we expect this Jenkins fellow to show? I must get home and ring up Ruth. She'll be horribly worried about me."

"Like I said," Dickson answered. "Jenkins will be here. We just have to wait."

And wait, they did.

Two o'clock came and went. Then 3 a.m. And before long, all three men could see the Sun begin to come up over the horizon.

"Dickson?" Jack asked, after an hour of silence. "Are you awake?"

"Yes," Dickson answered. "How's Corona?"

"Asleep. And so are both of my feet."

At the sound of Jack's voice, Corona began to rouse himself. "Good God," he said. "It's daylight."

"You have my heartfelt apologies, Corona," Dickson said. "I can't imagine where Jenkins..."

Just then, all three men heard the sound of a car slowly moving above them.

"Is it him?" Jack asked, as the car crept along the ridge. "Is that him?"

"Jenkins!" Dickson shouted, "Down here!"

"Jenkins!" Corona added, "You worthless, overpaid son-of-a-bitch! Get down here...*Now*!"

The three men heard the car stop with a sudden lurch, then heard the door slam and footsteps sliding down the grass toward the rocks. All three began to shout. "Jenkins! Down here!"

"Detective Dickson!" Jenkins called out. "Sergeant Corona! Where are you?"

"Trapped!" Corona answered. "Behind this car! Now, for Christ's sake, get us out of here before we starve!"

"I'm sorry, Sergeant," Jenkins answered, breaking into a jog and heading toward the overturned car. "I was in the middle of...the middle of..." he spied Dickson lying in the dirt, his wrist stretched upward and handcuffed to the steering wheel. "Detective Dickson! Is that you?"

"Do you have a set of keys for these things?" Dickson asked, referring to the handcuffs.

"Yes, sir," Jenkins answered. "I..." Jenkins had stepped toward Dickson when he caught sight of the dead body of Fantômas' henchman, still slumped over the driver's side door of the car. "Is he..."

"Dead, Jenkins," Dickson answered. "Yes, he is. Now, help me out of here so that the two of us can make our way around to the bottom of the car. Maybe with enough leverage, the four of us can tip it away from the cave so we can free the others."

Jenkins' eyes were glued to the corpse. "Uh...right, Detective, right."

Approximately 20 minutes later, all four men were piled into the police car with Jenkins at the wheel. "And just what took you so long?" Corona asked.

"Well," said Jenkins, "I was thinking about this whole Fantômas problem and I remembered that the great Nick Carter once solved a case in which no one knew the true identity of the blackmailer. So I went to the supply closet where I store all my old magazines and just started digging through them to see what Nick had to say about such things. And before long… I'm sorry, Sergeant. I don't know where the time went."

Dickson spoke up before Corona had a chance to respond. "Did anyone see you leave? That's more important."

"Too true," Corona agreed, "Too true. It's getting harder and harder to keep this Fantômas business under our hats."

"It may be about to get even harder," Jenkins said. "Our officers are still bringing in thugs because of the crime wave, and those crooks keep talking about Fantômas like they know him personally. The newspaper guys are starting to pick up on it."

"Dammit," Corona said, "I want Fantômas off the streets. Period! I want to flush him out of hiding and I want to dispatch him once and for all. I don't want the press to write about him and I don't want to answer any questions about him. My greatest wish, Detective Dickson, is for Fantômas to cease to exist. Immediately. We have enough problems in this city without master criminals leading us on wild goose chases along Long Island Sound. Enough is enough!"

Corona's pronouncement brought a hush of silence to everyone in the automobile, and within a few minutes Jenkins was pulling up alongside Jack Meredith's palatial Long Island home. "Get some rest, Meredith," Corona said. "I'll ring you up this evening and let you know our next plan of attack."

Jack Meredith, who was beginning to look the worse for wear after his night's adventure, stumbled from the car in the early morning mist and made his way up the walk toward his front door.

"If you don't mind, Jenkins," Dickson began before Jenkins had pulled the car away from Jack's house. "I think I'll get out here."

Corona looked at Dickson incredulously. "Here?" he asked. "What for?"

Dickson's face flushed red. "I could use the air," he said.

"And you'll what… walk back to midtown?"

"I have a friend," Dickson lied. "I thought I'd drop in on him."

Corona looked suspicious. "At 5:30 a.m.?"

Dickson turned away, pulled open the door and stepped onto the street. "He's a very old friend," he said.

"Whatever you wish, Dickson," Corona said through the car window. "But meet me at headquarters this evening. Fantômas has won this round and we must, at all costs, make sure that the next win belongs to us."

"Yes sir," Dickson said, and watched as the car pulled away, leaving him alone in front of Jack Meredith's house. He watched Jack stumble exhaustedly inside and shut the door. Then he steeled himself and began walking down the street toward Ruth Harrington's house.

Despite the danger that had taken place over the past 24 hours, Freddy Dickson was unable to shake Ruth Harrington from his thoughts. Their eyes had met moments before he last left her, and he was certain that the moment was as significant to her as it was to him.

Or maybe it wasn't.

Dickson turned around and walked back toward Jack's house.

What am I doing? he thought. *Ruth... Miss Harrington... is engaged. I would be foolish to come between them.*

He stopped, then turned around again.

On the other hand, she's engaged to an oafish clod. Maybe it's only because she's never met anyone else that might...

He pitched around once again, marching in the opposite direction.

But I'm a gentleman. Surely it shows a certain lack of respect to even think about wooing a taken woman, and...

He stopped. *If I could just talk to her.*

He turned around.

Standing in front of him was the Woman in Black.

Dickson leapt backwards. "You!" he said, startled.

"There is very little time," she said. "He is with her."

"With Ruth?" Dickson asked. "Who is with her?"

The Woman in Black leaned forward until Dickson could feel her hot breath as it blew through her thin black veil. "Fantômas," she said.

"Fantômas!" Dickson shouted.

"He wants her," the Woman in Black continued. "I think…" and Dickson could hear a trembling in the woman's voice. "I think he's in love with her."

"In love with her?" Dickson shouted incredulously. "Impossible!" Dickson bolted forward toward Ruth's house.

The Woman in Black clutched him firmly by the arm, causing Dickson to wince in pain. "You are needed elsewhere," she said.

"Ridiculous! Let go of me!"

"He won't hurt her. Not yet. There is someone else who is in more immediate danger."

Dickson wrenched himself free of the woman's grasp. "Who?" he asked.

"Before he can have Ruth Harrington, he must get rid of the one person who stands in his way."

A horrible realization crossed Dickson's mind. "Meredith!" he said, spinning around and sprinting toward Jack's house.

"Detective!" the Woman in Black shouted.

Dickson spun sharply around.

"Save her, if you can," she warned. "If Fantômas has her in his grasp, he won't be the worst danger she faces."

"No?" Dickson asked.

"No. She will have to face me." Dickson could hear the rage and jealousy tightening the woman's throat. He stared at her for a moment, uncertain of which way to turn. "*Go*!" she shouted, and Dickson turned and ran toward Jack's house as fast as his weary legs could carry him.

He didn't stop running as he reached Jack's front door, but pressed on, driving his shoulder into the door and knocking it off its hinges.

"Good God!" Jack shouted, "What's the meaning of this?"

Dickson could see that Jack was speaking into the receiver of his telephone and holding the earpiece to his ear. He froze and scanned the room until he saw a series of wires snaking along the wall and leading to the telephone.

Without a word, Dickson lunged forward, grabbed Jack by the shoulders and ran him toward the front door.

"What the Devil?" Jack yelled, resisting Dickson as much as possible. "Ruth is on the line! I think she's in trouble!"

"Later!" Dickson screamed, continuing to shove Jack through the door and out towards the street.

"Really, Detective," Jack snarled, his face red with frustration. "No matter the reason, your behavior is inexcusable!"

They felt the explosion before they heard it. The force of the blast knocked them forward and into the street, where they slid across the pavement. They remained still for several moments before turning around to see that Jack Meredith's house was bursting into flames.

"Oh, dear God!" Jack shouted in desperation. "My house!" He rose shakily to his feet and began limping toward his home. Another smaller explosion caused both men to turn their heads away and press their hands to their ears. A series of flames began to leap through the upstairs windows, setting the curtains ablaze while thick black smoke curled upwards toward the sky.

"Oh, dear God, no!" Jack fell to his knees.

Dickson rushed to him and helped him to his feet. "Later," he said. "We'll deal with this later. Fantômas has Ruth."

Jack stared into Dickson's eyes as his defeat turned to steely resolve. "Where?" he asked, his lips tight with rage.

"Can you run?" Dickson asked, placing his hand on Jack's shoulder.

"Yes. Let's go," Jack answered.

"They're at Ruth's house," Dickson said, and began running with Jack trailing close behind. The Harrington mansion was a block and a half away and the two determined men ran for all they were worth, ignoring their heavy fatigue.

"The front or the back?" Jack asked, as the mansion came into view.

"The front," Dickson ordered brusquely. "No time to be sneaky. We may already be too late."

Jack found a burst of energy and brought himself up beside Dickson. The two men increased their speed as they approached the front door. Instinctively turning their shoulders outward and placing their forearms in front of their eyes, they smashed the door in tandem. It exploded inward, swinging violently toward the wall and striking it with an enormous thud. Jack and Dickson stood in the doorway, their lungs aching for breath but their eyes burning with fury and determination.

Fantômas was still disguised as Emile Cortez. He was standing over Ruth Harrington's body, which was slumped backward on the sofa, her chin resting on her chest and her arms immobile at her sides with her hands facing upward. Her eyes were alert but her body was motionless.

"What's wrong with her?" Jack asked.

Dickson spied the empty syringe in Fantômas' hand. "She's awake," he said, "but paralyzed."

"Don't come any closer, gentleman," Fantômas said with a sneer. "I've only given her enough formula to render her helpless…for the moment. One more injection, however…"

Jack lurched forward. "Son of a bitch!" he cried out in frustration.

Dickson grabbed him by the shoulders and eased him back. "What do you want?" he asked Fantômas.

Fantômas removed Emile Cortez's bowler from his head and gave it a light dusting with his fingers. "Merely to leave here with my treasure intact."

"Not on your life," Dickson said.

"Jack! Detective!" Ruth was alert enough to speak, though her eyes were facing downward. "I'll be fine. He's not going to hurt me. Do as he says."

"Say goodbye to your fiancé, darling," Fantômas said to Ruth. "With any luck, you'll never have to lay eyes on his pathetically weak countenance ever again."

"Monster!" Jack shouted and leapt forward, grabbing Fantômas by the shoulders.

"Meredith! No!" Dickson tried in vain to hold Jack back but it was too late.

"Idiot," Fantômas said in a voice tinged with eerie calm. Suddenly, Jack clutched his neck and spun around so that Dickson could see the hypodermic needle that had been forced into the side of his face. The plunger had been pressed down, sending several inches of sharp metal through Jack Meredith's jaw and into his tongue. His face turned red and he began gasping for breath before collapsing to the floor.

Fantômas turned his back on the two men, then scooped up Ruth Harrington's body in an instant and carried her across the room. Jack stared up at Dickson with terrified eyes, struggling for all he was worth to tell Dickson to save Ruth but all that came out was a cry of pain. He clutched Dickson's shoulder in agony.

"Just relax," Dickson said. He glanced across the room in time to see that Fantômas was escaping by carrying Ruth… upstairs? "Just relax," he repeated, then dashed for the bathroom and returned a moment later with a small towel. He placed the towel on Jack's jaw, right at the base of the needle.

"Now," he said, "I'm going to pull it out. Press the towel to your mouth to squelch the bleeding."

Jack's eyes were still staring sharply at Dickson. He was on the edge of panic. "On the count of three," Dickson said. "One…Two…Three!" The needle slid from Jack's cheek as a geyser of blood erupted from his mouth, striking Dickson in the face. Jack grabbed the towel and pressed it to his mouth. He was still in pain, but he began to breathe easier.

"Are you all right?" Dickson asked.

Jack nodded, grunted, then motioned for Dickson to follow Fantômas.

"Just relax," Dickson said. "In a moment, you won't be able to move. The effects will wear off in an hour or so." Then Dickson bolted up the staircase, taking the steps two at a time. He reached the landing in time to hear the sliding of a window in Ruth's room, down at the end of the hall. He drove himself forward and as he entered the room he looked out the window and saw Fantômas and Ruth disappear upwards.

Upwards?

Why was Fantômas heading toward the roof?

Ignoring the trepidation brought on by a childhood fear of heights, Dickson climbed out of the second story window. He glanced upwards, making sure that Fantômas wasn't waiting to stamp on his hands and force him to the ground. Seeing no trace of the fiend, Dickson leapt for the edge of the drainpipe and caught it with his fingertips. The sharp metal pressed into the flesh of his hands as his feet let go of the windowsill and he dangled along the side of the house. "Ruth," he reminded himself. "He has Ruth." With a burst of adrenaline, Dickson pulled himself onto the roof, his muscles straining and beads of sweat forming on his forehead.

Not wanting to leave himself vulnerable to attack, Dickson jumped to his feet and spun around. Fantômas and Ruth were nowhere in sight. Where could they possibly have… then he saw Fantômas' jacket tossed haphazardly at the foot of the chimney, as well as the cables–two of them running parallel from the top of the chimney and down toward the ground. He rushed forward to the edge of the roof just in time to see Fantômas, with the motionless Ruth Harrington in his arms, sliding down the cables by way of two metal hooks rising from his shoulders, anchored by straps that circled his torso and fit snugly over his forearms. By the time Dickson had understood how Fantômas had escaped, the villain and his captive had disappeared into a grove of trees below.

Dickson glanced sharply around, desperately searching for a quick way down to the ground. The cables seemed to be the fastest way, but what if Fantômas had expected him to follow and rigged them to snap in two just as he was making his descent? To follow was too risky.

Before he had another chance to weigh his options, Dickson heard the sharp pistons of a motor car and saw puffs of smoke erupting from the grove of trees into which Fantômas and Ruth had vanished. Leaves blew upward as the black automobile forced its way out of the grove, around the house and toward the main road.

"Damn!" Dickson cursed to himself, stamping his feet in anger.

Then he heard another sound. Just as the grind of Fantômas' motor car was retreating into the distance, Dickson heard the sound of another motor. This one was approaching the house. He turned around in time to see the car pull into the Harrington mansion driveway.

Jenkins. It was Jenkins!

"Corona!" Dickson shouted. "Jenkins! Up here!"

Corona craned his head out of the passenger window. "What's happening?" he shouted. "We heard an explosion!"

Dickson didn't answer, but leapt off the back of the roof, clutching the twin cables in his hands and lowering himself, hand over hand, to the ground. Danger be damned! Ruth Harrington's life was at stake!

Once on the ground, he rounded the edge of the house and made a mad dash for Jenkins' squad car. "It's Fantômas!" he shouted, leaping into the backseat. "He has Ruth! I mean Miss Harrington!"

Jenkins turned toward Dickson, his face in shock. "Didn't you hear me, Jenkins?" Dickson shouted. "Follow that car!"

It wasn't easy. Fantômas already had a head start, but at this hour of the morning there were no other automobiles on the road. Once Jenkins had pulled out onto the main road, all three men could clearly see Fantômas ahead in the distance.

"Faster!" Corona shouted. "Dammit, Jenkins, can't you make this thing go any faster?"

"I'm trying, sir!" Jenkins said. "If I may, sir, this is terribly exciting!"

"Just drive!" Corona snapped.

Dickson leaned forward, his hands tightly clutching the back of the seat as if he could increase the speed of the auto through sheer will. Corona drew a handkerchief from his breast pocket and began dabbing beads of sweat off of his forehead. Jenkins pressed down on the accelerator as hard as he could and Dickson thought that he looked, for all the world, like the hero of a silent film serial–his face grim and taut with fury.

"The Hell with this!" Corona suddenly shouted and drew a gun from his jacket.

"Corona!" Dickson screamed. "No!"

Corona aimed the gun out of the passenger window and fired at Fantômas' car.

"Are you insane?" Dickson shouted, wrenching the gun from Corona's hand. "You'll hit Miss Harrington!"

Corona harrumphed and sat back dejected. Fantômas' car appeared to be inching closer.

"We're gaining!" Jenkins shouted with a burst of excited laughter. "We're gaining!"

They were, indeed, pulling themselves closer and closer to the rear of Fantômas' car. As they rounded a curve, however, Fantômas broke free from the road and sent his car skidding down a grassy hill toward the shoreline below. "What the Devil? Where's he going?" Corona asked.

"No idea," Dickson said. "Jenkins, can you follow?"

Jenkins turned and winked. "Is the Pope Catholic?"

Corona pressed his hands to his hat as the squad car bounced and shook down the hill, with Jenkins doing his best to stay on Fantômas' tail. Fantômas' car skidded to a stop along the shoreline and Corona clapped his hands and laughed in triumph. "Ha, ha!" he said, "The fiend has driven himself into a trap! There's nowhere to go but the water. We have him now! Nice driving, Jenkins!"

"Thank you, sir."

"Be careful," Dickson said with a hint of caution. "Something's not right."

As if on cue, Fantômas' car started up again. Its engine screamed and its tires spun into the ground, kicking up a wall of sand behind it. Then, the car shot forward and began driving.

Into the water. Fantômas was driving directly into the water!

"For the love of..." Corona stopped short when he saw that Dickson had leapt from the car while it was still coming to a halt. "Dickson!" he shouted. "Where are you..."

But Dickson was already gone and running toward the shoreline. Fantômas' car had driven into the surf. The water had risen to the car windows and Dickson thought, for a brief moment, that Fantômas had decided, in a fit of insanity, to drown himself and Ruth rather than be captured by the law.

Then, he watched as Fantômas' car began to rise. A mechanical buzzing noise came from the auto as all four wheels began to twist sideways until they were laying flat on top of the water. Then, with a loud hiss, all four tires began to inflate, growing three times their normal size. Buoyed on four cushions of air, the car continued to float away from the shore.

Dickson turned to see Jenkins and Corona standing outside the squad car with their mouths agape. "It's impossible," Corona was saying. "Impossible." But more and more, Dickson was beginning to understand that when it came to Fantômas, nothing was impossible.

Suddenly, Jenkins came running down the hill and set off along the shore. Dickson stared after him and noticed, for the first time, a set of boat docks. Moored there were three small boats with outboard motors. It took Dickson a moment to realize what Jenkins had in mind, but by then he was too far away.

The chase on Long Island Sound

"Jenkins!" Dickson shouted. "Don't!"

"Don't be a fool, Jenkins!" Corona said.

"It's OK!" Jenkins answered over his shoulder. "My wife's pop has one! He taught me how to drive it last summer!"

"Jenkins!" Dickson shouted again. "Don't be a fool!"

But it was too late. Jenkins had quickly unmoored the boat, started the motor, and was pulling away from the dock into the water of Long Island Sound. Fantômas' car was drifting away, but at a slow pace and it took Jenkins no time at all to catch up to him.

"It's OK!" Jenkins shouted again. "It's like Nick Carter in the Adventure of the River Bandits!"

The idiot, Dickson thought. *Didn't he understand this wasn't a game?*

Then he watched as the roof of Fantômas' car began to move forward and close. Large sheets of metal lifted themselves mechanically from the bottom of the windows, sealing themselves and turning the motorcar into an airtight container. Then, Dickson watched as something resembling a large gun barrel rose straight up from the roof of the car before bending backward and aiming itself directly at Jenkins.

"Oh, God," Dickson said aloud. "Dear God, no."

Jenkins was heading closer and closer to Fantômas. "I'm gaining!" he said to himself. "I'm gaining!"

"Jenkins!" Dickson shouted, "Turn back! For the love of God, man. Turn back!"

But Jenkins couldn't hear over the roar of the motor. By the time he noticed Fantômas' sinister visage peering out from the roof and taking aim with the large gun attached to the frame of the car, it was too late.

This isn't how it's supposed to happen, he thought. Nick Carter always wins. He always…

The first bullet struck Jenkins in the stomach and he slumped forward onto the steering mechanism of the boat. The boat began to spin in circles, giving Fantômas a split second to aim the gun at the gasoline tank. The second bullet pierced the tank.

Corona and Dickson grimaced and shielded their eyes from the explosion. The thick black smoke curled into the air, and pieces of metal and burning wood fell down all around them. Dickson could barely see as Fantômas smiled and gave him a quick salute before dropping back down into the car and closing the roof behind him. The car continued to move forward and soon disappeared beneath the water.

Chapter Fourteen: The Caverns of Hell

Even before the Great War, Hans Voitzel wanted to leave Germany and settle in America. His wife did not and insisted that his daughter wouldn't either, if she were old enough to have an opinion on such things. Indeed, by the time little Frieda was able to speak, she and her mother presented a more or less united front against immigrating.

The problem was that no one in Berlin understood Dr. Voitzel's genius. As the years went by, he found it more and more difficult to put up with the extreme prejudice from his colleagues. His idea for a car that could be driven straight into the water, thus turning itself into a kind of submersible, brought tears of laughter to the eyes of his fellow scientists who occupied themselves with boring things like new ways to package gun powder.

Dr. Voitzel insisted that the development of his submersible auto would make the difference in the outcome of the war, but he had trouble finding anyone who would listen to him. And so, against the protestations of his wife and daughter, he sold his family's belongings and set about moving them to America.

Helen was upset, of course, and didn't want to leave her parents behind. Frieda cried at the thought of never being able to see her nana again but Dr. Voitzel assured her that America would be better for them than Germany. With all the German immigrants that had settled there, one didn't even have to learn English. There were entire newspapers written just for Germans! Not to mention the fact that the Americans would be much more inclined to recognize Daddy's genius. Did she want him to be laughed at the rest of his life?

No, he didn't think so.

A shame then, that Frieda and Helen became so sick during the voyage to New York. Had they left on the next ship a month later, they might have been able to survive the outbreak of influenza that claimed so many of the passengers, as well as a good portion of the crew. Dr. Voitzel often asked himself why he was able to stay healthy through his wife and daughter's frightful coughing and high fevers. Before long, however, the question was moot. He had arrived in America. He was now alone, yes, but he also began to feel a certain kind of lightness. Without the burden of family, neither of whom really appreciated his intellect anyway, Dr. Voitzel became more confident than ever that within a short time, his fortune and reputation would be made.

Unfortunately, it's difficult to take the financial and scientific worlds by storm when you're living in an alley. And so Dr. Voitzel set about trying to find a place to live–nothing too ostentatious, he insisted, just something with enough room for all of the devices and inventions that he would undoubtedly be developing for various investors. "No," he'd say to the tenement owners with an exuberant smile. "I don't have any money at the moment, but if you'll just take a look at these schematics…"

Usually, the landlords would laugh before slamming the door in his face.

Why bother? If they couldn't appreciate his talents, he would rather not live in their tiny, flea-bitten apartments anyway. Father had always told him to surround himself with like-minded people who would appreciate his genius, and now that his nagging wife and whiny child were out of the way, life was beginning to show promise.

But then the days turned to weeks, the weeks to months, and Dr. Voitzel found himself spending night after night at the *Hog's Head* tavern–sketching intricate designs, that no one could possibly understand, on the napkins and drinking until he passed out.

One night, after a particularly brutal bout of drunkenness during which the good Doctor continued to sketch details on how his brilliant submersible auto might seal itself automatically to create a temporary "air pocket," his drink-addled head struck the edge of the table, sending him into unconsciousness. As the crowd dispersed, Voitzel became dimly aware of the arms of Geoffrey the Slasher lifting him, carrying him into the adjacent alley and tossing him to the ground. He could have brought himself to his feet at that point, but for some reason his mind drifted to Helen and Frieda. The thought crossed his mind that perhaps he was not a genius at all, and for the first time he began to feel a twinge of regret about the loss of his loved ones.

Thankfully, his mournful reverie didn't last long. As Dr. Voitzel lay there shivering in the early morning, he became dimly aware of a presence sharing the alley with him. He opened his eyes and spied a man clad entirely in black–his two thick, dark eyes peering at him quizzically.

"Hello, Dr. Voitzel," Fantômas said. "My name is Fantômas and I wish to make use of your talents."

Shortly after Fantômas' car entered the East River, the air began to grow stale. Ruth Harrington could feel a small amount of mobility coming back to her fingers but not enough to strike back or defend herself. The thought entered her mind that it was possible that Fantômas was superhuman somehow, and didn't need to breathe oxygen like everyone else–that he wouldn't even notice the lack of air and would continue steering forward while she choked to death, unnoticed, behind him.

"What a nuisance," Fantômas uttered, and threw back the throttle. Ruth could feel the car begin to rise to the surface. "We'll have to talk to the Doctor about a more substantial air supply," Fantômas said to no one in particular.

The metal plates covering the side windows slid down with a loud buzz. The light streamed in and the windows slid open just enough to allow air into the back seat. Ruth sucked in a deep breath and exhaled a sigh of relief.

"Of course," Fantômas said, turning toward Ruth. "We'll have to get out of sight as quickly as possible. A car floating in the East River at seven in the morning is bound to attract attention, don't you think?"

Fantômas pressed a button near the steering wheel and Ruth heard the hum of an outboard motor begin to churn through the water. As it spun faster and faster, the sound grew louder and louder, and Ruth felt the car tip backwards as its front rose and it began to build speed, shooting toward the shoreline. A large, metal, cylindrical tube came into view. Sewage was spilling from its edge, but Fantômas continued to drive the car forward, heading directly toward the dark circle. Ruth gasped as the car plunged into the large drain and continued to bump along the bottom of the pipe. She felt the wheels snap back into position and soon they were no longer floating, but driving through the sewer system of Manhattan. The next sensation to strike Ruth was the rancid smell.

"A bit rank in here, isn't it, darling?" Fantômas chuckled, then pulled a small lever in front of the passenger seat. Instantly, two tiny ventilation shafts opened on either side of the car, sending jet streams of perfume into the air. Fantômas must have noticed that Ruth's first impulse was to take a deep breath and hold it. He laughed. "Don't worry," he said. "There's nothing toxic about this particular scent. It's the smell of the Jardins du Luxembourg, if you're interested. The Luxembourg gardens. If you close your eyes and concentrate, you can catch a hint of apple and pear from the trees that blossom in the spring." Fantômas closed his eyes and took a deep breath. Ruth panicked for a brief moment, afraid that the car would go careening into the side of the drain, but it seemed to be driving automatically, pressing forward through the dark.

"A little trace of Paris," Fantômas continued. "Dr. Voitzel is really quite brilliant. Fashioned the scent using only my description and personal reminiscence. The pears were especially difficult." Ruth closed her eyes tight as the car continued to race forward.

Minutes later, Fantômas and Ruth emerged from the murky drain into a large concrete room. The water from the bottom of the pipe grew more and more shallow as the wheels of the car slowly righted themselves once again, sending it rolling up an incline onto a hard, dry surface. The car stopped and Fantômas turned toward Ruth. "Almost there, my love." He smiled, then stepped from the car and walked across the floor toward a large lever hidden among an outgrowth of rock. He grabbed the lever, pulled it down, and Ruth heard a loud hum that seemed to come from everywhere at once.

"Once again," Fantômas said, "this room is the brainchild of Dr. Voitzel. Quite a genius."

With a sharp lurch, the floor of the room began to lift them upward. Ruth looked up and watched as the ceiling slowly divided into two parts that folded upward as the floor rapidly continued to rise. Finally, the floor came to an abrupt halt and Ruth saw that they were now in another tunnel. Fantômas approached the car and opened the door. "Step lively, Miss Harrington," he said. "There is much to prepare for."

Her hands still tied together, Ruth stepped warily from the car as Fantômas clutched her tightly by the forearm. "Knowing you as I do," he said, "I'm fairly certain that you have already considered whether or not you should take the first opportunity to attempt an escape. Rest assured, Miss Harrington, it would be in your best interest to quell those impulses the moment they arise. That is, if you ever wish to see your father again."

Ruth stared sharply into Fantômas' eyes. "Dad?" she said, "If you've hurt him, I swear…"

"Please," interrupted Fantômas. "Don't swear." He ran the back of his gloved hand lightly across her cheek. "It's so unladylike."

"Mr. Fantômas! Mr. Fantômas!" The voice with the thick German accent came from the far end of the tunnel. Ruth looked over Fantômas' shoulder to see a small, balding, bespectacled man in a lab coat running toward them. "The car!" he shouted. "You used the car!"

"Ah!" said Fantômas, turning away from Ruth to greet the visitor. "Dr. Voitzel! How are you, my friend?"

“Mr. Fantômas!” Voitzel stammered. “The car was not ready. There is still much to do…”

“Pish-tosh, Doctor,” Fantômas grinned. “The car passed inspection marvelously.”

The scientist looked surprised. “It did? But… I still have not perfected the flying mechanism.”

“Yes, yes,” Fantômas said, placing his arm around Voitzel’s shoulder. “But the sailing mechanism was top-notch. The air could have lasted a touch longer, though. I was afraid our guest was beginning to suffocate.”

Dr. Voitzel put his hands to his face with horror and noticed Ruth Harrington for the first time. “Oh, my apologies, Miss,” he said. “Please understand. It’s not quite finished. Had I known the master was planning to use it, I would have increased the capacity of the air tanks.”

“Now, now,” Fantômas said. “The car performed admirably. See, not a scratch on her. In fact, she rather enjoyed the trip. Didn’t you, Miss Harrington?”

Ruth Harrington captured by Fantômas

Fantômas and Voitzel stared at Ruth, waiting for her to comment. Ruth narrowed her eyes and set her mouth tight, sending Fantômas the message that she refused to speak.

Fantômas approached her and spoke in a low voice. "Miss Harrington, the Doctor worked long and hard to make sure that your trip was a safe one. Please do not insult him. I will remind you once again that your father is waiting to see you."

Ruth turned away from Fantômas and looked at Voitzel. "It's a splendid contraption," she said. "I was very comfortable."

Dr. Voitzel clapped his hands with glee. "Thank you, Miss. And now, if you don't mind, I'd like to examine the automobile and see just what can be done to allow it further travel."

"Don't let us keep you, Doctor," Fantômas said, then grabbed Ruth by the arm and led her away. "Really, my love," he whispered into her ear. "If we're going to be together, you must learn to appreciate my business colleagues."

Ruth ignored him. "Tell me where my father is," she spat.

"Very well," Fantômas answered.

Fantômas led Ruth away from the car and down a long cavern lit by torches embedded in the stone. As they rounded a corner, Ruth could see the flickering of the flames create shadows on the walls and could hear the faint mewling of a small child. She broke free of Fantômas' grasp and rushed to the bars, gazing in horror on what she saw inside the cell. Sally Shea was seated on the dirt floor holding her child to her breast. Her ankle was chained to the wall and tears were streaming down her face. "Help me," she whispered, in the raspy voice of someone who hadn't spoken a word aloud in days.

"Who is she?" Ruth demanded of Fantômas.

"She is none of your concern," Fantômas answered quickly, shuffling Ruth away from the cell.

Ruth resisted Fantômas' grip. "What have you done to her?" she said.

Fantômas spun Ruth around and gripped her tightly by the shoulders. "Far less than I will do to you and your father if you refuse to cooperate," he said, his sunken eyes gazing hypnotically into hers. "Now," he continued, feeling Ruth's resistance beginning to wane beneath his grasp, "If you wish to see your father, come with me."

Ruth walked with Fantômas away from Sally Shea's prison, trying desperately to block out the sound of Sally's muffled sobs. Their journey took them around another eerily lit turn, and Ruth was struck with the realization that they were walking in a circle. The cavern was curved in a way that made it seem much larger than it was, but where exactly were they? Clearly they were underground, having risen directly from the sewer system. But what was above them?

Before she had time to consider the answers to these questions, Ruth found herself facing the barred door of another prison cell. This one was much larger and cleaner than Sally Shea's, with a bookshelf, a small table with a pitcher of water and an electric lamp, and an armchair where Professor Harrington was seated.

"Dad!" Ruth cried, rushing forward and reaching through the bars.

Professor Harrington said nothing, but bolted from his chair and reached through the bars to wrap his weary arms around his daughter's head.

"Are you OK?" Ruth asked, clutching her father's shirtfront in her fist. "Are you hurt?" She turned and shot Fantômas a venomous stare. "I swear to God if you've hurt him…"

"Really, Miss Harrington," Fantômas interrupted. "Why spoil a perfectly moving reunion with such bile? You have asked to see your father and I have brought you to him. As you can see, he is unhurt. Thus far I have had no real reason to hurt either one of you. This, however, could change if you fail to do as I say. Now," he continued, drawing a key from his jacket pocket, "if you would be so kind as to step aside for one moment."

Ruth watched as Fantômas inserted the key into the lock of the cell door. She glanced at her father and he looked back in turn. Her eyes shot to his leg, where she could see that he was not chained to the wall as Sally Shea had been. If the two of them had their wits about them, they might be able subdue Fantômas the moment he finished opening the…

"I wouldn't advise it," Fantômas interrupted Ruth's thoughts. "There is no way out of this corridor without my assistance and if you try to exit the way we came, you're likely to find yourself washed up on the shore of the Hudson with the rest of the sewage." He gazed at her, then shot her a brief smile. "Play along, won't you? It really is the only way."

Ruth looked back at her father, who nodded his head in agreement. She walked past Fantômas into the cell and embraced her father, listening to the sound of the large door as it clanged shut behind them.

Fantômas walked further down the corridor to one of the torches mounted on the cavern wall. Clutching the torch at its base, he drew it downward. With an audible snap, the lever triggered an opening in the rock. A doorway slid open, revealing a circular staircase. Fantômas stepped through the doorway and mounted the staircase as the entrance closed behind him. After walking up two flights of stairs, he stopped and reached for another lever on the wall. He pulled it downward and another door opened into Fantômas' chamber–the same one that contained his dining table, wine cabinet, bookshelves and the imprisoned Father Rose.

Fantômas heard the clanging of the chains as the authentic Father Rose shifted in his cage, craning his neck to see who had arrived. Fantômas didn't address him, but moved directly to his bureau. He opened it, drawing out one of his thick black face-masks. He quickly removed the false moustache and wig that he had used to adopt his Emile Cortez identity, and drew the mask over his face. He produced a pair of thick black gloves which he drew tight onto each hand.

The illusion of Emile Cortez was gone, and in his place stood Fantômas.

Fantômas walked to his dining table where the morning edition of *The New York Times* had been placed for his perusal. The headline leapt out at him: *Who is Fantômas?*

"Ha!" Fantômas exclaimed. "Excellent! Out of the shadows and into the light!"

Rubbing his hands together in satisfaction, Fantômas walked over to a small cylinder jutting from the wall and spoke into it. "I have returned," he said. "Please send the Torch to my chambers immediately." He then walked over to the cage that contained the sickly Father Rose. "If all goes well, I will have need of you very soon. Try not to fret. This evening, you will be well fed. I need you healthy for the big day."

Father Rose stared at Fantômas in silence. Despite the persistent discomfort of imprisonment, he found the idea of being released to do Fantômas' bidding even more terrifying.

A door at the far end of the chamber opened and the Torch entered carrying the briefcase he had secured from Corona the previous evening.

"Good evening, Torch," Fantômas said, clapping his hands together and rubbing them vigorously. "I see you have something for me."

"Yes sir," the Torch answered enthusiastically. "The reward Ruth Harrington offered for the Professor. A million dollars!"

"Really?" Fantômas replied, and the Torch noted a discomfiting sound of sarcasm in his voice.

The Torch abruptly ceased walking toward him. "Is something wrong?" he asked.

"Bring me the briefcase."

The Torch warily but quickly carried the case to Fantômas, who took it from him and placed it on the dining table.

"It's locked," the Torch said. "We'll have to find some way to…" Before he could finish, Fantômas had snapped the lock open with his bare hands, barely straining to do so. The Torch stopped speaking and felt a wave of anxiety well up in his throat. Fantômas lifted the lid of the briefcase.

"Fascinating," Fantômas said, pulling out a stack of bills. "Apparently the United States mint has ceased printing currency with anything on the back." He turned the bills over and flipped through them. The Torch could see that the backs of the bills were completely blank.

"Counterfeit," the Torch said.

"Hmm," Fantômas uttered. "And not even very good counterfeiting at that."

"But how? The money came directly from Ruth Harrington. Why would she risk her father's life by…"

Fantômas interrupted him once again. "Really, my friend," he snapped. "Are you so stupid that you are unable to add two and two together? You've been conned. It appears we have an enemy who is far more resourceful that I would ever have anticipated."

The Torch felt beads of sweat begin to break out on his forehead. "I don't understand."

"Sit down," Fantômas ordered. The Torch did as he was told. "Two evenings ago, you failed to retrieve the journal from Professor Harrington's safe."

"It was that Ruth dame! She's tougher than she looks! Besides, the book in the safe was a fraud."

"Indeed. Then, you didn't even attempt to retrieve the formula from Jack Meredith, even when you realized he had the authentic formula in his possession."

"I'll go back. I'll search his house."

"I already searched the house. The formula wasn't there, so I blew it up."

"Oh."

"And now, it seems, that the reward money you so craftily stole, after first causing the death of one of my drivers, is completely fake. Stage money."

"How could I know? Honest to God…"

"This is a church, Mr. Torch," Fantômas said, placing his hands on the arms of the chair and leaning in toward the Torch's face. "Please do not take the Lord's name in vain."

"I'm sorry," the Torch said, his anxiety and confusion giving way to panic. "Please. Don't…"

"I find your track record of failure to be highly distressing."

"Listen, I made a couple of mistakes I admit. But have I ever steered you wrong before?"

"Hmmmmm…"

"Honest!" the Torch's voice was quivering badly. "How can I make it up to you?"

Fantômas let go of the chair and backed away from the Torch. "You can kill Brian Shea," he said.

The Torch felt his face flush red. "But…I…"

"I was insulted the first time you lied to me, Mr. Torch. Please don't insult me again by perpetuating the same lie. I know that you allowed Brian Shea to live. It's very touching, this bond of friendship you seem to have with him, but his betrayal can simply not be allowed to go unpunished. I still have a need for your talents. Therefore, you have gained a temporary reprieve. But it is only temporary. If you wish to stay among the living, you will correct your past errors by killing Brian Shea. Am I understood?"

The Torch stared at Fantômas, his lips tight with grim determination. "Yes," he said.

Sally Shea closed her eyes, clutching her child to her chest. Denny was finally asleep, thank God, and exhaustion had set in. Moments before she was about to lose consciousness, she heard the sound of footsteps scraping along the floor of the cavern. She lifted her head and forced her eyes open a crack, but her tears only allowed her to see the visitor through a dim haze. Still, there was something familiar about him.

"Sally," the stranger said. "Sally, it's me."

The voice was unmistakable. Sally rose to one knee, pressed Denny to her chest and stumbled over to the door, dragging the ankle chain behind her.

"Brian?" she said.

"Yes, Sally," the stranger said. "It's me. Brian. Your husband."

The image of Brian Shea became clearer as she drew herself toward the bars. "Brian? Oh my God…" Sally reached through the bars and clutched Brian's hand.

"It's OK, Sally. I'm here now."

"Brian, you've got to help us. We've got to get out of here. Are you OK? Did Fantômas hurt you?"

"I'm OK, Sally. I'm here and I'm OK."

Sally pulled her hand back through the bars and panic rose in her throat. The voice was the same. The face was the same. But she suddenly knew it wasn't Brian. "Who are you?" she choked.

"Sally, it's me. Brian Shea. I'm going to be with you forever. I'll take care of you forever."

Sally backed away from the bars and pressed herself against the wall of her cell. "Why do you look like him?" she said, pressing her fists to her mouth. "Why would you make yourself look like him?"

The man began to grow frustrated and pressed his palms into his forehead. "My head," he said. "It hurts."

From the corridor stepped Fantômas–his face still clad in black. He placed his gloved hands on the man's face and turned his head toward his own. "Relax, Boris," Fantômas said in a soothing voice. "Your impersonation is good. Very good, in fact. You just need practice." Fantômas drew a ring of keys from his pocket and unlocked the door of the cell. "You and your lovely child seemed so lonely, Mrs. Shea," Fantômas said, opening the door and slowly leading Boris inside. "I thought it high time that you had some company. Boris misses his family and I imagine you do as well, so I thought perhaps we could kill two birds with one stone, as they say."

"Oh God," Sally pressed her hands against her eyes, attempting to block the horrible image from her vision. "He looks like Brian. Why did you make him look like Brian?"

Fantômas chuckled. "I'm afraid I can't take all of the credit. Boris has a talent for mimicry that is truly impressive. He just needs to be in the right environment. I promise that if you'll just submit to him and treat him with the appropriate respect that all women owe their husbands, you'll soon be unable to tell the difference between the original and the copy."

The baby began to cry and Sally tried to stifle her own whimpering as she gently bounced the child in her arms. "Sssshhhh..." she said, quietly. "Mommy's here. She's right here."

"Boris," Fantômas said. "Be a man and deal with the child."

Boris stepped toward Sally. Sally scurried to the corner of the cell and turned away from him, shielding the baby with her body. "Don't touch him," she snarled. "Don't you touch my child."

Boris stopped dead in his tracks and turned toward Fantômas. Fantômas placed a hand on Boris' back and pushed him forward. "For God's sake, Boris, don't be so shy. Mrs. Shea, surely you don't wish to keep your son from his father."

"Please," Sally cried. "Don't touch him!"

"Now, now," Fantômas chastised Sally. "No one is going to hurt your child. If anything, I think you'll find that Boris is a gentle soul."

Sally turned toward the two men and saw that the path to the door was almost completely blocked. She could try to make a run for it–perhaps she could even knock Fantômas off balance for a moment and try to escape–but what if her child were hurt in the struggle? It wasn't worth the risk.

Quietly, reluctantly, Sally handed her baby to Boris. Boris reached out carefully with his hands and a smile crossed his face.

"Support the head," said Fantômas. "We don't want to crack his little neck."

Boris began rocking the child, then hoisted it onto his chest and patted it gently on the back, all the while singing a soft Russian lullaby. Sally's hands were shaking as she tried desperately to keep herself from screaming in grief.

"Well," said Fantômas, "I see everything is settled here. Boris, I'm going to lock you in for the moment, but I'm certain you'll be fine. Everything you want is right here." But Boris couldn't hear Fantômas, so enchanted was he with the delicate life he held in his arms.

"Wait," Sally said. "You're going to leave him here?"

"Why not?" Fantômas answered. "Why not make your prison a little more like home?" He quickly stepped out of the cell, closed the door, and locked it behind him.

Fantômas continued down the corridor until he once again reached the cell occupied by Ruth Harrington and her father. "Knock knock," he said.

Ruth darted toward the door, wrapping her hands around the bars and staring into Fantômas' eyes. "Listen, you son of a bitch," Ruth snapped. "Do whatever you want to do with me, but let my father go. He's too old for this. He can't take it."

"Really?" Fantômas said with a tone of surprise. "I think your father is capable of withstanding a great many things. Being taken prisoner by a tribe of Amazonian savages, for instance." He drew a handkerchief from his pocket, dusted off the seat of a chair and sat down. "America, as I'm sure you're well aware, Professor, is a land of inconsistency. I find myself continuing to plunge myself into my criminal activities but I am...dissatisfied. There is something about the American way of life–the hypocrisy, the prejudice, the privilege–that I find intriguing. Wrapped up, as it is, in the fanciful notion that anyone can simply pull themselves up by their bootstraps. It's an illusion of freedom that keeps the poor immigrants blaming themselves for their own failures, while the same families that have always thrived continue to do so. There will be no storming of the Bastille here. No beheadings of queens. And quite frankly, I find that rather...boring.

"But the question remains–would I be able to create the same kind of fear and terror that I am accustomed to without ever breaking the law? Were it not for the stubbornness of that infernal Detective Dickson, I would be closer to finding out the answer by now. But he is little more than a nuisance that I will soon be rid of. In the meantime, my next step is finding a way to acquire your precious journal."

"Never," Harrington said.

"And yet," Fantômas continued as if he hadn't heard Harrington's response, "Man cannot live on gold alone, whether it's authentic or man-made. I find that the truly pleasurable things in life are the objects of beauty that one is able to steal and surround one's self with."

Ruth felt a cold shiver up her back. "What do you mean?"

Fantômas reached in his pocket, pulled out a small box and got down on one knee. He opened the box to reveal a large diamond ring. "Professor Harrington," he said. "I have come here today to ask for your daughter's hand in marriage."

"YOUR FATHERS LIFE DEPENDS UPON YOUR ANSWER"
WILLIAM FOX PRESENTS
FANTOMAS
1921 American Serial in 20 Episodes

Chapter Fifteen: Terror in the Tenement

"Where do we start?"

"Second one from the end. *The Hanging Gardens.*"

"They all look the same to me."

"Run down…filthy…"

"How can anyone live like this?"

"Even worse than where they come from originally."

"Everyone wants a piece of the pie."

"You said it."

"So…tell me again what has to happen?"

"We need information on Fantômas. Put a scare into them. If anyone gets fresh, break somethin'. A nose, a finger…"

"What about kids?"

"Threaten the kids. They'll say anything to keep us from hurting the kids."

The two men standing in the hidden corners of the dark alley are Number Two and Number Eight–members of the Council of Ten. We are back on the Lower East Side. It is just past 9 p.m., and although noise from one of the bars can be faintly heard in the distance, the street that the two men are watching is deserted. From their place, hidden among the piles of garbage tossed from the windows above, they can see their target across the street–a tenement building known as the Hanging Gardens.

The Claussens have lived on the first floor of this building for over 14 years. Max Claussen owns a shoe store on 12th Street. His wife, Freda, works as a seamstress in the Garment District. Ten-year-old Rebecca Claussen is the only native English speaker in the family, and Max and Freda have grown to depend on her speaking skills to help them deal with difficult situations. Rebecca hates missing school, but on more than one occasion it has been necessary for her to stay home and help her parents. For instance, there was the time that she had to help the policeman explain to her father that the sign to his shoe store was partially on someone else's property. "He says no one can see this sign anywhere else. How will they know where his store is?" Rebecca asked. The policeman shrugged his shoulders and pointed his night stick at Max. "Move the sign by tomorrow," he said, and although he couldn't quite understand the words, Max understood the threat just fine.

But the Claussen we are most concerned with at the moment is Max's brother Lukas. Lukas is 27 and for the past five years has been a rare visitor in the Claussen home. Tonight is an exception. After years of petty thieving, Lukas seems to have turned his life around and the Claussens are overjoyed. He seldom drinks any longer and he always seems to have money.

Perhaps it's all the time he's been spending at church, listening to the sermons of Father Rose.

"Where have you live?" Max asked Lukas, trying hard to impress his brother by speaking English.

"Here and there," Lukas said. "Some of us guys, we sleep in the church sometimes. Me and them and Father Rose… we get to talkin' late at night. About God and Jesus and things."

At the sound of her savior's name, Freda Claussen smiled and clasped her hands to her breast. Perhaps Lukas really had turned his life around. He looked good too–clean shaven, and the clothes he was wearing were definitely more expensive than the rags he used to wear.

"Yeah," Lukas continued. "Father Rose is a smart man. Brilliant man. He knows all about destiny and power and taking charge. It's all about having something that's your own, he says."

Lukas walked over to Rebecca who was sitting quietly, respectfully on the floor in the corner of the room. "How's my little niece?" he said, mussing her hair with his beefy hand.

"Fine," Rebecca said, smiling and feigning enthusiasm. Rebecca had a bad feeling about her Uncle Lukas. It was nothing, at the tender age of ten, that she could put her finger on. Her mother and father seemed happy enough that he was here, but still–there was something about the glint in his eye that made her feel uncomfortable and a little bit frightened.

She jumped when she heard the knock on the door.

Max shot his wife a questioning glance. Freda shrugged her shoulders with a worried look, then covered with a smile as she nodded to Lukas and walked toward the door.

She undid the deadbolt, turned the knob and opened the door ever so slightly. "*Wer ist dort?*" Freda asked.

"Freda Claussen?" one of the men asked. There were two of them, both dressed in long grey coats and wide brimmed hats that concealed the tops of their faces.

"*Ich bin traurig*," Freda answered. "*Ich spreche nicht Englisch*. No English."

"Is Max home?" Number Two asked.

Max walked to the door. "Yes?"

Number Eight squeezed his way in front of Number Two in order to see Max clearly. "May we come in?" he asked.

Max and Freda stared at one another.

"*Ist etwas falsch?*" Freda asked.

"Something is wrong?" Max translated.

Number Eight smiled at Max. "We realize it's terribly late," he said, "but we'd like to ask you a few questions about your brother Lukas."

"Lukas not here," Max said.

Number Eight snorted and turned toward Number Two. "I hate it when they lie," he said.

While Max and Freda's backs were turned, Lukas swept Rebecca up in his arms with one swift motion. "Listen to me," he said with a whispered, desperate urgency that frightened Rebecca. "Is there another way out of here?"

Rebecca nodded.

"How?" Lukas asked, shaking Rebecca by her shoulders.

Rebecca pointed toward the stove. "The window," she said.

Lukas looked at the heap of useless, rusted metal, but saw no window. "Where?" he asked. "Tell me!"

"Behind it," she said.

"We want to speak to Lukas Claussen and we want to speak to him now." Number Eight spoke in a quiet, subdued tone but there was no mistaking the threat.

"I sorry," Max said. "I no see my brother."

"*Lukas ist nicht hier*," Freda said, the panic in her voice giving her away.

Lukas pressed his shoulder against the stove and pushed with all of his might. Knowing what was going to come next, Rebecca clasped her hands over her ears. The stove fell apart, the large pieces of clunky metal crashing to the floor.

"Who else is there?" Number Eight asked, pressing his hand against the door.

"Let us in, Mr. Claussen," Number Two said.

Knowing that he had only seconds, Lukas began kicking the stove pieces away from the wall. The window was small, dirty, probably sealed shut but just large enough for a person to fit through.

Number Eight and Number Two were pounding on the door.

"You're only making things worse, Mr. Claussen!"

"Let us in, Mr. Claussen. Let us in now!"

Freda was screaming. "*Nein! Nein! Ihn allein lassen! Uns allein lassen!*"

Lukas picked up a piece of the stove and used it to smash the window. The noise made Freda scream and Rebecca covered her ears again.

"Lukas Claussen!" Number Two shouted. "I know that's you, Lukas Claussen!"

Rebecca felt the large hand grab her by the shirt and lift her into the air. "Go!" Lukas said to her. "Hurry! No matter what you hear, don't come back. Run as fast as you can.

Everything will be OK. I promise." And with that, Lukas Claussen shoved his niece through the window. She fell with a thud onto the dirty ground below, just as she heard the front door to her home splinter and break, followed by her mother's screaming and the distinct sound of bare knuckles striking flesh.

"Here!" She heard the voice of her Uncle Lukas whispering through the window. "For protection," he said, tossing his switchblade out the window. It landed at Rebecca's feet. She lifted it up and stared at it for a moment. "Go!" Lukas yelled.

Rebecca tucked the knife into her shoe. Despite the pain in her knees, she leapt up and ran forward into the night.

"Tell your wife to stop screaming." Number Eight had lifted Max Claussen by his lapels and pressed him against the wall. "Tell her," he snarled, "or I'll kill her."

"Freda," Max said, trying to catch his breath. "*Ruhig sein. Bitte. Alles ist fein. Sie verletzen uns nicht.*"

Freda pressed her hand against her mouth to hold in her screams. Number Two had retrieved Lukas Claussen from the remains of the broken stove and thrown him to the floor at Freda's feet.

"Good," Number Eight said, slowly lowering Max Claussen to the floor. "Now, the three of us are going to have a little chat."

"Sit down." Number Two said to Max Claussen, gesturing toward a bare mattress.

"*Hinsitzen*," Max Claussen said to his wife. Freda slowly lowered herself to the mattress and Max stumbled weakly toward her.

Lukas was laying face down on the floor, his head dripping with sweat. "Lift up your head," Number Two said. Lukas did so.

Number Eight settled down onto his haunches and stared into Lukas Claussen's eyes. "Tell me about Fantômas," he said.

"Fantômas is a myth," Lukas Claussen said. "He doesn't exist."

"Liar," Number Eight said, smacking Lukas Claussen's face with the back of his hand.

Freda screamed and Max put his arm around her. Number Two shot her a glance and she pressed her hands to her eyes.

Number Eight grabbed a handful of Lukas Claussen's hair and lifted his head. "We can do this all night, or we can be finished in just a few moments," he said. "The choice is up to you."

"I don't know what you're talking about," Lukas Claussen said.

Number Eight let go of Lukas Claussen's hair. His chin hit the floor with a thud. Number Eight turned toward Max and Freda. "You have a daughter," he said in a soft voice. "Rebecca. Where is she?"

Freda yelped and Max put his finger to her lips.

"She's not here." Lukas Claussen was smiling.

Freda began to panic. Where was Rebecca? Max grabbed her trembling hand. "She is with Aunt," he said.

Number Eight exchanged eye contact with Number Two and the two of them glanced around the tiny, one-room tenement.

"I thought you said you heard her," Number Eight said.

"I thought I did," answered Number Two.

Number Eight rolled his eyes and turned his attention back to Lukas Claussen. "I will ask you one more time," he said, drawing his gun and aiming it at Lukas Claussen's temple. "Where is Fantômas?"

Lukas Claussen looked across the room and met his brother's frightened eyes. When Lukas was ten and Max was eight, both boys lived with their parents on a farm in Vorpommern. Max's dog (it was more Max's than Lukas' since he was the one that found it) got loose in the kitchen. The dog wasn't allowed in the house, but since his mom was away all afternoon and it was raining outside, Max decided it would be a fun idea to play fetch indoors. In the frenzy of play, the dog leapt up and landed both of his paws on the counter, knocking over one of grandmother's hand-painted dinner plates in the process. The plate went crashing to the ground and smashed into a thousand pieces. Max chased the dog around the kitchen, trying in vain to wrap his tiny arms around the thick, plodding beast, but to no avail. Lukas came running downstairs to find his brother in tears, certain that his mother would never forgive him for destroying the precious heirloom. Lukas comforted his brother, then shooed the dog outside and promised to take the blame for the broken plate. Max remembers, hours later, hearing his brother cry as his father brought the strap down on his bare legs.

Lukas continued staring at Max. "What was that dog's name?" he thought.

Number Eight pulled the trigger. Lukas Claussen's head pitched backward with a jerk, sending a torrent of blood onto the wall behind him.

Freda screamed.

"Come on," Number Two said. "Let's go."

Number Eight put his gun away and turned around toward Max and Freda. "Tell everyone what you saw here today," he said. "The Council of Ten is looking for Fantômas and we intend to find him. Even if it means killing one person in every house, street by street, block by block, to do so. Tell your neighbors."

Max began to cry and buried his head in Freda's arms.

Back outside, Number Two and Number Eight stood on the corner under a streetlamp. "Nice night," Number Two said.

"Nice and quiet," Number Eight replied.

"What next?" Number Two asked.

"The Cavalier," Number Eight replied.

The two men walked across the street, entered the tenement building known as the Cavalier and walked down the hallway until they found the room they were looking for. Number Two rapped on the door. "Harold Steinberg?"

Number Eight yelled. "Open the door. We're here to speak with you."

The Musketeers of Pig Alley outside the Black Friar

Snapper hadn't yet told Glimpy and Muggs that he had been thrown out of his home. Not a really a big deal, since he didn't like his mom's new husband anyway. He was still welcome for dinner, which he went to every day for his mom's sake, but once the Sun fell he made his way to the basement of an abandoned tenement on 11th Street.

The tenement in question, a ratty, boarded up four-flat with the ironic sobriquet of the Black Friar, was flanked by two dirt-strewn lots on either side. Black Friar was originally one of three tenements that made up a slaughter-house in the late 1800s. At the turn of the century, the building was converted into three separate tenements–the Eaves, the Black Friar and the Canterbury. All three buildings shared a common cellar where, in defiance of new regulations, as many as 30 families lived at once. The Immigrant Aid Society discovered the travesty and ordered the tenements closed immediately.

Shortly after, the Eaves and the Canterbury burned to the ground, leaving the Black Friar scorched but intact.

Snapper, of course, had no inkling of the Black Friar's checkered past. All he knew was that the decrepit building was home to a cellar that was, magically, three times larger than the building itself. After climbing the fence behind the Schuler house, then crossing the patch of dirt that he and Glimpy and Muggs used for stick ball games, he would squeeze through a hole in a boarded-up window. It was dark inside but he had stashed a pillow, a blanket and a couple of copies of *Nick Carter Magazine* in the corner. Not bad for a makeshift bedroom. In fact, some nights it even made Snapper feel more like a grown-up. After all, who needs adults? One of these days, he was going to fold up his clothes in a blanket and hop a train car–see the country and live off the land.

On this particular night, Snapper squeezed through the window and made his way across the floor to his bundle. He groped on the ground for the candle he had left behind, lit a match and set the candle alight, the yellow flame bouncing shadows on the cold concrete walls. He looked down.

There was someone wrapped in his blanket.

A girl. A child.

Rebecca Claussen.

Her eyes were clenched shut in a desperate attempt to feign sleep. Snapper jostled her shoulder. "Hey, kiddo!" he said. "What are you doing here? Where's your mom and dad?"

Rebecca's eyes popped open and she stared at Snapper in panic. "Don't hurt me," she said. "I'm good. I promise."

"Easy, kid, easy," Snapper said, pulling his hand away. "I ain't gonna hurt ya. Are you OK?"

Rebecca nodded, and then skittered backward toward the wall.

"Honest, kiddo," Snapper said, crossing his heart, "I ain't gonna hurt ya."

Rebecca Claussen knew she shouldn't talk to this dirty boy in the torn cap and suspenders, but something told her to trust him. She told him everything–about her Uncle Lukas, about her parents and about the men in grey coats that came to the door.

"Jeez," Snapper said, taking off his cap and scratching his head. "That's tough, kid. Do ya think your parents are OK?"

Rebecca didn't answer, but began to shake as a tear suddenly crept out of the corner of her eye.

"Oh, Jeez," Snapper said. "I'm real sorry, kid. Listen… you can stay here as long as you want. I mean it ain't much but there's a lotta room. You can even use my blanket."

"Can my mom and dad stay here too?" Rebecca asked. "So the men in grey coats can't find them?"

"Huh? Sure, kid, sure. We're gonna help your parents however we can." Snapper scratched his head again. He knew he was out of his depth. If only Muggs were here. Muggs always had good ideas. In fact…

Snapper laid his hands lightly on Rebecca's shoulders. "Listen, kid," he said. "I'm gonna go away for a few minutes. But don't be scared, OK? I'm gonna go get some buddies o' mine. We can…I don't know…help your folks. Or somethin'. Anyway, don't go anywhere, OK?"

Rebecca nodded her head.

Snapper climbed back out the window, over the fence and back into the Shuler's yard. Rooftops were easier to travel at this time of night, so he climbed the four floors up the fire escape, taking pains to tiptoe past the window right next to Mr. Shuler's bed, and made his way to the top of the building. The nearby tenements were so close together that it was barely a hop to each roof. Snapper ran as fast as he dared, leaping over the narrow crevices between buildings and trying not to disturb the pigeon cages on some of the roofs. After a few blocks, he landed on the roof of the Harvester, a tenement on Broome Street.

Snapper shimmied down the fire escape to the third floor and crouched in front of Muggs' window. Muggs was sitting on a pail, back against the wall, smoking a cigarette and thumbing through a copy of *Flynn's Weekly*. Snapper tapped on the window and Muggs leapt up with a start.

"Holy Cow!" Muggs snapped. "You tryin' to give a guy a heart attack?"

"Sorry, Muggs," Snapper said. "Open the window a second. I gotta talk to ya."

Muggs slid open the window and shimmied out onto the fire escape where Snapper told him the whole story of the scared kid wrapped in blankets.

"Where's the kid now?" Muggs asked.

"Still there."

"Good. Any idea who was after her?"

"She said they was in grey coats."

"Oh, jeez," said Muggs. "Councilmen. That sure ain't good."

"I'll say."

"The Council ain't never bothered anybody outside of the saloons before. Whattaya think they're goin' around scaring kids for?"

"You got me, Muggs."

Muggs banged his fist on the iron railing of the fire escape. "Goddamn Council!" he said. "We gotta get back there."

"I thought we could pick up Glimpy on the way."

"Good idea. Where's he at?"

Snapper rolled his eyes. "Where do you think?"

A few minutes later, Snapper and Muggs opened the back door of the *Black Jack* saloon, one of the most disreputable sites of vice on the Five Corners. The front of the tavern looked as classy as a tavern could, chipped paint on the roman-style cornices not withstanding, but a quick walk over the dance floor and into the back room told a different story. Battered wooden tables, many of which had been tossed about more than once in various drunken brawls, adorned the smoke-filled, windowless room. The owner, an Irish immigrant by the name of Marty "Suicide" Gilligan, didn't mind kids coming in to gamble as long as they used the rear entrance and didn't disturb the clientele on the Bowery side.

On any given night, a visitor to the *Black Jack*'s back room could find at least a half dozen dice games or a hand or two of poker. Fridays, however, were something special. Snapper and Muggs saw the crowd of men gathered in a circle around the wooden pen, illuminated by a single dim bulb hanging from the ceiling. Tonight's fight was Jacob the Bulldog vs. a particularly toothy black raccoon that had been living on the roof of Glimpy's tenement. Glimpy caught him a week earlier, stuffed him in a bag and kept him hungry and angry all week long, convinced that he'd finally found a fighter who could take on Jacob–a mean-tempered bulldog that had left the floor of the *Black Jack* littered with rat and dog carcasses in his bid to become the undefeated Bowery champ.

Jacob's owner was smacking the red-eyed beast on the mouth, riling it up while the foam dripped from its thick lips. Glimpy was on the opposite side of the room giving a pep talk to a writhing burlap sack. "Now I want you to get in there and go for broke!" he shouted to the hissing and kicking raccoon. "Jacob's had a lock on this contest for long enough and it's time for someone to take him to the mat! You hear me?"

The raccoon couldn't hear or, at the very least, didn't care. "C'mon Glimpy!" said a toothless man holding a crutch near where his left leg used to be. "Time's a wastin'!"

Glimpy clutched the bag to his chest, trying to wrestle the raccoon under control as he carried it toward the makeshift ring. "C'mon, you crazy, rabid thing. You're gonna be good ol' Glimpy's meal ticket, if you know what's good for you."

Snapper and Muggs shoved their way through the throng and found themselves on either side of Glimpy. "Hey, Glimp," Muggs said. "Let's go. Something's up. Somethin' big."

"Hey, fellas!" Glimpy said, surprised to see his friends. "You come to see me and my new pal take on the pit champion? Whoa, there little guy…" The raccoon had started to squirm and Glimpy almost lost control of the bag.

"This is serious, Glimp," Snapper said. "We gotta go right now."

Glimpy turned to Muggs with an inquisitive stare, which Muggs returned with a look that said, "this is no joke."

"Awwww no, fellas," Glimpy said, pushing himself away from Muggs and Snapper and heading closer to the pit. "I been waitin' all week for this bout and I'm walkin' away from here with pockets full o' bills. Gimme an hour, at least!"

"Hey, Glimpy!" a large man sporting a thick, half-chewed cigar shouted above the din. "We ain't got all night!"

"This is big stuff, Glimp," Snapper said, grabbing Glimpy by the shoulder. "Life and Death stuff."

"Council of Ten stuff," Muggs added.

"Come on, kid!" the large man shouted.

For some reason, perhaps because it sensed tentativeness on Glimpy's part, the raccoon decided that it was time to make a break. He started squirming wildly in Glimpy's arms and Glimpy was just distracted enough to be caught off guard.

"Oh, Chee!" Glimpy shouted as the burlap bag fell to ground and the large hungry raccoon, teeth bared and vibrating with anger, bolted out of the sack and ran pell-mell into the crowd.

"Oh, Christ! What the hell was that?"

"Jesus, my ankle!"

"Ah! Leggoleggoleggoleggo…"

"Ah Chee, boys!" Glimpy threw his hands up in exasperation. "See what you've gone and made me do!"

The large man with the cigar leapt onto a rickety chair. His face was beet red and a sudden resemblance between him and Jacob the Bulldog became immediately obvious. "Glimpy!" he shouted. "Get control of that…that…thing! Before it gives every guy in here rabies!"

Glimpy bent over and ran along the floor, whistling and snapping his fingers. "Here, Snowball…" he said.

"Snowball?" Muggs rolled his eyes in amazement. "What are you, some kind of moron? The thing's black as pitch!"

"Sssshhhh!" Glimpy said. "You'll hurt his feelings!"

"Come on fellas! Time to go!" Snapper grabbed Muggs and Glimpy by the shoulders and dragged them through the back door out onto the dirt-covered lot. As the door swung closed, all three boys could see the clientele of the *Black Jack* leaping onto chairs as Jacob began to bark and Snowball continued to chatter and hiss.

A few minutes later, Snapper was leading Muggs and Glimpy through the Shulers' lot, over the fence and through the cellar window of the Black Friar.

"Hey kid!" Snapper whispered into the darkness. "You still here?"

"Yes." Snapper heard Rebecca's voice in the darkness. "I went and got them. You said it was okay."

"I don't understand, kid," Snapper said. "Went and got who?"

Snapper grabbed one of the candles he had left on the windowsill and lit it. He moved toward the sound of Rebecca's voice and extended the flame in her direction. She was standing upright against the back wall.

Right next to her father, Max, and mother, Freda.

And Harold Steinberg, his wife Marta and their two daughters.

And their four cousins–Benjamin, Lewis, Jerry and David.

"Thank you, young man," Max said in his broken English. "We are very need help. Thank you for letting us stay here."

"Uh…fellas?" Snapper said, turning toward Muggs and Glimpy. "We're gonna need a few more blankets."

Chapter Sixteen: In Sickness and in Health

The authentic Father Rose woke up with a start. His body had almost grown used to the cramped conditions of his cage and the lack of movement had made him weak enough to finally sleep, during which time he did little else but dream of heaven. When the door to Fantômas' study slid shut, however, he felt the familiar tide of panic starting to rise. As he heard the footsteps draw nearer, he drew himself to a sitting position and squinted into the darkness as Fantômas walked toward him.

Much to Father Rose's surprise, Fantômas withdrew a ring of keys from a hook on the wall, unlocked Father Rose's cage and lifted the top. Father Rose stared at the face covered in dark cloth, trying to discern a motive for Fantômas' actions, but his dark eyes stared straight down at the nervous Father Rose.

"Get up," Fantômas finally said after Father Rose had failed to rise. "The time has come. I have a use for your talents."

We are inside Detective Frederick Dickson's Broadway apartment. It is 48 hours after the destruction of Jack Meredith's house and Freddy Dickson's defeat at the hands of Fantômas. Jack has been dismissed from the hospital and has taken his damaged tongue and wounded ego to Dickson's crowded rooms.

It is night.

"Make yourself comfortable," Dickson said, clearing away a stack of newspapers from the tiny sofa along the back wall of the front room. "I'm sorry for the mess." Dickson looked up to see Jack staring out the window, seemingly oblivious to Dickson's awkward attempts at conversation. "Have no fear," he added. "You'll be back on your feet in no time. Houses can be rebuilt and this arrangement is only temporary. I'm sorry that there's so little room that…"

"You're fond of her aren't you?" The question caught Dickson off guard. Not only had Jack not turned around to ask it, but his trademark false British accent was nowhere in evidence. Without removing his eyes from the street, he quickly raised his hand to caress his sore jaw but made no utterance of pain or discomfort.

"I don't know what you mean," Dickson answered with no small amount of awkwardness. He knew exactly what Jack meant and had been trying desperately to hide his growing affection for Ruth Harrington, but despite his talent for disguises, Dickson had never been very accomplished at hiding matters of the heart.

"Good man," Jack replied with a short sigh. "You know exactly what I mean. You're in love with Ruth, aren't you?"

Dickson stared at the back of Jack's head, unsure of how to respond. "We're going to find her," he said finally. "We will save her and you will marry her. You have my word."

"I've seen the way you look at her…"

"She is your fiancé."

"And I've seen the way she looks at you."

Jack turned away from the window and looked at Dickson for the first time since the conversation began. His lips were pursed and his eyes were narrow. Dickson couldn't tell if he was staring at a man in the throes of worry or if it was something more troubling. "I think, Jack, that now is not the time for this conversation. You're tired. You're hurt. Try to get a good night's sleep and we will do our best to locate Fantômas' trail tomorrow."

Jack continued to stare at Dickson without speaking and Dickson began to note a hint of sadness in the red of his eyes. "You have my word," Dickson added. "That I would never attempt to take something, or someone, that is rightfully yours."

The two men locked eyes for a few moments before Jack finally broke his gaze with a loud peal of laughter, followed by a brief burst of pain in his mouth.

"Are you all right?" Dickson asked.

"Nothing to it, old man," Jack answered, his British dialect having returned. "It's all one, as they say in Shakespeare."

"I'm not sure I understand," Dickson stammered.

"My apologies, Detective," Jack answered with a gracious nod. "I fear the lack of sleep, coupled with a great deal of pain, has made me forget my manners. Here I am, a guest in your home, humble though it may be, and I have yet to offer you the slightest modicum of gratitude."

Dickson briefly contemplated returning to the heated topic of Ruth Harrington, but remembered the lateness of the hour and thought better of it. "We both need a good night's sleep," he said.

"And this attractive, rustic cushion looks like it will do the trick," Jack replied, practically leaping onto the sofa. His manner had changed dramatically since his arrival a quarter of an hour earlier, and he now appeared to Dickson as Jack Meredith, heir to the Meredith fortune, rather than Jack Meredith, the poor unfortunate whose house was destroyed while his fiancé was being kidnapped.

"Yes," Dickson said. "Is there anything else you need?"

"A pillow for my head and blanket for my weary bones and I'm as happy as lamb. Is that a phrase they say? Happy as a lamb?"

Dickson wasn't sure, so he didn't answer. "I'll wake you in the morning," he said. "We'll meet with Corona at the Broadway station and go over our next move."

"But first," Jack said with an exaggerated yawn, "sleep, my good man, sleep."

Dickson left the room and made his way to his bed. Minutes later the lights were out and Dickson, unable to sleep, lay awake staring at the ceiling. In the other room, Jack Meredith was sitting bolt upright on the sofa, doing his best to remain perfectly still. *Just another few minutes*, he thought, *and Dickson will be sound asleep*. He waited until he was confident that Dickson had drifted off, then made his way to the window once more.

The man in the grey trenchcoat with the cigarette between his teeth and hat pulled down over his brow was still visible under the streetlamp. Jack had spotted him while Dickson was talking (that damned detective did like to go on, didn't he?) and much to Jack's surprise, he saw that the man with the cigarette was staring directly up at him. On noticing that Jack had returned to the window, the Councilman extended his finger and motioned for Jack to join him outside.

Jack listened for any movement coming from Dickson. He knew he should wake the detective, but he also knew this was his chance to wrest the investigation from him and perhaps even find Ruth himself. He didn't know what the Councilman wanted with him, but he damn well knew that he didn't want Freddy Dickson saving his skin yet again.

Jack tiptoed across the floor, easing his weight onto each floor board as quietly as possible to avoid squeaking. Once he was convinced that Dickson was indeed asleep, he opened the front door, stepped out of the apartment and slowly eased the door closed behind him.

Dickson, who had been lying motionless in his bed, bolted upright when he heard the door snap shut. He had sensed Jack's distraction earlier in the evening and spotted the Councilman from the bedroom window moments later. Once he no longer had to feign sleep, he rose from his bed and stepped backwards, away from the window, just in time to see Jack join the Councilman outside. As quickly as possible, Dickson threw off his bed clothes and donned his James Dale suit, followed by the tell-tale bowler and false moustache.

Outside, Jack Meredith approached the Councilman with some trepidation, but held his head high in a desperate attempt to appear in control of the situation. "Mr. Meredith," the Councilman said.

"I don't believe we've had the pleasure," Jack answered.

"You have something that my boss wants and he'd like to strike a deal with you."

Jack, wrongly assuming the man was a confederate of Fantômas, made a bold move. "You can tell Fantômas," he said, "that I refuse to deal with him until I know Ruth Harrington is safe."

The Councilman did his best to suppress a smile. He had followed Meredith in an effort to procure the Professor's journal and was about to get information on Fantômas as well.

Will wonders never cease?

"Not here," the Councilman said. "Follow me."

Jack Meredith and the Councilman started off down the street. A block behind them, keeping a safe distance and darting from shadow to shadow, was James Dale. Block after block, the two men, followed by their pursuer, walked in silence toward the Lower East Side. As the streets began to grow more crowded with drunks and the homeless, James Dale began to allow himself more freedom. He eventually stopped hiding in the shadows and began to bury himself in the nighttime crowd. Soon, the lights of Broadway gave way to the Five Points, and a few blocks more led Jack and the Councilman to the *Hog's Head*. They entered the saloon while James Dale remained behind.

Dale breathed a sigh of relief when he realized their destination. Perhaps he could count on Geoffrey the Slasher if things got out of hand.

Jack and the Councilman made their way across the floor of the bar. The Councilman tipped his hat toward Geoffrey the Slasher, who returned the gesture with a quick nod. Rounding the corner of the smoke-filled room, the Councilman placed his hand on the back wall and pressed on it. The wall gave way and swung open, revealing a hidden room. Jack followed the Councilman inside.

Illuminated by a single bulb in the middle of the room, a dozen similarly garbed men sat around a table. In the middle of the table was the electronic box that allowed the leader of the Council to address his followers.

"Good evening, Mr. Meredith," the box hissed.

"Who said that?" Jack asked.

"You have nothing to be afraid of," the voice spoke again. "You're among friends. The men that you see here represent the strong arms of justice. You, my friend, are being given the golden opportunity to help restore order to this corrupt city."

Jack thrust his chin into the air as a gesture of defiance. "I will never cooperate with you… Fantômas!"

The men surrounding the table laughed at Jack's clumsy posturing. Jack's face turned beet red as he glanced nervously around at the men.

Once more, the voice of the leader emitted from the wired box. "I'm afraid you are mistaken, Mr. Meredith. I am not Fantômas, nor do any of us represent Fantômas. Fantômas is our common enemy."

The Councilman who had led Jack to the *Hog's Head* stepped forward. "Sorry to interrupt, boss," he said. "But Mr. Meredith here said that Fantômas had kidnapped his girlfriend. Isn't that right, Mr. Meredith?"

Jack's lips tightened in anger. "It's true," he said. "Fantômas has kidnapped her and I'll do anything to get her back."

"Interesting," the voice said. "If I'm not mistaken, you're engaged to be married to Miss Ruth Harrington, daughter of the noted explorer Professor James Harrington."

"Yes," Jack answered.

"And Professor Harrington is the owner of the journal that Fantômas is so desperately trying to steal, and which you are now in possession of."

"How did you…"

"Let's not waste time," the voice interrupted. "You have something we desire and we can assist you in obtaining something that belongs to you. Surely we can strike a deal. We will aid you in rescuing your fiancé, in exchange for information on Fantômas and the journal containing the gold formula."

Jack's eyes grew wide. "The formula isn't mine to give," he said.

"Really, Mr. Meredith," the voice said. "Selling out your love for a fistful of gold? Your greed will be your undoing."

"What right do you have to it?" Jack asked, his voice raising with indignity.

"The real question, Mr. Meredith, is what right does Fantômas have to it? His criminal network is made up of hundreds of the most devious and downtrodden members of society. Can you imagine the chaos that would result if those people were suddenly endowed with unimaginable wealth? No, Mr. Meredith, we cannot allow such a travesty to take place. Better that the cradle of wealth rests with us–the hidden faces of justice in this corrupt metropolis. Only we have the knowledge and good sense to deal with such a treasure."

"The problem is," Jack answered, "that the treasure doesn't belong to you. It is the property of Professor Harrington. He stole it, fair and square, from an Amazonian Indian tribe."

"In that case, Mr. Meredith, it appears that we have reached an impasse." The Council of Ten slowly rose from their chairs. "Either give us the formula, or face the consequences."

At the same time that Jack was meeting with the Council of Ten, James Dale was seated at a barstool in front of the Slasher.

"What'll it be?" the Slasher asked, not looking up.

"Some more information, my friend," James Dale answered, sliding a bill across the bar.

The Slasher looked up and recognized James Dale. "You," he said. "I wouldn't show your face here if I were you."

James Dale was taken aback by the Slasher's tone. "What do you mean?" he asked.

"Hey, boys!" a drunken man stood up and addressed the room in a raised voice. "Here's the fella we're looking for!"

We find it necessary, Dear Reader, to offer some explanation for the unusual event that is about to take place. To do so, we draw your attention to Detective Dickson's rather simple disguise–a bowler hat and false moustache. Now, we ask you to remember the last time someone, or rather two someones, donned similar disguises in this very establishment–Ruth Harrington and Fantômas. The average citizen, assuming he was sober and encountering James Dale in broad daylight, would probably have no trouble distinguishing him from the other two.

The patrons of the *Hog's Head*, however, still smarting from their broken bones and black eyes, can only see James Dale through the haze of drunken anger and assume that he is one or the other of the two men that instigated such violence a few nights earlier. At least a few of them believe he is a sorcerer capable of dividing himself in two. They won't believe this tomorrow morning, but tonight it feels perfectly logical.

A silence fell across the room as all eyes turned toward James Dale. Then, almost in unison, the patrons of the *Hog's Head* made their way across the floor and surrounded James Dale, pressing him against the bar.

"Thought you'd come back to finish the job?" one of them said.

"Son of a bitch knocked out two of my teeth."

"Wasn't you a lady under that moustache?"

"Knuckles are itchin' to teach him a lesson…"

"Gentlemen!" James Dale raised his hands to draw everyone's attention. "It's obvious that all of you have mistaken me for someone else, but I assure you I'm not here to cause any trouble. I'm just here to speak to my old friend Geoffrey, and then I'll be on my way."

"This guy an old friend of yours, Slasher?" a large man with a scar across his face said.

"Look," said the Slasher. "I know who you're looking for and this ain't him."

"Sure looks like him," another man said.

"Gentlemen," James Dale interrupted once again. "I'll ask you again to please turn around and go back to your tables."

"Or what?" an especially angry-looking drunk replied. "You'll break my other arm?"

Suddenly, an arm lashed out at James Dale's face. The punch caught him unawares and he dropped hard to the ground. He pushed himself up on his elbow, and a kick from a hard leather boot sent a shock of pain through his gut. A burst of air shot from his mouth as he dropped back to the floor.

"C'mon fellas," the Slasher said. "Not again!"

"All right," James Dale said, crawling to his knees. "I give up."

The men laughed. "Good thinkin'," one of them said.

Perhaps he had been inspired by Ruth Harrington's physical prowess, or perhaps it was just his overwhelming concern for her safety or just plain anger. Regardless of his reasons, Detective Dickson, feeling freer than ever in his James Dale disguise, suddenly found himself possessed of a ferocity that he had never experienced before. Instead of "giving up" as he had promised, Dickson brought both of his fists upward, striking two men simultaneously between the legs. They screamed in pain and doubled over, clutching their genitals. The rest of the group was dazed, which gave Dickson time to grab another man by the back of the neck and throw him forward into the edge of the bar. His nose smashed on the edge, sending a spray of crimson in all directions. The man collapsed to the ground as the rest of the men backed away from James Dale, giving him a wider berth. He lowered his guard briefly, silently hoping that the fight was over.

"So," a large man missing an ear said as he cracked his knuckles. "That's the way you want to play..."

As the fracas continued and grew noisier, the Council began to take note of the sounds of scuffling outside their meeting room. Jack turned around toward the closed door as the shouts grew louder.

"Sounds like another fight," Number Two said, rolling his eyes. "Someone made a drunken pass at the wrong woman."

But the sounds continued and the shouts grew in volume until it became obvious that this was no ordinary bar fight.

"What the Devil is going on out there?" the leader's voice hissed from the box.

"Not a problem, boss," Number Seven said, stepping toward the door. "We'll take care of it." He shot Jack a glance as he passed. "You stay here."

Just then, the door to the room cracked in half as the large body of one of the *Hog's Head* patrons came sailing into the room, the wood splintering beneath his large frame. The man rolled on his back and moaned in pain.

Like a cobra leaping from his charmer's basket, James Dale came flying into the room, arms outstretched, clutched the man by the collar and lifted him to his feet. The man's head lolled to one side and James Dale raised his fist and dealt him a blow that sent him spinning to the ground into unconsciousness.

The Slasher was standing on the bar, trying to calm the violence. The pitiful drunks had practically forgotten about James Dale and were busy beating the daylights out of one another. At least two dozen men had entered the fray, with the front door opening every so often to allow in new combatants–none of whom knew the reasons for the fight but were willing to smash a few jaws anyway.

It was, after all, a break in the routine.

All the while, mirrors were being smashed, tabletops cracked, chairs splintered and the front of the bar caved in, sending the Slasher's precious frozen pig head rolling into the melee.

Back in the Council's meeting room, Number Four pulled a lever, revealing a hidden passageway. "This way, Meredith," he said.

James Dale drew a pistol from his pocket. "Not on your life," he said. "Meredith comes with me."

"And who, pray tell, are you?" Jack cried.

"Shut up," James Dale answered. "Trust me."

"Trust me, he says!" Jack shouted in exasperation. "Bloody well good work trusting people has gotten me so far!"

James Dale ignored Jack's raving, wrapped his arm around Jack's chest and backed his way out of the room with the pistol pointed squarely at Number Seven. As he stepped carefully into the bar, he barely noticed that the sounds of fighting had come to a halt until he felt the tight grip of a fiercely strong hand on the back of his neck.

James Dale roughly shrugged the hand away, releasing Jack in the process. He spun around to face his would-be attacker–a small, wiry man in a thin white shirt and suspenders. Despite his size, his muscles bulged from a lifetime of hard, physical labor. A recent cut above his right eye sent a stream of blood running down his face. "This is the guy," he said to everyone in the room, all of whom were breathing heavily, preparing themselves for another bout of fisticuffs. "This is the guy what caused all the trouble."

James Dale didn't say a word, but grabbed Jack and spun on his heels in the opposite direction. He had intended to whisk Jack up the back stairs and, hopefully, to an exit. Instead, he found his flight blocked by the Council of Ten who had congregated in the bar, creating an immovable barrier preventing James Dale and Jack from escaping.

"Everyone move along!" Number Seven said aloud, addressing the throngs of bare-fisted bar patrons. "These men belong to us!"

The thin man flashed a toothless grin and pulled his suspenders off his shoulders. "Oh," he said with a laugh. "If it ain't the mighty Council of Ten. Well, run along, men. The troublemakers belong to us."

Geoffrey the Slasher was still standing behind his broken bar, desperately trying to take control of the situation. "Fellas, please!" he pleaded. "Take it outside."

But the thin man ignored him. “Maybe you fellas ought to turn around and take your Council with ya.” The other bar patrons laughed and the thin man joined them.

With a sudden movement, Number Seven leapt forward, wrenched the pistol from James Dale’s hand and shot the thin man squarely in the chest. The thin man flew backwards, his chest exploding in a splash of blood that spattered across the faces and clothing of everyone around him.

Number Seven had meant to stun the drunkards into inaction, giving the Councilmen time to secure James Dale and Jack, but his plan backfired. Already drunk more with rage than booze, the bar patrons shouted as one and charged the Councilmen. Number Seven tried firing the pistol again, but it was quickly knocked from his hand as the fists began to fly.

“This way!” James Dale shouted, pulling Jack to the ground. As the Councilmen scuffled with the drunkards, they crawled on all fours toward the back of the bar, where a staircase led upward to freedom.

“Who the Devil are you?” Jack asked again.

“The name’s James Dale. Just relax and I’ll get you out of here.”

“Thank you,” Jack responded. “Do you wish to know something, Mr. James Dale?”

“What’s that?”

“This is the best bloody time I’ve had in ages!”

James Dale looked at him aghast. “I beg your pardon?” he said.

“Guns pointed at my head, rescued by a mysterious stranger… these East Side taverns are every bit as exotic as one reads about! Just wait until Ruth hears that I faced off against a group of sinister, grey-garbed thugs! She’ll never look at that bloody detective again!”

James Dale felt the anger rise in his throat, but swallowed it when he saw one of the Councilmen look their way. “Time to get up,” he said, clutching Jack by the shoulder.

But it was too late. Number Six was making his way through the crowd toward them. "Go!" James Dale shouted.

"Go where?" Jack asked.

"Up! I'll try to hold them off!"

Jack considered, for a moment, staying behind to help his cohort–but only for a moment. Self-preservation quickly took hold and he dashed up the stairs like a frightened rabbit. James Dale threw himself at Number Six, swinging his fists wildly at the Councilman's jaw. Unexpectedly, Number Six clutched James Dale around the waist, lifted him in the air and squeezed. James Dale began striking Number Six on the shoulders as he felt a sharp pain shoot through his ribcage. Number Six barely felt the blows on his head and shoulders as they continued to grow weaker. James Dale felt his face flush red and it became harder to breathe. Sensing that his real quarry was escaping, Number Six tossed James Dale aside, where he rolled beneath the stairwell and continued gasping for breath. He heard the heavy footsteps as Number Six ascended the stairs after Jack.

James Dale tried to move but the pain in his torso was too great and his breath too weak. He lay on his back in the stairwell, hidden from the rest of the bar, and waited for his strength to return. Suddenly, he felt the wall behind his head give way. Before he could turn around, three sets of arms reached for him and pulled him into a passageway. Too weak and surprised to kick his way free, James Dale found himself in a small tunnel. The door leading to the bar slammed shut, and the six arms dragged James Dale down into the darkness.

At the top of the stairwell, Jack found himself face-to-face with a large wooden door. He could hear Number Six's footfalls approaching. Recalling Detective Dickson's shoulder-first dash through the door of his home days earlier, he leaned forward, aimed his shoulder at the door, shut his eyes tight and leapt forward. The door tore from its hinges and Jack landed with a thud on top of it. "Bloody hell!" he shouted, clutching his dislocated shoulder. "How the Devil does Sexton Blake do that week after week?" He stood up and found himself on the roof of the Hog's Head. Number Six was almost to the top of the stairs, so Jack ran forward to the edge of the roof. He looked down. Only four flights, but he was sure to break a leg. Besides, the rest of the Council was downstairs. He looked back. Number Six appeared in the doorway and charged toward him. Jack looked out again and considered his options. It was only five feet to the next building. Surely he could make it. After all, didn't he just knock down a door for God's sake?

Jack backed up a few feet, then dashed forward and took a running leap off the roof. Unfortunately, his back foot kicked the cornice and he found himself falling far short of his goal. With a burst of luck, he was able to twist around just in time to grab the edge of the roof with his good hand.

Hanging by his fingertips, Jack looked up just in time to see the sinister, smiling face of Number Six approach the edge of the roof. He stared at Jack in silence.

"See here, old man," Jack pleaded. "We can make a deal. You want the formula? It's yours. Just pull me up, all right? A fall from this height could be quite painful."

Number Six laughed.

"Actually," Jack said, his fingers weakening from the strain, "the others don't even have to know. You can tell them I escaped and later, in a few days when it's all blown over, I'll deliver everything to you–the formula, Fantômas, whatever you wish."

Number Six said nothing.

"What, then?" Jack asked. "What do you want?"

Number Six stepped forward, lifted his boot and drove his foot down onto Jack's fingers.

We regret ushering the reader away from the *Hog's Head* at this most desperate hour, but it's time to return to Our Lady of Perpetual Sorrow, where the most unholy of holy ceremonies is about to take place…

Fantômas, in his disguise as Emile Cortez, stood in front of his mirror adjusting his bow tie. "How do I look?" he said to the Torch who was standing beside him.

"You look fine," the Torch answered.

"So this is it," Fantômas said. "The big night. It's strange, isn't it? I find myself dreaming about all the other women in my past... Maud... Helen Dodler... Françoise Lemercier... There have been so many."

"Right," the Torch said.

"It's an odd feeling," Fantômas continued, "knowing that from now on, I'll be with the same woman, night after night, every night."

"Yeah."

"What happens on the inevitable day when I come downstairs–she's drinking tea in her attractive red kimono–and I look at her and suddenly don't wish to be married anymore?"

"I don't know," the Torch answered.

Fantômas stared at himself in the mirror and considered the conundrum. "I guess when that happens," he decided, "that I'll have to kill her."

The Torch glanced at Fantômas with no small amount of alarm.

"But that," Fantômas declared, "is in the future. Today is my wedding day and this is a celebration!"

"Boss," the Torch said with a tone of sheepishness in his voice. "Do you mind if I ask you something?"

Fantômas turned and the Torch could see his dangerous glare beneath the deceptively innocuous looking face of Emile Cortez. "Yes?" he asked, raising one eyebrow.

"Well…why are you doing this? Getting married, I mean."

Fantômas placed his hand on the Torch's shoulder and looked him in the eye. "Are you, by any chance, familiar with this country's Declaration of Independence?"

The Torch thought for a moment. "No, I'm not really…"

"After a rather hypocritical opening about freedom, the wordy, tiresome document goes on to state that everyone is created equal and is endowed with the right to life, liberty, and the pursuit of happiness."

"So?"

"The pursuit of happiness! This pitiful, arrogant rock felt that the selfish pursuit of happiness was so important that it deserved to be documented. Incredible! I can do as I wish in this country, simply because it makes me happy! Perhaps it lacks criminal flair, or perhaps it simply doesn't seem pragmatic, but I am marrying Ruth Harrington because I wish to do so. Because it makes me happy to destroy a family from within. It makes me happy to know that I have tamed that rabid, savage bitch into being my wife. It makes me happy to see the agony in Professor Harrington's eyes and to know that I have robbed Jack Meredith and Fred Dickson of their one true love. It makes me happy to see them suffer and to know that I am the cause of that suffering.

"Then, years later, when I have taken everything I can from Ruth Harrington, when I have robbed her of her chastity and her dignity, when I have numbed her to her own pain and when the spark of light has vanished from her eyes, it will make me happy–very, very happy–to kill her."

The Torch stared into Fantômas' eyes in silence, unsure of how to respond.

"Does that answer your question?" Fantômas said, leaning in so that the Torch could smell his foul breath.

"Yes," the Torch said.

"Good!" Fantômas exclaimed, dusting off the Torch's lapels with the back of his gloves. "Then let's go. Time to get married."

Fantômas stepped into the church expecting to see it full to bursting with his criminal apaches. He was disappointed to find that the room was nearly empty. A small group of men was huddled into one of the back pews and there were a few others scattered about the musty church. Some of them had put on neckties over their work clothes or dusty shirts, in a ridiculous attempt to add dignity to the proceedings. A handful had even managed to bathe before arriving. Several of the men, never having been to such an event before, took off their hats and placed them over their hearts as Emile Cortez walked down the aisle to the pounding music of a Bach chorale that screamed through the large pipes of the church organ.

Fantômas leaned in to the Torch. "Where is everyone?" he snarled. "This is my wedding, for God's sake. The happiest day of my damned life."

The Torch swallowed hard and adjusted his collar. "We put the word out," he said as a bead of sweat formed on his brow "but the thing is…we're not sure where everyone is."

Fantômas glared at the Torch, his eyes filled with anger. "In that case," he said, "we'll just have to make them pay, won't we?"

The Torch wiped his forehead with the back of his hand. "Yes, sir," he said.

The wedding of Ruth Harrington and Fantômas

Bound and determined not to let anything spoil the occasion, Fantômas strode down the aisle with confidence, savoring every moment of the ceremony. When he arrived at the front of the church, he was joined by the authentic Father Rose, who stumbled forward, fragile from hunger and weak from the atrophied muscles in his legs. His hair was matted and his skin was pale. He watched as Emile Cortez approached the front of the church.

Sitting next to Father Rose was Professor Harrington, who was bound hand and foot, gagged, and tied to a chair. Fantômas placed his hand on the Professor's cheek, leaned into him and whispered. "It's so hard, isn't it? Watching our little ones leave the nest."

Abruptly, the Bach chorale ended and was immediately replaced by Mendelssohn's Wedding March. Fantômas faced front and looked down the aisle. The congregation stood up and watched as Ruth Harrington entered the church.

She was dressed in a beautiful, white, floor-length gown. A tight gag was wrapped around her mouth and bit into her cheeks. Her ankles were strapped together with a length of heavy wire. Her hands were bound and holding a large, bright bouquet of roses. Blood dripped down the backs of her hands as the thorns from the stems pressed into her fingertips She was standing on the platform of a dolly, which leaned back as the Torch wheeled her forward down the aisle.

The crowd watched as the dolly slowly rolled by. Ruth Harrington's head rocked back and forth as she tried to shake herself free from her bonds. The organ music was punctuated by the occasional muffled scream as she traveled closer and closer toward her future husband.

"Darling!" Fantômas said, as the music ended. The dolly stopped by his side and Ruth Harrington was jolted upright. "So glad you didn't get cold feet."

Father Rose looked as if he were about to swoon and was forcing himself to remain standing by leaning on the dais.

"Ahem..." Fantômas cleared his throat to get Father Rose's attention.

Father Rose stumbled forward. "Dearly beloved..." he began, his raspy throat coarse from days of thirst.

"A little louder," Fantômas said. "They can't hear you in the back."

"Dearly beloved," Father Rose began again. "We are gathered here today to join this man and this woman in the bonds of holy matrimony. Do you, Emile Cortez, take this woman, Ruth Harrington, to be your lawfully wedded wife? To love and to cherish, for better or for worse, in sickness and in health for as long as you both shall live?"

Fantômas smiled. "I do," he said.

Father Rose wiped a bead of sweat from his brow and turned toward Ruth. "I'm sorry, young lady," he whispered.

Fantômas' smile turned to a sneer. "Get on with it," he said.

Father Rose continued. "Do you, Ruth Harrington, take this man, Emile Cortez..."

"Blah, blah, blah" Fantômas interrupted. "She does, she does, she does. Let's wrap it up, shall we?"

"Very well," Father Rose said, delivering Ruth Harrington one final, pitiful, glance. "I hereby declare you man and..."

The gunshot came from the back of the church and the explosion echoed through the high ceilings and shook the windows. The congregation dropped to the ground en masse and tried desperately to hide under the pews. At the end of the aisle, holding a large pistol with smoke wafting from its barrel, was the Woman in Black.

"Oh, Christ." Fantômas said, putting his hand to his face. He turned back to Father Rose. "Keep going," he said.

"But..."

The Woman in Black was charging down the aisle with her arm outstretched. She took aim again.

"Hurry!" Fantômas snapped at Father Rose.

Father Rose continued. "I now pronounce you man and..."

Ruth Harrington screamed behind her gag as the second shot exploded toward her and she found herself blinded by a splash of thick, dark blood.

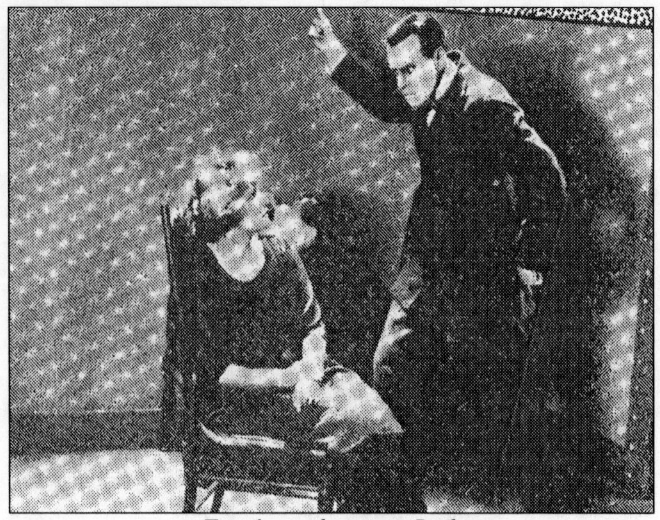

Fantômas threatens Ruth

Once again, Dear Reader, we fear that the act has come to a close. We are fast approaching the conclusion of our tale and things are bound to get worse before they get better. That is–if they get better at all. For the sake of his mental health, we suggest the reader try to spend a few hours in the sunlight before pressing on to Act IV–in which someone discovers the truth about James Dale, and Jack Meredith is menaced by a blind, albino knife-thrower.

ACT IV

In which someone discovers the truth about James Dale, and Jack Meredith is menaced by a blind, albino knife-thrower.

Chapter Seventeen: Mysteries of Manhattan

For a split second, Jack Meredith considered which of his two choices would be more cowardly. Choice Number One–continue clutching onto the edge of the roof despite the fact that the man in the grey coat was about to bring his oversized shoe on top of Jack's fingers which would then cause blinding amounts of pain. Choice Number Two–let go of the roof's edge, thereby avoiding the pain, but falling four stories to the ground resulting in certain injury and possible death.

Like every choice Jack Meredith had ever been faced with in his young life, this one demanded that he persevere–that he withstand the horrible pain long enough to find the inner strength to somehow propel himself back onto the roof to do battle with the sinister Councilman. Unfortunately, Jack Meredith had always opted out of immediate pain, even if it meant complicating his life months, days, or–in this case–seconds later. As the Councilman brought his foot down, Jack let go of the roof.

Before he had a chance to fully realize the consequences of his actions, however, Jack found himself dangling in midair somewhere between the second and third stories.

"Come on, fella! Climb in! Jeez, you're heavier than you look!" The voice came from behind him. Jack turned his head to see a man's face, his unshaved stubble pressing coarsely against Jack's cheek. Jack looked down and realized that he was still outside the building, two stories from the solid ground below. He felt two rough, calloused hands underneath his arms.

This unwashed man, whoever he was, had caught him.

"Pull me in!" Jack shouted. "Hurry!"

"Criminey-Jeez, fella!" the stranger said. "Quit squirmin', will ya? You already wrenched me arms out o' their sockets! Swing a leg up on the sill!"

Jack threw his leg over the edge of the windowsill, then grabbed the top of the frame with his hand and pulled himself inside. The stranger kept his arms around Jack's waist and the two men collapsed to the floor. Down below, Jack could hear the violence escalating, as if the drunken mob was dismantling the Hog's Head plank by plank.

Jack lay face-down on the floor, panting heavily, for several moments. "Thank you," he gasped. "That man… I think he was going to kill me."

"Nah," the stranger said. "The fall probably wouldn't have killed ya. Crippled ya for life, maybe, but you'da survived."

"Really," Jack gasped, lifting his head and eyeing the stranger with gratitude. "I can't thank you enough. I thought I was a dead man."

The stranger rose and dusted himself off. "Think nothing of it," he said. "Now get up. We gotta get you outta here before they come back."

Jack pulled himself to his feet in a hurry. "Yes, yes!" he said in a panic. "For God's sake, we've got to hurry! If they capture me, they'll torture me until I tell them where the formula is."

The stranger squinted one of his eyes and stepped toward Jack. "The formula?"

"Uh, yes…" Jack stammered and took several steps backward. "Formula for… You see, my nana makes the most sublime corn chowder. Really exquisite. And those men in grey are with some…secret…underground… culinary sect. Very mysterious, and…"

"Wait a minute," the stranger interrupted. "You're Jack Meredith, right?"

Jack thought for a moment, but was unable to come up with a suitable pseudonym quickly enough. "Yes," he answered. "I'm Jack Meredith."

"All right then," the man replied, removing a blackjack from his inside pocket and bringing it down on the side of Jack's head. Jack stumbled, then crashed to the ground, unconscious.

The stranger dashed quickly to the door of the room and opened it. "It's him, fellas," he hissed with a harsh whisper. "Hurry!"

Suddenly, five more men dressed head to toe in full black body stockings, stepped into the room. They surrounded Jack's body, then lifted it off the ground. "Good," the stranger said. "Take him to Fantômas."

So many things can go wrong at a wedding.

Imagine yourself, Dear Reader, standing in the shoes of the unfortunate Ruth Harrington. She has spent her entire short life diving headlong into adventures of the most dangerous sort. When she finally gave in to the persistent attentions of Jack Meredith, she began to imagine what her own wedding would be like. Although she had always disdained the image of the simpering, obedient bride, she surprised herself by dreaming, now and again, of being draped in a glorious white gown (her deceased mother's) and parading down the aisle of a church surrounded by her loved ones. Upon reaching the front of the sanctuary, she would be greeted by her childhood priest, then would turn and look into her lover's eyes.

Imagine her disappointment, then, at finding herself bound and gagged and watching the officiating priest being shot in the chest, the blood from his wound staining her lily-white gown.

"Darling!" Fantômas shouted. "I can explain!"

The Woman in Black continued down the aisle, aiming the gun directly at Fantômas.

"How could you?" she whimpered from beneath her thick black veil.

Fantômas leaned into Ruth. "Trust me," he said. "I'll handle this." With a quick movement, he tossed the still-bound Ruth Harrington to the ground, where her head came to rest beside the lifeless body of Father Rose.

"This isn't what it appears to be," Fantômas said to the Woman in Black, his hands turned upward in supplication.

"Stand back," the woman said, cocking the gun and leveling it at Fantômas' head.

"Darling," Fantômas said. "For God's sake… don't you see? I'm doing this for us."

The Woman in Black's hand began to shake as Fantômas approached her. "Please… tell me you love me. You do still love me…don't you?"

"Darling," Fantômas whispered, his voice as smooth as poison. "Of course I love you." he gestured toward Ruth, "She means nothing to me. You are the only one I will ever love."

The wrath of the Woman in Black

The Woman in Black felt her knees go weak as Fantômas gently pried the gun from her gloved hand. She felt the heat of his body as he stepped in closer to her, gently lifting her veil to reveal her trembling lips. He stroked her cheek with the back of his hand, then firmly grasped the back of her neck and sank his mouth into hers. She quivered as he quickly and unexpectedly pulled his face away. "Take Miss Harrington and her father back to their quarters," he said, addressing two mystified members of his gang that were crouched behind a nearby pew. "And when you're done, escort this woman into one of the empty cells."

The Woman in Black stepped backwards with a start. "What?" she cried, raising her arms to strike him.

Fantômas gripped her firmly by the wrists. "Sorry, darling," he said. "But I've come too far to allow you to jeopardize my plans. Rest assured you will be well looked after."

Two of Fantômas' apaches were dragging the Professor and Ruth Harrington out of the church. They stopped dead in their tracks when they heard the Woman in Black scream to the heavens. "No!" she shouted to the rafters. "How could you? I loved you!"

Fantômas turned to the Torch. "Take her down below. Gag her so she doesn't disturb the other prisoners."

The Torch drew a thin cord from the inside of his jacket and quickly tied the Woman in Black's hands behind her back. She continued to scream until he tore a piece of cloth from the back of her gown and wrapped it across her mouth.

Minutes later, the Torch, accompanied by two other members of the Fantômas gang, were walking the Professor, Ruth and the Woman in Black through the narrow, underground corridor beneath Our Lady of Perpetual Sorrow. Ruth's feet had been untied, allowing her to walk, but her hands were still bound in front of her, clutching the bouquet of thorny roses. She glanced sideways at her father who, although clearly weak, was eyeing her with grim determination.

Fantômas was still in the church. This was their chance.

The Woman in Black was loosely bound and could easily be released with a momentary distraction. Once at liberty, she could aid Ruth in subduing the three men and they could make their escape.

It would be just like the time Ruth saved the expedition party from the tribe of headhunters.

Before Fantômas' men had a chance to realize what was happening, Ruth leaned sideways to bite the hand of the thug holding her father. He screamed and drew his hand back, sending a spray of blood into the air. Ruth dropped to the ground and rolled forward into the Torch, causing his legs to buckle beneath him. He kept a firm grasp on the Woman in Black, who came tumbling to the ground after him. Ruth lurched forward, clutching the cord that bound the Woman in Black in her teeth and pulling it loose. The third man had rushed forward, releasing Professor Harrington in the process.

While the three dazed criminals were still finding their way to their feet, the Woman in Black freed herself, removed her gag and began running down the corridor. Ruth head butted one thug, then the other, knocking them unconscious, leaving the Torch the last one standing.

"Wait!" Ruth shouted after the Woman in Black. "Where are you going? But I thought… Back in the church–you saved me!"

The Woman in Black turned around and Ruth could feel her wicked gaze even through the thick, black veil. "Saved you? You pathetic fool. I never intended to kill that poor priest. I was aiming for you."

The Woman in Black rounded the corner and disappeared into the darkness. Ruth barely had time to shout "Wait!" before the Torch's blackjack crashed down on the back of her head, sending her spinning to the floor, unconscious.

The Woman in Black ran until she ceased hearing footfalls behind her. Many times she had roamed these corridors, hiding in the shadows, trying to catch a glimpse of Fantômas, wondering if her love would ever accept her back into his life. Now was not the time to dawdle, however. She knew where the nearest exit was–a hidden staircase that led to a secret door behind a false tombstone in the graveyard behind the church. All she had to do was make it to the staircase before Fantômas sent his remaining thugs after her.

Then, she heard the sound of a baby crying.

A dim candle light was shining from a cell, dancing in the darkness. She crept forward to the bars of the cell and glanced inside. Sally Shea was slumped over, staring weakly at a blonde man who was bouncing a child on his knee. The man was oblivious to the Woman in Black's presence, but Sally spotted her at once. Their eyes met and Sally silently pleaded with the Woman in Black for help. The Woman in Black was moved by Sally Shea's suffering but suddenly heard the sounds of footsteps running through the corridors, accompanied by the shouts of at least a half-dozen men.

They were chasing her.

With a quick dash to the staircase, the Woman in Black exited upward through the cemetery and was gone.

Detective Dickson slowly came to his senses. He remembered being dragged through a hidden doorway under the staircase of the *Hog's Head*, then striking his head on the stone wall while several sets of hands grabbed his ankles and drug him forward. He remembered hearing a voice say, "Nice work, Genius! Now he'll be out for hours!" Then… nothing.

Slowly, he opened his eyes. Above him was a ceiling of chipped concrete and cheap plaster, adorned with cobwebs. The air was permeated with the smell of unwashed bodies, mixed with the scent of stale beef being roasted over an open flame.

He slowly brought himself to a sitting position, his head still aching from the blow that had left him unconscious. As his eyes adjusted to the light, he found himself in a large cellar. Along the side of one wall was a row of small windows that barely allowed in the moonlight. In front of him were scores of people dressed in rags. The men were unshaven. The women looked weak and tired. The children who weren't sleeping were squealing in their parents' arms. There were dozens of them, all squeezed into the cellar, climbing over one another for bowls of food. In front of a large, steaming bowl of broth, an old woman with a ladle was serving up small portions of soup to the others.

"Where in God's name am I?" Dickson thought. Then, almost as an afterthought, he realized that his bowler and false moustache were gone.

Someone had removed his James Dale disguise.

"Who are you?" a familiar voice said. Dickson turned around to find Snapper, Glimpy and Muggs staring at him accusingly with their arms folded.

"Boys," Dickson started. "Let me explain…"

Snapper interrupted. "Are you a copper?" he asked.

Dickson paused, wondering how much of the truth he should reveal. "Yes," he said finally.

Muggs tore his hat off his head and dusted the floor with it in frustration. "I knew it!" he cursed. "I knew somethin' was fishy! He was too tricky! Too mysterious!"

"Boys, listen…" Dickson stood up and faced the three boys.

"You gonna bust us?" Snapper asked. "Tell the other cops that we're here?"

"Boys, believe me," Dickson pleaded. "I didn't want to lie to you. But disguising myself was the only way to get information."

Glimpy stepped back in shock. "You hear that, boys?" he said. "We was snitches and didn't even know it. Mr. Dale turned us into squealers!"

"Listen!" Dickson snapped, bringing the boys back to attention. "I'm sorry that I don't have time to explain everything. I'm on the trail of a very dangerous man. Someone who is a dire threat to you, everyone here…everyone in the entire city. And I must find him as quickly as possible. I know you have no reason to trust me, but…"

"Fantômas," Snapper said. "You're lookin' for Fantômas, ain't ya?"

"Yes," Dickson said. "I'm searching for Fantômas. He..." Dickson paused briefly, almost choking on the words. "He kidnapped the woman I love."

Glimpy and Muggs looked at Snapper for approval. "Listen, boys." Snapper said. "Mr. Dale may notta been Mr. Dale, but he never steered us wrong. He coulda turned us in for lootin' that time, but he didn't."

"That's right, Snapper," Glimpy agreed. "He didn't say nothin'."

"OK, Mr...." Muggs began. "Say, Mister. What's your real name anyway?"

"Dickson. Detective Frederick Dickson."

"OK, Mr. Dickson," Muggs continued. "You got our help. But a deal's a deal..."

"Don't worry, Muggs," Dickson said. "I know you fellas keep your noses clean."

"How can we help ya, Detective?" Snapper asked.

"First of all," Dickson said, rubbing the bump on his head. "Where am I?"

Snapper answered, "You're in a cellar in an abandoned building off Houston. Building used to be called the Black Friar"

"And all these people...who are they?"

"The Council of Ten started comin' around. They was lookin' for Fantômas too. Started going door to door, threatening everybody. Askin' where was Fantômas. Someone didn't know, they started shootin'. These folks barely got away and came here."

"And these people...they work for Fantômas?"

"Not most of 'em. Some of 'em used to. Some of 'em have brothers or cousins that work for Fantômas. Some of 'em didn't even know Fantômas was real. Council didn't care. They just started kickin' in doors and firin' pistols."

Dickson scanned the room until he spied a familiar face. "Brian Shea," he said out loud.

"Huh?" Snapper asked. "Oh, yeah… that's him. That's the guy you wanted us to follow. Used to work for Fantômas too. Some guy kidnapped his wife and kid. Burnt down his house. We thought he was dead for sure, but he stumbled in here last night. Won't talk to nobody."

"Stay here, boys," Dickson said, walking toward the corner where Brian Shea was sitting, protecting a bowl of soup.

"Brian Shea?" Dickson said.

Shea said nothing and turned away.

Dickson continued. "Brian Shea, my name is Frederick Dickson. I'm a detective and I'm searching for Fantômas."

Shea turned to Dickson with a start and seemed on the edge of confessing everything, then thought the better of it. "I can't," he said aloud. "He'll kill both of them."

"Listen," Dickson said, clutching Shea by the shoulder. "If you know where Fantômas is, you must tell me. He has someone I love too. If we don't act soon, they're as good as dead."

"No," Shea said. "She told me to wait. She said she'd come back and help me."

"Who?" Dickson asked, his voice growing more and more impatient. "Who told you to wait?"

"The Woman in Black," Shea answered.

Dickson wasn't alone. Brian Shea had seen the Woman in Black too!

"When?" Dickson demanded. "When did you see her?"

"Leave me alone!" Shea shouted. The room fell to a hush and everyone turned to look at Dickson. "She'll die if I say anything," Shea whispered. "Please. Leave me alone."

Shea turned away from Dickson. Dickson let go of his shoulder and walked back to the three boys. "How did I get here?" he asked. "The last thing I remember was being under the stairwell at the *Hog's Head*."

Snapper gestured to Dickson to follow him to the back wall of the cellar. "The boys and me was in one of the tunnels and heard the commotion."

"Tunnels?"

"The tunnels underneath the streets. They connect everything on the Lower East Side. Well… almost everything. Come see…"

Snapper pressed on the wall and a small portion of it gave way, revealing a narrow tunnel. "Follow me," he said.

With Snapper in the lead, Dickson and the other boys entered the crawlspace and made their way on all fours until they arrived at a large open cavern. "We're in the sewers now," Snapper explained. "The tunnels lead to almost every bar and flophouse along the Bowery. I learned about 'em when I was runnin' numbers. Every gambling joint has a secret door. Usually under the stairwell. That's how you got out if the pigs decided to raid the place."

Dickson was aghast. He had discovered the mysterious escape routes of the Fantômas gang. "Listen, boys," he said. "I can get rid of Fantômas, but I need your help. Do you trust me?"

Snapper looked at Muggs and Glimpy. "Yeah, Detective," he answered. "I guess we trust ya."

"All right then," Dickson said. "I want you to continue to keep an eye on Brian Shea. He knows where Fantômas is. The second he leaves, I want you to come to police headquarters and ask for me."

"Come to police headquarters?" Muggs shouted. "I ain't settin' foot in that place! No, sir!"

"Boys," Dickson begged. "You have to trust me. I'm not going to let anything happen to you."

"All right," Snapper said. "What else?"

"Snapper, you sound like you know these tunnels like the back of your hand."

Snapper smiled with pride. "I sure do, Detective."

"In that case, gentlemen," Dickson said. "I want you to draw me a map."

In another location, the Council of Ten was meeting again. Once the final member was seated, Number Four leaned over to adjust the volume on the electronic voice box.

"Are we all met?" the voice growled.

"Yes," Number Four answered.

"Report, please."

Number Four glanced around at the others with apprehension. "We raided over a hundred rooms on the Lower East Side."

"Splendid," the voice answered. "And Fantômas?"

Number Four took a deep breath and cleared his throat. "We still don't know where Fantômas is."

The voice box was silent for a few moments, and the Councilmen imagined that their leader was silently fuming with rage. "Are you trying to tell me," the voice said with grim fury, "that not one of the people you interrogated had any information about Fantômas?"

"That's just it, Master," Number Four continued. "We only found people in the first dozen tenements. Then, after that, everyone was just…gone."

"What do you mean gone?"

"I mean they all just vanished. Tenement after tenement. There was no one there."

"Master," Number Ten spoke up, "Do you think maybe they heard we were coming and bolted?"

"More than likely," the voice answered. "The question is, where did they go?"

"So what do we do now?" Number Four asked.

"Go home," the voice answered. "Lay low. Don't allow yourselves to be seen for awhile. I'll contact you when it's safe."

The Councilmen looked at one another quizzically. "Yes, Master," Number Ten said with some confusion. "Whatever you say."

In silence, the Councilmen rose from their seats and filed out of the room. In another room, just 50 feet away, the man behind the mysterious voice–the leader of the Council of Ten–

turned off his electronic device and sat back in his chair. "Sometimes," he thought to himself. "If you want something done right, you have to do it yourself."

Chapter Eighteen: Fantômas Triumphant!

When Jack was just a young first-year student at Oxford, he decided he'd do whatever it took to endear himself to the prominent upperclassmen that surrounded him. After all, his father had told him that his Oxford classmates would be the men who helped him make his fortune. Not that Jack had to worry about money, as Jonathan Meredith Sr. had plenty of it to go around, but finding one's place in society was just as important as wealth.

And so, Jack Meredith performed every humiliating task that was asked of him by the older sons of the British aristocracy. He kidnapped the mascot of a rival football team and would have faced expulsion if the senior Meredith hadn't guaranteed funds toward the future site of the Meredith Memorial Library. He frequently drank to excess, and on more than one occasion, swallowed a goldfish or three. The most difficult torture, however, came from attempting to lose his American accent. Every time Jack failed to affect the pristine British pronunciation of a word, one of his brothers would roll up Jack's sleeve and give him what was called an "Indian Burn," whereupon the flesh on the forearm was twisted back and forth until the skin turned a bright red and the recipient howled in pain.

Jack graduated from Oxford convinced that these curious initiation rites had made him a better man. After all, not only did he win friends but he strengthened his constitution. He often thought back fondly to those wild, carefree, campus days and was convinced that he could withstand just about any humiliation, no matter how painful or unpleasant.

Until now.

Jack woke with a start to find the hooded face of Fantômas leaning over him. "Good morning, Mr. Meredith," he said. "I trust you've had a good night's sleep."

Jack knew he had been captured, but the striking courage in the face of adversity, which he was convinced he possessed, asserted itself. "I know who you are, Fantômas!" he said a little too loudly, "And you may rest assured that I will never, ever cooperate with your sinister plans! And I will certainly not debase myself by taking part in whatever vile scheme you have concocted!"

Fantômas pinched the bridge of his nose in exasperation. "So," he said. "This is how we're going to play?"

"Play?" Jack asked, swallowing hard. "What do you mean?"

Fantômas pulled up a chair and sat next to Jack. From the inside of his coat, he drew out a cigarette. He offered it to Jack, who nervously took it and placed it between his lips. Fantômas struck a match, lit Jack's cigarette, then sat back in his chair and eyed Jack curiously.

Suddenly, a thought dawned on Jack and he quickly removed the cigarette from his mouth, staring at it in horror.

Fantômas laughed. "No, no," he said. "It isn't poison. Really, Mr. Meredith. Poison cigarettes? How passé. Far too 19th century for my taste. Give me some credit, will you? All I want is a little chat."

Jack nervously placed the cigarette in his mouth and eased back into his chair. "Chat about...what?"

"About Miss Harrington."

"Ruth? Where is she?"

"She is unharmed, Mr. Meredith, I assure you. You love her dearly, don't you?"

Jack looked puzzled. "With all my heart," he said.

"I can't say that I blame you, Mr. Meredith. I have fallen under her spell as well. In fact, just this evening I attempted to marry her."

"You...*What*?" Jack bolted upright from his chair but Fantômas shoved his palm into Jack's chest, knocking him back down.

"Relax, Mr. Meredith. We were interrupted by my former lover. Very awkward. Regardless, I don't think Miss Harrington was as delighted by the prospect as I was. Such a spirited young woman. Perhaps it's the difficulty inherent in trying to conquer that spirit that makes her such attractive prey. Women are a puzzle. Wouldn't you agree, Mr. Meredith?"

Jack's shoulders slumped, as if the air had slowly leaked from his body. "I love her," he said. "With all my heart."

"Interesting," Fantômas continued. "You love her so much that you are willing to risk your life…for what? A dusty journal full of nonsensical chemical formulas? Come, now."

Jack glared at Fantômas with vicious intensity. "It doesn't belong to you," he said. "You don't deserve it."

"Hmm…" Fantômas mused. "But you, perhaps, do deserve it? Why? Because you are Ruth Harrington's paramour?"

"No," Jack stammered. "That's not it at all."

"Tell me, Mr. Meredith. Why do you wish to be with Ruth Harrington so desperately?"

"I told you. Because I love her."

"Why?"

"Why?" Jack threw up his hands in exasperation. "What kind of a question is that?"

"It is a question I wish to have answered and you are in no position to refuse me."

Jack stared at Fantômas for a moment, then gathered his thoughts and leaned forward. "I am…who I am."

"Yes," Fantômas elaborated. "You are Jack Meredith–heir to the Meredith munitions fortune."

"Exactly. It is… who I am. It is my birthright. And Ruth… Ruth is…"

"One of the most beautiful, most eligible women in Manhattan society."

"Yes! And when someone like me wishes to have someone… wishes to marry… it must be with…a…a…"

"It must be with someone deserving of you."

"Yes!" Jack slammed his fist into his palm. "By God, that's correct! I must be with her because I deserve her! Because…" And suddenly, Jack Meredith's countenance became one of quiet severity. “Because she is mine. Do you understand? I have claimed her and she is mine.”

Fantômas eyed Jack quizzically. “Hmm…” he murmured again to himself. “Mr. Meredith, don’t ask me why, but I like you.”

“I beg your pardon?”

“You are foolish man, it’s true, but beneath your obvious absurdity, you have qualities that I…well, I was going to say ‘admire,’ but that’s not quite the word I’m looking for. Let’s say that there’s something about you that I understand.”

“And so you’re going to let me go?”

Fantômas chuckled. “Oh, of course not. But I might be persuaded to let you live, provided you give me what I’m looking for. Where have you hidden Professor Harrington’s journal?”

Jack spit on the ground, which elicited a slight chuckle from Fantômas. “Never. And you ask me why, Fantômas? Because despite who I am, I still have something to prove to Ruth Harrington. Perhaps it is because, as you have observed, I am often taken for foolish, but Ruth has, on occasion…” Jack snapped his lips tight, unwilling to divulge anything further.

Fantômas rose from his seat and approached Jack. “Allow me to finish, Mr. Meredith. On occasion, Ruth Harrington’s eye has…wandered?”

Jack turned his face away from Fantômas and stared at the ground.

“Come now, Mr. Meredith. It certainly wandered toward me when she thought I was Emile Cortez. Surely it has wandered toward others. Like Detective Frederick Dickson perhaps?”

Jack’s head snapped up to gaze at Fantômas. His eyes narrowed and his lips tightened to a sneer. “I will never, ever give you what you want,” he said.

Fantômas sighed. “And I had such high hopes for you.” Turning his back on Jack Meredith, Fantômas walked to the doorway of the cell, opened it and called out. “All right, gentlemen. It’s time.”

From the doorway came two men–each of them dressed identically in gaudy circus garb. Their faces were bleached white, with hair to match. Their pink eyes stared out from their narrow eyelids. The man on the right held the other by the shoulder, guiding him forward. The man on the left was clearly blind and was carrying a small black case by its handle.

Jack sat bolt upright and a fresh wave of fear overcame him. “What...I mean…who are they?”

Fantômas raised his arm to introduce the two men with a flourish. “When I first arrived in Manhattan several years ago, my wanderings to took me to one of those delightful attractions along Bowery. Surely you know what I’m talking about, Mr. Meredith. It was one of those frightfully exotic collections of human oddities designed to make pennies off the poor unfortunates by charging admission to members of the shocked and appalled upper-class. May I present to you, Zor and Zam! Or perhaps it’s Zam and Zor. I can never remember. Needless to say, I was rapt with attention the moment their act began and it was worth killing a half-dozen people in order to obtain their release and become their custodian.”

Jack swallowed hard. “Their…act?”

“I’ve always had a thing for knives, Mr. Meredith.”

Zor and Zam stepped forward. Zor–the blind one–held up the case and withdrew three legs from the bottom, turning it into a tripod that rested on the floor of the cell. Zam reached forward, unlocked and opened the case. The small amount of light from the single overhead bulb was enough to illuminate the knives that sparkled from within.

Jack was on the edge of panic. “Knives?” he sputtered. “Knives?”

Fantômas smiled beneath his hood. “Indeed. I’d never seen a knife throwing act in which the thrower is completely blind.”

"What?" Jack shrieked. "Wait a minute…"

"Tell me the location of Professor Harrington's journal, Mr. Meredith."

"But…but…"

"Not quick enough." Fantômas darted across the room and grabbed Jack by the neck.

"Don't struggle, Mr. Meredith, or my eyes will be the last thing you ever see."

"Oh, God. What are you going to…"

Fantômas drove Jack backward and pressed him against a wall at the back of his cell. Holding Jack tightly by the neck with one hand, he pried Jack's left arm upward and secured it inside a cuff that was embedded in the ceiling. He did the same with his right arm, then let go of Jack's throat, knelt down and secured his feet to the bottom of the wall. He then turned toward Zor and Zam. "Proceed, gentlemen," Fantômas said, stepping away and moving behind them.

Zor lifted one of the knives from the case and held it aloft.

"This is a joke, isn't it?" A bead of sweat formed on Jack's brow and quickly made its way down his cheek. "A blind knife thrower?"

"A little to the left," Zam said.

Zor moved a little to the left.

"A hair more," Zam said.

Zor shifted again, ever so slightly.

"Throw," Zam said.

Zor tossed the knife forward and sent it spinning quickly through the air with an audible "whoosh." Jack felt the wind from the blade as it narrowly missed his right ear and stuck into the wood, a fraction of an inch from his face. "Jesus Christ!" Jack screamed.

"Tell me the location of Professor Harrington's journal," Fantômas said.

"You're insane!" Jack shrieked.

Zor drew another knife from the box and held it above his head.

"A shade to the right," Zam said.

"Tell me the location," Fantômas said.

"Jesus, Mary and Joseph!"

"Throw," Zam said.

The knife spun through the air and found its resting place on the other side of Jack's face. The edge of the blade scraped his cheek before embedding itself in the wood, and a trickle of blood ran down Jack's face, staining his collar. "Ow! Christ!"

"One last time, Mr. Meredith–where is Professor Harrington's journal?"

Tears began to flow down Jack's cheeks and he began gasping for breath. "Please," he cried. "I can't tell you. I can't…"

Fantômas turned toward the knife-throwers. "Aim for the heart," he said.

"Oh God, no. Please no."

Zor clutched the final knife in his fist and lifted it above his head.

"Right," Zam said.

"No, please," Jack begged.

"A little lower," Zam said.

"God help me."

"Now, to the left."

"I beg of you, don't do this!"

"Throw."

It is 9:05 a.m. the next morning, Dear Reader. We are inside the First National Bank of Manhattan. In five minutes, three people will have died.

Jack Meredith stepped into the lobby. A guard spotted him and snapped to attention. "Good morning, Mr. Meredith!" he said, a little too loudly. One of the tellers heard the greeting and looked up in time to see Jack walking toward her. She turned to another teller. "Quickly!" she said, "Tell Mr. Simmons that Jack Meredith is here!" The second teller ran to the back to relay the message.

"Good morning, Mr. Meredith!" The first teller beamed.

"Call me Jack," Jack said, flashing his pearly white teeth at the young woman.

The teller grinned and blushed. "Withdrawal or deposit?" she asked.

Jack leaned in and gazed at her over the counter. "I'm afraid it's a withdrawal. But perhaps some other time you can help me with a deposit."

The teller bit her bottom lip and blushed some more. Jack winked and turned away as the Bank President bolted toward him with his arms outstretched. "Well, well, well Jack Meredith! As I live and breathe! How lucky we are to see you twice in one week!"

"Morning, Simmons," Jack said, clasping Simmons' hands and shaking them vigorously. "Always a pleasure."

"What can I do for you?" Simmons asked.

"I'm afraid I need access to that safe deposit box you obtained for me a few days ago."

"Already, eh?" Simmons said, then leaned forward and lowered his voice. "Bet a little too steep at the track, I'll bet."

Jack laughed. "That's it exactly. Lost a little too much at the track."

"Well, what's the point of having a little money if you can't also have a little fun, right?"

"That's what I always say."

"Not a problem at all, Jack. Just follow me."

Simmons stepped behind the counter and Jack followed. In moments, the two of them were surrounded by safe deposit boxes. "You know," Simmons said, "every time I see you I can't help but think how much you resemble your father."

"Yes," Jack said. "You would know best."

"You bet I would!" said Simmons with a laugh. "My best friend, your father. Got me into the banking business as a young man and it has been very, very good to me."

"Indeed," Jack said.

Simmons spun the dials on a small safe, opened the door and retrieved a small key. "Here we are," he said. "Box number 34. Now before I give you the key, you probably expect me to go through with all that silly password business, don't you?"

Jack frowned. "I beg your pardon?"

Simmons laughed again. "Exactly! Really, Jack. You are too much! Going on about how I should wait for you to say the password, even if I was certain that it was you. All that talk about a master criminal and how we must take extreme precaution. You really are a caution, Jack. You know that, don't you?"

"Yes, well..."

Simmons continued chuckling. "So go ahead," he said. "Say the password and we can be done with this little charade. Say hello to that lovely fiancé of yours, will you?"

Fantômas reached into his coat pocket and drew out a small pistol with a silencer on the end.

"Jack?" Simmons said, the smile falling from his face. "What are you..."

Fantômas pulled the trigger and the gun went off with a quick whistle. The bullet struck Simmons in the forehead and his body went tumbling backwards against the wall. Fantômas leaned over the corpse and pried the safe-deposit box key out of its hand. He quickly found box number 34, inserted the key and lifted the lid. There, sitting alone inside the box, was Professor Harrington's journal.

Fantômas smiled beneath his Jack Meredith disguise.

"Mr. Simmons, are you OK? I thought I heard..." The teller arrived just in time to see Jack Meredith standing above the dead body of Mr. Simmons, whose face was covered in blood–his eyes dead and staring.

The teller screamed. Fantômas leapt toward her. "I'm sorry, darling," he said, grabbing her by the back of her head and pulling her face toward his, "but I really can't stay." He leaned in and pressed his lips to hers. She tried to scream, but the sound was stifled against Fantômas' cold face. He pulled away and stared into her eyes. "Something to remember me by," he said. "And don't worry–Jack Meredith never forgets a pretty face."

Fantômas threw the teller to the floor, stepped over the body of Mr. Simmons and made his way back to the lobby. No one in the front of the bank had heard the commotion. Nevertheless, Fantômas made his way quickly toward the front door.

"Good day, Mr. Meredith!" the bank guard said, tipping his hat.

"Good day, Wilson," Fantômas answered.

"It's Thompson."

"Whatever."

"*Stop him*!" The teller had made her way to the counter and screamed at the guard. Every head in the bank turned. "Jack Meredith killed Mr. Simmons! Stop him! *Murderer*!"

Fantômas grabbed the bank guard firmly by the shoulders and threw him to the ground. "Sorry, Wilson," he said. Then, with the journal firmly in hand, he bolted out the front door. From behind, he could hear more people shouting.

"Police! Call the police!"

Fantômas muttered under his breath, "Damn Meredith and his damned password…"

Fantômas glanced behind him in time to see Thompson, the bank guard, racing after him, gun in hand. "Stop!" Thompson yelled. "Freeze!" Thompson fired his gun but his shaking hands ensured that the bullet came nowhere near Fantômas.

"For God's sake, Wilson!" Fantômas shouted. "Put the toy away! You're going to hurt someone!"

Thompson began firing blindly into the air, causing passersby to begin screaming and dropping to the ground. "Stop! Murderer!" Thompson continued to run forward, his arms outstretched, panting. Fantômas ran faster, however, and soon put distance between himself and the sweaty, out-of-shape bank guard.

The people on the crowded streets of Manhattan continued to drop to the ground as Thompson charged forward with his gun raised and his finger pressed tightly on the trigger. Soon, he lost sight of Fantômas and stopped running.

He leaned forward with his hands on his knees, trying to catch his breath. People began to rise from the sidewalks, staring at him in fear. “Police business,” he said. “Move along, everyone.” He gestured with his gun, causing everyone to move out of the way more quickly than they would have otherwise. “Move along.”

Slowly, Thompson placed his gun back into its holster and continued to walk down the street, his eyes scanning the crowd for a sign of Fantômas. Suddenly, over the din of traffic and pedestrians, he heard a man’s voice. “Help!” the voice cried. “He’s got a gun!”

Thompson charged forward once again and continued to run until he heard the voice a second time. “Help me! Please.” It came from an alley two buildings down. Thompson drew his gun again and crept down the alley. He could hear the sounds of police cars, presumably headed toward the bank.

What a career move it would be to capture Jack Meredith. And they told him he’d never be a “real” policeman.

“Such a shame you had to follow.” The voice came from behind Thompson. He barely had time to react before a hand reached forward and pried his gun from him. “A shame for you, that is.” Thompson spun around and looked into Fantômas’ eyes. “Very fortunate for me, however.” Fantômas drew his gun, placed it firmly into Thompson’s stomach and pulled the trigger. The silencer kept the sound from traveling, and Thompson clutched onto Fantômas’ coat as he slid slowly to the ground.

Fantômas ran to the edge of the alley and peered out. The police were leaving the bank and dashing back to their cars. The teller was pointing down the street in the direction that Thompson had run.

He had mere seconds.

Police Sergeant Maxwell Toomey led the cars on their chase. He rolled down the window and listened for shouts. He stared ahead, looking for any sign of Thompson.

Then he saw him.

Thompson was standing at the entrance to an alley two blocks away. Toomey couldn't be sure it was Thompson, but the man matched the description given to him by the bank teller. Sergeant Toomey pulled the car over and opened the passenger door. Thompson was crouched forward, holding his mouth.

"Thompson?" Toomey asked.

Thompson nodded.

"Get in!"

Thompson leapt into Sergeant Toomey's patrol car and shut the door behind him. "Was it really him?" Toomey asked, "Was it really Jack Meredith?"

Thompson nodded.

"What's wrong?" Toomey asked. "Why can't you speak?"

Thompson motioned frantically for Toomey to continue driving. "Just go!" he shouted, then clasped his hand to his mouth in pain.

"Did he hit you?"

Thompson nodded. "Broke…jaw…" he stammered, then placed his hands to his face again.

"We'll get you to the hospital," Toomey said. "As soon as we find Meredith."

Thompson nodded. The car barreled forward until it came to Times Square, at the divide between 7th and 8th Avenues. "OK," Toomey said. "Which way do you think he went?"

Thompson tried to speak, but there was too much pain for him to be able to form words successfully. He held his hand up and mimed writing on a pad of paper–indicating to Toomey that he needed a pencil and paper to write on.

Toomey pulled a pencil from his shirt pocket and handed it to Thompson. "Now I know I have a pad of paper around here somewhere…"

Fantômas leaned forward and drove the pencil into the side of Sergeant Toomey's neck.

Toomey gasped in horror, then let go of the steering wheel and began clasping frantically at his throat. Fantômas grabbed hold of the steering wheel and navigated the patrol car up 8th Avenue. “Stop squirming!” he shouted. “You’re liable to cause an accident!”

From behind, police officers Delaney and Heaney slammed on their brakes as Toomey’s patrol car began swerving all over the road. “Christ almighty!” Delaney said. “What the hell is Toomey doing?”

Toomey’s patrol car suddenly stopped. The door opened on the driver’s side and Delaney and Heaney saw a body clad in blue fly out of the car and land on the pavement. “Did you see that?” Heaney asked. The door to Toomey’s car closed and the car itself took off again, driving at top speed down 8th Avenue.

Delaney and Heaney leapt from their car with guns drawn. “Oh my God,” Delaney said as he approached the body. “It’s Sergeant Toomey.”

“Is he…?” Heaney put his hand to his mouth, unable to continue.

“Yeah,” Delaney said. “He’s dead.”

Heaney looked down 8th Avenue and saw Toomey’s patrol car fade into the distance. “Then who’s driving his car?” he asked.

It is 9:15 a.m., three blocks away from the First National Bank of Manhattan. Three people are dead and the secret of the Lost City of Gold now belongs to Fantômas.

Chapter Nineteen: Dickson's Gambit

It is later, the same afternoon and we are in the apartment building occupied by Detective Frederick Dickson. Sergeant Corona is, once again, attempting to mount a flight of stairs without giving himself a stroke.

Corona paused in front of Dickson's apartment, mopping his forehead with his handkerchief. He waited several moments to catch his breath before rapping on the door. "Dickson?" he shouted, suddenly changing his light knock to a full-fisted pound, "Are you there?"

Dickson jolted awake. He was clothed in the same suit he had been wearing for almost 24 hours. There was spirit gum still clinging to his face where his false beard had been applied. Following his adventure in the tunnels of Manhattan, Dickson had spent the next several hours interviewing the Musketeers, asking them everything they knew about the secret passageways. When he finally arrived home, spent and exhausted, he fell into bed without removing a stitch of clothing. He might have slept through anyone else's knocking but he was accustomed to snapping to attention when he heard Corona's voice.

"I'm coming," Dickson said, his voice betraying the intense pounding in his head. "One moment, please."

Dickson crawled out of bed, pulled his suspenders back over his shoulders, and shuffled sleepily to the door. "What is it, Sergeant?" he said, once the door was open and Corona had successfully elbowed his way inside.

"You all right, Dickson?" Corona said. "You look like hell."

"Yes, thank you." Dickson said. "I mean… yes, I'm all right. A little tired."

"Well perhaps, Detective, you could refrain from spending your nights at jazz clubs or what have you, and focus more on ridding this city of filth. Fantômas is still out there, you know."

Dickson began to protest, then thought better of it. "My apologies, Sergeant," he said. "What can I do for you this morning? What time is it?"

"It's 10 a.m., Dickson!" Corona said, a little too loudly, "Business started just an hour ago at First National, yet that was still enough time for our friend Jack Meredith to kill the bank manager, a security guard and a police officer!"

Dickson could hardly believe his ears. "I'm sorry, Corona. What did you just–"

"You heard me right the first time, Detective. Your friend, Mr. Jack Meredith, waltzed into the First National Bank, went with the Bank Manager to open a safe deposit box, shot him in the forehead, then ran out the front door, shot the guard in the gut, commandeered a police car, stabbed the driver in the neck and left his body in the middle of the street!"

"Impossible."

"I don't want to believe it either, Detective, but it happened in broad daylight and there were a fistful of witnesses, including one poor teller who seems to have gone into shock." Corona dropped into a chair and began fanning himself with his handkerchief. "Do you have any water, Detective, or are all of your visitors forced to suffer from heat exhaustion?"

Still stunned by Corona's revelation, it took Dickson a moment to hear his question. "Huh? Oh…of course. I'm sorry." He made his way to the sink where he poured Corona a drink. "What did Meredith steal?"

"What did he what?"

"From the bank, Sergeant." He handed Corona the water and waited while he gulped it down, spilling much of it on his shirt front, then wiping his mouth with the back of his hand.

"There was no money missing," Corona said with a slight burp. "And witnesses say that Meredith wasn't carrying anything."

"It was Fantômas," Dickson said.

"Christ almighty, Dickson," Corona harrumphed. "I want to believe Meredith's innocent as much as you do but Simmons, the Bank Manager, had known Meredith since he was a child. Their families have been friends for generations. If it were someone in a disguise, Simmons would have noticed."

"Fantômas is a genius, Corona. Surely everything we've seen so far has convinced you of that."

"I'll admit it is a bit of a stretch to imagine Meredith killing three fully grown men inside of five minutes. He's a good man, but I once saw him burst into tears after tripping over a polo mallet."

"Think, Corona, think!" Dickson said, pulling up a chair until he and Corona were face to face. "He went with Simmons to open a safe deposit box. What would Meredith keep inside a safe deposit box?"

Corona sighed. "I don't know, Detective. His will? A collection of dirty pictures?"

"The journal, Corona. The journal with Professor Harrington's gold formula and the maps of the Lost City!"

"Of course!"

"Furthermore," Dickson continued, his voice growing in intensity. "If Fantômas was disguised as Meredith, that means he wasn't afraid that the real Meredith was suddenly going to appear."

"Fantômas has kidnapped Meredith!"

"Kidnapped, or…or worse."

"Good God, Detective! You don't think…" Corona leapt from his chair. "Let's get down to the station! I want the entire force out there, searching for Jack Meredith!"

Dickson stood up as well. "No!" he said. "Fantômas believes he's gotten away with it. Let him continue to do so."

"Really, Detective! Unless you have a better plan…"

"I do," Dickson said, his eyes generating a fierce intensity. "I do have a plan."

Dickson rushed to his dining room table and motioned for Corona to follow. He brushed away the plates littered with stale scraps of bread and began smoothing down a large, wrinkled piece of paper.

"What the Devil is that?" Corona asked. The paper was covered with large diagrams, hurriedly scratched out in dull pencil. Areas of the paper were circled or adorned with "x" marks. A series of crude arrows suggested a navigation route.

"It's a map," Dickson answered, "of a series of secret corridors that thread throughout midtown Manhattan, along the Bowery and through the Lower East Side."

Corona squinted and shook his head, unsure if he was hearing Dickson correctly. "Excuse me, Dickson," he said, with no small amount of suspicion in his voice. "Do you mean to tell me that there is a network of secret tunnels underneath the city?"

Dickson smiled, his lips stretched thin across his teeth and his eyes alight. "That's exactly what I mean," he said. "This is how the Fantômas gang is able to invade every bar and gambling joint in the city, then disappear without a trace."

"And where, exactly, did you get this map?"

Dickson's heart sank as he suddenly realized that to reveal his sources to Corona, he would have to reveal everything about James Dale and the Musketeers of Pig Alley. "Do you trust me?" he said, finally.

Corona looked at him askance. "I'm not sure," he said.

"I can't tell you where I got this map," Dickson said. "But the people who drew it for me are utterly honest. You have my word."

Corona uttered a deep sigh. "So you have a map," he said. "So what?"

"Take a look," Dickson said, grabbing a pencil and tracing a series of lines connecting the arrows one to another. "The tunnels form a network of paths but if you follow each path to its final destination, without taking any of the detours that lead above ground, you wind up…here." Dickson circled a large area on the map near a label that read "the Five Points." "Look familiar?" he asked.

Corona leaned forward to examine Dickson's chaotic scrawl. "Certainly," he said. "It's Our Lady of Perpetual Sorrow, the oldest parish on the East Side. Father Rose has been a beloved community icon for years. You're not suggesting..."

"I'm not suggesting anything," Dickson interrupted. "I'm merely following a line of inquiry to its logical conclusion. The tunnels used by the Fantômas gang all lead to the church."

"So," Corona expounded. "Fantômas may be using the church as his headquarters!"

"That's one possibility, yes."

Corona slammed his fist on the table. "By God!" he shouted, his corpulent frame twitching with nervous energy. "We've got him! Where's your telephone, Detective? I'll phone headquarters immediately. We'll raid the church tonight!"

"No," Dickson said.

"No?" Corona said, aghast. "Am I hearing you correctly, Dickson? You wish to pass up our first opportunity to round up the Fantômas gang once and for all?"

"It's too dangerous. If the church is really under Fantômas' control, it's replete with death traps, secret exits and who knows what else? Detonators? Incendiary devices? We could be leading every member of the New York Police Department to their deaths, not to mention Professor Harrington, Ruth and Jack Meredith."

Corona pinched the bridge of his nose with his fingers. "And your plan is..."

"Cut off the head and the rest of the dragon will follow."

"I don't follow you, Detective."

"We lure Fantômas away from the church. Separate him from his gang. Once he's captured, arresting everyone else will be easy."

"Perhaps you're forgetting the events of the past few weeks, Dickson, but we haven't had much success arresting Fantômas up 'til now."

"That's because," Dickson said, clapping his hands together in a burst of enthusiasm, "until now, Fantômas has called the shots. He has dictated the time and place of every confrontation. It's time to turn the tables on him–draw him out and lead him directly to us."

"I take it your plan includes a way to do this?"

"It does." Dickson darted to the other side of the room where he retrieved a copy of *The New York Times*. He thumbed through it until he located the society column, then handed it to Corona. "Here," he said. "Read."

Corona took the newspaper and began reading. "*The flowers of high society will be in full bloom tomorrow evening at the Long Island estate of Samuel Cobblepot, heir to the fortune originally owned by his grandfather, the now deceased theatrical impresario Oswald Cobblepot.* The Times *has learned that the Grand Duke of the Duchy of Deux-Ponts-Veldenz, along with his beautiful wife, Duchess Penelope, will be in attendance along with many other society luminaries.*"

Corona folded the paper and dropped it back onto the table. "Blah, blah, blah," Corona said. "What does this have to do with Fantômas?"

Dickson searched his pockets and retrieved another scrap of paper. "Call the *Times*," he said. "Make sure this notice is on the front page."

Corona took the paper and read it aloud. "*This reporter has learned that the Grand Duchess Penelope, who will be in attendance at the Long Island estate of Samuel Cobblepot this evening, will be showing off her new acquisition–the Caderousse Diamond*." Corona stared at Dickson. "I'm confused, Detective. Why, pray tell, is a Grand Duchess visiting Long Island?"

"She's originally from Brooklyn."

"And you expect this notice to draw out Fantômas?"

"Precisely."

"And the Grand Duchess really has this jewel in her possession?"

"She does. I will contact her this evening and convince her to wear it."

"Surely, Dickson, Fantômas has plenty of jewels and baubles already. What makes this one so significant?"

Dickson smiled again. "Trust me," he said.

Corona sighed and walked to the other side of the room. "I'm putting an awful lot of trust in you lately, Detective, and we still have very little to show for it."

"Don't you see, Corona?" Dickson said, following closely on Corona's heels. "We are playing to Fantômas' vanity. Once he reads this notice, he will become obsessed with obtaining the Caderousse Diamond. Once we have him out of his element, he'll be ours."

"How many officers do you need?" Corona asked.

"No officers," Dickson replied. "The last time we tried an ambush like that, it cost Officer Gregory his life. No. You and I will go it alone."

Corona blinked rapidly and Dickson could see, for the first time that morning, a slight twinge of fear. "Just you and I, Detective? Are you sure that's safe?"

Dickson shook his head. "It's not safe in the least, Corona. But if we wish to capture Fantômas we must put aside our own personal safety."

Corona stared deeply at Dickson, his loose jowls barely able to mask his anxiety. "All right," he said, snapping up the *Times* notice and placing it in his pocket. "I'll call for you tomorrow night."

Jack Meredith was still bound upright, his arms above his head and the rest of his body tied tightly to the knife-throwing board. The cold metal of a knife blade rested against his cheek, the sharp tip embedded in the wood a fraction of an inch from his head. Two hours had passed since he revealed the location of Professor Harrington's journal to Fantômas. He was pathetically tired and emotionally drained. The knives thrown by Zor and Zam surrounded his body, each of them coming perilously close to an artery or some other equally important body part. Despite his fatigue, however, Jack Meredith was unable to give into the peace of unconsciousness. No sooner would his eyes begin to close, then his mind would flood with images–not of Fantômas and his hideous, knife-wielding accomplices, but of Ruth and Frederick Dickson. There they were, locked in a passionate embrace, their lips touching. He buried his face in her neck and she clutched his hair and pitched her head backward, her eyes closed in ecstasy, her mouth open and waiting for another kiss…

The images tore at Jack's brain and ate away at his insides. Wretched detective! Curse him for being the messenger of these hideous thoughts! If only Jack were free, he would show Ruth how much more deserving of her love he was than that mumbling civil servant! No sooner would Jack Meredith shake his head and force his eyes open, then the pressure of sleep would begin its descent once more until his eyes faded and the images would appear again.

From the corridor outside, Jack heard footsteps accompanied by a cheerful whistle. Peering through the bars of his cell he observed the man as he passed alongside the prison.

It was a police officer.

"Don't get too excited, Mr. Meredith," Fantômas said. "It's just the uniform of a poor, unfortunate guard who got in between me and something I wished to have." Fantômas reached inside his jacket and withdrew Professor Harrington's journal. "Luckily, he didn't succeed. I want to thank you for your cooperation in this matter, Mr. Meredith. It was hard-won to be sure. In the future, however, I would encourage you to be more detailed in your information. Three men died this morning, including your father's colleague, the manager of the First National Bank of Manhattan. And all because you neglected to let me know there was a password. If you ever see your father again, please extend to him my condolences. It's a horrible thing to lose a friend."

Fantômas resumed whistling his tune as he made his way down the corridor. Jack Meredith dropped his head to his chest and tried to force the image of Ruth and Dickson from his mind.

Dr. Voitzel spied Fantômas as he left Meredith's cell and rushed to catch up with him. "Master!" he cried. "You've returned. I hope your efforts were successful."

Fantômas smiled. "Like shooting fish in a barrel, as they say in America. Honestly, I'm not even sure what that phrase means. But never mind that. I have a need for your talents, Doctor."

Dr. Voitzel could barely contain his excitement. "Anything!" he said, rubbing his hands together with delight. "How may I be of service?"

"I want you to assist me in my dealings with Miss Harrington and her father," Fantômas answered.

Dr. Voitzel suddenly appeared downcast and his excitement began to wane.

"Something wrong?" Fantômas asked.

"No, no," Voitzel answered. "My apologies, Master. It's just that I've been observing Mr. Meredith and I find him…intriguing."

"Hmmm. How so?"

"Well," Voitzel continued, adjusting his spectacles. "It's difficult to explain. Since the moment you left, he's been in a bit of a daze. He continues to curse Ruth Harrington's name and has been referring to her with all sorts of unpleasant words. Then he cries 'Wretched detective!' and begins…well…spitting."

"Spitting?" Fantômas asked.

"Yes, well…spitting and cursing. Most unpleasant."

Fantômas smiled. "Thank you, Doctor. You are correct. I find that most intriguing. Perhaps Mr. Meredith shows more promise that I originally thought. It bears investigation, in any case. Meanwhile, I have other prisoners to attend to. I will call on you in a few moments."

"Yes, Master," Dr. Voitzel said, and headed back to his laboratory.

Fantômas continued further on to the cell shared by Professor Harrington and Ruth. Both were still awake and chained to walls on opposite ends of the cell. Their hands were cuffed behind their backs. "Good morning, dear family!" Fantômas chimed.

Ruth Harrington raised her head and eyed Fantômas with contempt. She briefly considered shouting a curse at the villain, but caught the outrage before it left her lips. "I know," Fantômas continued. "It's awkward between us. Here we were on the verge of lifelong bliss and one of my former conquests suddenly appeared and made me look–I'm not ashamed to say it–extremely foolish."

It was all too much for Ruth, who snorted her derision but refused to give Fantômas the satisfaction of her voice.

"Don't get me wrong," Fantômas said. "I know it was no picnic for you, but imagine how I felt! Here I was, about to pledge myself to one woman until death do us part and suddenly I'm forced to confront one of my past sins. I'm not happy about it, believe me. Still, I'm also not happy with the way you maimed one of my gang members and tried to escape."

"What do you want?!" Professor Harrington demanded.

"Never fear, Professor Harrington," Fantômas answered, holding up the journal. "I'm very close to having absolutely everything that I want."

At the sight of the journal, Ruth and Professor Harrington looked at one another, then hung their heads in defeat.

"By the way," Fantômas continued. "I'm sorry that I can no longer give you the freedom that you once had inside your cell but I simply don't trust either of you anymore." He glared at Ruth and the bemused glimmer in his eyes turned to one of pure sadism. "It's a terrible thing to suddenly mistrust the woman you intend to marry. Wouldn't you agree?"

Ruth stared at Fantômas but didn't respond.

“Still,” Fantômas said, drawing the key to the cell from his pocket and undoing the lock. “Perhaps that trust can be mended.” Fantômas opened the door to the cell and stepped inside. “As you can see, Professor Harrington, I have finally obtained your journal thanks to the collaboration of Mr. Jack Meredith.”

On hearing Jack’s name, Ruth’s head shot up and she glared at Fantômas. “See what I mean?” Fantômas said, turning toward Ruth. “It’s a horrible thing not to be able to trust the ones you love.” He turned back toward Professor Harrington. “Despite this acquisition, I am in further need of your assistance. The journal appears to be written in some kind of cipher and I imagine that you’re the only one who can translate it for me.”

“Not even to save your daughter’s innocence?”

Professor Harrington shot Fantômas a look of defiance. “I won’t do it,” he said.

“Really?” Fantômas replied. “Not even to save your daughter’s innocence?”

"What do you mean?"

"I'm giving you a choice, Professor Harrington. I will cease my pursuit of your hardly-virginal daughter in exchange for the information to decipher this journal."

"Don't do it, Dad!" Ruth could hold back her voice no longer. "It's not worth it. The formula will give him unlimited power. He'll be able to shatter the finances of every state in the country. He'll be unstoppable."

Fantômas didn't look at Ruth but kept his gaze steady on Professor Harrington. "All those things your daughter is saying are true. Once I have the formula, I will not stop until I am the wealthiest, most powerful man in the country. On the other hand," Fantômas leaned in until Professor Harrington could feel his hot breath, "if you do not cooperate, I will spend the rest of my life–day and night–corrupting and fouling your precious daughter until every last bit of her talent and reason have vanished beneath my will. Don't be a fool, Professor Harrington. A short while ago, I presented a similar choice to Detective Dickson. He also made what he thought was the noblest decision. You can see for yourself the results. To be honest, neither of you would be here now if it weren't for him. Don't make the same mistake, Professor Harrington."

Professor Harrington glanced across the cell at his daughter. "I'll do it," he said, his voice barely a whisper. "I'll do whatever you want."

"Splendid!" Fantômas cheered. "You've made me a very happy, very powerful man, Professor Harrington!" He turned to Ruth and the look on his face altered from one of joy to regret. "Oh, my dear," he said. "It would have been fun. Never fear. You still have your looks. I'm sure you'll find someone new in due course."

Fantômas drew a small syringe and a vial from his coat. "And now," he said, opening the vial and filling the syringe with a thick, bluish liquid. "In case you get any ill-advised ideas, like giving me an incorrect cipher or meddling with my plans in some other unforeseen way..." He plunged the syringe deep into Professor Harrington's shoulder and pushed the plunger until the blue liquid began to course through the Professor's veins. "Just something to relax you and prevent you from attempting to lie. Save yourself the struggle, Professor Harrington. Many people have attempted to hide secrets from me while under the influence of this drug and all they did was delay the inevitable." He placed the top back on the vial, then withdrew from the cell, locking the door behind him. "It will take effect in about ten minutes. Then, my colleague will pay you a visit and you will answer every question he asks. His name is Dr. Hans Voitzel. I'm sure you'll get along well. You have much in common. You're both geniuses." Fantômas continued down the corridor and soon Ruth could no longer hear his footfalls.

"Dad!" Ruth said, once she was sure Fantômas could no longer hear her.

"I'm sorry," Professor Harrington interrupted. "But I couldn't let him hurt you."

"No, dad," Ruth said. "We still have a chance to fix this."

"Fix what? What are you talking about?"

"I'm almost free of my handcuffs."

"What?" Professor Harrington was aghast. "But…how?"

"The bouquet of roses…from the wedding…Fantômas had them strapped to my hands."

"Yes, but…"

"I jammed one of the thorns as deep into my thumb as I could. About ten minutes ago, I was able to pull it free. From the moment Fantômas began talking, I've been using it to unlock these cuffs."

Professor Harrington shook his head in amazement. "Wait a minute," he said. "You're telling me that you're picking the lock of your handcuffs with a rose thorn?"

"I removed two infected back teeth from a hungry crocodile once. Picking a lock with a thorn should be no problem."

It took all of Ruth Harrington's will to focus on the task at hand. Professor Harrington stared at his daughter, still clad in the stained white wedding dress as beads of sweat formed on her forehead and fell into her eyes.

Finally…

“Got it!” Ruth shouted, then ran toward her father.

“This Dr. Voitzel will be here any second,” Professor Harrington protested, “there’s no way to escape.”

“I’m not trying to escape,” Ruth said. “Not yet.” Ruth grabbed her father’s forearm and tore away the sleeve. She found the tiny hole from the syringe, placed her lips over it, and began to suck out Fantômas’ serum, bit by bit, catching the drops between her teeth and spitting them on the ground.

Professor Harrington was wincing in pain. “This will never work,” he said.

“Are you forgetting about the time I saved our entire expedition party from snake bite?” Ruth asked.

“Just hurry,” Professor Harrington said. “For God’s sake, hurry!”

Chapter 20: At Home with Fantômas

We are fairly certain that you, Dear Reader, are currently in possession of a battery of questions, many of which pertain to Fantômas, Detective Dickson, Ruth Harrington, Jack Meredith and their various schemes, cross-purposes and unusual methods. For instance–how is it possible that Ruth Harrington can pick a lock with a rose thorn? How does one craft an automobile that can so easily convert into a submersible? And most of all–what, exactly, does a terrifying figure like Fantômas do to relax? In other words, how does the Lord of Terror, after of evening of theft and murder, spend his mornings?

It is the morning of the following day and we are in Fantômas' chambers. Although he has risen from his bed and is dressed in a long, elegant bathrobe sans mask, we will spare the reader a detailed description of his actual face. It would serve no purpose other than to shock the reader with its familiarity while at the same time triggering gasps of doubt and disbelief. While the revelation would be of historical interest, it has no significant bearing on the story at hand.

So, after Fantômas prepares his tea and butters his toast, he sits down at his dining table, which is adjacent to the large cage that once held the unfortunate Father Rose, God rest his soul, and peruses the headlines of *The New York Times*. Since the beginning of the recent crime wave, he has been delighted to see his name plastered on the front page in large bold type, followed by details of the Fantômas Gang's latest atrocities and the failed attempts by the heroic Detective Frederick Dickson to capture the fiendish menace to society.

This morning, however, Fantômas is dismayed by the lack of gruesomeness in the *Times*' headlines. Moreover, he is disappointed that his uninterrupted streak of daily press has been curtailed by something that would be better suited for the society column.

Just what the Devil is going on?

Fantômas skimmed the article quickly, searching for some reason that might aid him in understanding why an insipid society party might be more newsworthy than his most recent travesty. At the very least, he expected a healthy dose of speculation as to his true identity and when he might strike next. He knew that New York wasn't quite the same as Paris, but surely the Big Apple valued its blood and gore as much as the City of Lights.

Then, his eyes ran across an item of interest.

It seemed there was a duchess. And this Duchess owned a particularly valuable jewel.

The Caderousse Diamond.

"Hmm…"

Fantômas strode across the room and spoke into the voice tube embedded in the wall. "Torch?" he said.

"Yeah, boss?" The Torch's voice traveled down the tube.

"I want to see everyone in the church in exactly one hour."

The Torch paused just long enough for Fantômas to note a hint of trepidation. "Is there something wrong, Mr. Torch?"

The Torch cleared his throat. "No, boss," he said. "One hour."

An hour later, Fantômas, clad in his black suit and face mask, strode into the church. He wasn't used to appearing above ground in this house of God without his Father Rose disguise but there were no common parishioners here–only members of the Fantômas gang. The shades were drawn and the doors locked.

Only after Fantômas took a seat at the foot of the altar did he notice who was seated in front of him. Scattered throughout the two dozen pews were the Torch, Dr. Voitzel, Zor and Zam…

…and that was all.

"Mr. Torch?" Fantômas cocked his head at the nervous man sitting three pews away.

"Yeah, boss?" the Torch said, clearing his throat.

"I thought I instructed you to call in everyone."

"You did."

"Then where the Devil are they?"

Dr. Voitzel chimed in. "They are not here, Herr Fantômas."

Fantômas turned his head sharply toward the scientist. "Yes, Doctor," he snapped. "I can see that. And where, pray tell, are they?"

The Torch stepped forward, rubbing his sweaty palms against his shirt front. "The thing is, boss… we don't know."

Fantômas stood up slowly–a little too slowly for the Torch's comfort. "You don't know where they are?" he asked with a whisper.

"It's like this," the Torch continued. "It's the Council of Ten. You know they've been after you…"

"I am aware of that," Fantômas answered. "And thus far, they've been unsuccessful."

Voitzel walked forward. "They have not found you, Herr Fantômas, but they have found…everyone else."

Fantômas stared at Voitzel and the Torch, attempting to remain calm. "When you say 'everyone else,' you mean–"

"Everyone," the Torch answered. "Their rooms are completely empty. They picked up whatever they could carry and just left. Word on the street is that the Councilmen were going door to door, trying to force them into telling them where you were."

"While I'm grateful for their silence," Fantômas said, "do they not understand that being a part of my network of crime demands complete and utter allegiance?"

"Yes, Herr Fantômas!" Voitzel said. "They understand that. It's just…"

Fantômas stepped quickly in Voitzel's direction. "Just…what?"

The Torch answered. "It's just that they're more afraid of the Councilmen than they are of you."

The Torch and Voitzel both tried to imagine the rage that was contorting Fantômas' face and both silently thanked the Heavens that it was covered in thick, black cloth. "You mean to tell me," Fantômas said, his voice an eerie calm, "that my criminal empire has been reduced to…the five of us?"

Neither man spoke. They didn't have to.

"Well," said Fantômas. "No matter. I can obtain the Caderousse Ruby on my own. The fact that it's obviously a trap, designed by Detective Dickson and Sergeant Corona, matters not in the slightest. Besides, I still have Professor Harrington's journal. Were you able to coax the cipher from him, Voitzel?"

Voitzel walked forward, drawing a notebook from the pocket of his lab coat. "I interrogated Harrington for over an hour," he said. "He appeared to be heavily under the influence of the drugs."

"Good!" said Fantômas, rubbing his hands together. "And what did you come up with?"

"Well," said Voitzel, adjusting his glasses nervously. "I applied the cipher to the first few pages of the formula…"

"Splendid!" Fantômas cheered, raising his fist in the air. "All is revealed!"

"Well," Voitzel said. "Not…exactly."

"What do you mean, Voitzel?" Fantômas said. "Read me the formula."

Voitzel instinctively stepped backward. "I'm not certain that's such a good idea, Herr Fantômas."

Fantômas' lips grew tight and he growled at Voitzel. "Read it," he said.

Voitzel's quivering hands opened the notebook. He cleared his throat, adjusted his glasses, and read. "Fantômas is a pathetic man. Barely worth his salt, when you get right down to it. In fact, I'd rather drink year-old beer than give him the time of day. He's a poor excuse for a criminal and an even worse dresser…"

"That's enough." Fantômas said.

"It goes on for five more pages."

"I said, that's enough."

By the time Fantômas returned to his quarters, he was furious. He hardly noticed Boris "The Prince," still disguised as Brian Shea, seated in the corner, hugging his knees to his chest.

"Idiots!" Fantômas shouted, pulling wine bottles off the rack and shattering them against the wall. "Fools!" he screamed again, driving his shoulder into his bookshelves, sending them toppling one over another until hundreds of dusty volumes were scattered on the ground. He stood over the books, breathing heavily, then reached down and picked up a copy of *Struggling Upward* by Horatio Alger. "All I've done–the years of hard work–but at the first sign of difficulty, I am suddenly surrounded by cowards."

Fantômas remembered that Boris was seated in a huddle behind him. "Boris," he said, "why are you here?"

Boris lifted his head and gazed at Fantômas. "What?" he asked.

"I asked you a question, you idiot. I said, 'why are you here?' "

Boris' voice quivered with despair. "Sally Shea," he began. "She…"

Fantômas interrupted. "Ah, yes," he said, understanding. "You too have been rejected."

"Yes," Boris said.

"You tried your best. Gave everything you had, within reason, and applied force when necessary?"

"Yes."

"And still, she rejects you."

"She does."

Fantômas sighed deeply, then crouched down and began methodically stacking the overturned books. "Our problem, Boris," he began, "is that we depend far too much on other people." He picked up the Alger book again and began absent-mindedly thumbing through it. "It seemed so much easier when I first came to this country, so long ago, and I was all alone. When I was known as Mr. Melvil... If only I could…"

An idea flitted through Fantômas' thoughts and he snapped the book shut with a loud clap. "Yes," he said, more to himself than Boris. "Of course! I can begin again. Rebuild everything from the ground up. All I need is a clean slate. Sometimes, in order to have everything you want, it is necessary to give up everything you already have." Fantômas turned to Boris, who was staring at him quizzically. Fantômas smiled beneath his mask. "Tell me, Boris," he said. "If you could choose one person to be, out of all the people in the world, who would you choose?"

Boris answered.

Fantômas smiled.

Fantômas

We are in Detective Dickson's apartment. It is four hours before the gathering at the Cobblepot estate is due to begin but Dickson hasn't slept. He sits in his dining room chair, hunched over notebooks full of scribbled notes. His clothes are unkempt, as is his face and beard. His eyes are puffy and red. The unpleasant scent wafting through the room is, indeed, coming from him.

The previous evening found Dickson pacing the floor, counting down the hours until the Cobblepot affair when he knew he would be coming face to face with Fantômas. Upon reading the society notice in *The New York Times*, however, he was suddenly hit with a nagging feeling of unease. It lingered in the back of his mind, unable to come forth in a way that provided words to his confusion but nevertheless, the feeling made its presence known for hours.

Something was wrong. Dickson had missed something–some crucial fact or point of information. He had overlooked or forgotten something important.

"*Trust your instincts*," Cousin Harry had said, and Dickson had done so. Thus far, his instincts had allowed him to track Fantômas, but Fantômas had always gained the upper hand. Still, Dickson had forged ahead, never laying the facts out before him–never taking every incident, every observation, into account.

Never connecting the dots.

At 7 a.m., after tossing and turning all night long, he removed his notebook from his dresser, sat down at the table, and began to write. He began with the abduction of Professor Harrington, then pressed forward–through the appearance of the Council of Ten, the Torch's double-cross, the kidnapping of Ruth Harrington, the Musketeers of Pig Alley and the denizens of the underground tunnels. It was all connected, but not everything pointed to Fantômas.

He made lists of events, put them in columns and drew lines between them. Some lines linked events from both columns but other lines stopped cold. He stared at the notebook for hours, paced his room, then continued with his scribblings until the events finally made themselves clear.

He cursed himself for not having seen it before. If he had only made the discovery one day earlier…

But there was no time to curse himself. The Cobblepot affair began in four hours and unless he was sorely mistaken, the phone call he was about to make would tell him that he was about to attend the party, and face Fantômas, completely alone.

He picked up the phone, dialed and told the operator to connect him with the New York Police Department.

"NYPD," the voice on the other end answered.

"It's Detective Dickson," Dickson said. "Put me through to Sergeant Corona."

"Dickson!" the voice replied with no small amount of alarm. "We were just about to call you. Corona's not here."

"Not there?" Dickson asked, even though his worst suspicions were being confirmed.

"We tried to get him on the horn this morning but there was no answer. Some of the boys went to his flat. He didn't answer, so they kicked the door in. The place was a mess–drawers opened and thrown around, the clothes from his closet tossed everywhere… it looks like there was a fight. We think Corona's been kidnapped."

Dickson hung up the phone without saying goodbye. He stared out the window of his apartment, watching as the Sun began to descend. Then, he walked into his bathroom and began to prepare for the party.

We are back on the Lower East Side, watching the frightened residents with their collars pulled up around their faces try desperately to make their way back to the cellar of the Black Friar before nightfall.

The first flyer was seen that afternoon, attached to a light pole on Mulberry Street. One man read it silently to himself, straining to remember the meaning of each English word. He told two of his friends of the flyer's contents, but they were already in possession of several flyers themselves. The three men walked down Houston where more flyers had been attached to the boarded-up windows of abandoned buildings and reams more seemed to be blowing across the streets, forcing themselves into the faces of passersby. Groups of women in the Five Points shared copies with one another, reading them aloud and quietly shedding tears of hope. In a matter of hours, dozens upon dozens of flyers had found their way into the Black Friar's cellar that was serving as the secret hostel for the fearful men and women hiding from the Council of Ten.

Standing outside the building that housed the hidden sanctuary, the Woman in Black read a flyer to herself and knew instantly what it portended. She had been wandering the streets for hours, trying to get the image of poor Sally Shea out of her mind. She had seen the man inside Sally Shea's cell, knew that he was a pawn of Fantômas, and saw within Sally Shea's eyes echoes of her own suffering. The Woman in Black had been seduced by Fantômas' evil and had fallen deeply, profoundly in love with him. There was no hope of redemption for her. But poor Sally Shea could still be saved, if only the Woman in Black would dare to betray the man she loved in order to save an innocent soul.

The Woman in Black hid in an alley as the shadows began to fall. As the streets began to grow more and more deserted, she followed the people holding flyers until they led her to the ground floor window that led into the abandoned cellar. Making herself part of the crowd, all of whom hid their faces as they glanced furtively around them, she crawled through the window and saw the masses of people crowded into their corners. She heard the babies squealing and held her nose against the scent of unwashed bodies. She walked through the room with barely anyone taking notice of the black clad woman striding through their midst.

At the back of the cellar, the Woman in Black spied her quarry. Brian Shea was hunched in a corner, reading one of the flyers. She approached him quickly.

"Brian Shea," she said.

Shea looked up, recognized her and clutched her by the arm.

"Do you remember me?" the Woman in Black said.

"Remember you? My God," Shea answered. "I've been waiting for you. Is it time?"

"It is time," the Woman in Black answered. "I have seen your wife."

"Sally!" Brian said with a choked whisper. "Is she…"

"She is safe. But if that paper in your hand is to be believed, she may not be safe much longer."

Brian looked ahead to see groups of people, flyers clutched tightly in their hands, making their way through the window to the outside. "They're leaving," he said.

"Then we have less time than I thought. Come," the Woman in Black said, taking Brian Shea by the hands and lifting him to his feet. "We must work quickly."

Snapper was helping the tiny Rebecca Clausen adjust her makeshift bed when he looked up and noticed the Woman in Black leading Brian Shea from the cellar. He watched them leave, then turned around in time to see the Clausens pick up their daughter and carry her toward the window. It was then that he noticed the mass exodus of the crowd.

"Muggs! Glimpy!" Snapper yelled across the vast expanse of the room as the inhabitants were quickly abandoning their belongings to head outside. Muggs and Glimpy ran to Snapper's side. "What the heck's going on?" Snapper asked.

"I dunno," Glimpy said. "It's a stumper. Everything was quiet, then there was some hubbub and everyone got up and started moving."

"Maybe it has something to do with this," Muggs said, handing Snapper one of the mysterious flyers.

Snapper snatched the flyer from Muggs' hand and read the contents. "Oh God," he said. "We gotta get this to Detective Dickson right away."

Geoffrey the Slasher is standing among the broken tables, smashed counters and caved-in walls that once made up the *Hog's Head*. Twenty-four hours earlier, he had been enjoying good business–making a poor, but adequate, living. He kept his head down, made friends with the right people and, for the most part, kept his nose clean. Then the Councilmen and that James Dale character–the so-called Saint of 14th Street–started a skirmish that brought his business crashing down around his ears at the hands of dozens of angry, drunken men.

Yesterday he had a life. Today he had nothing.

Geoffrey brought the pint glass to his lips and began drinking the last of the whiskey, salvaged from one of the only barrels that had survived the previous night's brawl. He threw his head back and didn't come up for air until he could see the bottom of the glass. The alcohol made his head swim and he braced himself on the only intact chair to keep from falling over.

He looked down at his feet, and through his blurred vision spied a large, brown object. On closer inspection, he could see the whiskers still attached to the chin and snout. A waft of foul-smelling air drifted upward, burning his nostrils with the stale stench of rotting pork. Geoffrey carefully lowered himself to the ground and stared intently at the severed pig head.

"Well, old friend," he slurred. "Here we are. Just you and me, I guess. Feh! I prefer it that way! People can be so... disappointing. But you've never let me down. Always there when I needed you. Yes sir."

Unlike a lot of his friends, Geoffrey was born right here on the Lower East Side. His father owned a dry-cleaning business on the Bowery and his mother sewed lace onto tablecloths that were sold in "some of those big stores uptown." Once when he was a child, during one of his family's rare visits to Midtown, his mother had taken him to a shop window where a dining room table and four chairs were on display. She pointed to the tablecloth and told her son with pride that it was her hands that stitched the lace.

Unfortunately, Geoffrey's mother didn't live much longer. Although Geoffrey's father made a decent living, he enjoyed spending it on dice games and booze. One night, during a heated argument with his mother over money, Geoffrey's father wrapped his fingers around his wife's throat and began to squeeze. Geoffrey was afraid but he knew his father would stop just in time, break into tears and beg his wife for forgiveness. This was, after all, what had happened so many times in the past.

This time, however, his father grabbed a razor from his shaving table and drew the blade across his wife's delicate white neck. The lifeless body of Geoffrey's mother slid from her husband's grasp and sank to the floor. Geoffrey's father, sickened by his drunken act of violence, turn the blade on himself and gazed at his son as he sliced open his jugular, sending torrents of blood across his shirt front until the light faded from his eyes and he fell sideways onto the floor in a slump.

Thereafter, Geoffrey was raised by a distant cousin who let him work in his butcher shop. He developed a reputation, not just for his work ethic, but for the speed with which he was able to slaughter the livestock, easily doubling the work output of older, stronger men with twice as many years' worth of experience.

Geoffrey was a hard worker. He was well-liked. He saved his pennies and eventually bought the building that he transformed into the Hog's Head.

But that was yesterday. Today, he was a broken man.

"So this is it, eh?" Geoffrey asked the pig head. "This is what it's come to."

The pig head remained silent.

"What's the matter?" Geoffrey asked. "Ain't you got nothin' to say?" He slapped the pig lightly on the snout. "Nah," he continued. "You're just gonna sit there and keep rottin' away, like the rest of us. Just sit here and rot." Geoffrey once more clutched the back of the chair and drew himself upward. "Well, not me!" he said, a little more loudly than he had intended. "I ain't gonna rot! You hear me?"

He stumbled over to the pile of splintered wood that used to be the bar counter. "Now," he mumbled to himself. "Let's see what we've got here." He tore through the wood, tossing aside plank after plank, until he found the object he was looking for. "Aha!" he cried aloud. He picked up the antiquated, rusty razor, covered in sawdust and grit, and held it aloft. "You had the right idea, Dad." He said. "Both you and Mom are far better off where you are."

Sitting among the broken wood that was once his life, Geoffrey the Slasher placed the blade to his throat.

"Now, now, friend. Is that any way to behave?"

The voice came from the doorway.

"Who's there?" Geoffrey called, squinting through the darkness. He could barely make out the figure of a stranger, clad entirely in black.

"Put the blade down, Geoffrey. A chapter of your life has come to a close, it's true. But a new chapter, a new glorious chapter, is about to begin."

Geoffrey removed the blade from his neck. The stranger drew closer to Geoffrey and gently pried the razor from his hand. "Who are you?" Geoffrey asked.

The stranger smiled. "My name," he said, "is Fantômas. And I am in need of your talents."

Chapter 21:
The Affable Members of the Long Island Chapter of the Saint James Society

Among the residents of Long Island, the Saint James Society was the *crème de la crème* of New York's elite. Young men applied for membership years before being accepted and even New York's favorite sons often found themselves excluded for the most unusual reasons. Jack Meredith, for instance, applied for membership seven times before he was accepted into the inner circle. Unfortunately, his membership lasted a scant three months before Oxford beat Cambridge in a rowing competition, which angered the Long Island chapter president (a Cambridge alumnus) so greatly that he subsequently saw to it that all Oxford alums had their memberships revoked. No matter. The Saint James Society members went about their business completely Oxfordless and no damage was done to their reputation.

The young, influential Saint James men met weekly at their Long Island headquarters where they smoked the finest tobacco, drank the most expensive wine, discussed current events and played epic games of chess. Then, every Friday evening after midnight, they traveled en masse to the Bowery where they slept with prostitutes.

It was on one of these late night sojourns that longtime Saint James member Samuel Cobblepot invited his new acquaintance, the Grand Duke of Deux-Ponts-Veldenz, to join him and the other members in their downtown debauchery. The Grand Duke was only too delighted to oblige, having spent several months away from his wife who was tending to the home fires in Europe.

Less than an hour after arriving at the most profane–and therefore most exotic–flophouse on the Lower East Side, the Grand Duke found himself enchanted with a young showgirl from the Bronx by the name of Penelope. Within four hours, the Duke had invited Penelope to be his Duchess.

Not officially, of course. The Duke, after all, had no desire to face the wrath of his wife back home. Instead, he rented a room for Penelope on Broadway (all the better for her burgeoning theatrical career) and visited her once a year when business brought him back to Manhattan. Often, the Grand Duke and Duchess Penelope stayed with Samuel Cobblepot at his home in Long Island. On these occasions, the Duke showered his Duchess with the finest clothes and most expensive jewels. It was a masquerade that Penelope was only too happy to indulge.

Tonight we are at the private residence of Samuel Cobblepot. Cobblepot's wife passed away several months ago, leaving Samuel to care for his 15-year-old son, Oswald, a rotund child with the manners of serpent and the gait of a malformed penguin. Detective Dickson has just pulled his car into the circular driveway. Since his realization that he would be facing Fantômas alone this evening, Dickson has been attempting, without much success, to keep his hands from shaking and his heart from palpitating. At the very least, he is gratified to know that due to the size and prestige of tonight's gathering, he will be able to mill about the estate completely unnoticed.

What a surprise it is when he steps into Samuel Cobblepot's foyer only to be greeted with a round of applause.

"Here he is!" Samuel Cobblepot exclaimed, clapping his oversized palms on Dickson's shoulders. "This is the man I was telling you about! The man who daily braves the evils of New York's criminal classes in search of the elusive Fantômas!"

Dickson silently cursed *The New York Times*.

Cobblepot put his arm around Dickson and led him into the parlor. "We've all read about your exploits, of course," he said.

“If it’s all the same to you,” Dickson said tentatively, “I’d prefer to keep a low profile this evening. As I’m sure you’re aware, I have reason to believe that Fantômas…”

“Is this the man?” A jovial man nursing an expensive cigar joined the conversation, cutting Dickson off in mid-sentence. He immediately grabbed Dickson’s hand and began pumping it wildly. “How great it is to meet you!” he said. “The name is Sedgwick. Edward Sedgwick. I write for Hollywood. You know…motion pictures?”

Dickson smiled. “I’m afraid I don’t get out much,” he said. “I’ve never actually seen…”

“Never seen a motion picture?” Sedgwick exclaimed.

“Try to relax, old man,” Cobblepot intervened. “Not everyone has the luxury of time that would allow for taking in a moving picture. Not when there are so many other things to do in New York. I’m sure you’re a theater-goer. Are you, Detective?”

“Well…uh…” Dickson stammered. “Again, it’s been a while since I had the time to do anything like that. I really should, though…”

“Indeed you should!” Cobblepot said. “A man can’t spend every day of his life ferreting out master criminals.”

“Which brings me to my proposition!” Sedgwick said. “If you don’t mind, Cobblepot, I’d like to speak to Dickson confidentially for a moment.”

“Not at all,” Cobblepot said with a laugh. “I’ll see you later in the evening, Dickson.”

“Sir,” Dickson said, calling after Cobblepot as he walked away. “I think you don’t quite understand the seriousness of…”

“Cigar?” Sedgwick asked.

“No, thank you,” Dickson answered.

“Listen,” Sedgwick said, “I’m only going to take a moment of your time. Obviously, I’ve been reading about your exploits for weeks now and it has occurred to me that your story might make a swell chapterplay.”

“Chapter…what?”

"Aw hell, Dickson. You know what I mean. There's a main feature, see? But before the main feature there's a chapter from a chapterplay. It lasts about 20 minutes and it always ends with you driving off the edge of a cliff or about to get stabbed or something. Gets the audiences to come back to the theatre a week later so they can see what happens."

"And you want to make a chapterplay about…me?"

"About you," Sedgwick leaned in conspiratorially, "and Fantômas."

"Oh…" Dickson said. "I don't think…"

"Look," Sedgwick said. "It doesn't have to be exactly what happened. We bend it a little, twist the truth a bit. Make it a little less violent so it's easier to swallow. Before you say yes or no, there's someone I want you to meet." Sedgwick put his thumb and forefinger between his lips and sent a shrill whistle across the parlor. "Hey!" he shouted, "Roseman! Get over here! I got someone I want you to meet!"

A dashing man with dark, slicked-back hair dressed in an immaculately pressed tuxedo walked across the room to where Dickson and Sedgwick were standing. "How are you, Sedgwick?" Roseman said.

"Just fine, Roseman, just fine. Remember that chapterplay idea I was telling you about?"

"Sure I do," Roseman answered. "The Fantômas thing."

Sedgwick clapped Dickson on the back. "Detective Dickson here is gonna tell us everything he knows about the guy."

"Gee," Roseman smiled. "That's swell. You've actually met this Fantômas?"

"Uh…yes," Dickson stammered. "A number of times, and I should tell you…he's no joke. In fact, this very evening I have reason to suspect…"

Sedgwick and Roseman continued to talk as Dickson glanced at a large grandfather clock against the wall. Fantômas had entered through such a clock in Professor Harrington's living room. Could he do the same here? Had he burrowed tunnels beneath the foundation of this house? Were all the doors and windows secured?

"Listen, Dickson," Sedgwick continued. "I know you don't get out to the pictures much but this guy here has been in some of the most exciting stuff I've ever seen."

Roseman blushed. "Oh, go on…"

"No, I mean it! Roseman, what was that picture you did where you played the Russian prince?"

Roseman laughed. "It was called *The Tiger Woman*," he said.

"Scary stuff!" Sedgwick chortled. "This guy," he said, turning the conversation back to Dickson, "would make the best Fantômas you can imagine. Mark my words, someday they're gonna call Ed Roseman the 'Man of a Thousand Faces!' "

"Gentlemen!" Dickson shouted, a little too loudly. "I'm terribly sorry, but I'm here on business, not pleasure. However, I'd be more than happy to talk to you on Monday if you want to come by the station."

"That's great!" Sedgwick said. "Roseman and I will drop by around five and we'll talk."

"Splendid," Dickson answered, pulling himself away from the men. "See you then."

Dickson made his way across the foyer, eyeing the doors, windows and any large piece of furniture that might conceal a secret entrance. He stared up at the skylight, thankful that there was a full Moon rising. If the chase for Fantômas led him outdoors, he would at least be able to see where he was going.

More guests continued to arrive until Dickson felt he was swimming through an ocean of cocktail dresses and cummerbunds. The scent of clove cigarettes filled the air until Dickson found himself squinting through his tears to examine separations in the wallpaper. He paid particular attention to the faces of the servants, searching in vain for the telltale line of Fantômas' jaw. His investigation had progressed no more than a couple of minutes when a voice called his name.

"Frederick Dickson."

Frustrated at the interruption, Dickson turned around. "I beg your pardon," he said. "I'm sure it's very exciting to meet someone that's been in *The New York Times* repeatedly and, yes, I have been searching for the master criminal known as Fantômas. But I am here to see to the security of the guests and I really can't afford to banter."

The man raised one eyebrow and extended his right hand. "Charles West," he said.

Dickson shook the man's hand. "Do I know you?"

The man shot Dickson a wry smile. "We met at a couple of shareholder meetings when you took over your father's business."

"Yes," Dickson said. "Yes. I remember you."

West opened his eyes wide in mock surprise. "Oh you do, do you? Do you remember all the other shareholders or just me?"

"I don't… is there something I can do for you, Mr. West?"

West drew a cigarette case from his jacket. "Smoke?" he offered.

"No thank you."

"Your father was a genius," West said, pulling a cigarette from the case and inserting it between his lips. "An industrial visionary. I became a wealthy man when I invested in his properties."

Dickson frowned, unsure of where the discussion was headed. "Well, I'm…glad to hear that," he said.

West looked bemused. "Are you?" he asked. "You know when your father passed away, I thought–we all thought–that his leaving the business in your charge made perfect sense. Surely, the Dickson business acumen runs in the family, we thought. Even when profits began to plummet and other shareholders began to sell, I held on tightly. After all, I had invested a considerable sum in Dickson Amalgamated and I wasn't about to give up on it so easily. You see, I had faith in the business."

"Mr. West," Dickson said, feeling a bit nervous about where the conversation was heading. "This isn't really the time or the place to…"

"And then, when you sold the property," West continued, "I thought to myself, there's a wise man who knows when to call it quits and put his work into the hands of someone more capable than he. I trust, Mr. Dickson that you remember what happened."

Dickson's forehead broke into a cold sweat as he recalled the day his father's business burned to the ground. "Yes," he said. "Of course I remember."

"Perhaps if it had merely been a case of property damage, Dickson Amalgamated might have risen like a phoenix from the ashes, but all those people trapped inside… How many were there again?"

Dickson felt his knees begin to buckle. "One hundred forty-seven," he answered.

"One hundred forty-seven lives lost," West said. "There was no returning from that. I lost a great deal of money that day, Mr. Dickson. I had tremendous faith in the Dickson name and you failed me and a lot of other foolish, trusting people. Oh, I didn't lose everything. I still maintain my place in society but it's all a sham, really. I'm simply not the man I once was. I'm wearing my father's tuxedo tonight, Mr. Dickson. It's a casual reminder of a simpler, more lucrative time. Within two years I expect to find myself penniless. I try not to think about what my life will be like when that day comes to pass. And while I'm trying desperately not to think unpleasant thoughts, I turn to drink. And often, when I'm drunk, I read the newspaper. Imagine my surprise to find out that the hope of Manhattan currently lies in your hands, Mr. Dickson. Perhaps there are any number of fools out there who believe such twaddle but I know you, Mr. Dickson, and I know the truth. If you are all that's standing in the way between the good men and women here tonight and the evil of Fantômas, well then all I can say is, God help us all."

Dickson stared at West, his face flushed red with shame.

"Good day, Mr. Dickson," West said, walking away.

Dickson made his way to an open window and kept himself upright by leaning on the sill. He tried to push the unpleasantness of the conversation out of his mind and focus on the task at hand, but he found his thoughts growing clouded and muddy. In truth, the words of Charles West hadn't been the sole agents of Dickson's lack of confidence, but they had brought all of his apprehensions and fears to the fore. The thought that he had never truly succeeded at anything he had attempted his entire life was always flitting about his subconscious but his single-minded efforts to track down Fantômas and bring him to justice had kept him from dwelling on his own inadequacies. Now that he was here, alone, and the lives of Ruth, Professor Harrington and Jack Meredith were at stake, he felt himself begin to crumble.

"There you are, Dickson!" Samuel Cobblepot said, charging across the room with his monstrous son in tow. "I want you to meet someone. This is my only son Oswald. Named after his grandfather. He's a voracious reader and has followed the Fantômas stories with a great deal of interest!"

Dickson extended his hand to the young man with the squinted eye and beak-like nose. "Pleased to meet you," he said. Oswald's hand was cold and damp to the touch.

"Waugh!" Oswald said.

"Indeed," Dickson countered.

Before he could engage the young man further, Dickson heard a tumult of noise on the other side of the foyer.

"Ah!" Cobblepot exclaimed. "Finally, the guests of honor!"

From the front door came the Grand Duke of Deux-Ponts-Veldenz and the Duchess Penelope. Dickson's ears immediately perked up, listening for any untoward sounds that might be a signal of Fantômas' invasion. "Come with me, Dickson!" Cobblepot said. "I want you to meet the Grand Duke!"

Dickson followed Cobblepot across the room. The Grand Duke was an abnormally tall man wearing a van dyke beard.

His dinner jacket was adorned with a large red cloth sporting dozens of gold and silver medals. The Duchess Penelope, looking decidedly uncomfortable in her evening gown, was next to him.

"Duke, this is Detective Dickson," Cobblepot said.

"Your highness," Dickson said with a slight bow.

"Ze pleasure iz all mine!" the Duke said.

"And here," Cobblepot added, placing his arm lightly around the Duchess' shoulders, "is this evening's *pièce de resistance*!"

"Oh!" Penelope said. "So charming!"

"Not you, my dear," the Duke said. "Herr Cobblepot is speaking of your diamond."

"Yes!" Dickson said, doing his best to focus on the jewel. "The Caderousse Diamond."

"Oh," the Duke said, raising an eyebrow. "You've done your homework, Herr Dickson."

"Tell me again, your highness," Cobblepot said in a commanding voice, urging the room to listen, "about the fascinating history of this stone."

"Well!" the Duke said, removing his monocle and polishing it with a handkerchief. "The diamond came to my mother by way of a family descended from, believe it or not, a common hotel owner. It seems the man did a very good deed at one point and a mysterious stranger delivered the jewel to him as a thank you. Legend has it that the man was…"

"Edmond Dantès," Dickson interrupted. "Also known as the Count of Monte-Cristo. The diamond originally belonged to the Borgias, of course, before it fell into the hands of Abbé Faria. He hid the jewel, along with the rest of his vast wealth, on the island of Monte-Cristo before he was imprisoned at the Chateau d'If. It was there that he revealed the location to the wrongly imprisoned Edmond Dantès."

The room fell to a hush as everyone acknowledged Dickson's telling of the story.

"All you told me was that it belonged to your mother," Penelope said.

"That was the short version," the Duke replied. "You've outdone yourself, Herr Dickson. I hear that you are a trustworthy man. Obviously you are also very well educated."

"It is one of my favorite stories," Dickson said. "When I was young, my mother used to read me Alexandre Dumas' account of Edmond Dantès' life."

"Look," Cobblepot suddenly chimed in, clapping his gloved hands to gain the attention of the crowd. "It would be impolite to invite the Grand Duke and his lovely…uh…bride without asking the fair Duchess Penelope to grace us with a song."

The crowd applauded.

"Oh, I couldn't!" Penelope squealed, although it was obvious she had been anticipating the request. Nevertheless, very few people batted an eye when the piano player began plunking away at a tune entitled *The Devil's Ball* right on cue, destroying the illusion that the performance was completely impromptu.

Dickson cursed silently with frustration. How was he to protect these people when they weren't taking the threat of Fantômas seriously? They had read the newspapers, heard the stories and no one any longer voiced doubt about Fantômas' existence. So why this willing, blissful ignorance? Glancing around at the room, watching the well-dressed gentlemen and ladies sip their cocktails and absent-mindedly finger their cigarette holders, the reasons became obvious. These were the privileged sons and daughters of New York–born into wealth and guaranteed that their good fortune was limitless. With the exception of Mr. Charles West, very few of them suffered a misfortune that couldn't be explained away as "God's will" or "the result of bad decisions." They were untouchable, and the thought that someone as evil and treacherous as Fantômas could be a threat to them and their divine providence was simply too impossible to believe. And so they sang and danced and drank and smoked and would continue to do so until the roof caved in.

Which, moments later, it did.

The piano music was bouncing away as the Duchess Penelope flashed her white teeth to the crowd, beat time on the piano with her hand, and began to sing.

I had a dream, last night,
That filled me full of fright.
I dreamt that I was with the Devil below,
In his great big fiery hall,
Where the Devil was giving a Ball,
I checked my coat and hat and started gazing at
The merry crowd that came to witness the show
And I must confess to you
There were many there I knew.

The Duchess left the piano and began to work the crowd. Dickson was surprised that her impossibly brash Bronx dialect seemed to vanish as the song caught fire and the masses began to tap their hands and feet in rhythm.

At the Devil's Ball,
At the Devil's Ball,
I saw the cute Mrs. Devil so pretty and fat,
Dress'd in a beautiful fireman's hat.
Ephraham, the Leader man,
Who led the band last Fall,
He play'd the music at the Devil's Ball,
In the Devil's Hall,
I saw the funniest Devil that I ever saw,
Taking the tickets from folks at the door
I caught a glimpse of my Mother-in-law
Dancing with the Devil,
Oh! The little Devil,
Dancing at the Devil's Ball.

Dickson was almost tempted to give in to the joyful lure of the music but he began to feel the familiar pang of danger crawl up his spine. He scanned the room, searching for Fantômas. Was he, perhaps, disguised as a party guest? Samuel Cobblepot? The Grand Duke himself? His gaze rested on Charles West, who was staring directly at him. West lifted his champagne glass and shot Dickson a toast. Suddenly, he began to hear a slight buzzing sound, barely rising over the sound of the Duchess' voice, but growing progressively louder.

The Duchess finished her song with a flourish and a high note that seemed to go on forever. It was joined by the dissonant screeching of the young Oswald Cobblepot, who suddenly pointed at the ceiling and cried aloud.

"Waaaugghhh!"

The skylight.

Dickson looked upward just in time to see two black-clad feet crash through the skylight, sending a rain of glass onto the partygoers. The women screamed. The men tried in vain to shield the women from the shower of glass. It was Fantômas. And somehow, he was slowly lowering himself from the skylight into the foyer.

He was dressed in a full tuxedo and top hat. His face was disguised by a cloth domino over his eyes. In one hand, he held a bright red rose. In the other hand was a long, black tube of some sort that looked for all the world like the handle of an umbrella. At the top of the device was a series of blades that were rotating so quickly that they caused a deafening "whup, whup" sound and kicked up enough wind to send all the sheet music on top of the piano flying. The device had clearly acted as a flying mechanism of some sort, allowing Fantômas to defy gravity and lower himself slowly from the sky.

Fantômas spied Dickson right off the bat and winked. Dickson drew his pistol and aimed but by the time he pulled the trigger, Fantômas had tipped the flying mechanism forward, deflecting the bullet and sending it ricocheting around the room. Dickson heard a man choke on the other side of the foyer and glanced in that direction to see Charles West grab his head while a spray of blood vaulted onto the white curtains.

Dickson looked back at Fantômas in time to see him reach for the Duchess Penelope and tear the Caderousse Diamond from around her throat. He tucked it inside his jacket, waved to Dickson, then bowed to Duchess Penelope while handing her the rose. He then pointed his flying mechanism into the air and floated upward out of the Cobblepot mansion and into the sky.

Dickson wasted no time, bolting out the door and into the driveway. He stared into the moonlit sky and saw that Fantômas was hovering just over the mansion–not traveling forward or back, just suspended in midair as if he were waiting for something.

He wants me to follow him, Dickson thought. He knew it was probably a trap but he also knew he had no choice. Caderousse Diamond be damned. Ruth Harrington's life was at stake.

He ran to his car, got inside, started the engine and drove toward Fantômas. Despite the distance between them, Dickson almost swore that he could see a smile cross Fantômas' lips as he drifted away from the mansion and began soaring over the rooftops of Long Island. Dickson continued to drive, keeping Fantômas in sight. Fantômas, for his part, never strayed too far from the roads but allowed Dickson to continue following. The chase continued like this for several miles until Dickson found himself completely and utterly lost.

The land became dark and the neighborhood mansions faded away until there was nothing left but open fields in the moonlight and the sound of water crashing against rocks. The road Dickson drove angled upward and he was vaguely aware that he was leaving the most inhabited part of the island behind.

Suddenly, Dickson could see a large mansion looming in the distance. This one was unlike the modern homes occupied by Samuel Cobblepot and Professor Harrington. This one was clearly at least a hundred years old and looked as if it had been, until very recently, completely abandoned. Weeds had overgrown the land around it and ivy crawled up the antique turrets. Dickson looked ahead to see Fantômas drifting over the roof of the house and landing somewhere behind it. He stopped his car and got out.

He didn't hear a sound at first. Then there was a quick flash of bright blue light that emanated from the window of the house and disappeared as quickly as it came. The light was accompanied by a short, electronic buzzing sound. The blue light flashed again, and in the fraction of a second before it disappeared, Dickson glimpsed three faces in the window of the mansion. He waited for the light to flash again and this time saw that the three faces belonged to Ruth Harrington, Professor Harrington and Jack Meredith.

There was no doubt in his mind that Fantômas was luring him to his death. Without a second thought, Dickson steeled himself and walked forward toward the house. All at once he realized that his final confrontation with Fantômas was about to begin.

And so at the end of Act IV, our players take their places onstage for our final act. If you, Dear Reader, feel confident that your nerves can emerge from this tale undamaged, you are welcome to continue on to Act V–in which all questions are answered, mysteries are resolved and Detective Dickson finds redemption at the hands of Fantômas.

THE TORTURE CHAMBER
WILLIAM FOX PRESENTS
FANTOMAS
1921 American Serial in 20 Episodes
FROM THE WORLD FAMOUS STORIES OF MARCEL ALLAIN & PIERRE SOUVESTRE
SCENARIO AND DIRECTION BY EDWARD SEDGWICK
EPISODE FOUR
"BLADES OF TERROR"

ACT V

In which all questions are answered,
mysteries are resolved and Detective Dickson finds
redemption at the hands of Fantômas

Chapter 22: Under the Guillotine

Ruth Harrington awoke to find herself sitting upright in a chair beside a small table adorned with an ornamental teapot. The room was sparsely furnished and although it was very brightly lit, Ruth could see no windows, nor could she discern any source of light whatsoever.

Sitting across the table from her was the Woman in Black.

"Tea?" the Woman asked, pouring herself a cup.

Ruth watched as the steam from the teapot wafted into the air. "No, thank you," she said. "Where am I? How did I get here?"

"Tea?" the Woman in Black repeated, leaning across the table and filling Ruth's teacup.

"I don't understand," Ruth said, raising her voice. "What am I doing here?"

The Woman in Black refused to answer, then drew a vial of white powder from her cloak and emptied it into Ruth's teacup. "Drink up!" she said.

Ruth stared at her aghast. "You're trying to poison me," she said. "What's going on here?"

The Woman in Black continued to stare at Ruth through her long black veil. "Drink the tea," she said.

Ruth looked over the woman's shoulder and spied a doorway on the far side of the room. "Curious," she thought. "It wasn't there before." With a sudden movement, she leapt from the table and darted for the door. Much to her surprise, the Woman in Black made no attempt to follow after her but merely chuckled to herself as Ruth bolted through the doorway and found herself…

"In the same room," Ruth said aloud. "I'm in the same room." The Woman in Black was seated at the same table. The tea was steeping in the pot and the woman motioned for Ruth to sit down.

"Tea?" the Woman in Black offered.

Ruth clamped her eyes shut. "I'm dreaming," she thought. "I must be." When she opened her eyes again, she found that the room itself was unchanged but now the Woman in Black had been joined by two more occupants–men clad entirely in black from head to toe who were seated at the table and seemed to be involved in a game of dice.

The first man rolled the dice. "Box cars!" he yelled in triumph.

The second man clutched the dice, blew on them, then sent them spinning across the table. "Snake eyes!" he cried.

A sick feeling begain to grow in the pit of Ruth's stomach. "What are they playing for?" she asked the woman.

The Woman in Black extended her hand toward Ruth. "For you, my dear," she said. "Unless of course you'd like to make the choice yourself."

Ruth had no time to respond. From behind, someone tapped her on the shoulder. She spun around to see a man dressed in a suit standing next to a gramophone.

Fantômas.

Fantômas lifted the arm of the player and lowered onto the cylinder. The sound of music wafted through the air. Ruth recognized Tchaikovsky's waltz from his *Serenade for Strings in C Major*. "And now, my dear," Fantômas said. "We dance."

Without warning, one of the men in black clutched Ruth around the waist and began awkwardly waltzing with her around the room. He spun Ruth wildly around and she glimpsed Fantômas and the Woman in Black clapping along with the music–keeping time as her head grew ever more dizzy. Feeling herself begin to panic, Ruth reached for the man's black hood and tore it from his head, revealing the face of Detective Frederick Dickson.

"Miss Harrington!" Dickson said. "Thank you for choosing me."

"Wait just one minute, Old Bean!" The voice came from behind Ruth and she turned to see the second man remove the hood from his head. It was Jack Meredith. "After all," he said, "I was here first!"

Ruth pushed herself away from Dickson. "I don't... I don't understand," she said. "What's happening?"

"Isn't it obvious, darling?" Jack said. "It's time for you to decide." For the first time, Ruth noticed that Jack was carrying a large club.

"Don't be absurd, Meredith!" Dickson cried, drawing a large net from behind his back. "The lady has made her choice and I'm afraid you've drawn the short straw."

Ruth clamped her eyes shut and tried to shake away the images but the moment she opened them again, Dickson and Meredith were advancing on her. She ran to the gramophone, wrenched the bell-shaped speaker from the device and held it in front of her. "Stay back," she warned. "I once held off a horde of razor-toothed pygmies with a wooden bucket!"

Meredith and Dickson stopped dead in their tracks which gave Ruth all the time she needed. She spun around and found herself in front of a window that gave way to a lush green field. Leaping through the opening, she suddenly realized that the field had vanished and there was nothing beneath her but the waves of Long Island Sound crashing against the jagged rocks. Just as she thought she was plummeting to her death, she felt an arm reach out and clutch her wrist, stopping her descent.

"Hold on, Ruth!" a man yelled. Ruth recognized the voice as that of her father. "Hold on," Professor Harrington repeated. "Listen to me! None of this is real!"

"Dad?" Ruth cried. "Dad? What's happening?" She looked to one side and saw Dickson next to her, hanging from the edge of the cliff.

"Don't be afraid," Dickson said in a soothing voice. "I'll save you."

"Don't listen to a word that dullard says!" Jack shouted.

Ruth turned to see Jack hanging on the other side of her. "That idiot detective couldn't save a dime on a penny stick of candy! I'm the only one that can get you out of this scrape!"

"Ruth!" Professor Harrington's voice returned. "Listen to me! You're hallucinating. You ingested some of the potion you drew from my shoulder and it's causing you to hallucinate."

Ruth turned back toward Dickson and was surprised to see that he had let go of the cliff and was hanging in mid-air. "Don't let me fall," he said.

"Don't listen to him!" Jack shouted. "Ruth, darling, tell me you love me. Please. Tell me you're not in love with that wretched detective."

"Don't say anything, Ruth!" Professor Harrington shouted. "Whatever you think you see right now–it isn't real. You're going to wake up at any moment! Don't say something you might regret!"

Ruth looked at Dickson. "Don't let me fall," he said.

She turned toward Jack. "I love you," he said.

Ruth felt tears well up in her eyes. "I'm sorry, Jack," she said. "I'm so sorry."

Jack smiled. "It's all right, darling," he said. "God bless." He let go of the edge and Ruth watched as he went plummeting to the ground and crashed onto the rocks below.

She woke with a jolt. The cliff was gone. She felt a wooden floor beneath her knees. She tried to lift her head but a large plank of wood kept her neck tightly secured and head facing the floor. "Are you all right?" Professor Harrington asked. Ruth craned her head as much as the mysterious trap would allow. "It was Fantômas' drug," her father said. "You're awake now but hardly in a better situation. I'm afraid we're prisoners, darling–prisoners of Fantômas."

Ruth looked the other direction and saw that Jack was next to her. How much had she said aloud? What had he heard? "Jack?" Ruth asked. "I just want you to know–"

"Don't say a word, darling." Jack said, his lips tight with anger. "There's no need. I understand. I'm going to get us out of here. Just you wait and see."

We are now beneath the streets of Manhattan.

The caverns dripped in the darkness. The moist walls and wet floor, covered in rotting sewage, gave off a hideous stench that attacked the senses of the Council of Ten the moment they slid the secret door to one side, allowing the light from *Casino Joe's* to illuminate the tunnels.

"Jesus," Number Ten said aloud. The others coughed and choked, covering their faces with their hands.

"Silence!" said their leader, who seemed to be unaffected by the smell. "Hold your lanterns high and stay close!" The Councilmen did as they were told. This was the first time their leader had dared to appear before them in person, which made it very clear that this was a mission of some great importance.

"Wait!" said Number Two. "What's that sound?" The Councilmen stood still and listened.

Number Six snorted with derision. "I don't hear…"

"There it is!" Number Seven shouted. "I hear it too!"

"Silence!" the leader shouted again and they all listened intently until they heard the sound of something sloshing toward them in the darkness, making its way through the muck. "Nobody move…" the leader said, then slowly, calmly drew his pistol from his trench coat and fired into the water. Sewage sprayed everywhere, coating the faces of the Councilmen in grime. The sounds of the gunshots were deafening as they echoed off the rocks. "Got it," the leader said.

The Councilmen leaned forward to shine their lanterns on the pile of gore lying at their feet. "Goddamn alligators in the sewers," the leader said.

"I'll be damned," Number Four said. "I always heard there were alligators in the sewers but thought it was a rumor."

"Come on," the leader ordered. "Stop gawking at the thing and let's get moving. We've got a job to do."

The Councilmen stepped over the bloody corpse and followed their leader into the darkness.

The search for Detective Dickson

We are inside police headquarters.

The typically busy night of phone calls, interrogations and collars has erupted into chaos as police officers from every precinct crowd into the tiny station, shouting over the constant clanging of the telephones.

"Geez," Glimpy said, struggling to keep up with Snapper and Muggs as the three of them stepped lively up the stoop to the door of the station. "What's goin' on, ya think?"

"Cut it, you guys," Snapper whispered. "Somehow, we gotta get past the pigs to find Mr. Dale…I mean Mr. Dickson."

"How we gonna do that, Snapper?" Muggs asked, pushing his fingertips under the rim of his hat to rub his forehead.

"Leave it to me," Snapper answered. Muggs and Glimpy fell in step behind him as he pushed open the doors. Almost immediately, the three boys were assaulted with the sounds of panic. Snippets of shouted conversation caught their attention.

"Corona kidnapped…"

"Signs of a struggle…"

"Who saw him last…"

"Anything touched? Anything moved?"

"Door knocked off its hinges…"

Snapper brushed past a rookie officer about five years away from filling out his freshly scrubbed face and baggy pants. "Excuse me, sir?" Snapper said, trying to get his attention. The officer didn't even notice him and kept walking.

"C'mon, Snapper," Muggs said with no small amount of exasperation. "What are we doin' here? No one gives information to guys like us."

"We just haven't found the right mark, yet," Snapper said, his eyes suddenly lighting on a bored secretary filing her nails at a nearby desk. "Stand back, boys," he said, turning up his collar, "and watch me work."

Glimpy and Muggs took two chairs by the front door while Snapper thrust his hands into his pockets and sauntered over to the flaxen-haired beauty who was unsuccessfully attempting to stifle a yawn. "Hello, Madam," Snapper said, trying to keep his voice from cracking.

"You wanna report something, you need to get a form from Officer Petrowski only he ain't here right now," the woman said, her voice even more shrill than Snapper had imagined.

"No, my good woman, I am not in need of reporting a what do ya call it… a criminal incident, shall I say…"

"We don't give handouts here," the woman interrupted. "This is a police station."

Snapper laughed heartily. "Oh, my dear woman," he said. "You misjudge me! I am merely here because I have an appointment with Detective Frederick Dickson. Could you please inform him that I've arrived?"

The woman looked down her nose at Snapper. "What business you got with Detective Dickson?"

"Well," Snapper stammered, "It's rather private business that I wish to discuss with him in private. Tell him a Mr. Snapper is here to engage him in, how shall we say, important conversation."

The woman snorted as a tall man sporting a badge and a handlebar moustache approached her desk. "This fella givin' ya trouble, Maggie?" the man said, his chin pressed against his chest and his fists against his sides.

"Says he wants to see Dickson," Maggie said.

"He does, does he?" the officer said. "Well, Dickson ain't here, young man."

Snapper dropped the man-about-town act and turned his attention to the policeman. "He ain't here? Well when's he gonna come back?"

"He's outta the city, Sonny," the officer answered. "He'll be out all night." Just then, the officer's attention turned to something on the other side of the station. "Hey! You! Just what do ya think you're doin'?"

Snapper didn't even have to turn around to know the officer was talking to Muggs and Glimpy. "Them fellas with you?" the officer asked Snapper.

"Uh…I…" Snapper turned around to see Muggs and Glimpy staring wide-eyed at him, each one with a fresh cigarette in their hands, while the man they had lifted the tobacco from was running his hands through his pockets to make sure his wallet was still there.

"You damn kids!" the man yelled. "Why I oughtta…"

"What?" Glimpy said. "We was gonna pay for 'em!"

"All right, you," the officer said, clutching Snapper by the ear and dragging him toward the front door. "It's good for you there's important business going on here tonight, 'cause any other night I'd slap you in a cell for 24 hours just to see how you'd like it!"

"Ow!" Snapper said, squinting his eyes from the pain in his ear. "I wouldn't like it at all!"

"Now," the officer said, planting Snapper next to Muggs and Glimpy and letting go of his ear. "Beat it, 'afore I change my mind."

"Come on, fellas," Snapper said, leading his friends back out onto the street. Just as they were heading down the stoop, six police cars pulled up to the curb and at least a dozen officers filed out of them and ran up the stoop, taking two steps at a time and nearly knocking the three boys off their feet.

"Jeez!" Muggs said. "Watch where you're goin', fellas!"

"Hush up!" Snapper hissed. "You got us in enough trouble already!"

As the policemen continued to ascend the steps, Snapper overheard more snippets of conversation.

"What about that Detective? The one Corona's been working with on the Fantômas case?"

"Dickson?"

"That's the fella. Anyone heard from him?"

"Out on another case on Long Island…"

Snapper grabbed Muggs and Glimpy and led them to the side of the building. "You hear that fellas? Mr. Dickson is on Long Island!"

"Where on Long Island?" Glimpy asked. "Long Island's a big island."

"I'll bet I know where," Muggs said. The others turned to see Muggs staring into a newspaper box.

"What are you talkin' about, Muggs?" Snapper asked.

"Take a look at this."

Glimpy leaned in and stared over Muggs' shoulder. "*Mayor announces expansion of trolley system*," he read.

"No, dummy!" Snapper said, smacking Glimpy on the back of the head. "I see what Muggs is talkin' about. The society column underneath."

Glimpy read for a few moments, his lips moving all the while. "I don't get it," he said.

"Fantômas?" Snapper asked Muggs.

"Fantômas," Muggs answered. "We gotta get to Long Island. And fast."

"How we gonna do that?" Glimpy said. "The train'll take too long."

Snapper turned his attention to the row of police cars. "I got an idea," he said.

Moments later, all talking inside the police station came to a halt as a rookie officer with his desk overlooking the street began shouting. "Hey! Hey! *Hey*!" All eyes in the station landed on the young officer as he leapt to his feet. "Three kids outside! They just made off with one of the squad cars!"

Inside the stolen police car, Snapper pressed the gas pedal to the floor and began steering the vehicle wildly through the darkened midtown streets. "Snapper?" Glimpy said. "You sure you know what you're doing?"

"Yeah," Muggs shouted, a fearful tremor in his voice. "You ever drive a car before?"

"A couple a times," Snapper laughed. "Hell… a kid's gotta learn sometime!"

Snapper made a sharp right into an alley. "What are you doing?" Glimpy yelled.

"Don't worry," Snapper said. "This alley goes all the way through. We just have to lose the cops, then circle around to the bridge."

Muggs turned around to see a row of police cars passing the alley. "You lost 'em, Snapper!" he said, clapping Snapper on the shoulder. "You did it!"

"Now," Snapper said, "we gotta get to the Cobblepot mansion and find Mr. Dickson!"

At that moment, Frederick Dickson was stepping out of his car and marching towards the darkened house, its windows still illuminated by the sudden bursts of electric light revealing

Ruth, Jack and Professor Harrington. The safety of Ruth Harrington was uppermost in his mind as he charged forward, unmindful of the danger that awaited him. He burst the front doors open and stepped into the darkened foyer. In the blackness, he was able to make out a staircase. From the floor above, he could hear the random buzzing sounds that accompanied the flashes of blue light, but as he began to ascend the stairs, he heard another sound weave its way into the mix–Tchaikovsky's waltz from his *Serenade for Strings in C Major*.

Fantômas threatens Professor Harrington

Dickson tried to keep himself from growing afraid as he continued up the staircase. The music grew louder, and once he reached the top of the stairs he found himself staring down a darkened hallway lined with closed doors. From underneath the furthermost door, the blue light continued to shine along the floor at irregular bursts, accompanied by the buzzing sound and the music.

Dickson drew his gun and crept silently down the hall. Surely Fantômas knew he was in the house and Dickson knew his only hope of rescuing Ruth was to press forward and try to anticipate Fantômas' movements. In seconds, he found himself outside the door. The buzzing sound now included a strange clicking noise, like pieces of wood slapping against the floor.

With both his hands on his gun, he lifted the weapon in front of him and kicked open the door. He was completely unprepared for what he saw.

The large room sported a high ceiling framed in gold crown molding. Every wall sported at least a dozen paintings–all of them masterworks that had disappeared from various exhibits and museums over the past year. In the center of the room was a dance floor and on it were several masked couples waltzing to the lyrical strains of Tchaikovsky's serenade. On close inspection, however, Dickson could tell that the dancers were not real. They were wooden mannequins attached to tracks in the floor. Those tracks led to a large generator along the far wall that delivered bursts of electricity through the floor and sent the mannequins spinning and dancing through the room. The blue light that shone intermittently from the generator gave the room an eerie glow as the mannequins continued to promenade through the ballroom in time with the music coming from the phonograph.

The image was disarming, yes, but the real horror settled into Dickson's gut when he looked past the spinning wooden toys to the center of the room. Arranged with almost perfect symmetry were three large wooden objects sporting shiny blades suspended from the top.

Guillotines. And strapped beneath them were Jack Meredith, Ruth Harrington and her father.

"Freddy!" Ruth shouted. "Don't come any further! He's here! He's…"

"Well!" the voice came from above. "Mr. Dickson. How delightful of you to join our little soiree."

Dickson looked up to see Fantômas and a man in a lab coat–the man we know as Dr. Hans Voitzel–perched on a small veranda. At Dr. Voitzel's back was a large metal contraption with dials and switches. To his left were three large levers.

Dickson pointed his gun upwards and pulled the trigger. Three bullets seemed to stop in mid-air before reaching Fantômas and ricochet into the adjoining walls. "A waste of time, Mr. Dickson," Fantômas said. "The good Doctor here has crafted a glass that appears to be impervious to bullets. I don't know how he does it, but who am I to look a gift horse in the mouth? I would advise you not to attempt such a stunt again. One of the bullets might wind up hitting one of your friends or, worse yet, an original Matisse. Drop the gun immediately, Detective, or all three of your friends here will be separated from their attractive little heads."

Dickson lowered his gun, then tossed it to the floor.

"Welcome to my home away from home, Mr. Dickson–a little piece of Parisian paradise in the middle of this boring little island. And nothing says Paris to me like the guillotine. Wouldn't you agree?"

"What do you want?" Dickson asked.

"You couldn't leave well enough alone, could you, Detective?" Fantômas answered. "You had an opportunity to choose what direction my life would take and you refused to do so."

"You asked me to choose one evil over another. It wasn't a choice at all."

"Blah, blah, blah, Mr. Dickson. Now it is your turn to choose again. Only this time, you will choose the direction of your own life."

"What are you talking about?" Dickson asked.

"Three people that you have continually risked your life for, Mr. Dickson. Here they are in front of us. With a single command, I could end their lives and yours as well. Instead, I will be merciful. I will allow you to save two of them, while I kill the third. All you have to do is choose."

"You're insane," Dickson shouted. "Kill me. Let them go and kill me."

“Wouldn’t that be oh so noble and convenient? No, I’m afraid that won’t do. Please try to remember that you are in no position to negotiate the rules of this particular game, Mr. Dickson. Choose one, only one, who you wish to die. Then you must live with the ramifications of that decision.”

While Fantômas spoke to Dickson, Jack Meredith was focused on setting himself free. Shortly after he was whisked away from Fantômas’ lair beneath Our Lady of Perpetual Sorrow, he had managed to secure a small piece of broken glass beneath the cuff of his jacket. It was lying along the shore of Long Island Sound, following the trio’s exit from Fantômas’ submersible. Jack had to feign a coughing fit in order to throw himself to the ground, but was able to hide the tiny shard without Fantômas noticing. For the past few minutes, he had been sawing at the rope behind his back, breaking it a strand at a time and loosening his bonds. In mere moments, he would be free. He could rescue Ruth, save her father and defeat Fantômas. Maybe, if he was lucky, Freddy Dickson would be fatally injured during the ensuing melee. Ruth would forget all about the pathetic detective and Jack would have won back her heart.

If only Dickson could keep Fantômas talking for a minute longer.

“Let’s consider the options, shall we?” Fantômas said. “Professor Harrington is an old man. Certainly he was a significant figure in the anthropological and chemical fields at one time, but now? Honestly, this whole situation has been very bad for his constitution. How many more good years can he have left in him anyway? Whereas Miss Harrington and Mr. Meredith are youthful! Vigorous! Why, one can easily imagine them going on to great things. They have many more years ahead of them than the good Professor has.”

Dickson was trying to block Fantômas’ words from his mind. Behind Fantômas stood Dr. Voitzel. Next to him were three levers–one for each guillotine. The levers were mounted in a box. The box sprouted wires that snaked along the wall, down to the ground where they joined another box, embedded in the wall behind the three guillotines.

"But," Fantômas continued, "I understand that ordering the death of such an upstanding citizen would be very upsetting and you'd probably be raked over the coals in the local press. Perhaps you haven't quite the stomach to put Professor Harrington to death. Hmm..." Fantômas thought for a bit, then his eyes lit up with a new idea. "It's quite simple isn't it, Detective? Of the three people up here, the only person you wish to have out of the way is Jack Meredith!"

Jack stopped sawing at his bonds when he heard his name and looked across the room at Dickson. Dickson returned Jack's glance, then flushed a deep shade of red.

Killing Jack Meredith was obviously exactly what Dickson had been thinking.

Jack continued working away at the rope. Just another minute...

Dickson stared at his gun out of the corner of his eye. If he were able to grab it and fire a single shot at the electronic box on the floor, he could stop the current leading to the guillotines before Dr. Voitzel threw the switch. But no–the gun was too far away. Dickson turned his attention back to Fantômas as the spinning mannequins continued to dance in front of him.

"Of course!" Fantômas said. "With the foolish Mr. Meredith out of the way, you can have your heart's desire–the brilliant and alluring Miss Ruth Harrington. And who could blame you? After all, you were a victim of that evil Fantômas. You had no choice in the matter. What a sadist!"

Dickson ignored him. The gun was out of arm's reach but the mannequins were not.

"Or," said Fantômas, "perhaps we should be pragmatic. Allow the men who actually contribute to society to live and let the useless female die."

Sweat pored down Jack Meredith's face. He was almost free.

"Meredith," Dickson said aloud.

"I beg your pardon?" Fantômas asked.

Dickson stepped closer. "I choose Meredith. Kill him if you must. I have no use for him."

Dickson watched as Dr. Voitzel brought his hand to the lever that would trigger Jack's guillotine.

"You idiot!" Jack shouted. "No! Please, God! No!"

Dickson swiftly reached for the arm of one of the mannequins and tore it from its body. Then he hurled the wooden limb toward Jack Meredith and prayed that his aim would stay true. The arm sailed forward and lodged itself just above Jack's neck, stopping the blade before it continued its fall.

Dr. Voitzel was momentarily stunned by Dickson's action, giving the detective enough time to yank the head off of another mannequin and rush forward toward the electric box feeding power to the deadly trap. Voitzel reached for the remaining levers with both hands and pulled them down. The generator sizzled as the current traveled along the wires. Dickson held the wooden head over him, then plunged it down with all his might on top of the box, shattering the cover and dislodging the wires. The lights flickered, the wooden dancers came to a halt, and Tchaikovsky's waltz slowed until the phonograph ceased spinning.

"No," Jack Meredith whispered to himself. "I was almost free. I almost saved her."

Dickson heard a small explosion on the veranda, then a scream came from Dr. Voitzel. The box containing the levers had short circuited, sending the burst of electricity back at him.

Dickson opened the tops of the death-traps, allowing all three to remove their necks from the paths of the blades.

"Thank you, old boy," Professor Harrington said. "I thought I was a dead man."

"We're not safe yet," Dickson said. "Fantômas will be down here in moments, and then…" Dickson spun around.

"What is it, Freddy?" Ruth said.

"Where is Fantômas? Where did he go?"

"There!" Ruth shouted, and Dickson looked up in time to see Fantômas through the window, running along the front lawn.

"Fantômas is running away?" Dickson said. All three were incredulous. "Since when does Fantômas simply run away?"

"Go," Ruth said. "Go get him. We'll be fine."

"Ruth, I…"

"Go, my boy!" Professor Harrington interrupted. "You heard the girl!"

Dickson stood up and bolted from the room. He leapt down the staircase and headed out the front door.

"Jack," Ruth said after they were all free. "Are you OK, darling?"

"Whore," Jack muttered under his breath.

"What did you say?" Ruth said. "Jack, you don't look well." Ruth placed her hands on either side of Jack's face and brought his head around until she was staring into his eyes. The familiar, happy Jack was gone and his face was seething with anger.

"Tramp!" Jack yelled, pushing Ruth to the ground. "Trollop!"

"Meredith!" Professor Harrington yelled. "What in the name of God…"

"I know what you did!" Jack yelled, staring down at the shocked Ruth Harrington. "I know what you did with him!"

"With who?" Ruth said. "Listen to me, Jack. You're not well."

Jack continued to scream at her. "I know what you want to do with him! I know what you're dreaming of doing with him!"

Ruth Harrington's understanding had reached its breaking point. "Jack Meredith!" she said, standing up and dusting herself off. "If you're implying what I think you're implying…"

"Listen, the two of you," Professor Harrington interrupted. "Not that I don't have a few choice words for Mr.

Meredith myself but I think Mr. Dickson may need our assistance."

Jack snorted with derision.

"Come on, Jack," Ruth said, taking her father by the hand and leading him out of the room. Once they arrived at the doorway, Ruth turned around to see Jack still standing next to the guillotines, glaring at her.

"Come on, Jack!" Ruth repeated. "Are you coming or aren't you?"

Jack didn't answer but continued to stare at her, his eyes blazing with hatred.

"Come on, darling!" Professor Harrington said, taking his daughter by the arm to usher her down the stairs.

"Suit yourself," Ruth said over her shoulder.

Not everyone, Dear Reader, is unlucky enough to be driven to the brink of insanity. For those of us with a strong constitution and a strong moral sense, losing our minds is merely an expression we use when the stress of daily life begins to take its toll. On this night, however, Jack Meredith is losing his mind in a different manner entirely. Perhaps it was his torture at the hands of Fantômas, or the slow realization that he could never be the man that he had always wished to be. Perhaps Jack Meredith was simply a fragile man to begin with and this most recent combination of horror and humiliation has unhinged him. Regardless of the cause, we find that Jack Meredith has, indeed, tragically lost his mind.

Ruth and her father had been gone for mere seconds when Jack heard Dr. Voitzel begin to stir above him on the glassed-in veranda. Jack slowly, and with an uncommon amount of confidence, circled around the back of the room until he found the circular staircase leading up to where the scientist lay. He could hear the Doctor sputtering and coughing back into consciousness as he rounded the final turn and stepped onto the platform, finally stopping when he was standing above Dr. Voitzel's wounded body.

Dr. Voitzel's face was a mass of red blisters, due to the electric shock he had received moments before. His eyes were very nearly swollen shut but he was able to see Jack's approach. "Herr Fantômas?" he said. "Is that you?"

Jack bent down over Dr. Voitzel, clutched him by the lapels and lifted him until he was staggering on his feet. "Wretched detective," Jack whispered.

"You're not Herr Fantômas," Dr. Voitzel said, his vision beginning to clear. "Mr. Meredith? How did you–"

"*Wretched detective*!" Jack shouted, slapping Dr. Voitzel with the back of his hand.

The scientist tumbled back to the ground and raised his arm in front of his face, shaking and cowering beneath Jack Meredith's gaze. "Please," he said, "You must understand. You were merely an experimental subject. Don't take it personally."

Jack lifted Dr. Voitzel to his feet again and dragged him across the floor and down the circular staircase. "What are you doing?" the scientist demanded. "Where are you taking me?" But Jack remained silent, even as he dragged Dr. Voitzel across the floor to the three guillotines and lay him down beside them.

"Listen," Dr. Voitzel said, his voice betraying a note of panic. "You appear to have escaped with your life. Perhaps we can let bygones be bygones and…"

Jack lifted the top of the first guillotine, then clutched Dr. Voitzel by the back of his lab coat. "Wait," the scientist said. "What are you doing?" Jack threw Dr. Voitzel across the guillotine until his neck was resting in the appropriate position. "Wait!" Dr. Voitzel shouted. "You can't…you mustn't!"

Jack lowered the top of the guillotine onto Dr. Voitzel and secured it until his neck was trapped. "Wait!" the scientist shouted again. "No!"

Jack clutched the top of the blade and brought it down with all of his might. The blade sliced cleanly through Dr. Voitzel's neck, separating his head from his body and sending it tumbling across the floor.

After a few moments, Jack Meredith pulled Dr. Voitzel's headless body from the guillotine and dragged it by the ankles across the room and through the doorway. He tossed it down the stairs and watched as it tumbled awkwardly, limb over limb, until it came to a halt in the foyer. He turned around, walked back into the room to retrieve the head, then returned to the staircase, tossing the disembodied head down the stairs, watching it bounce until it came to a rest on top of Dr. Voitzel's chest.

Then he wiped his bloodied hands onto his pant legs, straightened his tie, and slowly descended the stairs, carefully stepping over the corpse to exit the house. Once outside, he could hear the sounds of a struggle coming from his left, so he set out in the opposite direction and walked off into the night.

As Jack Meredith was becoming dangerously unhinged, Detective Dickson was chasing Fantômas across the grounds of the mansion. His pursuit was growing ever more confounding as Fantômas began to scream with panic. "No!" he shouted. "This wasn't supposed to happen!" He spun around, drew an object from his coat and hurled it awkwardly at Dickson. Dickson instinctively raised his arms to defend himself and caught the object in his hand.

The Caderousse Diamond.

Fantômas stopped running when he reached a cliff, 50 feet above the jagged rocks and tossing waves of Long Island Sound. He turned around and held out his arms toward Dickson. "Please," he said. "I'm sorry."

"No tricks, Fantômas," Dickson said. "You're under arrest."

Fantômas fell to his knees, panting and gasping for air. "Please," he said. "No more."

A feeling of horror settled into Dickson's gut. He had been in Fantômas' presence many times and, despite the multitude of disguises, he always found himself looking into the same eyes.

"Look at me," Dickson demanded. "Look at me!"

Fantômas stared into Dickson's eyes. "Good God," Dickson said. "You're not Fantômas. Who are you?"

Boris "The Prince" Zaitsev began to plead with Dickson. "He asked me who I wanted to be more than anyone. He said he'd give me a chance. He'll be so disappointed with me." He pressed his palms into the sides of his head. "My head…oh God… it hurts…"

"Who are you?" Dickson shouted. "Where is Fantômas?"

"I thought I was good enough to be him," the Prince said, slowly bringing himself up to his feet. "But no one is good enough to be him. How could I ever have thought that? I'm so, so, sorry."

Dickson grabbed the Prince by the front of his shirt and began shaking him. "Listen to me! Tell me what's going on here and where Fantômas is or I'll…" But he was unable to continue his threat as the Prince began to struggle against Dickson's strong arms. "Stop it you fool," Dickson shouted. "You're too close to the…"

The Prince brought his hands back to his head in an effort to blot out the pain. He began to lose his footing and Dickson reached out for him, but only grasped a small object around his neck. Whatever it was came loose as the Prince tumbled backward off the edge of the cliff, screaming all the way down until his body struck the jagged rocks below.

Dickson stepped away from the edge and opened his hand. Resting in his palm was a necklace he had seen before. The charm at the end was a gold tooth.

"Freddy! Are you all right?" Ruth and her father were hand in hand, racing toward Dickson.

"Where's Meredith?" Dickson asked.

Ruth and the Professor exchanged looks. "As far as I'm concerned," Professor Harrington said, "I never want to see the little bastard again."

"What happened to Fantômas?" Ruth asked.

"It wasn't him," Dickson answered.

"I don't understand."

"It wasn't Fantômas. We've been duped. It was one of his lackeys. Fantômas obviously predicted the trap I laid for him and played me for a fool. He was trying to lure us away."

"Away from what?" Ruth asked. "If that man wasn't Fantômas, then where is Fantômas?"

"I have no idea," Dickson answered. "Damn me and my stupidity! For the second time, I've failed to see the obvious truth staring me in the face!"

"Second time?" Professor Harrington asked.

"Later," Dickson answered. "First, we…" Dickson's speech was interrupted when he noticed a lone figure stumbling away from them in the distance. "Is that Meredith?" he asked.

Ruth spun around and stared into the dark. She could barely see the lumbering shadow shrinking into the night. "Jack!" she called out. "Jack, where are you going?"

Professor Harrington rested his hand on his daughter's shoulder. "Enough, my dear. Clearly, Jack Meredith no longer wants anything to do with us and, quite frankly, I want nothing more to do with him either."

Ruth turned to her father, a tear falling down her cheek. "I don't understand," she said. "Why would he…? I don't understand."

"Courage, my dear," Professor Harrington said, patting Ruth on the hand. "I never liked the whiny little sissy anyway."

Ruth looked at Dickson as she was struck by a sudden thought. "The other one. The one in the lab coat. Where is he?"

"Whoever he was, he didn't strike me as the kind of person to wait around for the authorities. I need to get you two to safety, then return the Caderousse Diamond."

"And Fantômas?" Professor Harrington asked.

"Obviously had a good reason for not showing up tonight. And I'm afraid to find out what that reason might be."

Dickson ushered Ruth and Professor Harrington into his car, then drove through the night toward the Cobblepot mansion.

The guests at the Cobblepot mansion were still in a state of mild panic. The police had yet to arrive (no doubt because they were all in search of Sergeant Corona and the stolen squad car) and the few party-goers that hadn't been injured were busy trying to extract the shards of broken glass from the faces and arms of the others. The men were cursing, the women were crying and the outspoken Charles West was busy pontificating while another man–a local Doctor–was nursing the bullet wound on Charles' scalp. "Lucky, lucky, lucky!" he shouted. "We're all damned lucky it wasn't worse!"

"Mr. West," the Doctor said, "you've got to calm down. You've lost a lot of blood."

"Very fine!" West snapped. "I've lost my blood, I've lost my fortune… If that Detective Frederick Dickson were here, I'd…"

It was then that Dickson strode into the living room, followed by Ruth Harrington and her father. "You'd what, West?" Dickson said. He strode across the floor with grim determination toward West, who was seething–his face flushed with indignation.

"You!" West said, slapping away the hands of the Doctor who was adjusting his head dressing. "It seems all you have to do is step into a room and everything goes to Hell. Do you know I could have been killed, Dickson? As if it's not enough for you to cost me hundreds of thousands of dollars of my family's money, you have to make sure my father no longer has an heir as well?"

"Listen to me, West," Dickson said, meeting his eyes. "I'd love to stay and chat with you about how incorrigible, irresponsible and unholy it is for you to blame your minor misfortune on the tragedy of others, but the truth of the matter is that I doubt you've ever known a seriously unpleasant day in your life. Oh, I'm sure you may have woken up with a cold now and then and fretted away the midnight oil wondering whether or not you should put your summer home in the Hamptons on the market or keep it and sell your railway stock instead. But true suffering? You don't know the meaning of the word.

"Like I said, I'd love to stay and tell you all of this but I have a master criminal to catch and quite frankly you're in my way and becoming a damned nuisance and an unforgivable waste of time."

West's lips pursed and his eyes grew wide. "You insufferable…public servant. Do you realize what I can do to you? What the people I know can do to you?"

"Yes," Dickson replied. "And I don't care." Dickson turned on his heel and left the perpetually angry Charles West behind. He approached the Duchess Penelope and drew the Caderousse Diamond from the inside of his jacket. "Your jewel, madam," he said.

The Duchess craned her neck forward as Dickson placed the necklace over her head. "Thank you," she said. "And I will tell my husband not to invite Mr. West to any more parties."

Dickson bowed and nodded.

Suddenly, a large commotion erupted on the front porch. The doors to the main foyer swung open and the crowd turned around to hear the butler shouting at a group of men forcing themselves inside.

"For the last time," the butler cried. "You can't go in there! This is a private party!"

"We've got to see Detective Dickson!" one of the voices replied.

Dickson stepped around to the entry way and saw the butler struggling to keep Snapper, Muggs and Glimpy from darting into the ballroom. He had two of them by the shirt collars and a third under his arm. He turned to Samuel Cobblepot. "My apologies, sir," he said. "They pulled up in a police car and it took me a few moments to see that they were…"

"A police car?" Cobblepot interrupted. "What in Sam Hill is going on?"

"Let them through!" Dickson yelled. "I know them."

The butler shot a glance at Cobblepot. "Do as he says," Cobblepot said.

The three boys fell to the ground when the butler let go of them, then quickly bounced to their feet and dusted themselves off. "Mr. Dickson," Snapper said, pulling a flyer from his pants pocket and walking toward him. "Something's going on at the church. Everyone in the cellar, they just packed up and left. We found this."

Dickson snatched the flyer from Snapper's hand. Ruth ran to his side and read it over his shoulder.

"*Dear Friends*," the flyer began. "*It has come to my attention that the unthinkable has happened. You have been threatened and abused in a most ungodly manner, much as many of you were in your home countries before you wisely sought shelter here in America. No doubt you felt you left all that fear behind, yet here you are, afraid once again. Afraid to return to your own homes and afraid to walk the streets of your own neighborhood.*

"*But there is one thing that you need not be afraid of, my friends–the power of God. In hiding from the danger that surrounds you, you have also hidden from God and that is something that we must never do. For blessed are the righteous that dare to step forth into the light and bravely declare their allegiance to the Lord, for theirs is the Kingdom of Heaven.*

"*There is no reason to hide, dear friends. Father Rose requests your attendance at Our Lady of Perpetual Sorrow where we can join together in worshipping He who is the Lord and Savior of all. The Devil will not tread where angels dwell. God has spoken and Father Rose has heard the call. He will see to your safety and well being.*

"*This special mass begins tonight at 11 p.m. Father Rose requests your prompt arrival, as no one will be allowed to enter or exit once mass has begun.*"

Ruth turned and stared at Dickson. "What does it mean?" she asked.

"Dear God," Dickson whispered. "He's going to kill them all."

We are in the Church of Our Lady of Perpetual Sorrow. The greeter on the left, dressed in his finest attire, is the Torch. Throngs of people have come out of hiding from the cellar of the Black Friar and other hidden shelters throughout the Lower East Side, dozens of people have walked to the church, hand in hand, rushing through the streets hoping that none of the Council of Ten are lurking in the shadows with their guns drawn. The Torch is graciously escorting the older residents to their seats, while whole families clutch one another and make their way into the church. They kneel at the side of their pew, remove their hats and make the sign of the cross before being seated.

Fantômas, in his disguise as Father Rose, approached the Torch and pulled him to the side. "Why is this taking so long?" he said. "Don't they know what it means to be on time?"

"I'll handle it," the Torch said.

The Torch stepped outside and stood at the head of the stairs leading into the church. "Come quickly!" he shouted, "Father Rose wishes to speak and salvation waits for no man!"

The street slowly emptied as the last of the parishioners stepped through the doorway. The Torch closed and locked the doors behind them.

Once everyone was seated, the quiet mumbling among the congregation ceased and all eyes went to the altar as Father Rose stepped up to the podium. He stood still for a moment, luxuriating in the silence and reveling in his feeling of power. A tight-lipped but sincere smile crossed his face as he gazed at the fearful masses gathered before him. "My children," he said, "for you are all, all of you, my children. As you know, I have, for many years, made it my solemn duty to minister to the sick of my parish. And I'm not just referring to those with physical sickness but to the spiritually sick as well. To the sick at heart. And I know that recent events–for some of you, very tragic events–have made you sick at heart.

"But know, my children, that you are not to blame for these events. When tragedy and hardship seem to be occurring all around you, you begin to wonder, 'What have I done to deserve this? What have I done to make the Lord hate me so, so much?'

"I know, my friends! I have felt it too! Yes, even I, who must speak for the Lord, often feel as if the Lord has abandoned me in my time of need. But it isn't true. It isn't true for me and it isn't true for anyone in this room because we are believers. We believe in the Lord's infinite mercy and because of that, we are saved."

Father Rose thrust his hand into the air. "He is your savior! He is the truth and the light! Join me as I gaze into the heavens and plead with the Lord for salvation! Stand up, my friends! Stand up!"

The people, enraptured by Father Rose's sermon and fearful of the dangers that lay outside the church, stood en masse at his command.

"Look up!" Father Rose cried. "Look up to the Lord for salvation! Everyone! I want every one of you to look up! Turn your eyes heavenward and look…up!"

The moment every member of the congregation was staring upward, Fantômas gave the signal to the Torch, who was standing at the back of the church. The Torch reached upward for a rope and pulled down on it with all of his might. The rope was attached to a small system of pulleys that controlled a half dozen giant tubs that were suspended above the heads of the congregation, hidden in the rafters. As all heads were turned toward the ceiling, the tubs tipped, spilling gallon after gallon of foul green liquid into their faces. The congregation immediately screamed, their hands darting to their faces as the liquid made its way down their throats and behind their eyes.

Father Rose chuckled as he watched his parishioners struggle against the burning sensations in their eyes and throats and begin to climb over one another in a mad dash to escape the church. "Your panic is wholly unnecessary," he said to the crowd. "The doors are locked. There is no escape. In seconds you will feel your joints begin to stiffen and shortly after that, you will remain conscious but will completely lose the ability to move. There is nothing any of you can do about what is happening to you at the moment, so as Father Rose might say, 'give yourselves up to He who has complete control over your destiny.' "

The congregation continued to struggle until, after only a few seconds, they had all ceased moving. Some had fallen to the floor and others had fallen between the pews. Still others had remained standing. Their voices were unimpaired, however, and they continued to cry, scream and pray as their eyes stared forward, wide open and unmoving.

Then, at another signal from Father Rose, the Torch opened a panel in the side wall, revealing a large crank with a handle. He spit on both of his hands, then began turning the crank as quickly as he could. From everywhere, ropes that had been woven throughout the pews and hidden under the congregation's feet, began to snake through the crowd–wrapping around their ankles and constricting tightly until everyone in the church was bound tightly to one another.

Fantômas stood at the front of the church, hands pressed together in front of his chest, and smiled at his handiwork. "Soon," he thought to himself, "my work here will be done."

Chapter 23: He Who Lives by the Sword

We are in the cemetery behind Our Lady of Perpetual Sorrow. The Woman in Black, lantern in hand, has led Brian Shea to this spot.

"Why are we here?" Shea asked. "What's going on inside the church? I want to know where my wife is. Do you hear me? Tell me or I'll barge through those doors, grab Fantômas by the throat and force the information out of him!"

"And in the attempt," the Woman in Black countered, "you would seal the fate of your wife and child. Patience, Brian Shea. I have brought you back here for a reason."

The reason soon revealed itself as the Woman in Black knelt over a tombstone and leaned into it, pushing it to the side with a mighty shove until the ground gave way to an underground staircase. "Your wife is down there," she said. "Two stories down lie the caverns beneath the church. When you reach the bottom, turn left and follow the corridor about a hundred yards. Your wife is locked inside one of the cells."

Brian Shea didn't answer but leapt down into the earth, taking the stairs two at time. "Hurry!" the Woman in Black whispered fiercely into the dark ground. "If what I suspect is true, you have very little time before everything comes crumbling down around you!"

Brian Shea only half-heard the Woman in Black's final warning as he pressed forward, stumbling on occasion and scraping his hands along the black dirt that made up the sides of the pit. Soon, the dirt gave way to rock as the staircase ended. Shea leapt from the final step and landed on the floor of the cavern. Most of the torches had been extinguished but there were still a few of them leaking light through the grim tunnels, the orange glow flickering and dancing along the stone walls.

Shea rose to his feet and wiped the dust from his hands. He ran to his left about a hundred yards, and the bars of Sally Shea's cell came into view. He threw himself at the cell door.

"Sally!" he hissed. "Are you there?" As his eyes adjusted to the darkness, he could see his wife hidden in the corner, holding their child.

Sally looked up, startled–a sharp shriek beginning, then stopping, in her throat. "Monster!" she cursed. "Get away from me. How dare you. How dare you!"

"Sally!" Shea said. "It's me! It's Brian!"

"I know who you are," Sally snarled, still convinced that the man before her was an imposter. "You're that…man. That idiot that works for Fantômas. You can't touch me and you can't touch my child. I won't be fooled twice!" She held tight to her child and turned away from Shea, toward the wall.

Shea ran to the wall of the cavern and pulled a lit torch from its place in the rock. He returned to the bars and held the torch as close to his face as he dared so the light would illuminate his features. "Sally," he said. "Look at me." Sally slowly turned her head to look at Shea, a scowl still sitting upon her brow. "At our wedding," Shea continued, "The Justice of the Peace, Judge Trimarco, took our hands in his and placed them on the Good Book. Then he took his own cracked, weather-beaten hand and gave you a squeeze on the shoulder. You looked up at him and he winked and you dropped your head for a moment because you didn't want me to see you smile."

Sally gazed at Shea and her lips began to quiver. "Brian?" she asked, a tear falling from her eye. "Oh my God. Brian…" Shea thrust his arms between the bars and Sally crawled forward to meet them. She pressed her cheeks against his hands and kissed his palms. "Are you OK?" she asked.

"I'm fine," Brian said. "Everything's going to be fine. My God, you're so beautiful."

Sally held their child so Shea could see him. "See," she said. "Denny knows it's you. He didn't smile once at that…other man."

Shea pulled his arms out of the cell and immediately began tracing his fingers along the bars, stopping at the lock and holding the torch in front of him to examine it. "We're gonna be fine, Sally," he said. "But I've got to get the two of you out of here. Something's happening upstairs."

"How?" Sally said. "Fantômas and that man who looked like you are the only two people with keys."

Shea clutched the two bars protruding from the lock and threw himself at the door of the cell with all his might. "It's a Samuels lock," he said.

"What?"

"Garrison Samuels. He's a locksmith in Boston. There's no way to undo the lock without a key. Even if I had my lock picking equipment with me, the pins are too far away from one another." He looked into Sally's cell. "Hand me those rocks in the corner."

Sally retrieved several large rocks and passed them to Shea through the bars. He used them to create a makeshift stand for the torch so that it would stand upright and continue to illuminate the ground. "Do you have a dinner plate or a cup or something in there?"

Sally passed a small dish to Shea. He began using it to dig into the hard dirt of the cavern floor, just around the bottom of the bars that led to the lock. "I can't pick the lock," he said, "but it secures the door by extending the bars into two couplings–one under the dirt, here, and one in the ceiling. If we can expose the couplings, between the two of us we might be able to break the lock and open the door."

"What should I do?" Sally asked.

"Try using a stone to chip away at the ceiling above the center bar."

Sally grabbed a large stone, stood on her tiptoes and began bashing away at the ceiling, sending dust and dirt spilling into the cell. Suddenly, Brian noticed the chains binding her wrists as they clanged away at the bars of the cell. "Oh my God," he said, "You're chained to the wall."

Sally stared at him again, the look of hope on her face turning to sorrow. "Don't worry, Sally," Shea said. "Everything will be fine. We'll get the cell door open, then I'll deal with the chains." Sally nodded and tried to smile but her fear continued to mount.

And on the opposite end of the cavern, another door opened as someone else penetrated Fantômas' private sanctum.

Dickson's late night study of the maps made by Snapper, Muggs and Glimpy served him well. After driving the Musketeers, Ruth and the Professor back to the city, he set off for Good Time Charlie's Pub–point A on the map. He barged into the bar and darted for the staircase, much to the consternation of the bar's owner, who didn't like people making a mess in his establishment. By the time the owner had made his way around the counter and to the staircase, Dickson had vanished behind the secret panel he knew would be in the stairwell. The bar owner calmly scratched his head, then racked the incident up to just another hallucination and resolved to stop drinking on the job.

Dickson made his way through the tunnel, hands groping along the wet walls until he reached the end. Here, he knew, was an entryway leading to Our Lady of Perpetual Sorrow. He felt along the walls until the rock gave way to the smoothness of a large door. He pressed against it with his shoulder until it began to give way, the bottom of it scraping against the ground and the hinges sending out a squeal that echoed through the tunnel. Flame from torchlight became visible as Dickson eased the door open. He stepped through the doorway and found himself in the underground cavern beneath the church.

Despite his resolve, Dickson began to feel foolish. Firstly, he had insisted that Ruth escort her exhausted father back home, despite her loud and accusatory protestations. Now that he was in the devil's lair he found himself wishing he had told her how much he cared for her before they had parted.

Secondly, he had forgotten to replace the gun he had lost at Fantômas' mansion in Long Island.

Still, there was no turning back and with a determination that bordered on madness, Dickson continued walking through the curved cavern. An impulse told him that one of the unlit torches in the wall looked out of place and, when he pulled it downward, a wall opened up in front of him revealing a staircase. He took the steps two at a time until he found himself in Fantômas' study. The bookshelves were still overturned and an empty cage stood in the middle of the floor. He made his way to the circular staircase and climbed upward until he found another door blocking his way. He felt along the wall until he discovered the lever. The door opened and for the second time that night Dickson found himself staring at a scene of unbelievable horror.

He was in the church now, standing in the doorway at the altar. A priest was in front of him, his back to Dickson, walking up the aisle with his eyes turned heavenward. Above the priest, hanging from the rafters, were at least a hundred people–young men, old men, women and children. All of them were upside down, hanging from ropes that bound their ankles. They looked for all the world like pieces of meat hanging in a slaughterhouse and it occurred to Dickson that perhaps that was exactly what they were. For a brief moment, Dickson feared that they were all dead. Then he heard whimpering and crying coming from above and it became obvious that Fantômas wasn't through with them yet. Destroying them wasn't enough. He wanted them to die slowly. He wanted them to watch one another die.

Most of all, he wanted them to be afraid of him.

"My friends," Fantômas addressed his victims, unaware that Dickson was standing behind him. "The time has almost come to meet your maker. For many of you, I'm sure the time is coming quite a bit sooner than you expected. But try to think of it this way–given your lack of position in life, your poverty, your ill health and general laziness, I'm probably saving you from a much more painful death that you would have incurred otherwise. Many of you would have died from tuberculosis in the next few years or smallpox or diphtheria or some other painful plague. Or perhaps many of you would have been murdered for the handful of pennies you kept clutched tight to your chests. Regardless, please try to remember that the Lord has a plan and tonight that plan includes me. It grieves me to do this, as I've gotten to know so many of you over the past months, but it's time for me to vanish, so all of you must vanish as well. My parting gifts to all of you are your next several minutes of consciousness so that you may all make peace with your God."

"*Fantômas*!" Dickson surprised himself with the brutality of his shout. It did the trick. Fantômas spun around to see Dickson standing on the altar. Dickson could tell from the look on Fantômas' face that he hadn't expected Dickson to be there.

"Impossible," Fantômas said under his breath, then caught himself and regained composure. "Mr. Dickson!" he said with a smile. "What a pleasant surprise. And tell me… exactly which one of your poor friends did you choose to die? I so wanted to be there for that character-defining moment but as you can see I've been busy."

"Let them down," Dickson said, his voice eerily calm. "All of them."

"Surely you're kidding. You know I'll do nothing of the sort. As far as I can tell, Mr. Dickson, you're not even armed or you would have shot me already. Now tell me, which one of them died? Of course it wasn't your beloved Ruth Harrington, although I wonder whether or not she found a way to sacrifice herself for the others. And not the Professor. What kind of bastard sends an old man to his death? No, it must have been Meredith! Tell me I'm right!"

"They're all alive and well, Fantômas. You've failed."

Fantômas' smile remained unbroken. "Impossible," he said.

"Your look-alike lackey, however, took a tragic tumble onto the rocks along Long Island Sound, I'm sorry to say." Now it was Dickson's turn to smile. Fantômas was clearly taken by surprise.

"You're bluffing," Fantômas said.

"Not at all," Dickson said, reaching into his pocket to retrieve the necklace with the golden tooth. He tossed the trinket to the ground and it slid to a stop at Fantômas' feet.

Fantômas knelt down, picked up the necklace and held it up to the light. "And here I thought this was such a good luck charm. It has brought me nothing but grief."

"Let them go," Dickson repeated.

Fantômas stared at Dickson with exasperation. "Let me try to understand, Mr. Dickson. Here I am and here you are, completely unarmed and defenseless and you wish to save these worthless miscreants behind me."

"They aren't worthless," Dickson said. "They simply have not begun to live. And as long as there are people like you exploiting and threatening them, they will never have a chance."

"Don't make me laugh, Detective! You think that I'm the only thing standing between this human chattel and the good life? The people that run this city don't want them in the way of progress any more than I do. I tried to give them something to live for and all I asked in return was their allegiance. And their gratitude? They ran from me. Betrayed me. Trust me, Mr. Dickson. People focused on basic survival aren't dependable. I much preferred the criminal classes of France. At least, we were honest about the possibility of the poor becoming wealthy. There was no chance! The criminals accepted their lot in life and even reveled in it. But here, your leaders have propagated this...myth that these people–these pathetic, diseased people–are the future of the country."

"It isn't a myth."

"Really?" Fantômas stepped onto the altar. "If you are so convinced of their worth, Detective, defend them." He reached for two crossed swords hanging on the wall and pulled them free.

"What?" Dickson felt his panic rise.

"These swords belonged to one of General Washington's men and were used to shed the blood of the British oppressors.

They were given to the real Father Rose as a gesture of thanks upon the completion of this church–a reminder that 'he who lives by the sword, shall die by the sword.' " Fantômas tossed one of the swords to Dickson. It landed heavily in Dickson's hands. "*En garde*," Fantômas said.

Dickson held the sword in front of him with both hands. He had virtually no experience fencing and had never even touched a weapon of this weight before. Still, upon hearing the whimpers and cries of the people hanging from the rafters, he raised the sword in front of him and prepared himself for Fantômas' first strike.

The blows came faster than Dickson could have anticipated–from the left, then right, then above. He blocked each blow, but just barely, and the smile on Fantômas' face told him that he was simply toying with Dickson. "Come now," Fantômas laughed. "You're going to have to do better than that if you want to save the future of America!"

Fantômas leapt at Dickson again, driving him backward among the throngs of bound people swinging from the ceiling. Dickson found himself eye-to-eye with the upside-down prisoners as he weaved back and forth, attempting to dodge the thrusts of Fantômas' sword all the while.

Lunge. Left. Right. Lunge. Right.

The sounds of fear among the trapped crowd began to increase and Fantômas drove Dickson deeper into the morass. Dickson was too afraid of striking one of them to charge forward and so remained on the defensive.

Fantômas lowered his sword momentarily. "See this man beside me, Mr. Dickson?" he said, stroking the upside-down head of a man hanging eye-level with Fantômas. "One of the quietest, most skillful criminals I've ever met. His wife and family are hanging here beside him. As long as he worked for me, he was able to put food on their table. But at the first sign of trouble from that damned Council of Ten, he took his family into hiding. Regardless of how much he might be crying at the moment, he is a criminal. And you think he's worth saving?" Fantômas shoved the man to the side, sending him swinging like a pendulum, to and fro, between himself and Dickson.

"You and I are not judges of these people!" Dickson cried as Fantômas thrust his sword forward every time the man swung past, nearly striking Dickson every time.

"Interesting," Fantômas said, continuing to lash out at Dickson as the man swung right, then left, then right again. "Because it seems to me that you and I are the only people with any interest in him whatsoever. Not a single policeman besides you has even attempted to enter this church. No doubt they are otherwise occupied soothing the egos of Samuel Cobblepot's wealthy friends. You are alone, Mr. Dickson. You are alone and a nobody. A *tabula rasa*. Nobody knows who you are and I would be very much surprised if even you knew who you were. Your foolish attempts at significance have failed and you will be lost to history as the people around you go down in flames."

Fantômas stopped fighting for a moment, as the man swung to a stop. He struck a pose with his hand above his head and sword arm outstretched. "For the last time, Detective," he said. "*En garde*."

Dickson lowered his arms and tossed his sword to the ground. "I am not alone," he said. "I know who I am." Dickson leapt forward with his hands reaching for Fantômas' throat. Fantômas was so thrown off guard that he was unable to defend himself with his sword. Before he knew it, Dickson was on top of him and had wrestled him to the ground. Dickson straddled Fantômas' torso as the villain twitched and writhed beneath him. "I am the man that destroyed Fantômas," Dickson said, pressing his thumbs upward into Fantômas' throat until the criminal began to gasp for air. "It's over, Fantômas," Dickson said with an eerie calm. "Finally over."

Fantômas still had his hand wrapped around the hilt of his sword but there was no room to maneuver the blade between them. His face turned a deep crimson and his legs began to relax as his vision grew dark. In a final desperate attempt to free himself, he turned the sword around and thrust upward with the handle into Dickson's ribcage.

It worked.

Dickson relaxed his grip just long enough for Fantômas to struggle free. Dickson fell to the ground and attempted to crawl away but the pain in his side kept him from standing. Fantômas slowly stood up, sword still in hand, and stared down at Dickson as he held onto his side and gasped for breath. "It has been a pleasure crossing swords with you, Mr. Dickson," Fantômas said, massaging his sore neck. "But our struggle, like all good things, must now come to an end." Fantômas raised the sword above his head and stepped over Dickson's body, prepared to thrust the blade into Dickson's chest.

The gunshot came from the direction of the altar and echoed throughout the church. The crowd let out a collective gasp as the bullet struck Fantômas in the shoulder and he dropped the sword. Dickson shifted to one side as the sword fell to the ground, its blade penetrating the floor and its handle vibrating. It missed Dickson's face by inches.

Fantômas stumbled backward and clutched at his shoulder with his opposite hand. He grimaced in pain and brought his hand up to his face. It was covered in blood. He turned toward the altar to see who had fired the shot and his lip twisted into a sneer. "I might have guessed," he said.

Dickson turned around as well and struggled to get to his feet. It took a few moments for him to understand what had happened, but once he realized the identity of the mysterious gunman, all the pieces fell into place.

"You!" Dickson cried aloud.

Chapter 24: The Council of Ten

Standing on the altar were ten men, all dressed identically in dark grey coats and matching hats. The Council of Ten had arrived to pass judgment on Fantômas. Their guns were drawn and standing in front of them was their mysterious leader.

Sergeant Corona.

"Step to one side, Dickson," Corona said. "Our business is with Fantômas."

"You don't believe for a moment that you're safe from Corona, do you, Dickson?" Fantômas asked, still grimacing from the pain in his shoulder.

"No," Dickson said. "Not for a moment."

"Good!" Fantômas smiled. "Despite everything, Detective, I'm glad to know I didn't underestimate your powers of deduction."

"I will admit," Dickson said, "it took me longer to figure it out than it should have. I attributed every criminal activity to you until I realized that that was an impossibility."

"Ah, Detective," Fantômas sighed. "You flatter me."

"After all," Dickson said, facing Corona. "No one else knew of the journal's hiding place in Professor Harrington's bedroom except myself, Ruth, Meredith and Corona. Meredith substituted the false journal, preventing the Council from obtaining the real one so it was clear he wasn't working with them. Corona, on the other hand, was the only one with the opportunity to communicate the hiding place to the Council. Indeed, he's the only one that could have clued the Council into the journal's very existence."

"Very good, Detective!" Fantômas said. "And I think that if we were to search the good sergeant's rooms right now we might even find a suitcase containing Miss Harrington's million-dollar reward. The money I received was counterfeit."

"Shut up!" Corona shouted. "Both of you! I'm not interested in how clever either of you are. The Council has arrived to pass judgment on Fantômas and retrieve Professor Harrington's journal from him!"

"Ha!" Fantômas laughed. "Do you hear that, Mr. Dickson? Was I lying about the hypocrisy of authority? The Council isn't interested in serving justice. They want Harrington's formula all for themselves. How typically American you are, Sergeant."

"Corona," Dickson said, appealing to his sense of righteousness. "We have to free these people. Arrest Fantômas, take him to prison and this will all be over."

Corona laughed. "Dickson, you're as naïve as ever. I don't care an ounce about these people. As far as I'm concerned, the streets are better off without them. The Council and I want Harrington's journal before Fantômas is tried and punished. No one else can be trusted with that kind of power. The Council will see to it that Harrington's work is used wisely. I should thank you, Detective. Without your hard work, particularly that detailed map of the underground tunnels, the Council and I would never have gotten this far."

"You plan to use Harrington's work wisely?" Dickson said, his temper rising. "Then why did you feign your own kidnapping? Perhaps you intended to disappear with the journal, leaving the rest of the Council to fend for themselves."

Fantômas continued to weigh in. "Certainly, a journal containing the darkest secrets of alchemy coupled with Miss Harrington's million-dollar reward could help a man to disappear and never be heard from again."

Corona began to huff in frustration. He turned to the rest of the Council, all of whom had begun to eye him suspiciously. "Surely you don't believe either one of them!" he said. "It's all lies! They seek to escape the hand of justice through deception! We cannot allow that to happen!"

Suddenly, Fantômas began to laugh. Corona spun around and aimed his gun at Fantômas' head. "What's so funny?" he asked.

"You, Sergeant." Fantômas answered. "And not just you but your entire misguided Council."

Corona sneered. "And why, pray tell, do you find us so amusing?"

Fantômas stared Corona directly in the eyes. "Because I find the image of ten dead men in grey with knives protruding from their chests to be very, very funny."

Corona was alarmed. "What are you talking about?"

First, Number Seven cried out in pain as the dagger struck him in the heart. He dropped his gun and staggered forward. Number Three instinctively tried to help him but was subsequently also struck. The dagger landed in his chest with a thud, staining his coat with blood.

Dickson dropped to the ground in confusion while Fantômas continued to laugh uproariously. Number Two clutched his chest and fell forward. The remaining seven men began firing their guns wildly into the air, causing screams of panic to erupt from the hanging crowd. Dickson stared into the rafters, searching for the source of the daggers until he finally spied two men, their skin a bleached white. One of them was guiding the other by the arm while the other continued to draw knives from a table and fling them at the Councilmen. "A little to the left," Dickson heard the first one say. "Now lower, and…throw!"

Number Four choked and fell to the floor, followed in quick succession by numbers One, Five and Eight. Corona took cover behind the podium on the altar. The gleam of the knives caught his eye and he turned his attention to the rafters where Zor and Zam continued to fling their weapons with uncanny accuracy. As the last of the Council members fell to the ground, Corona took careful aim and shot Zam in the stomach. Zam clutched his abdomen and rocked back and forth in confusion. Zor grabbed hold of him and in moments the two had lost their balance and went tumbling from the ceiling. They landed with a sickening thud across the back of a pew, their spines twisted and broken as they slid to the ground.

The church grew silent save for the sobbing coming from the children. Corona emerged from behind the podium with his gun drawn. He slowly made his way to the secret door in the altar, never taking his eyes or gun off of Fantômas. "You have won this round, Fantômas," Corona said. "Congratulations. But I will find you again and I will have Professor Harrington's journal."

"With all due respect, Corona," Fantômas said. "I think not."

The blade pressed into Corona's neck. He dropped his gun to the ground and his hands shot to his throat. His eyes grew wide as he brought his hands to his face and stared in shock at his blood-covered palms. The knife cut smoothly through his flesh and his jugular began to erupt, sending a sharp spray of crimson down the front of his gray suit and creating a thick puddle around his feet. The wound was so deep that the color drained from Corona's face in an instant. "Goodbye, Sergeant Corona," Fantômas said. "Godspeed."

Corona dropped to his knees, his eyes rolled back into his head and pitched forward until his dead body fell with a thud on the church floor. Standing behind him, bloody knife in hand, was Geoffrey the Slasher.

"Yes," Fantômas said to his new recruit. "I think you'll do just fine."

From the depths of his soul, Dickson's anger rose and he emitted a hoarse shout as he darted across the room and leapt at Fantômas. But he was still weak from the blow to his ribs and he clutched his side in pain before he could lay a hand on the villain. Fantômas walked over with an air of calm and took Dickson's chin in his hand. "A shame," Fantômas said. "Such a waste of intelligence on people that don't deserve it." He reached down and picked up his sword.

"No," Dickson said. "Please. Let them go."

"We're through," Fantômas said. "You and I, Detective, are through." He struck Dickson on the head with the hilt of the sword. Dickson lost consciousness and fell to the floor in a heap.

"Well," Fantômas said to Geoffrey. "That was exhausting."

We are back in the caverns beneath the church and rejoin Brian and Sally Shea in their struggle to open the door of Sally's cell. Shea is still digging beneath the bars with a small dish while Sally is chipping away at the dirt in the ceiling. Both of them are growing exhausted and their muscles have begun to ache. Sweat drips down Brian Shea's face and bits of rock and dust are falling into Sally Shea's eyes and mouth. Still, the two of them continue to chip away at the prison.

"Can you see the coupling?" Brian Shea asked.

"Yes," Sally said. "I have it."

"Grab the bar above the coupling and on the count of three, press down. I'm going to press toward you and we may be able to break the lock."

"OK," Sally said. "OK."

"One…Two…Three!"

The two lovers pressed against one another with all of their might, but the lock didn't budge. They continued pressing until Brian let go and fell backward onto the cavern floor, exhausted. "Just a few moments," he said. "And we'll try again."

But Sally knew it was no use. The two of them didn't have enough strength and no matter how many times they tried, the lock would hold firm. She crawled to her child, picked him up, and carried him to the bars. "Take him," she said.

Brian Shea lifted his head. "What?"

"Take Denny and go."

Shea could hardly believe his ears. "I'm not leaving you here," he said.

"Come back for me, but let's get Denny out of here. At least he'll be safe."

Shea wiped the sweat from his forehead with the back of his hand. "Sally, listen…"

"No," Sally Shea interrupted, "you listen. We can dig all we want but that lock isn't going anywhere. If we stay here, Fantômas will find us and we'll have no chance. You need to get help and, if you're going, I want you to take Denny with you. At least one of us will be safe."

Shea hated the idea but he knew Sally was right. "I love you," he said.

"I love you too, Brian. Now take him, quickly, and go." Sally passed Denny through the bars and Shea took his child in his arms.

"I'll be back," Shea said.

"I know," Sally answered.

Shea ran back through the cavern until he found the hidden staircase leading up to the tombstone entrance. Putting Denny over his shoulder and holding onto him with one arm, he used his other to lift the two of them onto the bottom rung. Once he had secured himself on the ladder, he climbed up as fast as he could. He noted with relief that the Woman in Black had left the entrance open so that he could escape. He reached upward and placed Denny on the ground outside the entrance, then pulled himself out of the hole, picked up Denny and hurried to leave the graveyard.

"Well, well," a voice behind him said. "Isn't this damned lucky?"

Shea turned around. The Torch was standing behind a tombstone with a gun. "I'm sorry, Brian," the Torch said. "I truly am."

"Don't do this," Shea said. "I just want to take my wife and child and leave. Help me save Sally and I'll disappear."

"You had your chance to disappear, Shea," the Torch answered. "It's too late."

Shea clutched his child to his chest. "You're going to kill me."

"Yes," the Torch said. "Give me the child."

Brian Shea held Denny in front of him and kissed the child on his cheek.

"I have to do this," the Torch said. "My future with Fantômas depends on this. I didn't want to do it but he calls the shots. You know that. Damn it, Shea! Why didn't you just obey orders? None of this would have happened."

The two friends stared at one another, each of them knowing how it was going to end. Shea handed Denny to the Torch. "Don't let Fantômas have him," he said. "And make sure nothing happens to Sally."

"I will," the Torch answered. He took Denny and sat him on the ground under a tree. "Now," he continued. "Turn around."

Brian Shea turned his back on the Torch. "Get on your knees," the Torch said. Shea did so. The Torch placed his gun to Shea's head and pulled the trigger. The bullet pierced Shea's skull and embedded itself in the ground. Shea's body slumped forward and fell to the dirt.

The Torch walked back to the tombstone and retrieved a can of kerosene which he then proceeded to pour over Shea's corpse. Once Shea's clothing was soaked, he drew a match from inside his coat, lit it and set the body on fire. The flames spread quickly, sending bright jets of orange and red high into the air. The Torch stared into the heat, becoming gradually hypnotized as the spirals of color danced in front of his eyes. As the fire worked its magic and began to possess him, his grief over his friend's death gave way to an overwhelming feeling of joy.

"Snap out of it, my friend," Fantômas said, sidling up alongside the Torch and waving his hand in front of his eyes. The Torch came to his senses.

"I did it," the Torch said. "Shea is dead."

"Yes," Fantômas said. "Several days later than I intended but I suppose better late than never. Where is the child?"

The flames continued to grow and engulf Shea's body. The Torch walked to the tree, picked up Denny and handed him to Fantômas. "I promised Shea he wouldn't be hurt," the Torch said.

"Heavens," Fantômas said. "Perish the thought. What kind of monster would hurt a child?" He took Denny from the Torch and held him in the crook of his arm.

"Now," the Torch said. "I've done everything you've asked me to."

"Yes, Mr. Torch, you have."

"What's next?" the Torch asked with some eagerness. "What happens now?"

Fantômas lifted one eyebrow. "I assure you, Mr. Torch," he said, "that you're about to get everything that's coming to you."

Geoffrey the Slasher had crept up behind the Torch and in an instant cut the Torch's throat from ear to ear. The Torch pitched forward and landed face first into the dirt. He was dead in an instant.

"We're almost through, my friend," Fantômas said to Geoffrey. "Soon this long night will be over."

Geoffrey began to grow afraid. "Are you gonna kill me too?" he asked.

Fantômas smiled. "No, my friend," he said. "You have done everything I've instructed you to do and loyalty is all I ask." Fantômas handed the child to Geoffrey. "Stay a safe distance from the church. All hell is about to break loose."

Chapter 25: The Redemption of Frederick Dickson

The first sensation Detective Dickson experienced upon awakening was a sharp pain in the back of his head that seemed to spread all the way over his skull and across his eyelids. This was quickly followed by the realization that he was, in fact, not dead but that his hands and feet were curiously bound. Once he was able to open his eyes, he realized he was still in the church, suspended upside-down from the rafters alongside the rest of Father Rose's congregation. The crowd had ceased their cries and now seemed possessed of a hopeless silence. Dickson could tell many of them were staring at him, their last hope, and had resigned themselves to their fate.

Quietly, Frederick Dickson resolved to do the same.

After all, Dear Reader, I am sure we all agree that there is only so long that one can struggle against evil, persist in a battle against injustice, before acknowledging that the forces of malevolence often overwhelm the forces of good. It is in this state of mind that we now find Detective Dickson. He has been beaten, humiliated, defeated and left to die with scores of other victims, all of them casualties in the war against Fantômas.

Dickson reminded himself as he hung there, blood rushing to his head and eyes blurring, that he had saved Ruth and Professor Harrington. He decided as he went to his death, that that would be enough. When combating an evil as pervasive as Fantômas, one had to be satisfied with small victories. It would take more people to come along after him in order for the war to be won.

Dickson closed his eyes and waited for Fantômas' inevitable final stroke and wondered what it would be. A church filled with poison gas? Or perhaps he planned to kill each one of them one by one, satisfying his mounting blood lust well into the next decade. While Dickson was considering these possibilities, he heard the sound of crying coming from beside him. He opened his eyes and saw a young girl. She couldn't have been more than eight years old.

Rebecca Clausen.

Although he had never met her, Dickson decided that his last act should be ministering to the poor girl. Perhaps if he could bring her a small moment of peace, he could ease her suffering as she passed from this world into the next.

"What's your name?" Dickson asked.

Rebecca stared at Dickson, her eyes swollen with tears. "Rebecca," she answered.

"Rebecca," Dickson continued. "We all must face this inevitable moment sometime. Let us face it together. We won't be afraid and we won't cry."

Rebecca Clausen shot Dickson a confused look. "I'm not crying because I'm afraid. I'm crying because I have a knife in my shoe and it hurts."

Dickson's eyes immediately blazed with energy. "You have a knife in your shoe?"

"Yes," Rebecca answered. "My Uncle Lukas gave it to me."

"Well, now," Dickson said. "That's very interesting, Rebecca. Why don't I try to swing toward you and we'll see what we can do about that knife in your shoe."

Dickson's comment was overheard by several other people who were still conscious and they focused all their attention on him as he wriggled his body, trying to gain enough momentum to swing back and forth. Eventually, he began drifting to and fro until he could feel the fabric from Rebecca's dress brush past his bound hands. "OK, Rebecca," he said as he swung past her. "The next time I go past, I'm going to grab your hands. I need you to hang tightly to me until we stop swinging. OK?"

Rebecca nodded.

Dickson swung his body alongside Rebecca's and clutched her hands tightly. His weight pulled her sideways and the ropes suspending them were pulled taught, forming a V between them. “Hold on,” Dickson said, “and be brave.” He used his tightly bound hands to pull himself along her back, working his fingers into the fabric of her dress until he made his way to her legs. He could hear Rebecca begin to groan with discomfort as he slowly pulled himself to her feet. “Just another moment, Rebecca,” he said. Dickson slowly worked Rebecca’s shoe off of her foot, but in the final second lost his grip. He let go of Rebecca and they swung back into place. The shoe went plummeting down to the floor. The people that could see what was happening gasped in horror.

All was lost.

“Dammit!” Dickson cried.

“It’s in the other shoe,” Rebecca said.

Dickson rolled his eyes and sighed. “Now, she tells me.” He began swinging again, clutching onto Rebecca and pulling himself back to her remaining shoe. This time, he removed the shoe and felt the warm metal press into his palm as he let go of Rebecca and swung away. Some of the people began to cheer.

“Sssshhhh!” Dickson chided them. “Fantômas could return at any…”

Fantômas re-entered the church. He was holding a lit torch in one hand and a jug of kerosene in the other.

“Oh, God,” Dickson thought.

Fantômas marched to the altar and held the torch aloft so everyone could see. “And now, my friends,” he announced with a flourish. “I’m sure you’ll forgive me for not leaving you with any words of hope or wisdom, but quite frankly I’m sick to death of all of you. Besides, I hate long goodbyes.”

Dickson started to work at his bonds, feverishly pressing the blade against the rope in an effort to free his hands. Fantômas began splashing the kerosene on the altar, making sure every piece of wood and ornamental fabric was saturated.

Dickson’s hands were free. He bent upward while Fantômas’ back was turned. Pain shot through his abdomen until he was able to clutch onto the rope and begin sawing away at it.

Fantômas held the torch to the altar cloth and the table was immediately engulfed in flame. He calmly walked over to a tapestry hanging to the side of the altar and set it alight as well. The crowd felt the heat almost instantly as the flames spread and leapt into the air.

Dickson severed the final fibers of the rope and fell toward the ground, twisting himself to get his feet underneath him. He landed with a sharp thud and pain shot through his ankle. It was clearly broken.

Fantômas turned around when he heard the noise. It took him only a moment to determine which rope no longer held its hostage. "*Dickson*!" he yelled. He drew a pistol from his coat. "Show yourself or I swear I will begin shooting these people! It's your choice, Dickson! Kill them now or let them burn alive!"

Dickson could tell that Fantômas was desperate by the sound of his voice. Ignoring the pain in his ankle, he pulled himself along the ground, behind the side pews, until he was within feet of Sergeant Corona's body. The enflamed tapestry was right beside him and he crunched his face tightly against the painful heat.

"How about that little girl, Dickson?" Fantômas screamed. "One bullet will end her precious life! Show yourself on the count of three or I fire! One…Two…"

Dickson lifted Corona's body and found his gun. He held the gun up and aimed it at Fantômas.

"Three!" Fantômas shouted, but the bullet from Corona's gun had struck him in the stomach. Fantômas' gun tumbled to the floor and he clutched his abdomen. He turned to see Dickson crouched behind Corona's body, the gun still smoking in Dickson's hand.

Fantômas grimaced in pain, then smiled and turned away from Dickson, flinging the torch at the other tapestry. The painted cloth burst into flames.

Dickson fired the gun again. The second bullet struck Fantômas in the back and he howled in agony. Dickson rose to his feet, wincing in pain. Fantômas stumbled forward, blindly clutching at the air until the flaming tapestry fell from its mooring and landed on top of him. He screamed again until the flames from the tapestry merged with those from the altar and he vanished into the blaze.

Dickson ran to the group of people and stared up at them. No way to reach the ropes. He ran to the back of the church and found the crank that lowered and raised the ropes. He began turning it, but the rope around the crank had been severed and was no longer connected to the netting that suspended Father Rose's parishioners from the ceiling. He pulled the bar from the front doors and pushed them open. Outside, a small crowd was beginning to form. "Get help!" he shouted. "Now!" He spotted a stairwell next to the door and leapt up the stairs, ignoring the biting pain in his ankle, until he found himself in the rafters. He looked out over the ledge and found that he was now above the dozens of people hanging from the ceiling. He put the knife between his teeth, then crawled out onto a thin beam. He found Rebecca Clausen and, figuring she was the lightest one, grabbed hold of her rope and began pulling it upward.

The altar was now completely engulfed in flame and small pockets of fire were breaking out along the floor, edging further down the back of the church.

Once Rebecca was safely in the rafters, Dickson clutched her by the shoulders. "Listen," he said. "I want you to run down the stairs, out the doors and as far away from this building as possible. If you see a policeman, I want you to flag him down and tell him to call the fire department. Do you understand?"

"My mommy and daddy," Rebecca said. "They're still down there."

Dickson looked down between the beams. "I'll get them," he said. "I promise. But you need to get out of here."

Dickson could hear Rebecca's footsteps echo through the stairwell as he began hauling up a young, thin man, probably 20 years old. He cut the young man's bonds. "Down the stairs," Dickson said. "Get out of here."

"No," the man said. "I'm not leaving you here. I'm helping you."

Dickson almost protested but the enormity of the task before him was starting to look more and more like an impossibility. The flames had now spread halfway through the church and the ceiling above the altar was beginning to buckle and creak. "What's your name?" Dickson asked.

"Harry," the man answered.

"I'm Detective Dickson. Harry, I only have one knife. I want you to look around for something that will cut these ropes."

Harry began crawling across the beams, scanning the rafters for a tool of some sort when a glint of metal caught his eye. "Something like this?" he said, holding up a small case full of Zor and Zam's throwing knives.

Dickson smiled. "Yes! Something like that exactly!"

Harry withdrew a knife from the case and the two men began hauling up the prisoners as the flames continued to snake their way through the church. Harry released a young Polish dress maker named Sarah and handed her another knife. Dickson lifted a Russian butcher named Nicholas. The four of them, armed with knives, continued to pull members of the congregation into the rafters, then set them free. Soon, the four were joined by a newspaper boy named Ben. Rebecca Clausen's parents were next, as was a shabbily dressed, bearded Irishman who failed to identify himself but promptly grabbed a knife and helped the others. Soon, the crowd in the rafters had grown to a dozen people. The supply of knives was exhausted but they continued to pull, tossing the blades back and forth and freeing one another as quickly as possible. Twelve turned to 20, then to 30. A family of Italians joined in to rescue their shockingly heavy Irish neighbor, while a tailor named Hans rescued Sammy the baker. And so it continued, on and on.

Dickson saw that the floor of the church was now covered in flames. At least two dozen people were still suspended over the fire and the rafters were growing too crowded. Sarah the dress maker began to swoon, then fainted. "Listen," Dickson said. "There isn't enough room up here. I need some of you to escort the women and children down the stairwell and into the street. The rest of you need only stay if you feel confident that you still have the strength." The thick black smoke was beginning to cloud everyone's sight, making it difficult to see who was still trapped below. About half of the crowd began to escort one another to the stairwell. Ben the paperboy threw Sarah the dressmaker over his shoulders and carried her to safety. About 15 people were still in the rafters when the roof over the altar gave way and a ton of burning wood went crashing to the ground. The men began choking from the smoke but continued to pull the ropes and free the rest of the crowd. The remaining prisoners were now unconscious from the heat. "All right!" Dickson shouted. "The rest of you need to get these people to the street. Quickly! Before they suffocate!" Dickson remained behind while the dozen or so people that were still conscious carried the rest outside. He watched them descend the staircase, then returned to the beams to try and get a clearer look at who was left. The entire church was covered in smoke and the flames had leapt up the walls and were now tickling the beams beneath Dickson's feet. He began coughing from the smoke, and the heat from the flames now made the burning sensation in his face overwhelming.

First he heard the creaking, then he felt the beams start to buckle beneath his feet. The rafter finally collapsed in a roar of flame and Dickson felt himself falling to the floor into the center of the abyss. He crashed to the ground and landed on his side. He felt a sharp pain shoot through his ribs and was certain that they had broken. He opened his eyes as the flames circled him. It was over, he knew. Nevertheless, he smiled and rewarded himself on a job well done. And as his sight began to fade, the smoke gave way to an angel, haloed by a circle of light. She stared down at him and held out her arms.

"Come on, Freddy!" she cried. "Give me your hands, for Chrissakes!"

"Miss Harrington?"

"For the love of God, Freddy, wipe that silly smirk off your face and climb on my back!"

"No! Miss Harrington… get out. Please. You'll never be able to carry me and save yourself."

"Are you kidding?" Ruth said, picking up Dickson and tossing him over her back. "You think I rushed into a blazing inferno so I could just run right back out again without you?"

"Can you support my weight?"

"Listen," Ruth said, "if I can carry a lioness through a hurricane to get her back to her cubs, I can surely lift a single, infuriating detective!"

Ruth rushed toward the doors, ignoring the sound of collapsing wood and the roar of the fire. She carried Dickson outside and both of them felt the sudden blast of cool, fresh air on their faces. Once she had moved him a safe distance from the blaze, she lowered him to the ground. Dickson looked out among the streets and saw that dozens of Fantômas' prisoners had made it to safety.

Escape!

Ruth turned around when she heard the sound of the fire brigade pull up to the church. "Well it's about damn time," she said.

"Ruth!" Dickson said. "Tell them there are still people inside! Tell them…"

"Easy, Freddy," Ruth said, smoothing Dickson's hair back with her hand. "There's no one left inside. You saved them."

"I did?"

"Yes, Freddy," Ruth said, tears welling up in her eyes. "You saved all of them."

"I saved all of them," Dickson said, his eyes beginning to close from exhaustion.

"Yes," Ruth said, soothing him with her voice. "Now relax. Everything's going to be fine. Finally."

Dickson allowed himself to settle back into Ruth's lap as she cradled his head in her arms. The last thing he saw before his eyes closed was an unfamiliar woman carrying a baby. She was walking through the crowd calling out a name. "Brian?" she said. "Brian? Where are you?" She began asking people to help her. "Have you seen my husband?" she asked. "His name is Brian. He was right here a moment ago. He vanished." The strangers shook their heads in sympathy. Dickson wondered, briefly, where the woman had come from, then drifted quietly into a deep, dreamless sleep.

Chapter 26: Slippery as Sin

After the fire destroyed Our Lady of Perpetual Sorrow, life in Manhattan seemed to return to normal. There were the regular murders and riots, of course, but no master criminals to speak of. In a small amount of time, the press abandoned the Fantômas story and moved on to other things. In homes on the Lower East Side, Fantômas left the realm of daily life and became, once again, a legend–his name spoken in whispers. Fortunately, the legend of Fantômas and his misdeeds had now grown to include the brave detective who risked his life to save dozens of innocent souls on that fateful night.

Once the rubble from the church was cleared, a team of officers began to search the caverns beneath the streets, but they found little evidence of Fantômas' existence. A few books here and there, along with a mysterious-looking cage just large enough to hold a person, but nothing pointing to Fantômas' true identity. The doorways to the underground tunnels were sealed off, as were the individual entrances around the city that allowed members of the Fantômas gang to elude police.

At the house on Long Island, investigators tallied the value of all the stolen items into the millions. The paintings were returned to the museums or their respective owners. The curious, automatic guillotines were purchased by an anonymous collector and later made an appearance at the 1939 New York World's Fair. None of the investigators, however, happened upon Dr. Hans Voitzel's decapitated body.

Nobody discovered the true identities of the Council of Ten, as the fire had rendered their bodies unrecognizable. Over the next year, however, several missing persons reports were filed that gave some hint as to the possible makeup of that secret organization. They included a local physician, a prominent politician, several wealthy businessmen and, oddly, the man who had purchased Frederick Dickson's textile mill in

1912. Dickson examined the report with some interest and ascertained that justice had been served.

Two weeks after the burning of the church, Detective Frederick Dickson was back on the job. He had been promoted to sergeant and given a new office, complete with windows that looked out onto the Manhattan streets. He was initially reticent to accept surroundings that seemed far too lofty for someone of his humble nature, but he had grown to love the city and began to enjoy watching life parade back and forth from his window. The police department didn't trumpet Dickson's promotion to the press due to the mysterious disappearance of Dickson's predecessor. They thought it best to sweep that particular embarrassment under the rug. It was time for the city to heal.

We are now in Sergeant Dickson's new office. His face is still flushed from the fire. His ribs are tightly bandaged and he walks on crutches, but his movements betray a lightness and energy that have endeared him to his colleagues. Police officers who claim never to have noticed Dickson before the fire, now shake his hand warmly and stand at attention when he walks by. They tell stories of Dickson's exploits to their families and, for a brief time, are proud to be members of New York's Police Department.

"Sergeant Dickson?" the young woman said as she opened the door to Dickson's office.

"Yes, Margaret," Dickson answered. "What can I do for you?"

"There's a Ruth Harrington here to see you."

Whatever confidence Dickson may have felt moments earlier vanished with the announcement of Ruth's presence. "Sendherin," he mumbled.

"I beg your pardon, sir?"

"I said send her in!" Dickson replied, a little too loudly.

Margaret stepped away from the door, and moments later Ruth Harrington entered Dickson's office. She was even more shockingly beautiful than Dickson remembered.

"How are you, Freddy?" Ruth asked.

"Miss Harrington!" Dickson said, leaping to his feet. Unfortunately, he had forgotten that his left ankle was encased in plaster and he dropped to the ground with a thud.

"Oh, God!" Ruth said. "Let me help you!"

"No, no," Dickson said. "I'm fine, Miss Harrington, just fine." He rose, dusted himself off, then limped painfully back to his chair and sat down.

"How are your…injuries?" Ruth asked.

"Oh," Dickson waved his hand through the air dismissively. "Not a problem. The Doctor says I'll be as good as new in a month or so."

"That's good news," Ruth said.

"Yes," Dickson answered.

The two stared at one another awkwardly for several moments until Ruth broke the silence. "You wanted to see me?" she said.

"I did?" Dickson said. "Yes! I wanted to give you something." He reached under his desk and pulled out a briefcase. Ruth took it from him, laid it on top of his desk and opened it.

"It's the reward money," Ruth said.

"One million dollars," Dickson replied. "Your entire trust fund. Apparently our friend Corona had replaced it with counterfeit bills in an effort to swindle Fantômas. I suppose he planned to take the money and your father's journal, abandon the rest of the Councilmen and then…who knows? Maybe he wanted to become a master criminal himself."

"The journal," Ruth remembered. "Have you found–"

Dickson interrupted her with a woeful shake of his head. "Not a trace," he said. "Most everything in Fantômas' Lower East Side lair was destroyed in the fire. My guess is that your father's journal is scattered among the ashes."

Ruth sighed. "He'll be disappointed but perhaps that's just as well. And Fantômas?"

"We found his body. Apparently he managed to stumble outside the church. His features were burned but the body was still wearing the scraps of Father Rose's robes."

“Then he’s finally gone?” Ruth asked.

“Yes, Miss Harrington. I believe Fantômas is finally gone.”

Ruth slowly moved closer to Dickson, resting her hand on his chest. “You know,” she said, smiling. “You don’t have to call me Miss Harrington any more. I think we know one another better than that.”

Dickson flushed and laughed. “Yes,” he said. “All right… Ruth.”

“See?” Ruth said. “Much better.”

Once again, the two friends stared at one another unsure of what to say. Each of them waited for the other to speak but both wondered if perhaps the events of the past month had made any sort of intimacy an impossibility. Could two people dare to grow closer after witnessing such horror?

“Well,” Ruth said at last, turning her head away in embarrassment. “I suppose I should go.”

“Yes,” Dickson replied, starting to rise then remembering the cast on his ankle and sitting back down. “Well…perhaps you will…stop by again…some time.”

“Yes. Perhaps I will.” Ruth headed for the door to Dickson’s office, opened it, then turned back around. “Freddy?” she said.

“Yes?”

“Jack and I have split.”

“Oh!” Dickson said, trying to restrain a smile. “I’m…sorry to hear that.”

“Yes, well. He’s not quite the man I thought he was. I’m not sure he was ever the man I thought he was. Or something.”

Dickson nodded and, because he could think of nothing else to say, said “Well…”

“I just thought,” Ruth said, “that perhaps you might be…interested in knowing that. About Jack and I splitting.”

“Yes. That’s…well…that’s very important information.”

They stared at one another, nodding their heads.

“Well I better go then,” Ruth said, quickly exiting and shutting the door behind her.

“Yes, well, goodbye then.” Dickson said.

Dickson continued to work well into the night, organizing his files and making his office more presentable for a man in his new position. As the light of day began to fade, he found himself thinking more and more of Ruth Harrington. By the time the streets were enveloped in night and the Moon had risen, he had summoned the courage to call her. It was, of course, ridiculous that two lonely people such as they would spend such a beautiful evening alone.

He picked up the receiver and dialed the operator, then heard the sound of someone crying. It was coming from outside his window. He hung up the phone, picked up his crutches and made his way across the room. Looking out onto the street, he saw a woman standing under a streetlamp, her head buried in her hands, sobbing.

The Woman in Black.

She stopped crying for a moment and looked up at Dickson’s window. She shook her head mournfully, then began to cry again. Slowly, she turned away from him and strode off down the street, into the night. Dickson briefly considered going after her but there was no need. Her message to him had come through loud and clear.

Fantômas was still alive.

And now, Dear Reader, we give you the opportunity to close this book, close your eyes and drift peacefully asleep. With Fantômas no longer an immediate threat, Dickson and Ruth’s safety assured, with the promise of romance between them, we wouldn’t blame you if you wished to stop reading now. You may consider the tale completely told with only minor hints of loose ends that are easy enough to dismiss with a shrug. If you are the kind of reader who requires such neat and tidy endings, we request that you not continue on. You may simply consider the next few pages of no consequence.

If, however, you wish to learn the truth of what happened during the final struggle between Detective Dickson and Fantômas, read on.

It is six months later. We are seated in a midtown pub. Next to us is a man who has clearly fallen on hard times. His once immaculate suit is now wrinkled and mottled with sweat. His tie hangs awkwardly around his neck. He bears the visage of a man who once owned the world, yet is now little more than a coarse drunkard.

The bartender places a drink–his third–in front of him and the man raises it to his lips and swallows it with the speed of an experienced lush. Between his hands is a newspaper turned to the society column. The man blinks, trying to focus on the words, and reads the column for the umpteenth time that evening.

"*Wedding bells will soon be ringing for one of Manhattan's favorite sons! Sergeant Frederick Dickson of the New York Police Department, who gained notoriety last year for his handling of the Fantômas affair, will soon wed the delightful Ruth Harrington, daughter of the esteemed chemist and explorer Professor James Harrington. Word has it that the shy and retiring sergeant wishes to handle the nuptials with discretion, but seeing as how every bachelor in New York will want to mourn the loss of one of the city's most charming and beautiful single ladies (Sorry, fellas!), the* Times *suggests a more public affair!*

"*Rumor has it that the esteemed law officer popped the question during dinner at Delmonico's and was immediately besieged by reporters, one of whom was lucky enough to overhear the exchange and alert his colleagues. While Sergeant Dickson's romantic request had to be mumbled several times before the delicious Miss Harrington understood what he was saying, the future Mrs. Dickson herself was heard to exclaim, 'Well, it's about time!'*

"*Be careful, Mrs. Dickson! What will your future children say?*

"*In any case, the editors of the* Times *wish to congratulate Professor James Harrington and especially Sergeant Frederick Dickson. You lucky, lucky man!*"

Jack Meredith pushed the newspaper to the side and ordered another drink. He hardly noticed the blond man in the dark jacket that sat next to him.

"The next round is on me," the blond man said.

"No, thank you, friend," Meredith slurred. "I really must be going. What would Mother say to me if she saw me in this condition, hmmm?"

"Ridiculous," the blond man replied. "Sit and have one more drink with me."

Meredith made a useless effort to straighten his tie and smooth back his hair, then turned to address his new companion. "Awfully kind of you, old sport!" he said, extending his hand. "The name is Jack Meredith! And you are…?"

The blond man shook Meredith's hand. "Shea," he answered. "Brian Shea."

"Well! It's very pleasing to meet you, Mr. Shea. Did you know that I used to have absolutely everything? No, it's true! I had the love of a good woman, my own business and an impossibly large amount of money. And somehow it all slipped through my fingers."

"And why is that?" Brian Shea asked.

Meredith picked up the newspaper and thrust it into Shea's face. "Because of him!" Meredith said. "Detective Dickson! That phony. Why, given half the chance, I could have defeated that Fantômas fellow."

Shea raised an eyebrow. "Really?" he said.

"Why certainly!" Meredith boasted. "I'd have defeated Fantômas, won back the heart of the woman I love and I never would have–"

"Would have what, Mr. Meredith?"

Meredith pressed his palms against his eyes, as if trying to blot out a painful memory. "Nothing," he said. "I really don't feel well, I'm afraid."

Shea turned until he was facing Meredith directly. "Mr. Meredith, are you trying to tell me that you would never have lost your mind and beheaded that poor man in Fantômas' Long Island mansion?"

Meredith turned toward Shea and gazed with horror into his eyes. "You!" he whispered.

"Yes," Shea answered. "It is indeed your old friend."

Meredith tried to leap to his feet, but Shea grabbed his wrist and held him fast. "Now, now, Mr. Meredith. You needn't run away. I hold no grudge against you for Dr. Voitzel's death. In your position, I might have done the same thing. You needn't worry about repercussions. I did away with the good Doctor's body and made sure that your reputation remained free and clear from any embarrassment."

Meredith slowly sat back down. "But I thought you were…everyone thinks you're…"

"Yes," Shea smiled. "For a while, I thought I was too. But bullet wounds are like broken hearts, Mr. Meredith. If they do not kill us, they only make us stronger."

Meredith swallowed hard. "What do you…what do you want with me?"

"Relax, Mr. Meredith. I only wish to have a chat. Can't two old friends have a chat?"

"I suppose so."

"It has taken me a while to heal and find myself in a place where I feel it's safe to go public again. The time is not yet right but it soon will be and I need your help."

"My help?" Meredith asked. "Why me?"

"Because," Shea laughed, "this country will be built by people like you and me. Look at us, Mr. Meredith. I'm a murderer with the soul of a poet and you're a foolish romantic with the heart of a murderer."

"I could never…"

"Please, Mr. Meredith," Shea said, rolling his eyes. "Don't tell me you could never be like me. You already are like me. You became like me the night you relieved Dr. Voitzel of his life. That is now who you are. A murderer. You can go through your life a tortured soul, hiding your shameful secret because of some misguided feelings of guilt, or you can do as I did. Accept it. This is who you are, Meredith. And accepting that will be your key to success."

Meredith was still eyeing Shea with suspicion but his words were beginning to make sense. "What do you need from me?" he asked.

"In my current identity, I have a great deal of freedom," Shea said. "But it's unlikely that anyone will grant me the keys to society that I so desperately need in order to achieve my goals. But you, Mr. Meredith, can introduce me. You were born into wealth and you know the men who run this city. Let me be your companion until I get what I want."

"And what do I get in return?"

Shea laughed, "Already I like the way you're starting to think! You, Mr. Meredith, will get the one thing you want more than anything in the world." Shea lifted the newspaper and held it in front of Meredith.

"Ruth…" Meredith sighed.

"How dare that upstart detective rob you of what was rightfully yours. How dare he."

Meredith stared at the newspaper for a moment, then snatched it from Fantômas and crushed it in his fist.

"What do you say, Mr. Meredith?"

Meredith extended his hand. "Call me Jack," he said.

Shea gave Meredith's hand a firm squeeze. "And you may call me Fantômas," he said.

"There's a problem," Meredith said.

"Already? But we've just begun?"

"My business is failing. I haven't exactly been in the best condition to run it lately, and I'm afraid I'm losing money by the fistful every day."

"Not to worry, Jack. Very soon, America will find itself embroiled in the Great War and every munitions plant in this country will be booming!"

Meredith snorted. "If I last that long. I need capital–something to pay off the debts until I can get my feet back under me."

Fantômas stood up from his barstool, took a handful of coins from his jacket and laid them on the counter. "Thank you, Geoffrey!" he called to the bartender.

"Likewise," Geoffrey the Slasher said, giving a wink to Fantômas as he cleared their glasses.

"Come on," Fantômas said.

"Where are we going?" Jack asked.

"Follow me."

Night had fallen and Meredith followed Fantômas to the Lower East Side, then to the Five Points and the former site of Our Lady of Perpetual Sorrow. The cemetery behind the church had remained untouched by the fire and the two men walked among the headstones until Fantômas stopped. "Here," he said.

"Here…what?" Jack asked.

Fantômas reached behind a nearby tree and brought forth two shovels. "Start digging," he said.

The two men began digging in front of the headstone as the hours passed. In the wee hours before the Sun was about to break, they stood in the six foot hole and their shovels struck wood. "Finally," Fantômas said. "Help me lift it out."

Meredith looked around, to make sure they were safe from prying eyes but Fantômas seemed to have no such worries. "Climb out," Fantômas said. "I'll hand it to you."

Meredith climbed out of the grave and reached down to grab the handle on the side of the coffin while Fantômas pushed from underneath. After a series of heave-hos, the coffin slid onto the ground and Fantômas leapt out of the grave, dusting off his hands. "Now," he said. "Open it."

"Me?" Meredith said. "I could never…"

"Mr. Meredith," Fantômas replied, "please don't insult my intelligence by pretending to be horrified by the sight of a dead body."

Meredith shrugged, reached down and opened the lid of the coffin to reveal the badly decomposed body of the authentic Father Rose.

"Good God," Meredith said. "Why–"

"Just give me a moment," Fantômas answered. He knelt by the coffin and pulled the tattered robes from Father Rose's body, revealing his bare torso. Father Rose's chest was little more than a bare skeleton with scraps of skin and muscle hanging from the bones. Fantômas rubbed his hands together, then reached into the dead man's chest and drew forth…

"Dear God," Meredith said. "Professor Harrington's journal!"

"Yes," Fantômas smiled. "What hiding place could be safer than the heart of a priest?"

Meredith snorted and sat down on the ground in disgust. "This is why we've spent the better part of the night digging through a graveyard? I hope I don't have to remind you, Fantômas, that the journal is useless without Professor Harrington to decipher it. You had him in your grasp and you lost him!"

Fantômas stared at Meredith with confusion, then his head rolled back and he roared with laughter.

"What is it?" Meredith asked. "What's wrong?"

"Yes," Fantômas said. "I had Professor Harrington and I lost him. If I may, Jack, your problem is that you come from a world in which you were born into a fortune. I, on the other hand, have had to work my way up from nothing. And people like me have an old saying."

"What is it," Meredith asked.

"If at first you don't succeed, Mr. Meredith, you merely try…try…again."

It was early morning by the time Brian Shea returned to his tenement on Houston Street. Sally and Denny were still asleep in the bed. Sally woke up when Shea walked through the door. "Go back to sleep, Sally. It's Saturday," Shea said.

Sally reached out her arms. "Lie here with us," she said.

Shea crawled into bed next to his wife and child. Sally nuzzled up next to him and pressed her face into his chest. "You poor thing," she murmured. "Did you have to work all night?"

"Yeah," Shea answered. "Those crates won't unload themselves, you know."

"I had a dream," Sally said.

Shea stroked her hair. "What was it?"

"I was back in that cell. And I could hear the screaming coming from above and smell the smoke. And I wondered where you had gone and if you were ever coming back." Sally looked up in her husband's eyes. "But then you did come back."

"That's right, Sally," Shea said. "I came back. And I'm never going away again."

Sally lay with her head on her husband's chest and her breathing grew heavy as she fell back to sleep.

Fantômas lay in bed next to his new wife and child, watching the Sun rise through the window. After a few minutes, he closed his eyes, fell asleep and dreamt of America.

THE END

Printed in the United States
96117LV00001B/3/A